CHAPEL HILL
PUBLIC LIBRARY

NIGHTMARE RANGE

NIGHTMARE RANGE

The Collected
George Sueño & Ernie Bascom Stories

MARTIN LIMÓN

Introduction by Timothy Hallinan

SOHO CRIME

Published by
Soho Press, Inc.
853 Broadway
New York, NY 10003

The stories contained herein originally appeared, in slightly different form, in the following publications: "Nightmare Range," *Pulphouse*, Vol. 2, Issue 2, 1993. "The Black Market Detail," *Alfred Hitchcock Mystery Magazine*, January, 1991. "Pusan Nights," *Alfred Hitchcock Mystery Magazine*, May, 1991. "A Piece of Rice Cake," *Alfred Hitchcock Mystery Magazine*, June, 1991. "The Woman from Hamhung," *Alfred Hitchcock Mystery Magazine*, July, 1991. "The Gray Asian Sky," *Alfred Hitchcock Mystery Magazine*, October, 1991. "Seoul Story," *Alfred Hitchcock Mystery Magazine*, January, 1992. "ASCOM City," *Alfred Hitchcock Mystery Magazine*, Mid-December, 1992. "Night of the Moon Goddess," *Alfred Hitchcock Mystery Magazine*, October, 1994. "Seoul Mourning," *Alfred Hitchcock Mystery Magazine*, Mid-December, 1995. "Payday," *Alfred Hitchcock Mystery Magazine*, February, 1998. "The Mysterious Mr. Kim," *Alfred Hitchcock Mystery Magazine*, April, 2002. "The Filial Wife," *Alfred Hitchcock Mystery Magazine*, March, 2003. "The Widow Po," *Alfred Hitchcock Mystery Magazine*, September, 2003. "The Cold Yellow Sea," *Alfred Hitchcock Mystery Magazine*, January/February 2004. "The Opposite of O," *Alfred Hitchcock Mystery Magazine*, July/August 2008.

Library of Congress Cataloging-in-Publication Data

Limón, Martin, 1948–
[Short stories. Selections]
Nightmare range : the collected Sueno and Bascom short stories / Martin Limón
p. cm

ISBN 978-1-61695-332-4
eISBN 978-1-61695-333-1

1. United States. Army Criminal Investigation Command—Fiction. 2. Military intelligence—Fiction. 3. Sueqo, George (Fictitious character)—Fiction. 4. Hispanic American soldiers—Fiction. 5. Bascom, Ernie (Fictitious character)—Fiction. 6. Americans—Korea—Fiction. 7. Korea (South)—Politics and government—Fiction. 8. Political fiction. I. Title.

PS3562.I465N54 2013
813'.54—dc23   2013009578

Interior design by Janine Agro, Soho Press, Inc.

Printed in the United States of America

10 9 8 7 6 5 4 3 2 1

TABLE OF CONTENTS

INTRODUCTION
Timothy Hallinan

Cool and hot. Yes and No. Head and shoulders. Matter and anti-matter. Laurel and Hardy.

Sueño and Bascom.

Martin Limón has created my favorite crime-solving team since (and, perhaps, including) Holmes and Watson. He's taken a perfectly balanced union of opposites and put them into a whole landscape of opposites. Army grunts versus Army brass. The rigidity and pragmatism of the US 8th Army versus the truculence and tradition of Korean officialdom. On a larger scale, the permanent war between North and South Korea.

It's in the intermittently neutral spaces between all these grinding jaws that Limón sets the stories in which George Sueño and Ernie Bascom right wrongs caused by crime, betrayal, stupidity, misunderstanding, prejudice, drugs, and heartbreak. This is American-occupied Cold War South Korea, long after the armistice that resolved nothing and long before the miracle explosion of the economy. So, in addition to all the other opposites in Limón's books and stories, we have a vast economic and political division between haves and have-nots, between the powerful and the weak.

Martin Limon *owns* this world in a way that very few writers can claim their setting and characters. He learned it first-hand, over the course of a decade spent with the Army in Korea. Like

George Sueño, he opened himself to Korean culture and learned the language. Like Ernie Bascom—who will walk through a wall when it's the shortest distance between two points—he developed a healthy loathing for the cover-your-ass obstructionism of Army procedure.

So he had the experience to tell these stories. But hundreds of thousands of people graduated from that same school of experience, and none of them came up with George and Ernie. None of them came up with the AWOL soldiers in the Ville, none of them came up with the tragically exploited working girls, the Army's boneheaded officers and lost boys, the hard-eyed Korean cops, the whole landscape of want and desperation, invisibly layered with a rich and deeply spiritual culture thousands of years old.

And that's because Martin Limón is a writer of the very first rank. He's a poet of the people, although without the political connotations that phrase might suggest. He looks at people of at least two cultures and at every level, and he sees all the way through them, and then he uses his gifts to put them on the page so fully the reader feels that he or she can walk around them. And then, sometimes, he allows them to be broken into tiny pieces, and as we readers retreat to our fundamental conceptions of right and wrong and our comfortable certainty that right will prevail, George and Ernie's investigation reminds us forcefully that in this particular world, that's often not the case. Sometimes tiny victories are the only ones in sight, and sometimes you have to search even for those.

I discovered Limón when his first novel, the astonishing *Jade Lady Burning*, came out. I waited, often impatiently, for each succeeding book. It got to the point where all I had to do was open the cover to smell the charcoal cookers, feel the cold, see the eyes of the people—almost know what was around the corner—because the world Limón creates is so consistent, so thoroughly *known*, in a way that only the very best writers' fictional worlds are. If you think of, say, a prose description of a street as the point of view of a camera that's been placed there, Limón is one of those rare writers who could tell you instantly what's behind the camera and what's out of view to the right and the left. (He can do the same with the internal landscape of his characters.) I soon learned to put aside a big chunk of time when the new Martin Limón novel finally landed in my lap, because I wasn't going to be home, or anyplace close to home, until I'd finished it.

When I set out to write my own books about the emotional and spiritual collision between two cultures, Martin Limón was my primary inspiration. In thinking about my books, I read Limón not for events or characters or tropes but for the particular wizardry with which he keeps the larger perspective in view even while he's got his reader at the level of details. When we see a movie, we're rarely conscious of the lens the director has chosen, even though it can have a huge impact on how we see the scene. For Limón, it seems to me, this ever-present awareness of a cultural gulf is the lens through which we view the action in his books and stories, and it brings everything into a very clear and specific relief.

I am not a short-story reader, so it came as a complete surprise to me when Soho told me this volume was in the planning stages. All I can say is that it's a bonanza on the King Solomon's Mines scale, probably the best news of my reading year. I invite you to read these tales slowly or fast or however you do it (I really had to take my time because they're so rich and so many of them are so overpowering), and once in a while, ask yourself whether you know *any other writer* who could do what Martin Limón does here.

And if you think of one, send me his or her name.

NIGHTMARE RANGE

The mama-san didn't know how long the body had been out there. "Three, maybe four days," she said. Her girls had just conducted their business a few yards farther away from it each day.

"Where is it now?" I asked.

"Policeman take go." She waved her cigarette, and smoke filtered through the darkened gaps between her teeth.

The morgue was in Chorwon-ni, ten miles to the south. Ten miles south of Nightmare Range, and fifteen miles from the Demilitarized Zone that slashes like a surgeon's knife through the heart of the Korean Peninsula.

The war had been over for twenty years but still it lingered: a big dumb ghost that refused to go away. No peace treaty had been signed—just a cease-fire. So the fourth and fifth largest armies in the world, armed to their squinting eyeballs, faced each other across the line, fingers on trigger housings, knuckles white, dancing to the sound of no breathing.

Our police escort, Lieutenant Pak, stood back, arms crossed, glaring at the squatting woman. He was a tall man for a Korean, slim but muscular. His khakis were starched and fit as if he had been born in them. I didn't ask him why it had taken so long to dispose of the body. The non-person status of a "business girl" follows her into death.

One by one the doors to the hooches slid open and groggy

young women, their faces still puffed with sleep, gaped at us curiously. Some squatted in long underwear, their arms crossed over their knees, while others lay on the floor, beneath the wrinkled patchworks that were their blankets. All of the girls were ugly in some way: ravaged complexions, tufted hair, splotches of discolored skin. It seemed more like a ward for the incurably ill than a whorehouse.

Maybe it was both.

Lieutenant Pak asked a series of questions of the old woman and I managed, struggling, to keep up with most of it. There had been a number of American units in the field that day and just before nightfall the old woman had stationed a few of her girls near each encampment. As darkness approached, the girls called to the young GIs from just outside the concertina wire.

I'd seen the game before. Sometimes the GI would wade out into the tall grass and lie on the blanket, both he and the deformed girl protected by the enshrouding night. Sometimes the bolder fellows would bring the girls into their tents, risking the wrath of the Sergeant of the Guard and sneaking in and out of the camp with the stealth of a North Korean infiltrator.

I pulled out a map, showed it to the mama-san, and pointed to the area around Nightmare Range and the village of Mantong-ni. The old woman looked at it carefully and consulted with some of the girls. A few of them were up and dressed now. They chattered for a while and then came to a conclusion. With my pen, I marked the area beneath the old woman's gnarled fingernail.

I asked what type of unit it was. Big guns, they decided.

Lieutenant Pak wiped his hands on the sides of his khaki trousers and took a step toward the gate.

"Mama-san," I said. "This girl. What was her name?"

"Miss Chon," the old woman said. "Chon Ki-suk."

I wrote it down. "Do you have a picture of her?"

The mama-san barked an order and one of the girls handed

me a tattered piece of cardboard folded in half like a small book. A VD card. Chon Ki-suk peered out at me from a small black-and-white photograph. She had a round face with full cheeks that sagged like a bloated chipmunk. All visible flesh had been pocked by the craters of skin disease. She differed little from her sisters now breathing heavily around me, a timid little girl awaiting death.

Lieutenant Pak stomped into the mud.

I stood up and walked with him to the gate. As he stooped to get through the small opening, I looked back at the rows of blemished faces sullenly watching our every move. None of them smiled. None of them said goodbye.

My partner, Ernie Bascom, was in the jeep curled up with a brown-paper-wrapped magazine from somewhere in Scandinavia. He unfolded his six-foot frame as we approached and started up the jeep. Some people said he looked like the perfect soldier: blue eyes behind round-lensed glasses, short-cropped sandy-blond hair, the aquiline nose of the European races. What had blown it for him was Vietnam. Pure horse sold by dirty-faced kids through the wire, women taken on the dusty paths between rice paddies, the terror rocket attacks during innocent hours. His placid exterior hid a soul that had written off the world as a madhouse. Looks were deceiving. Especially in Ernie's case.

We dropped Lieutenant Pak off in Mantong-ni. A dozen straw-thatched farmhouses huddled around the brick-walled police station as if longing for an extinguishing warmth.

Ernie popped the clutch, our tires spun, and we lurched forward into the misted distance.

The roads were still slick, but all that was left of the early morning rain were ponderous gray clouds rolling like slow-motion whales through the hills surrounding the long valley. We plunged into a damp tunnel, and when we came out, the valley widened before us. Dark clouds in the distance glowered at us like fat dragons lowering on their haunches for a nap.

"Nightmare Range," Ernie said. "Where generals meet to see how much their boys can take." He pumped lightly on the brakes and slid around a sharp curve. The water-filled rice paddies on either side of the road strained impatiently toward our spinning tires. This valley had been the scene of some of the most horrific battles of the Korean War. Americans, Chinese, Koreans, had all died here, and the bones of some probably still embraced each other deep beneath the piled mud. I had looked it up in the military section in the library, how many had died here. All I remember is that there was a number followed by a lot of zeros.

The austere cement-block building of the Firing Range Headquarters was painted in three alternating shades of green. Inside, a brightly colored relief map of Nightmare Range covered a huge plywood table.

A ROK Army sergeant with short, spiky black hair and a crisply pressed khaki uniform thumbed through a handwritten log of the units that had been using the training facility. He came to the correct date and the correct position and pointed to the entry: Charlie Battery, 2nd of the 71st Artillery. They had returned to their base at Camp Pelham.

"Our next stop, Camp Pelham," Ernie said.

We returned to the jeep.

"Tough duty, pal." Ernie leaned back in a patio chair at the snack stand just inside the front gate of Camp Pelham, sipping a cold can of PBR. We were dressed the same way: blue jeans, sneakers, and black nylon jackets with brilliantly hand-embroidered dragons on the back. Standard issue for GIs running the ville.

The outfit usually got us over. We were the right age, both in our early twenties, and we both had the clean, fresh-faced look of American GIs. If we played with the girls enough, laughed, horsed around, toked a few joints, no one would suspect that we were conducting a criminal investigation.

Ernie looked like the typical GI from the heartland of America. I looked like his ethnic sidekick, taller than him by about three inches, broader at the shoulders, with the short jet-black hair of my Mexican ancestors. My face often threw people. The nose was pointed enough, and the skin light enough to make them think that maybe I was just one of them. But I'd grown up on the streets of east LA and I'd heard the racial slurs before. When some GI started in on "wetbacks" somebody usually elbowed him, whispered something in his ear, and looked nervously in my direction. They didn't have to worry though. That's part of America, after all. I wouldn't deny them their fun.

The afternoon was glorious but cold. The crisp, clear blue sky of the DMZ, far away from the ravages of industrialism, seemed to welcome even the likes of us.

Camp Pelham is in the Western Corridor, about twenty miles from the Division Headquarters at Camp Casey and forty miles from Nightmare Range. The Western Corridor was the route the North Korean tanks had taken on their way to Seoul in the spring of 1950. It was expected to be the route they would take again.

The camp was small—you could walk around it in ten minutes—but it still managed to house the battalion's three batteries of six guns each. The big howitzers of Alpha and Bravo Batteries pointed to the sky, their barrels snugly sheathed in plastic behind protective bunkers. Charlie Battery was out in the field again but scheduled to return that afternoon.

We heard distant thunder and ran to the chain-link fence. Across the narrow river, rows of dilapidated wooden shacks sat jumbled behind a main street lined with nightclubs and tailor shops.

Charlie Battery rumbled down the two hundred yard strip. A small jeep maintained the lead while six big two-and-a-half ton trucks barreled after it as if trying to run it down. A half dozen 105-millimeter howitzers bounced behind the big trucks like baby elephants trotting behind their mothers.

The men of Charlie Battery stood in the beds of the trucks, shouting, their winter headgear flapping wildly in the wind.

An M-60 machine gun crowned the cab of each truck, partially hidden behind bundles of neatly tied camouflage netting.

Rolls of razor-sharp concertina wire, draped over stanchions on either side of the truck bed, swayed lazily with the rattling of the trucks like huge and sinister gypsy earrings.

Some of the villagers of Sonyu-ri waved happily at the unstoppable convoy. Others scurried to get themselves and their children out of the way.

When the Camp Pelham gate guards swung open the big chain-link fence, the men yelled and laughed and the drivers gunned the truck engines. Diesel fumes billowed into the air.

The jeep sped by and headed for the Battery Orderly Room. The truck turned in the other direction to get hosed down at the wash point and topped off with diesel at the fuel point.

We finished our beers and walked down the road. In front of the Orderly Room a disheveled-looking little man rummaged through the back of the jeep trying to locate his gear. I spotted his name tag. Sergeant Pickering, the Chief of the Firing Battery.

"Chief of Smoke," I said.

He looked up and squinted, a crooked-toothed weasel who hadn't shaved in a couple of days. "Who are you?"

I showed him my identification. "George Sueño, Criminal Investigation Division. This is my partner, Ernie Bascom."

He looked at the badge and turned back to his gear. "Why ain't you wearing a coat and tie?" he asked. "I thought you guys always wore a coat and tie."

"Not undercover," Ernie said.

The Chief of Smoke ignored us and continued to rummage through his things, sticking his hand way down into the depths of his dirty green canvas pack.

"Here's the son of a bitch," he said. "Kim! Kim! I found it."

His Korean Army driver came running out of the Orderly Room as the Chief of Smoke wrenched his hand free from the enveloping material. He held up a dirty, unwrapped white bread sandwich and they both beamed. He tore it and handed half to the Korean. They munched contentedly and the driver, smiling, returned to the Orderly Room.

"Kimchi and bologna," the Chief of Smoke said. "Made it myself." His mouth was open. The odor of the hot pickled cabbage flushed the diesel fumes from my sinuses. He didn't offer us any.

"The last field problem you were on," I said, "you were at Nightmare Range."

The Chief looked at me, still chewing with his mouth open, but didn't say anything.

"There was a problem," I said. "Somebody from your unit went a little too far with one of the girls outside the wire."

He closed one eye completely. "What do you mean, 'too far'?"

"He killed her."

The Chief of Smoke chomped viciously on his sandwich. Cabbage crunched. "Probably deserved it." He continued to chew, turning his head to squint at the brilliantly outlined hills in the blue-sky distance. "I know my first wife did."

"Did you notice anything unusual that trip? Anything that might have . . ."

"Had to be Bogard. Only one mean enough to do it. And he was always messing with those girls out in the field. Didn't pay 'em, I don't think. Never had enough money anyway what with all the trouble he's been in."

"Trouble?"

"Yeah. Article Fifteens for not making formations, over-purchasing on his ration card, shit like that."

"Where's he at now?"

"Don't know."

"He's not in your unit anymore?"

"Well, we're still carrying him on the books. They say he's down in the ville." The Chief of Smoke swallowed the last of his rancid sandwich, turned away from the hills, and looked at me. Bread and bologna still stuck to his teeth. "He's been AWOL ever since we came back from Nightmare Range."

She propped her half-naked breasts atop my belt and rubbed her nipples against my stomach. She wore only shorts and a halter top, and her straight black hair swung back as she looked up at me and smiled through a mask of makeup.

"Where you stationed?" she asked.

"Starlight Club," I said.

She pulled back and punched me in the stomach with her small fist. "You not stationed Starlight Club. I stationed Starlight Club." She turned to Ernie. "You buy me drink?"

He pulled his beer back a few inches from his mouth and looked at her as if she were out of her mind. She left.

We were leaning against the bar of the Starlight Club and this was the fifth joint we'd been in. The place was packed with GIs, mostly playing pool, and Korean girls, scantily dressed in outfits designed to inflame the male hormonal system. Some of them gyrated their bodies on the small dance floor, moving to the beat of the overpowering rock music. Various colored lights flashed on and off around the club, stabilized by the steady glare of the fluorescent bulbs above the pool tables.

"Tits and ass," Ernie said.

"Yeah. It's not easy being a hunter."

A group of GIs walked in and one girl shuffled and squealed across the room, throwing herself into the arms of a young man with a wispy mustache and blond hair parted in the middle of his head.

The tallest member of the group stood aside and surveyed the club from the doorway. He was exceedingly thin but energy seemed to emanate from his body. Even though he stood still, some part of his anatomy seemed always to be quivering and about to explode into movement.

His name was Duckworth. The Chief of Smoke had pointed him out to us as he sped by in his deuce-and-a-half, the first driver to finish his chores at the wash point and make it to the motor pool. "They're all into whacko weed. He'll know where Bogard is."

Duckworth and his buddies entered the club, mingled with some of the pool players, and soon he was leaning against the jukebox, sparring and flirting with one of the girls. His buddy was still enveloped by a feminine bear hug and had to hold his elbows high to tilt back his beer. The group was in constant motion, all with seemingly little adult motive, like children frolicking on a nursery room floor.

Ernie took a sip of his beer. "Shouldn't we roust him out back?"

"I don't think there's any need. As ornery as the Chief of Smoke said Bogard is, these guys probably will be glad to be rid of him."

We ordered two more beers. One of the girls walked up, and this time Ernie grabbed her. We weren't in any hurry.

Duckworth and his buddies around the jukebox yelled into one another's ears. The wall of music between us stopped any sound from getting through. They took some of the girls with them and walked past the men's latrine and out the back door.

We gulped down our beers, not even giving the suds time to settle in our stomachs. Ernie let go of his sweet and rotund young girl and followed me out the back door.

The group stood in the mud in the dark and narrow alley. They didn't move when the light from the club followed us outside, just stared at us with hugely dilated cat's eyes. A joint came toward me and I reached out my hand. The GI hesitated and looked at Duckworth. When he nodded, the small, burning ember was passed to me.

I took a hit and handed it to Ernie. I held the smoke in my lungs while I spoke. "I'm look for Bogard."

Everybody laughed.

"Usually," Duckworth said, "people are trying to get away from him."

"Why?"

Duckworth shrugged. "He's mean, he's broke, and he doesn't take no for an answer—on anything."

The GIs and the girls sniffled and snorted in their efforts not to lose any of the precious herbal fumes.

"Where can I find him?"

"If you got money, he'll find you."

I waited.

Duckworth broke the silence. "Find the River Rat and you'll find Bogard."

"The River Rat?"

"Yeah. He lives with her. Sort of."

"Sort of?"

"She catches a lot of GIs," Duckworth said, "but usually just before curfew, when he needs a bunk, Bogard goes over to her hooch. If there's somebody there, he's just shit out of luck. Bogard tosses him out into the street."

The GIs giggled and snorted some more.

"How do I find the River Rat?"

"She lives by the river," someone said. The rush of air through nostrils increased.

"She walks the streets," Duckworth said. "And since there's only one street in the village, you can't miss her."

She blocked the way.

A GI stopped and listened to her for a moment and then shook his head. He stepped around her, but she grabbed him by the arm and seemed to be pleading with him. Keeping his hands in his pockets, he roughly pulled his elbow from her grip and continued past.

She smiled and waved her hand a little, as if saying goodbye to an old friend.

It was getting colder. Scattered flakes of snow hit the oil-splattered blacktop and vanished as if they'd never existed. GIs and half-dressed Korean girls scurried from club to club, running away from the small, blustering snow clouds that chased them like restless apparitions.

As she walked toward us, I turned to Ernie. "She's got to be the River Rat."

Her small breasts only slightly pushed out the thick, gray

material of her baggy sweatshirt. She wore a pair of bedroom slippers and loose-fitting, dirty-yellow pants that were short enough to reveal her tall brown socks. Her face was plain but pleasant and seemed removed from the mundane consideration of life by the half smile that controlled it. Her unwashed black hair dripped to her shoulders.

She talked quietly to herself and looked around, not at other people but at objects on the ground and on the walls and in the windows of the small shops that lined the street. She seemed delighted by her conversation and occasionally nodded or waved with an easy twist of the wrist. A fine lady gently accentuating some important point.

She appeared happier than the people trying to avoid her. If she'd actually had a companion, looked at some of the people staring at her, or made some effort to clean herself and make herself presentable, I might not have thought she was mad.

When she got close, I spoke. "*Anyonghaseiyo.*"

She seemed surprised by the interruption. But the small smile quickly regained control of her face and she turned and pointed with her thumb back down the street. "You go?"

I gestured with my head toward Ernie. "We go."

She looked at both of us and smiled. "No sweat," she said. We followed her down the street.

About fifty yards past the Starlight Club, she turned off the main road and wound through some mud-floored alleys that got progressively narrower and darker. The stench from the river got harder to take as we went downhill. Finally, she stopped and crouched through a gate in a fence made of rotted wood. The shore of the river lapped listlessly up to within a few feet of the entranceway.

We followed her in. She kicked off her slippers, stepped up on the wooden porch, and slid back the panel leading to her room. She motioned for us to follow.

"Just a minute," I said. "We wait."

I sat down on the porch facing the entranceway. Ernie found a wooden stool and pulled it over behind the gate so anyone enter-ing wouldn't be able to see him. He reached into the pocket of his jacket, pulled out two cans of Falstaff, and tossed one across the courtyard to me. I caught it with two hands, popped the cap, and sucked on the frothing hops.

The River Rat didn't question us but squatted on her haunches and waited. Just like I'd told her to do.

Ernie settled down on the stool, sipped on his beer, and checked under his jacket. His face calmed as he touched the shoulder holster that held the .45.

The wind gained strength and elbowed its way noisily through the cracks in the old wooden fence. The snow came down with more purpose now and began to stick on the mud, making for a slippery and clammy quagmire.

Just before midnight, I spotted a shadow lumbering along the edge of the river. At the gate, the shadow bent over and filled the entranceway completely for a moment and then popped into the compound.

At first I wasn't sure if he was human. He looked more like a moving mountain of green canvas. A small fatigue baseball cap balanced atop his big, round head, and two flaming eyes shone out from within glistening folds of black skin. His shoulders were huge and broad enough to be used as workbenches. The arms tapered slightly, like drainage pipes, and as he walked, they worked their way methodically around the gargantuan girth of his torso. The two large sections that were his legs moved alter-nately toward me.

My throat was suddenly dry. I held my breath and didn't move. When he got up close, he hovered for a moment, like a storm blotting out the sky, and turned and sat down next to me on the small wooden porch. It shuddered, groaned, and then held. He tilted his red eyes heavenward and took a drink from a small, crystalline bottle that seemed lost in his huge black mitt of a hand. He swallowed, grimaced, and then grinned, first at me and then at Ernie. His teeth were square blocks of yellow chalk, evenly spaced along purple gums.

He growled from deep in his throat. Laughter. And he was quivering with it. "Been waiting for you guys."

He leaned forward and reached out the bottle to me. *Soju.* I took it, rubbed the lip with the flat palm of my hand, and drank. I got up and handed it to Ernie. Ernie drank tentatively at first, and then tilted the bottle up quickly and took an audible gulp. He returned the bottle to Bogard, and walked back and leaned against the fence.

The River Rat bounced back and forth to the kitchen, running around as if she were going to prepare some snacks to go with our rice liquor. She mumbled to herself and flitted about, touching Bogard lightly on his back.

He reached out with one huge paw, grabbed her by the shoulder, and sat her down on the porch next to him. She got quiet and stared serenely at us like a schoolgirl waiting for the presentation to begin.

Bogard's eyes were viciously bloodshot.

"Tell us about Nightmare Range," I said.

Bogard grunted a half laugh and looked at the ground.

"It was a mistake," he said. "She shouldn't have struggled like that." He looked up at me. "They always want to check you out, you know? Check to see if you got any shit. But by the time she got me checked out, there was no turning back."

"The clap?"

"No. Chancroid." It was one of the more popular venereal diseases. "They wouldn't let me come out of the field to take care of it. Just a little hole in my pecker, nothing serious. She shouldn't have looked. Then we wouldn't have this problem."

"*We* don't have a problem," Ernie said.

Bogard looked up and grinned. "You will."

I spoke too quickly, trying to pretend that I didn't understand the threat implied in his answer. "So what happened? You held her down?"

"I hit her first. But the little bitch kept struggling." He pouted and looked at his fleshy underarm. "She bit me. So I held her."

"By the throat?"

"Yeah. And when I finished, she wasn't moving anymore. There was nothing I could do for her."

The River Rat got up and started to flutter around in little circles, like a wounded bird with one good leg. She mumbled some more and made squeaking noises.

Bogard spoke to her tenderly. "Shut the fuck up."

She shut up.

"Finish your *soju*," I said. "Then you're coming with us."

Bogard let out a chortling laugh that seemed to cause his shoulders to bounce. He raised the half-empty *soju* bottle to his mouth and took huge, breathless gulps. The level of the clear, fiery liquid fell straight down into his gullet.

He burped and handed the empty bottle to the River Rat. She took it as if it were a great gift and carried it with two hands to deposit it in a safe place.

"I ain't going," Bogard said.

Ernie stood away from the fence and jammed his hands further into the pockets of his jacket.

"Think for a minute, Bogard," I said. "You've got no place to go. You can't leave the country. You have no income, except for dealing a little drugs or whatever. You can't stay here and you can't get away." He just looked at me, amused. "The last GI convicted of murder here in Korea got four years." I waited for that to sink in. "After he finished the time they sent him back to the States. No sense making it harder on yourself. Come with me, and we'll get this shit over with."

The River Rat came back into the courtyard, stopped, and stood stock still for a moment. She started flitting back and forth again, humming and talking to herself, walking amongst us on imaginary errands, a gracious hostess serving her guests.

Bogard bared his block-like teeth. "I ain't going," he said. "And it's going to take more than you two guys to bring me in."

Ernie took his hands out of his pockets and stepped away from the wall. I reached behind my back and pulled out my handcuffs. Bogard stood up, his feet shoulder-width apart, still smiling, and put his drainage pipe arms out slightly as if he were ready to embrace us.

I took a step toward him. He crouched, and I stopped. He would pulverize me. And once I got in close, Ernie would be unable to use the .45.

Ernie pulled the big pistol out of his shoulder holster, slid back the charging handle, and shot Bogard in the leg. The River Rat screamed. Bogard doubled over, grabbed his leg, and bellowed like a wounded bear. I moved forward and snapped one of the cuffs around his huge wrist. When he realized what I was doing, he let go of his leg and swung an enormous paw at me. I went down. The River Rat jumped on Ernie; screaming and clawing at his face like a wildcat tearing the bark off a tree.

Bogard hopped on his good leg toward Ernie, his enormous girth rising and falling thunderously with each hop. I jumped up, ran at him, and rammed my shoulder into the green expanse of his side.

The foot of his wounded leg hit the ground, he screamed, and we all slammed to the ground in a huge pile. Things crunched. I rolled to my side, groped for the cuffs, and managed to get both of Bogard's hands shackled before he could recover from the pain.

Ernie hopped up and held the gun on him. Bogard rolled on the ground, his big, square teeth clenched in pain. The River Rat didn't move.

I checked her out. Her breathing was shallow. I left Ernie in the hooch and walked carefully along the lace covering of newly fallen snow to the main road. I trotted a few clubs down to an MP jeep and had them radio for an ambulance. They followed me to the mouth of the alley so they could guide the medics to the hooch.

When I returned, a few of the neighbors stood around outside talking amongst themselves. Ernie sat on the porch, hunched over, holding the .45 loosely in his hands. Bogard was still on the ground but sitting up now, slowly trying to shake the fresh snowflakes off his massive head. He clutched the upper part of his thigh, but a puddle of blood continued to grow beneath him. The River Rat hadn't moved.

The medics brought a stretcher. Cursing and howling, Bogard managed to roll up onto it. It took four of us to carry him out of the hooch, down the alley, and then hoist him up into the ambulance. One medic stayed in the back with him, the other was about to climb into the cab.

"What about the girl?" I asked.

"Can't do nothing for her," he said. "You know that."

"You can treat civilians when it's an emergency."

"Only on the compound." He closed the door and started up the engine. Ernie climbed into the back of the MP jeep. I told him to wait, and I trotted back down the alley to the hooch.

The River Rat still lay on the ground, unmoving, and a few of the neighbors had wandered inside. I checked her pulse. Faint. She was becoming pale.

I talked to one of the old women. She told me that the hooch's owner had been notified and was on her way. In Korea, going to a hospital requires front money, in cash, and I didn't have much. The MP jeep honked its horn. I ran back down the alley, got in the jeep, and we spun our tires all the way back to Camp Pelham.

Bogard was all right. The bone had been broken, but not shattered, and the chopper came and took him to the army hospital in Seoul.

Ernie and I spent some extra time on the paperwork. The shooting meant that if it wasn't done right, it would be our ass.

The MPs at Camp Pelham treated us like heroes, slapping us on the back and congratulating us. They were glad to have Bogard out of their village.

■ ■ ■

It was well past curfew, but I managed to convince the desk sergeant to give me a jeep. At the main gate the guard came out in the snow and rolled back the fence for me, just wide enough for the vehicle to squeeze through.

The village of Sonyu-ri was completely dark. Not even the glimmer of stray light from behind shuttered windows was visible to mar the beauty of the moon-cast glow on the white shrouded street. The road was slippery, and I drove slowly.

I parked the jeep, locked the security chain around the steering wheel, and felt my way down the pitch black alley. The stench from the river seemed lessened now, and the murky waters lapped peacefully against the glistening mud of the shore.

The gate was open. Inside, the moonlight shone down on the unsullied snow, and the River Rat lay on the ground where I had left her. I brushed the frozen lace from her hair and pressed my fingers into the base of her neck.

I waited a long time. When I got up, I brushed the snow from my knees and walked away from the unblinking eyes that followed me.

THE BLACK MARKET DETAIL

A full-length dress clung to the soft, round parts of her short body like cellophane on a peach.

"Looks like we've found our culprit," Ernie said.

We'd been sitting in the parking lot of the Yongsan Commissary for about thirty minutes, sipping acidic coffee, watching the housewives parade in and out, trying to decide which one to pinch for black-market activities. None of them had been good-looking enough. Until now. She pushed her overflowing shopping cart toward the taxi stand and smiled at the bright spring day. A voluptuous Oriental doll come to life.

"Instant coffee, strawberry jam, a case of oranges, about twenty pounds of bananas. Is she black marketing or what?"

"Either that or she owns a pet gorilla."

The bag boy helped load her booty into the trunk of the big PX taxi. The driver closed the door for her after she climbed in the back seat, ran around, and started the engine.

Ernie tossed his Styrofoam cup onto the pavement and choked the old motor pool Jeep to life. He slammed the gear shift into low, we jerked forward, and I barely managed to keep what was left of my coffee from splashing all over the front of my coat and tie.

Shadowing hardened criminals is never easy.

Ernie slid expertly through the busy afternoon Seoul traffic and stayed within a few yards of the cab. In Itaewon the cabby turned left, ran the big Ford up a steep hill through a walled residential area, and took a quick right. Ernie waited at the base of the hill until he was out of sight and then, the sturdy old engine whining all the way, charged up after him. At the corner he turned off the Jeep and wedged us up against a stone wall.

I got out and peered around the corner. The cab driver was helping her unload the groceries. I went back to the Jeep and waited.

Most Korean wives of GIs will finish their black market activities in the afternoon before their husbands get home from work. They don't want to jeopardize his military career by getting caught selling a few jars of mayonnaise and maraschino cherries for twice what they paid for them in the commissary. Sometimes the husbands are a little squeamish about the whole thing, but most of them like the extra income just as much as their wives do. An extra four or five hundred dollars a month. Easy. And if they get serious, go for the big ticket items—TVs, microwaves, stereo equipment—they can make as much as fifty thousand dollars during a one-year tour.

Ernie and I usually get stuck with the black market detail. Our job is to bust housewives, embarrass their husbands, and cut back on the flow of duty-free goods from the US bases to the Korean economy.

So far we'd managed to keep the deluge down to about a couple million dollars a week. Exactly what it has always been.

The cab driver finished unloading the groceries, accepted his tip with both hands, bowed, and in a few seconds the walled street was empty and quiet.

Ernie and I walked by her front gate. Stopped. Listened. Nothing I could make out.

Down about fifteen yards on the other side of the road was a small neighborhood store, fronted by an ice cream freezer and a couple of rickety metal tables under an awning emblazoned with the Oriental Beer logo. We rummaged around, Ernie bought some gum, and the old woman smiled as she came up with two paper cups to go with the liter of beer we bought. We sat outside, under the awning, and waited.

Spring was becoming summer in Korea and the afternoon was clear and bright but not hot. It reminded me of the endless days of sunshine I'd survived in foster homes throughout East LA. The sun had been as glaring and unrelenting as the gaze of the adults I'd been forced to live with. I'd cursed my mother for dying and my father for disappearing into the bottomless pit south of the border.

It hadn't all been grim. One of my foster parents, Mrs. Aaronson, made sure I brought my schoolbooks home and then took the time to correct my homework. She showed me that arithmetic and spelling and science are all puzzles. Games. The greatest games. And as I lost myself in these games for hours, I looked forward, for the first time in my life, to being praised by the teacher and respected by the other children for something besides my fists.

The first payoff was when I joined the army and my high test scores earned me a brief stint in the military police. Later, I found myself graduating from the Criminal Investigation School—and on my way to Korea.

Ernie and I had gravitated toward each other somehow. The two duds of the CID Detachment. The first sergeant kept us together mainly to keep an eye on us. We both had this bad habit of following an investigation even after the right slots had been filled in the provost marshal's statistical charts. They wanted a body count of GIs caught selling coffee in the village—not a report on how it was a customs violation for a general's wife to ship Korean antiques back to the States at government expense and then sell them at a three hundred percent profit.

There was no briefing chart for that.

By all rights Ernie should have been in Georgetown trying to pass the bar exam or working his way up through the ranks of young stockbrokers on Wall Street. His dad, a big honcho somewhere in the government, expected it of him. But for Ernie, Vietnam had interrupted everybody's plans.

Most people would blame his choices on the pure China White he was able to buy there from snot-nosed boys through the wire. But I knew him better than that. It was the loathing of routine, of predictability, that had caused him to reject a life of seeking riches in the States and caused him to reenlist in the army. And besides, he'd put down the heroin now—you couldn't buy it in Korea anyway—and replaced it with the duty-free, shipped-at-taxpayer-expense, happy-hour-priced booze that gushed from the army warehouses like crude from a grounded tanker.

A Korean man wearing sandals, a T-shirt, and loose-fitting gray work pants rode past us on a sturdy bicycle.

Ernie elbowed me. "Must be the pickup, pal."

The produce displays kept the man from seeing us, and Ernie and I got up, taking our beer with us, and faded deeper into the darkness of the grocery store.

The man parked his bicycle in front of the doll's front gate and rang the bell. In less than a minute the door opened and the man went through, carrying some flattened cardboard boxes and some string.

We sat back down and finished our beer. Ready for action.

A rag dealer pushing a wooden cart on oversized bicycle tires rolled past us. He clanged his big rusty metal shears and wailed something incomprehensible to his prospective customers. A woman down the street, across from the doll's house, came out from behind her big metal gate and bartered with the rag dealer for a while, finally selling him a brown paper bag filled with flattened aluminum cans.

The Koreans have been recycling for centuries.

The rag dealer tried to interest her in some bits of clothing but she shook her head and demanded money instead. A few coins changed hands, the woman went back behind her protective walls, and the rag dealer clanged down the road, turned left, and was out of sight.

In the distance his clanging and wailing stopped for a while and I figured he must have found another customer.

The man on the bicycle reappeared carrying two large cardboard boxes wrapped in string. He struggled beneath their weight but managed to hoist them up onto the heavy-duty stand on the back of his bicycle. He secured the boxes with rope, hopped on the bike, and rode off. The gate behind him had long since been closed.

"Let's go, pal." Ernie and I trotted down the hill after him, and then jumped in our Jeep and followed at a safe distance as he crossed the Main Supply Route and went about a half mile farther into the heart of Itaewon.

A steep alley turned up a hill, and the man jumped off his bicycle and pushed it slowly up the incline. Ernie pulled over, and I got out of the Jeep. I followed the man to the top of the hill and down a couple of alleys, and watched as he parked in front of a small house surrounded by a decrepit wooden fence. He unloaded his boxes and entered. Then he took his bicycle in and closed the gate.

On the way back to the Jeep I stopped at a public phone and called the Korean National Police liaison officer.

By the time I returned to where Ernie was waiting, a small blue and white Korean police car was just pulling up. Two uniformed KNPs got out, and the four of us walked up into the catacombs of the Korean working class neighborhood.

They kicked the door in. In about ten seconds the man was face down on the floor of his home, his wrists handcuffed securely behind him. Some of the fruit was smashed and the US-made canned goods rolled slowly across the room. They took him to the Itaewon police station.

Ernie and I popped back to the doll's house and knocked on the door. There was no answer. We waited for a while and then a GI sauntered toward us carrying a briefcase. He was tall and thin, with a pencil-line mustache and the strut of a Southern aristocrat.

The insignia on his neatly pressed khaki uniform identified him as Chief Warrant Officer Three Janson. Medical Corps.

"What do you want?"

I flashed my badge. "To question your wife concerning black market activities."

"No way."

Janson opened the door and told us to wait, but it didn't take long because we barged in when we heard his scream.

The voluptuous Oriental doll lay dead on the floor, blood seeping from a hole in her side where her ribs should have been.

The big red brick building that was the headquarters of the CID detachment seemed to be waiting to swallow us as we approached.

The first sergeant wasn't in his office, but down in the admin section barking into telephones and ripping off teletype reports.

"What the hell happened with you guys?" he said when he noticed us. "I send you on a simple black market detail, and you turn up with a corpse."

Ernie sat down on the edge of Miss Kim's desk and offered her a stick of gum. She smiled and accepted a piece with her long manicured fingernails.

"Bascom! Get down to my office! You too, Sueño!"

The ass chewing was royal. You would've thought we'd killed the girl ourselves, and in a way that's sort of what he said. At least we'd been in the vicinity and had the opportunity—if not the motive. He told us that if she'd been raped we'd probably have been charged and locked up by now.

Shows you the high opinion our leadership has of us.

He'd given the case to Burrows and Slabem, affectionately known around the office as the Boot Hill Brothers, his favorite investigators when it came to burying inconvenient facts. When the dependent of a US serviceman gets murdered, all hell breaks loose up at the Eighth Army Headquarters. Colonel Stoneheart, our provost marshal, was briefing the commanding general right now. The first sergeant felt that only a trustworthy pair of sleuths like Burrows and Slabem could properly handle the case.

"You mean properly cover it up," Ernie said.

The first sergeant freaked, chasing us out of his office and warning us to stay off the case unless Burrows and Slabem had some questions for us that weren't covered in our initial report.

We wandered down the long hallway.

"What would we do without the first sergeant's hoarse voice echoing down the halls?"

"I wouldn't know how to act."

Ernie winked at Miss Kim on the way out, and we jumped in his Jeep and went directly to the Itaewon police station.

Exactly what the first sergeant had told us not to do.

Burrows and Slabem were there. Burrows, tall and skinny with a pockmarked face; Slabem, short and round with a pimply face. The Korean police wouldn't talk to them. Neither would we. They harrumphed and tried to look officious. Chins met necks. Except in Slabem's case.

I greeted Captain Kim, commander of the Itaewon police station, and spoke to him in his own language.

"Were you told anything by the offender?"

"Yes. He told us everything."

"How did you get his confession so quickly?"

Captain Kim slammed his fist into his cupped hand. "The lie detector."

He ushered us back to the cells and the guy on the bicycle lay on a moist cement floor. I recognized him because of his clothes. His face was a puffed hive of purple welts.

Burrows and Slabem, the Boot Hill Brothers, glared at us as we walked out. Somehow I didn't think they'd keep our little visit a secret from the first sergeant.

We talked to a lot of the folks in the neighborhood, covering much of the same ground the Korean police had already covered. The only thing unusual anyone had noticed was me and Ernie hanging around. The man on the bicycle had been conducting black market business with the GI wife in the neighborhood for many months, without incident as far as anyone knew.

The whole thing was a mystery to me. Why would a black marketeer kill one of his sources of income?

Ernie thought it might have been Janson. Husbands are always a first suspect in a murder case. But we checked the back of the building. The walls were ten feet high, sheer, with shards of glass embedded in cement on the top. When we had seen Janson, his uniform was still neat, with no more wear than one would expect from a hard day's work at the office.

We couldn't interrogate him. Burrows and Slabem would be handling that, on compound, in conjunction with the chaplain who was giving him counseling and trying to pull him through this crisis.

"Might as well forget it," Ernie said. "If it wasn't the black market guy, Burrows and Slabem might figure out who it was. And anyway the first sergeant said to stay off the case. We're potential suspects. Nothing we can do about it."

But we both knew what was at stake. The guys who played everything by the regulations considered us a couple of screw-offs anyway. And a young woman, a US army dependent, had been murdered while we were actually staking out her home. We both planned a long career in the army, preferably in the CID, and I wasn't going to walk into one assignment after another with the stigma of an unsolved murder, one that happened right under my nose, hanging around my neck.

"We have to find out who killed her," I said.

Ernie shrugged.

We went back to the compound and started making some phone calls. Calling in every favor we had out there. Tracking Janson.

■ ■ ■

Somehow all our investigations seem to lead us directly to the Itaewon nightclub district.

In this case we found out that Janson was the chief inspector for the Preventive Medicine division. They're the guys who give the mess sergeants and the Officers' club managers a hard time about the cleanliness of their kitchens, the temperatures of their food storage facilities, stuff like that.

Janson's NCO-in-charge, the guy who actually ran the operation, was Sergeant First Class Billings. Billings was sort of a soft guy. I'd seen him before at the NCO Club. A little out of shape. Never with a woman. Suspect. And he always puffed on his scroags through a cigarette holder.

Word was that he was a real brown-noser. His boss, Chief Janson, or anybody else up the chain of command, could do no wrong as far as he was concerned. The privates who worked for him, though, could do nothing right, and he made their lives miserable. Much to the pleasure of Chief Janson, who felt that suffering subordinates meant a well-run ship.

Captain Bligh in khaki.

Sergeant Billings's desire to please his superiors extended beyond the working day, and we had heard from one of his cronies that Billings and Chief Janson regularly ran the village of Itaewon together. The guy had heard Billings mention the Spider Lady Club, a little hole-in-the-wall amongst the bigger, gaudier nightclubs, as their favorite hangout.

Ernie and I had changed into our running-the-ville outfits: sneakers, blue jeans, and a nylon jacket with a golden dragon embroidered on the back. It was nighttime and we were in the Spider Lady Club, having a welcome cold one and checking out the exceptionally attractive ladies. The music was mellow. The place was lit by red lamps and the flickering blue light from a row of tropical aquariums.

"Janson has good taste," Ernie said. "First his late wife and now this joint."

"Living his life to the full."

After about twenty minutes, Billings walked in, which didn't surprise us much, but what did surprise us was the guy he had in tow. Chief Janson.

We were at a table in a dark corner; my back was to them, and Ernie adjusted his seat so his couldn't be easily seen from where they sat at the bar.

"Looks like the chaplain's counseling has done wonders for Janson," Ernie said.

I heard their laughter as the excited barmaids brought them drinks without their having to order. Regulars. Through the smoke-covered mirror on the back wall I made out the smiling woman who leaned over to serve Janson. She was tall, thin, and elegant. Gorgeous, all in all. Black hair billowed around her pale, heart-shaped face. Her eyes slanted up, painted heavily with shadow.

The Spider Lady.

Ernie had checked with one of the girls earlier and gotten her story. She owned the joint, having apparently earned the initial capital outlay from working as a nurse. Some of the girls claimed it didn't come so much from her salary but from making extra-curricular arrangements with a few of the doctors. On a cash basis.

That would explain her infatuation with the white-coated types who worked in the Preventive Medicine division.

I wondered if she knew that Janson was actually a veterinarian—a horse doctor. But maybe it was just the rubber gloves that turned her on.

Could this be it? Could it be as simple as Janson's wanting to break free from his present old lady to hook up with the Spider Lady? We waited until Janson walked into the latrine and Billings was deep in conversation with one of the Spider Lady's girls, then we slipped out of the club.

We walked into the crisp night air of Itaewon, rejected two propositions, and sauntered down the hill toward our favorite beer hall.

"We have the motive," Ernie said. "All we have to do now is find the opportunity."

The big beer hall was on the outskirts of Itaewon. We drank draft beer, rubbed elbows with Korean working men, and bantered with the rotund Mongolian woman who slammed down frothing mugs in front of us.

All I could think about was the small Oriental doll and how she had looked with that bloody gash beneath her breast.

In the morning we slipped out of the office as early as we could, supposedly on our way to pump up Colonel Stoneheart's black market arrest statistics but actually on our way to see Captain Kim and get the key to Janson's house. It went smooth. Captain Kim liked the way we didn't try to revamp four thousand years of Korean culture every time we ran into a procedure we didn't approve of. He gave us the key.

The first sergeant would have had a fit if he'd known we were entering the restricted premises of a murder site. But we didn't plan on telling him.

Janson had moved most of his stuff out and was staying in officers' quarters on the base. White tape in the shape of a small woman surrounded a caked blot of blood. The Korean police usually use tape instead of chalk since it's hard to make an outline of the victim with chalk on vinyl floors that are heated from below by hot-air ducts. The floor we walked on in our stocking feet was cold now.

We surveyed the apartment. It was a one-bedroom job with a small kitchen and a cement-floored bathroom. There was no beer in the refrigerator.

Metal clanged and I heard an old man wailing for his life.

The rag dealer.

We put our shoes back on and hurried out to stop the old man and ask if he'd seen anything unusual yesterday afternoon.

I greeted him in Korean, "*Anyonghaseiyo.*"

The old man halted his cart, smiled, and his leathery brown

face folded into so many neat rows that I almost thought I heard it crinkle. He kept his mouth open and didn't seem to know what to say. Talking to Americans wasn't exactly an everyday occurrence for him. Folks in the UFO society probably have more conversations with aliens.

"Yesterday," I said, "we were sitting in that store over there when you came by."

The old man nodded. "Yes. I saw you."

"You bought some aluminum cans from this woman in this house here."

"Yes, yes. That's right."

"And then you went around the corner, down the hill."

"Yes."

"Did you notice anything unusual?"

"Unusual?"

"Yes. Did you see any American people in the neighborhood?"

"No. I saw no American people. The Korean police already asked me that. Look, I am an old man and I have to support myself and a sick wife. Do you want to buy something?"

"No. We don't want to buy anything."

We went back into the house and the old man trundled his cart down the road, clanging his metal shears and wailing his plaintive song.

We searched the grounds, passing through a narrow passageway that ran between the side of the apartment and the big sandstone brick wall that separated the building from the two-story house next door. Out back, a small cement-floored courtyard sat behind Janson's apartment and the landlord's apartment next door. It was enclosed by the big ten-foot masonry wall topped with the shards of glass.

The entire complex was on a corner, formed by the alley that ran up the steep hill we had originally come up in our Jeep and the street that ran in front of the little store from which we had conducted our surveillance.

The only way for someone to enter this house while we

were watching from the store was over the back wall, which seemed unlikely since it faced other people's residences, or over this ten-foot stone wall, which faced the public street. We had already checked the other side and it was sheer and very difficult to climb. But the inside of the wall was not as high since the level of the back courtyard was higher than the street by a few feet. It also provided a number of footholds, from a clinging vine and from some protruding rocks imbedded in the wall.

The wall had been designed to keep out intruders. But from inside it could be easily climbed.

So I climbed it. Ernie stayed on the ground, clicking his gum and telling me—sarcastically, I think—to be careful.

The tricky part about the climb was the handholds on the top of the wall, since you had to be careful to grab a spot between the randomly spaced shards of glass. If you were in a hurry you'd cut yourself for sure.

The jump down into the street would be rough also, although not impossible. About twelve or fourteen feet, depending on which part of the rapidly descending pavement you landed on. An airborne trooper, with a good hit and roll, would have no trouble with it.

As I gazed over the wall and out into the street, I noticed something fluttering in the gentle breeze. It was blue and stuck to the base of one of the shards of glass. Fiber. Wool maybe. A clump of it. I reached out and pulled the material off the jagged edge of the glass. It was soft and blue. Baby blue.

It didn't look worn. It looked new, but it would impossible to tell much about it without a lab analysis and that would be difficult since I wasn't officially on the case. And anyway the lab was in Tokyo. Before a packet could be sent there it had to be approved by the first sergeant.

So much for high technology. I fell back on my meager allotment of common sense.

It looked like threads from a woman's sweater. Maybe a

woman climbed this fence and got part of her clothing caught on these jagged shards of glass. It would be easy, of course, with a ladder, but the Korean police had already interviewed everyone in the neighborhood and no one had seen any workmen or anyone setting up any sort of apparatus.

I climbed down and showed the fiber to Ernie.

He thought for a while and then he said, "The problem is how did she get over the wall? It would have to be something that would give her a lift without causing any particular notice from the neighbors. Trashcans maybe?"

That was it. "Or a trash cart?"

Ernie and I ran outside and scoured the neighborhood until we found the old rag dealer.

"Yesterday, when you rounded the corner away from the store, you stopped calling and clanging your shears for a while. You had a customer."

"Yes."

"Who was it?"

"A beautiful young lady. Very tall. Very fancy." The old man slashed his fingertips across his eyes and up. "She locked herself out of her house."

"So she had to climb the wall?"

"Yes. I rolled my cart over and tilted it up. She climbed over easily."

"And then what?"

"And then I went about my business." The old man looked at the ground, shaking his head slightly. "But she was a very strange woman. Later, down at the bottom of the hill, I saw her again. She was all out of breath from her climb and she had torn her sweater."

"Her sweater? What color was it?"

The old man reached under some stacks of cardboard. "Here. She sold it to me, cheap, because it had been torn. My wife repaired it, and it looks fine now. I should be able to sell it for a good price."

The old man held it up to us, and I reached into my pocket for my small wad of Korean bills.

It was soft and fluffy and baby blue.

Since the Spider Lady was a Korean citizen and therefore not under our jurisdiction, we contacted Captain Kim and had him go along with us to make the pinch.

She was behind the bar of the Spider Lady Club, just getting ready for the evening's business, laughing and joking with the other girls.

Ernie and I came in the door first, wearing our coats and ties, and when she saw Captain Kim behind us and the blue sweater in my hand, the exquisite lines of her face sagged and her narrow eyes focused on me, like arrows held taut in a bow. Blood drained from her skin, and she stood stock-still for a moment. Thinking.

Then she reached under the bar and pulled out a long glistening paring knife, and as her girlfriends chattered away she kept her eyes on me and pulled the point of the blade straight down the flesh of her forearm.

She kept pulling and ripping until finally the other girls realized what was going on and by the time we got to her, her arm was a shredded mess.

Her nurse training had come in handy because she knew that stitches weren't likely to close arteries that had been cut lengthwise. We applied a tourniquet, but somehow she managed to let it loose while she was in the ambulance and, turning her back to the attendant, kept her secret long enough to do what she wanted to do: die.

Janson was put on the first flight out of the country by order of the commanding general, his personal effects packed and shipped to him later.

Billings spent a lot of time at the NCO Club, restricted to

post. He spun romantic tales about his two friends and what he saw as their self-sacrificing love.

The girls at the Spider Lady Club told us the truth. About how proud the Spider Lady had been to be marrying a doctor.

Through it all, from bar to bar, all I could think about was the doll-like woman with the nice curves.

Whose smile had been filled with life.

PUSAN NIGHTS

"The last time the USS *Kitty Hawk* pulled into the Port of Pusan, the Shore Patrol had to break up a total of thirty-three barroom brawls in the Texas Street area. Routine. What we didn't expect was the fourteen sailors who were assaulted and robbed in the street. Six of them had to be hospitalized.

"From eyewitness accounts, the local provost marshal's office ascertained that the muggings appeared to have been perpetrated by Americans, probably the shipmates of the victims. However, no one was caught or charged with a crime."

We were in the drafty headquarters building of the 8th Army's Criminal Investigation Division in Seoul, two hundred miles up the Korean Peninsula from Pusan. When the first sergeant called me and Ernie into his office, we expected the usual tirade for not having made enough black market arrests. What we got was a new assignment. The first sergeant kept it simple.

"First, make sure you take the right flight out of Kimpo. Then, when you land in Pusan, infiltrate the waterfront area and find out who's been pulling off these muggings."

Ernie adjusted his glasses and tugged on his tie.

"Maybe the gang who did it has left the navy and gone on to better things."

"Not hardly. The *Kitty Hawk* was here only six months ago.

The tour in the navy is four years, minimum. Not enough time to break up the old gang."

Ernie got quiet. I knew him. He didn't want to seem too anxious to take on this assignment, an all-expenses-paid trip to the wildest port in Northeast Asia, and he was cagey enough to put up some objections, to put some concern in the first sergeant's mind about how difficult it would be to catch these guys. That way, if we felt like it, we could goof off the whole time and come up with zilch, and the groundwork for our excuse was already laid.

I had to admire him. Always thinking.

"And you, Sueño." The first sergeant turned his cold gray eyes on me. "I don't want you running off and becoming involved in some grandiose schemes that don't concern you."

"You mean, stay away from the navy brass."

"I mean catch these guys who are doing the muggings. That's what you're being paid for. Some of those sailors were hurt badly the last time they were here, and I don't want it to happen again."

I nodded, keeping my face straight. Neither one of us was going to mouth off now and lose a chance to go to Pusan. To Texas Street.

The first sergeant handed me a brown envelope stuffed with copies of the blotter reports from the last time the *Kitty Hawk* had paid a visit to the Land of the Morning Calm. He stood up and, for once, shook both our hands.

"I hate to let you guys out of my sight. But nobody can infiltrate a village full of bars and whores and drunken sailors better than you two." His face changed from sunshine to clouds. "If, however, you don't bring me back some results, I guarantee you'll have my highly polished size twelve combat boot placed firmly on your respective posteriors. You got that?"

Ernie grinned, a little weasel-toothed, half-moon grin. I concentrated on keeping my facial muscles steady. I'm not sure it worked.

We clattered down the long hallway and bounded down the

steps to Ernie's jeep. When he started it up, he shouted, "Three days in Texas Street!"

I was happy. So was he.

But I had the uneasy twisting in my bowels that happens whenever I smell murder.

By the time we landed in Pusan I had read over the blotter reports. They were inconclusive, based mainly on hearsay from Korean bystanders. The assailants were Americans, they said, dressed in blue jeans and nylon jackets, like their victims and like all the sailors on liberty who prowled the portside alleys of Texas Street. The Navy Shore Patrol had stopped some fights in barrooms and on the streets, but they were unable to apprehend even one of the muggers.

By inter-service agreement, the army's military police increased their patrols near the dock areas when a huge naval presence moved into the port of Pusan. The aircraft carrier *Kitty Hawk*, with its accompanying flotilla and its over five thousand sailors, more than qualified as a huge naval presence.

The MPs were stationed, for the most part, on the inland army base of Hialeah Compound. They played on Texas Street, knew the alleys, the girls, the mama-sans. But somehow they had been unable to make one arrest.

Sailors and soldiers don't often hit it off. Especially when the sailors are only in town for three days and manage to jack up all the prices by trying to spend two months' pay in a few hours. It seemed as if the MPs would be happy to arrest a few squids.

Something told me they weren't trying.

We caught a cab at the airport outside of Pusan and arrived at Hialeah Compound in the early afternoon. We got a room at the billeting office, and the first thing we did was nothing. Ernie took a nap. I kept thumbing through the blotter report, worrying the pages to death.

There was a not very detailed road map of the city of Pusan

in a tourist brochure in the rickety little desk provided to us by billeting. Hialeah Compound was about three miles inland from the main port and had gotten its name because prior to the end of World War II the Japanese occupation forces used its flat plains as a track for horse racing. The US Army turned it into a base to provide security and logistical support for all the goods pouring into the harbor. Pusan was a large city, and its downtown area sprawled between Hialeah Compound and the port. Pushed up along the docks, like a long, slender barnacle, was Texas Street. Merchant sailors from all over the world passed through this port, but it was only the US Navy that came here in such force.

Using a thick-leaded pencil I plotted the locations of the muggings on the little map. The dots defined the district known as Texas Street. Not one was more than half a mile from where the *Kitty Hawk* would dock.

Ernie and I approached the MP desk.

"Bascom and Sueño," Ernie said. "Reporting in from Seoul."

The desk sergeant looked down at us over the rim of his comic book.

"Oh, yeah. Heard you guys were coming. Hold on. The duty officer wants to talk to you."

After a few minutes, a little man with his chest stuck out and face like a yapping Chihuahua appeared. He seemed lost in his highly starched fatigues. Little gold butter bars flapped from his collar.

"The commanding officer told me to give you guys a message." We waited.

The lieutenant tried to expand his chest. The starched green material barely moved.

"Don't mess with our people. We have a good MP company down here; any muggings that happen, we'll take care of them; and we don't need you two sending phony reports up to Seoul, trying to make us look bad."

His chest deflated slightly. He seemed exhausted and out of breath.

"Is that it?"

"Yeah."

Ernie walked around him and looked back up at the desk sergeant. "How many patrols are you going to have out at Texas Street tonight?"

"Four. Three MPs per jeep."

"Three?"

The desk sergeant shrugged. "We'd have four per jeep if we could. The advance party of the *Kitty Hawk*'s arriving tonight."

"All patrols roving?"

"No. One in the center of the strip, two more on either end, and one patrol roving."

"You must put your studs in the center."

"You got that right."

"Who performs your liaison with the Shore Patrol?"

The desk sergeant shrugged again. "The lieutenant here, such as it is. Mainly they run their own show, out of the port officer's headquarters down by the docks."

"Thanks. If we find out anything—and there's time—we'll let your MPs make the arrest."

"Don't do us any favors. Those squids can kill each other for all I care."

The lieutenant shot him a look. The desk sergeant glanced at the lieutenant and then back down at the comic book on his desk.

We turned to walk out. Ernie winked at the lieutenant, who glared after us until we faded into the thickening fog of the Pusan night.

Texas Street was long and bursting with music and brightly flashing neon. The colors and the songs changed as we walked down the street, and the scantily clad girls waved at us through beaded curtains, trying to draw us in. Young American sailors in blue jeans and nylon jackets with embroidered dragons on the back bounced from bar to bar enjoying the embraces of the "business girls," who still outnumbered them. The main force of their shipmates had not arrived yet, and the *Kitty Hawk* would not dock until dawn. But Texas Street was ready for them.

We saw the MPs. The jeep in the center of Texas Street was parked unobtrusively next to a brick wall, its radio crackling. The three MPs smoked and talked, big brutes all. We stayed away from them and concentrated on blending into the crowd.

Ernie was having no trouble at all. In bar after bar we toyed with the girls, bought drinks only for ourselves, and kept from answering their questions about which ship we were on by constantly changing the subject.

One of the girls caught on that we were in the army by our unwillingness to spend too much money and by the few Korean words that we let slip out.

"Don't let the mama-san hear you speaking Korean," she said. "If she does, she will know that you're in the army, and she will not let me talk to you."

"What's wrong with GIs?"

I could answer that question with volumes, but I wanted to hear her version.

"All GI Cheap Charlie. Sailors are here for only a short time. They spend a lot of money."

We filed the economics lesson, finished our beers, and staggered to the next bar.

Periodically we hung around near one of the MP patrols, within earshot of their radio, waiting for a report of a fight or a mugging. So far it was a quiet night.

Later, a group of white uniformed sailors on Shore Patrol duty ran past us, holding onto their revolvers and their hats, their nightsticks flapping at their sides. We followed, watched while they broke up a fight in one of the bars. A gray navy van pulled up, and the disheveled revelers were loaded aboard.

We found a noodle stand and ate, giving ourselves away as

GIs to the wizened old proprietor by knowing what to order. Ernie sipped on the hot broth and then took a swig of a cold bottle of Oriental beer.

"Quiet night."

"No revelations yet."

"Maybe tomorrow, when the entire flotilla arrives."

"Flotilla. Sounds like the damn Spanish Armada."

"Yeah. Except a lot more powerful."

Just before the midnight curfew the Shore Patrol got busy again chasing the sailors back to the ship or off the streets.

We had taken a cab all the way back to Hialeah Compound before we heard about the mugging.

"One sailor," the desk sergeant said. "Beat up pretty bad. The navy medical personnel are taking care of him now."

"Any witnesses?"

"None. Happened right before curfew. Apparently he was trying to make it back to the ship."

In the morning, before our eggs and coffee, we found out that the sailor was dead.

The buildings that housed the port officer's headquarters were metal Quonset huts differentiated from the Army Corps of Engineers' Quonset huts only by the fact that they were painted battleship gray while the army's buildings were painted olive drab. Slightly less colorful than Texas Street.

The brass buttons on the old chief's coat bulged under the expanding pressure of his belly. We showed our identification.

"Who was the sailor who got killed in the mugging last night?"

The chief shuffled through some paperwork. "Petty Officer Third Class Lockworth, Gerald R."

"What ship was he on?"

"The USS *Swann*. One of the tenders for the *Kitty Hawk*. They say he was carrying a couple months' pay."

"Nothing left on him?"

"No."

"Maybe the girls got to it first."

"Maybe. But I doubt it. He was three-year veteran of the Pacific Fleet."

"What was the cause of death?"

"Massive hemorrhage of the brain."

"Have you got your eyes on any particular group of sailors that might be preying on their shipmates?"

"Not really. The brass tends to think that it's some Korean gangs working the streets. Maybe they've developed a taste for the Seventh Fleet payroll. That would explain why there haven't been any arrests made."

"The police here want to protect the sailors. There's a lot of pressure from the ROK Government to make the US Navy feel welcome."

"Maybe. But at a lower level, policies have a habit of being changed."

"Do you buy all that, Chief?"

"Could be. I keep an open mind. But in general I tend to go with the scuttlebutt."

"What's that?"

"That it's some of your local GIs that got a taste for the Seventh Fleet payroll."

"If the average sailor starts to believe either one of those viewpoints, it could cause a lot of trouble down here on Texas Street."

"Yeah. I wouldn't want to be a dogface on liberty in this town tonight."

"Thanks for the encouragement."

"You're welcome."

The *Kitty Hawk* finally pulled in at noon, and standing by the dock were the mayor and the provincial governor and the US Navy's 7th Fleet band. The sailors lined the deck of the huge gloating edifice, their bell-bottoms and kerchiefs flapping in the breeze. The ship's captain and his staff, in their dazzling white uniforms, bounced down the gangplank to the tune of "Anchors Aweigh," and were greeted by a row of beautiful young Korean maidens in traditional dresses who placed leis over their necks and bowed to them in greeting.

The governor made a speech of welcome and the captain answered with a long rambling dissertation on the awesome firepower of the *Kitty Hawk*. Greater, he said, than the entire defense establishments of some countries.

"I thought he wasn't supposed to confirm or deny that they have nuclear capability," I said.

Ernie smirked. "He's also not supposed to confirm or deny that he's a jerk."

After the tedious ceremony was over, the sailors—free at last—poured like a great white sea into the crevices and alleys of Texas Street.

The night was mad. The Shore Patrol ran back and forth, unable to keep up with all the explosions being ignited by the half-crazed sailors. Even the MPs had to keep on the move. They were tense. Alert.

I saw different faces in the jeeps tonight and asked one of the MPs about it.

"We're on twenty-four hour alert while the *Kitty Hawk* is here, but we have to get some rest sometime."

"Twelve-hour shifts?"

"Or more, if needed."

Ernie and I wandered away from the bright lights, checking the outskirts of the bar district. Like all beasts of prey, the muggers would look for stragglers, strays who'd wandered from the main herd.

It was mostly residential area back there, high walls of brick or stone and securely boarded gates.

There were a few bars, however, and a few neighborhood eateries. Some sailors were wandering around, those who wanted to get away from the hubbub.

A couple of big Americans about a block in front of us turned a corner. They looked familiar to me somehow. We trotted after them, but by the time we got to the dimly lit intersection they were gone.

"Who was it?"

"I'm not sure."

We walked into a bar closer to Texas Street proper and ignored the girls until they left us alone with only two cold beers for company.

"We're not getting anywhere," Ernie said.

"Something's got to break soon."

"It better. It's not just muggings any more. It's murder."

I felt my innards sliding slowly into knots.

"We got to stay out tonight. Through curfew if we have to."

"Yeah."

I looked at Ernie. "Could it be the Koreans?"

"It could. But if the Korean National Police really believed it, they'd be cracking down on every local hoodlum hard, trying to squeeze the truth out of them."

"What if the local police are in on it?"

"Then we're in trouble. But I don't believe it. Too much pressure from up top. The Koreans need us to ensure that their Communist brothers to the north don't pour down here like they did two decades ago. And maybe more important nowadays is that they need the foreign exchange the fleet brings in."

"And if the navy seriously believes that the Koreans aren't doing everything they can to stop the assaults on their sailors, they could stop coming into port here."

"They'd lose dock fees and re-supply money . . . "

"Not to mention tourism."

We both laughed.

"Somebody in the navy then. In the advance party."

"Could be that, since the *Kitty Hawk* was still at sea last night."

I thought about the map I made and the blotter reports.

"The last time the *Kitty Hawk* was here, there were no muggings until they had docked."

"So?"

"We've been assuming that it's probably a gang of sailors aboard the *Kitty Hawk* that have been preying on their own shipmates."

"Yeah, but maybe there's more than one group. Ideas like this are catching."

"That's possible. But maybe it is somebody in the advance party or maybe it's somebody who's here all the time. Somebody who knows the terrain, the lie of the land, the ins and outs of all the back alleys."

"And if it's not Koreans . . . "

"That's right. GIs. GIs who spend a lot of time down here."

"Village rats."

"All the GI village rats have gone into hiding until the fleet leaves."

"So it seems."

I took a sip of my beer. I didn't like what I was going to say. "That leaves the MPs."

Ernie thought about it for a minute. "That would also explain why there were no arrests made in the past."

"It sure would."

He looked at me. "But why do the muggings only occur when the *Kitty Hawk* is here? And not other navy ships?"

"That I don't know yet." I looked around. "Let's find a phone."

"A phone?"

"Yeah. I got a call I want to make."

The desk sergeant didn't want to answer any of my questions at first because he could see what I was getting at, but I reminded him that this was an official investigation and he would be obstructing that investigation if he didn't cooperate in every reasonable way.

I borrowed paper and pencil from the mama-san and wrote furiously, trying at the same time to keep one finger in my ear to drown out the insane rock music. I seriously considered asking Ernie to hold his finger in my ear, but he was busy flirting with a couple of the girls.

Besides, there are limits to a partnership, even for crimebusters.

I had what I needed. Ernie looked at the sheet. A bunch of names, ranks, and times scribbled across the wrinkled paper.

"What's that?"

"No time to explain. Let's go."

The girls pouted on our way out.

The MP jeep that held the central position on Texas Street was cruising slowly down the crowded block. I waved them down, and they came to a halt. I looked at my notes and read off thee names to them.

"Have you seen any of these guys? Tonight? In civilian clothes?"

I'm not too good a judge of whether someone is telling the truth or lying, but this time I had an edge. The young buck sergeant on the passenger side let the muscles beneath his cheek flutter a couple of times. Then he blinked and said, "No."

I thanked him for the information. He'd given me more than he knew.

We walked off into the darkness away from the men, heading from the center of Texas Street toward the place a few blocks away where I had seen the two big Americans turn down a dark alley and disappear. We wandered around for a while, and in order to cover more ground we split up, agreeing on our routes and where to meet in fifteen minutes.

A couple of blocks later I saw the big guy I had seen before, standing at the mouth of an alley. He looked into the alley at something and then back at me, as if undecided what to do.

I shouted, "Hey!" and started running toward him.

He hesitated for a second and then ran. I let him go and turned down the alley he had been protecting. It was dark. I could see nothing. Then I tripped, sprawled, and something hit me from behind.

When I came to, Ernie was looking down at me, surrounded by some sailors in their dress whites and Shore Patrol armbands. I was never so happy to see squids.

They got me into their van and took me somewhere. Ernie told me, but it didn't register. Nothing much did. On the way there, I passed out again.

The next morning when I woke up I waited for a while and then asked the medic when he walked into the room.

"Where am I?"

"The dispensary. On Hialeah Compound. Had a pretty nasty bump on the noggin last night."

"What's my condition?"

"Hold on."

The medic left the room, and after a few minutes a doctor came in. He looked at my head, checked some X-rays up against a lightboard, and then pronounced me fit for duty.

No shirkers in this man's army. I could've used a few days off.

While I was getting dressed, Ernie showed up. He consoled me by reminding me about the Happy Hour at the Hialeah NCO Club tonight.

"Exotic dancers, too," he said.

I smiled but it hurt the back of my head.

The bright sun of southern Korea was out. In force.

"Personnel? Why personnel?"

"I want to check something out. Leonard Budusky."

"Who?"

"An MP who I think is an acquaintance of mine."

After we showed him our identification, the personnel clerk got Budusky's folder. "He came to Korea over six months ago," I said.

The bespectacled clerk ran his finger down a column of typed entries.

"Seven," he said.

"What state is he from?"

"Virginia."

I held up my hand. "Wait a minute. Let me guess. Norfolk."

The clerk looked up at me, his eyes almost as wide as his mouth. "How the hell did you know that?"

Ernie tried to pretend that he was in on the whole thing, but when we got to the Main Post Snack Bar, he bought me some coffee and threatened me with disembowelment if I didn't tell him what was going on. Considering the pain I was in, I probably wouldn't have noticed it much if I'd let him go through with it. Instead, to humor him, I explained.

"First of all, to find the culprit, we've got to figure out motive and opportunity."

"I remember that much from CID school."

"The motive seemed to be money. Now, that narrows our list of suspects down to anybody in the Seventh Fleet, any GI stationed near Pusan, or any of the Korean citizens of this wonderful city.

"The next step is figuring out opportunity. That brings us closer because that narrows it down to the four thousand or so sailors who had liberty during the stopover, the three hundred or so GIs who had passes, and again, all the Korean citizens of this fair city."

"So it's a tough job. We knew that."

"But the mugger got anxious. On the first night, when only the advance party was in, he attacked. That eliminated all the sailors who were at sea with the *Kitty Hawk*. When Petty Officer Lockworth died, it also eliminated, in my mind, the Korean civilian populace. Because there is no doubt that the Korean authorities would take the mugging of American sailors seriously, but they realize the enormity of the bad public relations they would get back in the States if a Korean was found to have done the killing.

The fact that they still didn't launch an all-out manhunt meant to me that they must be confident, through their own sources, that it wasn't the work of one of their local hoodlums.

"That leaves the GIs. When the fleet is in, soldiers tend to be conspicuous. They stick out, by virtue of their stinginess, from their seafaring compatriots, and the girls down in the village can spot them a mile away.

"We wandered all over Texas Street for two nights and didn't see any, did we?"

"Not except for the MPs."

"Exactly, and except for the two big guys we saw in that alley that looked familiar to me. After I called the desk sergeant and got the names of all the MPs who had duty on the first night, it started to click. The three big studs in the central patrol had all stayed on duty past curfew. Of the four patrols, theirs was the only patrol that did. Of the three of them, the desk sergeant told me that the biggest and meanest was Corporal Leonard Budusky. I remembered their faces. Two of them were the guys we saw scurrying down that alley. When the MPs on duty denied having seen them, I knew it had to be a lie. When MPs are in the village having fun, they will seek out the on-duty patrol, to let them know where they're at or just to say hello.

"When that young buck sergeant on duty realized that the notorious out-of-town CID agents were asking about his part-ners, his first reaction was to lie and protect them."

"So you know two MPs were on duty the first night, when the guy got killed, and you know they were out the second night, off duty, when you got beaned. You still don't have any proof."

"You're right about that. And they'll know it, too. Probably just go about their work as if nothing happened and if we ask them any questions deny everything. But the one thing I do have, that the killer doesn't know about, is the motive."

"Money?"

"Partially. But mainly his motive is something that abounds in a city with a big naval base like Norfolk."

"What's that?"

"Hatred." I took a sip of the hot bitter coffee. "Hatred of the US Navy."

It was a lot easier stalking Texas Street now that we knew who we were looking for. The desk sergeant had already told me, but I checked all four MP jeeps just to be sure. Leonard Budusky and his burly partner were not on duty tonight. They had pulled the day shift and got off about two hours ago.

Ernie had been disappointed when we missed Happy Hour at the NCO Club, and the exotic dancer, but I told him it would be in both our best interests if we remained sober.

The Pusan streets were filling again with fog. It was damp, cold, and dark.

This time we had weapons. A roll of dimes for me. Ernie had a short, brutal club, a wooden mallet, tucked into the lining of his jacket.

We patrolled methodically, keeping to the shadows. The Texas Street area is big, but not that big. Eventually we found them.

They were coming out of a bar, laughing and waving to the smiling girls.

"Spending money like sailors on shore leave," Ernie said.

"Must have come into an inheritance."

Budusky was tall, about six foot four, with squared shoulders and curly blond hair. His partner was the young guy who had enticed me into the mouth of the alley last night. He was tall, almost as tall as Budusky, and just as robust. I'm pretty big myself, and have had a little experience on the streets of East LA, but Ernie was a lightweight in this crowd, only about a hundred and seventy pounds.

We followed them carefully, one of us on either side of the street, hiding as we went. They weren't paying much attention thought, still laughing and talking about the girls.

Finally, when the alleys ran out of street lamps, they stopped. They took up positions, one behind an awning, the other behind a telephone pole, as if they'd been there before. I wished I had brought my little map, to check the positions of the previous muggings. It didn't matter much now, though. The opening to a dark, seemingly pitch-black alley loomed behind them. They had chosen their position well.

Ernie and I remained hidden. We could see each other from across the street, but the two MPs couldn't see us.

It took twenty minutes for three sailors, lost in their drunkenness, to wander down the road. They were little fellows, in uniform, hats tilted at odd angles. Two of them had beer bottles in their hands, and each had his wallet sticking out from beneath his tunic, folded over his waistband.

The navy's into tradition. Even if it's stupid. Or maybe especially if it's stupid. No pockets.

We let the sailors pass us. I was glad Ernie didn't warn them. Of course, he wasn't the type to warn them anyway.

They didn't see us as they passed. They were laughing and joking, and I doubt they would have noticed a jet plane if it had swooped down five feet over their heads.

What did swoop down was Budusky and his partner. Two of the sailors went down before the third even realized what was happening. He swung his beer bottle, but it missed its mark and he was enveloped by the two marauding behemoths.

Ernie and I slid out of our hiding places and floated up the hill, my roll of dimes clenched securely in my right fist. Ernie smashed his mallet into the back of the MP's head, and I knew all our problems were over with him. But just as I launched my first punch at Budusky, he swiveled and caught the blow on his shoulder. I punched again, but I was off balance from having missed the first blow, and he countered and caught me in the ribs. It was hard, but I've had worse, and then we were toe to toe, belting each other, slugging viciously. It could have gone either way, and I was happy to see Ernie looming up behind him. I jabbed with my left and backed off, waiting for it all to end, but then, as if a trapdoor had opened beneath his feet, Ernie disappeared. I realized that one of the sailors had gotten up and, thinking Ernie was one of the enemy, had grabbed him and pulled him down. Another of the sailors came to, and now the three of them were rolling around on the ground flailing clubs and beer bottles at each other, cursing, spitting, and scratching.

Something blurred my vision, and Budusky was on me. I twisted, slipped a punch, and caught him with a good left hook in the midsection. He took it, punched back, and then we were wrestling. I lost my footing, pulled him down with me, and we rolled down the incline. I threw my weight and kept us rolling, I wasn't sure why. Just to get us into the light, I guess. Our momentum increased our speed, and finally we jarred to a stop.

Blind chance had determined that it would be Budusky's back that hit the cement pole with the full force of our rolling bodies. I punched him a couple of times on the side of his head before I realized that he was finished. I got up in a crouch and checked his pulse. It was steady. I slapped his face a couple of times. His eyes opened. Before he could pull himself together, I rolled him over on his stomach, pulled my handcuffs out from the back of my belt, and locked his hands securely behind the small of his back.

I heard whistles and then running feet. The Shore Patrol surrounded me and then a couple of MPs. The MPs stood back, as if they wanted nothing to do with this.

I lifted Budusky by the collar and pushed his face back to the pavement.

"Why? Why'd you kill Lockworth?"

His face was contorted, grimacing in pain. His eyes were clenched. I lifted him and slammed him back again.

"It was your dad, wasn't it? Your dad was a sailor. And he left you, you and your mother."

It was an old story and didn't take a great leap of imagination. An illegitimate kid from Norfolk, growing up to hate the navy, joining the army as an MP, finding his opportunity to take his revenge. A few bumps, a few bruises, a few dollars, and a sailor would get over it. It was the least they owed him for what his dad had done to him and his mother. Until he went too far. And killed.

I heard Budusky talking. It was choking out his throat.

"He left us. So what's it to you?"

"And when you last heard from him . . . "

"Yeah." The tears seemed to be squeezed out of his eyes. "When the last letter came, he was on the *Kitty Hawk*."

Ernie and I left the next day with the date for Budusky's court-martial set for next month.

Back in Seoul the first sergeant requested that the venue be changed about sixty miles north, to Camp Henry in Taegu. Ernie and I had to appear in court as witnesses, and it wouldn't be smart to give the MPs in Pusan a chance to get at us.

I could understand their feelings. They saw us as traitors to the Military Police Corps. Maybe we were.

But none of those MPs ever sat down to write a letter to the parents of the late Petty Officer Third Class Gerald R. Lockworth.

I did.

A PIECE OF RICE CAKE

It seemed that half our blotter reports lately had something to do with gambling.

Maybe it was the beautiful autumn in Korea, when the green leaves of summer turn to orange and yellow and brown and people realize that they are heading for that long cold winter we call death.

"Take a chance! You only go round once."

Not what Buddha or Confucius would have said, but this is the modern Korea and the rules are changing. And the GIs stationed here have nothing better to do than throw away their money.

I thumbed through the blotter reports. A Korean businessman busted in a poker game on the compound; an NCO Club bartender rifling the night's receipts to cover his "flower card" losses; a GI collared running a shell game in the barracks. And so when the first sergeant called me and Ernie into his office and gave us our assignment, it didn't come as much of a surprise.

"Somebody stole the football pool on the Army and Navy game over at the Officers' Club."

We stared in mock horror. Ernie spoke first.

"Has Eighth Army been put on alert?"

"Yeah, wise guy. On alert. This may not seem too serious to you two, but the Eighth Army chief of staff is about to soil his shorts. 'Besmirching the honor of the Army-Navy tradition,' he said."

Whenever they start talking tradition, honor, or country, look out for your brisket.

"How much money did he have invested?" I said.

The first sergeant sighed, took a sip of his lukewarm coffee, and ignored me.

"I'd put Burrows and Slabem on the case—they have more respect for the officer corps—but they're on a case out at ASCOM City. So all I have left is you two."

"Thanks for the vote of confidence, Top."

"Don't mention it."

The first sergeant set down his coffee and smiled at us. There was a warning in that smile. Something about not screwing up.

"The pool money was collected by the bartender, Miss Pei . . ."

"A female bartender? On a military installation? I thought the union didn't allow that."

"Normally they don't, but this is the Officers' Club and the union honchos want to keep the Eighth Army staff happy."

"At the Enlisted Club, all we have to look at is the crusty old Mr. Huang."

"You should have gone to Officers' Candidate School."

"Too late to become a brown-noser," Ernie said.

The first sergeant shook his head. "All right, Bascom. And you too, Sueño. I don't care what your personal feelings are about the Officers' Club. This is a simple matter, and I want you to keep it that way. No nosing around for things that don't concern you, and no mouthing off to those officers over there."

Ernie pointed to his chest and mouthed a silent, "Us?"

"Yeah, you! Miss Pei is over there now, tending bar for the lunch crowd. At about thirteen hundred I want you to check it out and give me a complete report. Keep it simple, keep it neat, and don't get yourselves into any trouble."

"Piece of rice cake," Ernie said. "Not to worry, Top."

The first sergeant frowned as we rose from our chairs and

walked toward the door. All I could think about was the number of times I've gagged on a wad of thick chewy rice cake.

Terrible stuff.

Halfway down the carpeted hallway of the 8th Army Officers' Club I was slapped with the familiar aroma of stale beer, sliced lemon, and liberally sloshed disinfectant.

Home.

Miss Pei was behind the bar, cleaning up and doing her post-lunch-hour inventory. There weren't any officers left in the bar, as the chief of staff keeps the place closed during the afternoon.

Miss Pei stood up as we approached. Her face was flushed, and she appeared nervous. It hadn't been a good day. A wisp of straight black hair hung down across her forehead, and she brushed it back with her chubby hand and short brown forearm.

"You CID?" she asked.

"That's us," Ernie said. "Criminal Investigation Division, Yongsan Detachment."

Miss Pei wore a neatly pressed white blouse and a red skirt. She was a very attractive young lady and I could see why the chief of staff preferred this young flower gracing his cocktail lounge to some old curmudgeon like Mr. Huang.

"All the money is back," she said. "I made a mistake. There is no problem."

We looked at her for a moment, not sure what to say, and then a tall, thin American in a baby blue three-piece suit hustled out of the hallway and wound through the cocktail tables.

"George! Ernie! I tried to get in touch with you, but your first sergeant told me you'd already left. It was all a mistake. We found the money locked in the liquor cabinet and it's all there and there's nothing to worry about. But I'm glad you guys came anyway. Can I buy you a drink?"

"I thought the bar was closed?"

"For chumps. For you guys it's always open."

"I'll take a beer," Ernie said.

I shrugged. What the hell. It wasn't often that Freddy bought anything. Not unless you had him over a barrel. I turned to Miss Pei. "I'll take a Falstaff."

"Two Falstaff?" She held up two stubby fingers. Ernie nodded. I looked at Freddy. "How the hell did you get over here? They kick you out of the NCO Club?"

"Naw, nothing like that," Freddy said. "That mush-for-brains Ballard was losing money here, so they sent me over two months ago. Already we're back in the black. Made a profit of two thousand dollars last month, and we're climbing."

"You must know how to handle these officers."

"Nothing to it. Tell 'em that they're smart and make them feel like they're getting something for free and they'll let you manage the place the way you want to manage it."

"You mean, steal the club blind."

"Come on, George. You know better than that. We're audited all the time."

"A guy like you, Freddy, should be able to outsmart an auditor any day of the week."

His eyes sparkled at that, but he didn't say anything.

Ernie finished his beer and ordered another one from Miss Pei. As long as it was free, he didn't have time to talk.

"You say it was a mistake?" I said.

"Yeah," Freddy replied. "This new clown of an assistant manager, fresh out of club management school, he told the chief of staff about it before he got his head out of his ass and checked with me. The money was just misplaced, that's all. I counted it myself. It's all there."

"Miss Pei said that the money had been 'put back.'"

Freddy shot her a look. She froze, like a squirrel in front of a hunter.

"Just a figure of speech, that's all."

"Let me see the money, Freddy."

"Sure. No sweat, George. No sweat."

He snapped his fingers, and Miss Pei bent down into her

liquor cabinet and soon reappeared with a gigantic brandy snifter full of crisp green bills.

"And I'll need the chart, or whatever you use to record the
money put into the pool."

Freddy went around behind the bar and helped Miss Pei take
down a large cardboard poster that was taped to the mirror.

She laid it on the bar. A hundred squares, ten by ten, were
drawn on the board. Across the top and down the left side, each
square was numbered zero to nine. For a set amount you bought
a square, and if your numbers were, say, three and seven, and
the final score of the game turned out to be twenty-three to
seventeen, the two last digits matched yours and you won the
pool—the total amount of money bought in for. If each square
cost a dollar, and they were all sold, your take would be a hundred dollars. In this case it was a little steeper.

"Five dollar pool," I said. "Serious money."

"The Army-Navy game," Freddy said. "Half these guys were
cadets at West Point way back when Christ was a corporal. It's
like a religion to them."

I noticed a number of entries marked "SMF" in red felt pen.
The chief of staff's initials.

First I started to count the number of blocks that were filled
in with somebody's signature, but there were so many of them
that I just counted the empty blocks. There were five. Ninety-
five were filled in. That meant there should be a total of four
hundred and seventy-five dollars in the brandy snifter. The
bills were crisp, and I had to peel them off one another carefully. Twenty-three twenties, a ten, and a five. The money was
all there.

"It balances out, Freddy."

"You want another beer?"

"No."

But Ernie did. Miss Pei served him, deftly and silently.

I could have let it go. All the money was there, each square
in the poster was accounted for, but there was the crispness of

the bills. They hadn't been collected by the bartender as she went along during the workday over the weeks preceding the game; a five dollar bill here, a twenty dollar bill there. These bills had all been put in together. Even the serial numbers were in sequence. Fresh stuff. Right out of the Finance Office. My guess was that when somebody blew the whistle on him, Freddy had hustled into his cashier's cage, gotten the money, and replenished the brandy snifter so everything balanced.

"You mind if I take a look at the liquor cabinet?"

"No. Go ahead."

I walked around behind the bar. Stepping on the planks, I realized that I towered over Miss Pei. She was much more in control when us foreign monsters were seated on the other side of the counter. The liquor cabinets had sliding wooden doors with hasps and padlocks. None of them appeared to have been tampered with, and there was no evidence of recent repair work. Whoever had gotten to the brandy snifter had access to the area while the liquor cabinets were open, or they used a key.

While I was down there checking, I noticed Miss Pei's clipboard with her daily bar inventory on it. It listed all the various types of liquor and beer served in the 8th Army Officers' club. She had accounted for each shot poured, multiplied that total by the cost per drink, and compared the grand total to the amount of money taken in during her shift. It matched to the penny. Not an ounce of liquor had been wasted.

I stood up and rotated my back to loosen it up. "No sign of tampering with the locks."

"I told you," Freddy said. "It was all a mistake. The money's all here, what are you worried about?"

I ignored him and walked to the front of the bar. "Let's check the cashier's cage, Freddy."

As I walked toward the front lobby, Freddy followed. "You don't have a right! You came here to check out the football pool, not to rummage around in my cashier's cage."

I stopped when we reached the hallway and put my finger up to Freddy's nose. "I'm in the middle of an investigation, Freddy, in a government-owned facility. If you try to interfere, I'll arrest you."

Freddy stared at me, his thin brown mustache quivering with rage.

"You're an idiot, George."

Ernie passed us on his way to the cashier's cage, his Falstaff still in hand. "That's what everybody tells him. Doesn't do any good, though. He's still the same."

The middle-aged bespectacled woman in the cashier's cage stood up as we entered. I went right to work. The total amount of operating funds for the club was posted on the side of the safe and signed by the Yongsan Compound Director of Personnel and Community Affairs. The total was eight thousand five hundred dollars in US money and fifteen hundred dollars' worth of Korean *won*. Any monies above that would be cash receipts and would have to be accounted for with a form called the Daily Cashier's Record.

The big safe was open, and the money was neatly arranged. With Freddy and the cashier watching us, we counted it quickly. It was all there with the addition of the two hundred seventy-three dollars and eighty-five cents taken in by the bar and the six hundred forty-seven dollars taken in by the kitchen during the just completed lunch hour.

There was only one problem. Instead of fifteen hundred dollars' worth of *won*, the Korean operating bank had nineteen hundred seventy-five dollars' worth of *won* and the US dollar operating bank was depleted by exactly four hundred seventy-five. It all balanced out, but they had too much Korean money and not enough US money. And the difference was exactly the amount found in the big glass brandy snifter.

"You took up a collection, didn't you, Freddy?"

"Not me." Freddy put his hand to his chest and took a step out of the cashier's cage. "I don't know nothing about it."

"Or maybe you didn't want to know nothing about it."

"What the employees do with their own money is up to them. I had nothing to do with it."

Ernie snorted.

Freddy turned and fled back to his office.

Talk about standing up for your staff.

The situation didn't look too serious. Apparently what had happened was that Miss Pei noticed that the football pool money was missing from the brandy snifter, informed the new assistant manager, and he told the 8th Army chief of staff, who is also head of the Club Council. The chief of staff got on the horn and told the CID to get down here right away. Hot stuff. Money missing from the Army-Navy football pool—some of it his.

Meanwhile, Freddy and the club employees got wind of the situation and for some reason decided to take up a collection in *won*, the Korean currency; change it into US dollars at the cashier's cage; and replace the money in the brandy snifter. Why they did this I didn't know. One reason could have been to keep the heat off the club. Those bar inventories looked too precise to account for normal human activity. Bartenders sometimes spill liquor or open the wrong can of beer, or a customer sends a drink back because it isn't what he ordered. Inventories shouldn't come out even down to the last ounce of liquor and the last can of beer. Not real inventories. But when you're pulling a scam, you might decide to make everything balance perfectly so you don't attract attention. So you won't have a couple of nosy CID agents wandering around your club.

Or maybe the employees collected the money for some other reason. I didn't know. But most important, I couldn't figure who had stolen the money in the first place.

I looked at the cashier. "Who took the money out of the brandy snifter?"

She stared at the floor. Slowly she began to shake her head. I tried again.

"Where did all this extra *won* come from? Did you take up a collection?"

Still she said nothing, as if she were tremendously ashamed, and just kept shaking her head.

I stood up. I knew I wasn't going to get anything here. Ernie stood up and threw his empty beer can into the wastebasket. We walked out into the hallway.

Ernie said, "They're trying to cover something up."

I said, "You got that right."

Two cute young Korean girls, bundled in sweaters and scarves, bounced down the hallway toward the main exit. Lunch hour waitresses, heading home. I stopped them and spoke in Korean.

"Young lady. Who is the head of the union here?"

They both stopped abruptly, breathless and wide-eyed.

"Mr. Kwon. The bar manger."

I thanked them; they giggled and continued on their way.

Ernie looked after them. "Nice legs."

"That's all you could see of them."

"That was enough."

We wandered down the red carpeted hallway, took a couple of lefts, and found the bar manager's office. Mr. Kwon stood up when we walked in. He was a tall man, close to six feet, maybe in his mid-fifties, and he had the scholarly air of someone who works with books and ledgers—not like most of the bartenders I was used to back in the States. He wore slacks and a white shirt with a black tie. His hair was oiled and combed straight back. I tried to imagine him in the white pantaloons and tunic of the ancient Korean with the hair long and knotted on the top. He looked like a Confucian scholar caught in modern times.

His eyes widened slightly. "Yes?"

"It's about the money you collected," I said, "to replace what was missing from behind the bar. Why?"

Mr. Kwon sighed and indicated the chairs across the small cubicle. "Have a seat."

We sat.

"This morning," he said, "when Miss Pei came to me and told

me the money was missing, we decided to take up a collection and replace it."

"We?"

"The Korean employees here. It is not good to leave something shameful like the disappearance of money unattended to. This is our home. We take care of it."

"But Miss Pei had already told one of the Americans, the assistant manager."

"A mistake. We should not have bothered you about this matter."

"Who took the money?"

Mr. Kwon looked down for a second then up at me. "The money is back now. There is no reason to worry about who took it."

"Maybe not. But I need to know. Otherwise, I won't know whether to worry or not."

"And besides," Mr. Kwon said, "now that the chief of staff is interested in this matter, you are nervous and if you don't find out the truth it could be bad for you."

Bingo. I was hardly admitting it to myself. If this had been the Enlisted Club and the money had been returned and none of the 8th Army honchos had known about it, I wouldn't have bothered to look any further. As it was, the first sergeant would be breathing fire if we didn't wrap this thing up.

Ernie jumped in. "Don't you worry about the chief of staff. You just tell us who stole that damn money."

Mr. Kwon looked at him steadily. "One of our waitresses stole it. Miss Lim."

Ernie said, "Why haven't you turned her in?"

"We will take care of it. Our own way."

There was something about this situation that was bothering me. If the Korean staff had a bad apple among them who was embarrassing everybody by stealing the Army-Navy football pool money, I could understand their trying to get rid of her quietly in order to save face. But what I couldn't understand was why they would donate their hard-earned money to cover for her. Their chances of recouping their donations were nil. So why not just admit the thievery, run her out of town, and forget it? Were they that embarrassed that they'd shell out cash to avoid the wrath of the 8th Army chief of staff? I knew I wouldn't. Of course, years of doing without in East LA had taught me to be somewhat parsimonious. And the Koreans had risen from the ashes of a devastating war less that two decades ago. They were even thriftier than I was. It didn't make sense.

"What is it about this Miss Lim," I said, "that makes you want to protect her?"

Mr. Kwon shifted in his seat and then looked back at me. Maybe he decided that we weren't going to give up so he might as well lay it on the table.

"We know why she stole the money," he said. "She has a baby and the baby is sick and she had to take it to the hospital."

"What about her husband?"

"She's not married."

I waited. Mr. Kwon continued.

"There was an officer here. Not a good man. I warned her. She stayed with him while he spent his year in Korea. He told her that he would divorce his wife and return for her and the baby. After he left for the States, he wrote to her maybe two or three times, sent her some money, and then stopped writing. I've seen it many times. I've seen many young Korean girls with their hopes too high. They are blinded by their love for the United States."

"Not their love for the GI?"

"No." Mr. Kwon's face didn't move.

Ernie pulled out a stick of chewing gum, unwrapped it, and after a few chomps got it clicking. He didn't believe that line any more than I did. Shooting for sympathy. With a half-American baby.

"Where does this Miss Lim live?"

Mr. Kwon sighed again. He lifted the phone on his desk,

dialed, barked a question, and then wrote something on the notepad in front of him. After he hung up the phone, he ripped the paper off the pad and handed it to me.

"Do you read Korean?"

"If you write clearly." It was an address. "This is where Miss Lim lives?"

"Yes."

I thanked him. We stood up and left the room. He looked after us as we walked down the long hallway. Maybe it was his resigned manner. Maybe it was the ancient cast of his features. But something told me that he'd been through this before.

Unlike the lush gentility of the 8th Army compound, Itaewon was alive with milling people and rows of produce, chickens, hogs, and fish wriggling in murky tanks. Miss Lim's alley was right off the Itaewon Market, but the noise of commerce shut off abruptly as we slid into the narrow walkway. Ten-foot-high brick and stone walls loomed over us. I checked the number on the gateways to the homes. They didn't seem to be in order, as if things had changed too much over the centuries for a simple one, two, three, four. Finally I found the gateway to 246-15 and pounded on a splintered wooden gate. Hens squawked as an old woman put on her slippers and shuffled toward us.

"*Yoboseiyo?*" she said.

"Miss Lim," I said. "We're looking for Miss Lim."

The old woman opened the door. Trusting. We were Americans, not thieves.

"*Ae Kyong-ah!*" She called for someone. I thought it would be Miss Lim but it turned out to be an interpreter. A woman, about thirty, in blue shorts and a red T-shirt emerged from her hooch.

"Are you Miss Lim?" I said.

"No. She went to the hospital. Her baby is very sick."

"Which hospital?"

She spoke to the old woman in rapid Korean and then turned back to me. "The MoBom Hospital in Hannam-dong."

"Which room does she live in?"

"The one on the end. There."

Ernie and I walked over. It was just a hovel. Raised foundation, little plastic closet in the corner, folded sleeping mats on a vinyl floor, and a small pot-bellied stove in the center of the room with rickety aluminum tubing reaching to the ceiling. An American officer in dress greens stared at me out of a framed photograph. He looked to be in his mid-thirties, maybe twenty pounds over his fighting weight, with curly brown hair and a big jolly smile. Gold maple leaves on his shoulder glittered along with his white teeth.

I turned back to the women. "How long has Miss Lim been gone?"

"She came home from work late last night. The baby never stopped crying. She waited until the curfew was over and then left for the hospital."

"Before dawn?"

"Yes."

"And she's been there ever since?"

"Yes."

The old woman waited patiently, not understanding. I smiled at her, thanked them both, and we turned to go. The woman in the blue shorts and red T-shirt called after me.

"Hey!"

We stopped and turned around.

"Why you GI always make baby and then go?"

I didn't have an answer for her. Ernie stopped clicking his gum. We turned around and left.

The waiting room of the MoBom Hospital was packed. An attractive young Korean woman with a snappy white cap pinned to her black hair sat behind a counter near the entrance. Behind her was a list of basic fees. It was ten thousand *won*, up front, to see a doctor. Fourteen bucks.

I told her about Miss Lim and her sick baby and asked where

we could find her. She thumbed through a ledger but kept shaking her head. She wanted to know Miss Lim's full name. I told her she was the woman with the half-American baby. She perked right up.

"Oh, yes. She is in Room three fourteen. The stairway is over there."

The room held about thirty tiny beds with plastic siding on them. Next to one of them, Miss Lim sat on a wooden chair, her face in her hands. I showed her my identification.

"Hello, Miss Lim. We're from the CID."

It seemed that her face was about to burst with redness. She was a plain woman, young and thin with a puffy face that looked even more bloated from crying.

"Is your baby going to be all right?"

"The doctor is not sure yet. I must wait."

Ernie didn't like it here. He fidgeted with the change in his pocket and then drifted toward the door. My signal to wrap it up quickly.

"The money you took from behind the bar, it has already been replaced. I will talk to everyone. Explain your situation. I don't think you have anything to worry about."

Her head went back into her hands, and this time she clutched her red face as if she were trying to bury it in her palms. I couldn't be sure, but I think her shoulders convulsed a couple of times. I looked down at the baby. It was scrawny. Unconscious. Sweat-soaked brown hair matted against its little head.

We left.

Neither one of us spoke as the sloe-eyed stares followed us out of the hospital.

Ernie zigzagged his jeep through the heavy Seoul traffic as if he were in a race to get away from the devil.

"Well," he said. "We wrapped up another one."

"I'm sure they won't do anything to her," I said. "I'll type up the report to make her look as good as possible. Even the Eighth Army chief of staff has got a heart."

Ernie didn't say anything. I turned to him.

"Right?"

He shrugged. "If you say so, pal."

The chief of staff didn't want to prosecute, but in his capacity as the president of the Officers' Club Council he did demand that Miss Lim appear before the next board meeting and explain her actions. The word we got was that he was upset because she could have come to the Club Council at any time, explained the nature of her financial emergency, and they would have helped out. Thievery wasn't necessary, according to him.

When Ernie heard that, he snorted. "Nobody likes a person with a problem until that person has already solved the problem."

Also, the Club Council could have set up a mechanism to help employees with emergency medical expenses at any time in the past, but they never had. Better, apparently, to make them come begging for it.

Ernie and I went to the Enlisted Club that night for Happy Hour and paid thirty-five cents for a tax-free beer and forty cents for a shot of bourbon.

The stripper had eyes like a tigress.

"She was a real trouper," Freddy said. "Appeared before the Club Council looking sharp, standing up straight, and didn't bat an eye when they told her that she'd been suspended for thirty days."

"How have the other Korean employees taken it?"

"The place has been like a morgue. They do their jobs all right, but they won't look at me and they won't say anything. The laughter's gone."

"It'll come back." Freddy looked skeptical, but I knew it would. I'd learned that in East LA.

■ ■ ■

At first the Korean National Police Liaison Officer tried to keep it from us but Yongsan Compound is like a small town plopped in the middle of the huge metropolis of Seoul and word spreads quickly. Especially amongst the MPs and the CID.

Ernie didn't chew gum on the way to Itaewon, and he drove carefully.

Neighbors clogged the narrow alleyway leading to Miss Lim's hooch, but we pushed our way through them and at the gate we flashed our identification to the uniformed Korean policeman. Captain Kim, commander of the Itaewon Police Station, was there. He didn't say anything when we steeped to the front of Miss Lim's room.

The baby looked pretty much the way I'd seen her before. Thin. Still. But she wasn't sweating any more. She lay on the vinyl floor as if she'd rolled away from her mother's bosom. Miss Lim's mouth was wide open and so were her eyes. They were white. Without pupils.

When I turned around, Captain Kim stood right behind us.

"Carbon monoxide poisoning," he said.

I looked at the aluminum tubing above the heater. There was a hole in it, as if someone had punctured the thin metal with a knife, and twisted.

The photograph of the brown-haired major lay face up on the floor. Smiling at me.

THE WOMAN FROM HAMHUNG

We wound through the jumbled alleyways of Seoul's East Gate Market, past freshly washed fish in packed blue ice and mounds of Chinese cabbage glowing green in the canvas-covered darkness. In the heart of the catacombs a few large spools of industrial copper wire waited for a buyer. Ernie wrote down the case lot numbers.

"Hot off the compound," he said.

The black market had been going strong here since the end of the Korean War, primarily because of the lack of indigenous industry and the exorbitant import taxes levied on foreign goods. Guarding the plethora of US-made building supplies on army compounds were always a few GIs willing to go after some easy money.

At least sometimes the money was easy.

Our job was to stanch the flow of these supplies. Some of them. At least for a while.

A wrinkled forehead over a big red dress waddled toward us. She shrieked and waved her arms. Ernie put his notepad away, snapped his gum between his front teeth, and stalked off in the general direction of the rushing traffic on the main street.

"Not your typical Korean hospitality," I said.

Ernie snorted.

Our next stop was SP51, 8th Army's biggest supply point in Seoul.

We flashed our badges to a sullen corporal, thumbed through a small mountain of paperwork, and in a couple of hours had determined that the case lots in question had all been shipped north to the 2nd Infantry Division. After a few phone calls to the 2nd Division logistics office, we found out that some of the numbered spools had been issued to Camp Howze and some to Camp Edwards.

"Which one's closer to the DMZ?" Ernie asked.

"Edwards. But they say it has a better NCO club. And besides, I've already been to the village outside Howze."

"Then it's Edwards?"

"Right."

When we reported to the first sergeant, he stood in front of a metal urn of coffee tipping the last dregs into his big porcelain cup.

"What'd you get?" He didn't look at us.

"The copper wire's coming out of Camp Edwards," Ernie said.

"All of it?"

"Yeah."

"Then that's where we'll go." The first sergeant mixed some cream and sugar into his coffee, returned to his desk, and took a sip of the lukewarm concoction. A grimace split his face. "When is that Miss Kim going to learn how to make coffee?"

"When you quit riding her," I said.

The first sergeant shot a look at me, thought better of some remark, and took another careful sip of his bitter brew.

"One of you is going to have to go undercover up there," he said.

"For a few spools of wire?"

"It's more than just that. The Korean National Police are complaining that their construction sites have been flooded with US-made black market goods for the last few months. It's cutting into the sales of their local industries."

"The big shots are getting hurt," Ernie said.

The first sergeant glared at him. "Which one of you is it going to be? For the undercover, I mean."

Ernie touched his long bony fingers to his ribs. "Me, I've got to nurse my war wounds."

"Yeah. That's right." The first sergeant turned to me. "Sueño, you'll be the undercover man up there. We'll have orders cut for you today. Tomorrow you'll report to the Replacement Company up at the Second Infantry Division. Bascom, you'll be his control. Keep him out of trouble."

"I always get the hard jobs," Ernie said.

We left the first sergeant's office, clattered down the long hallway of the Criminal Investigation Division headquarters, and hopped in Ernie's jeep. The two-story brick building loomed over us as the sturdy little vehicle roared to life.

"The only wounds you got from Vietnam," I said, "are the scars on your liver."

"Yeah," Ernie said. "But they run deep."

Snow speckled with coal dust swirled behind us as the little jeep lurched forward into the dark afternoon.

My name is George Sueño. My partner Ernie Bascom and I had been kicking around Korea for the last few months as army CID agents, solving a few cases, blowing a few others, getting in trouble.

The CID Detachment first sergeant wasn't too happy with us, but that was because we had a bad habit of not knowing when to wrap up a case, even if some nefarious activities seemed to be pointing in the direction of someone with a little rank. At the 8th Army headquarters, rocking the boat is considered to be a mortal sin.

Even so, Ernie and I had managed to hang on. Barely.

I'm what you might call an orphan. The army's my home now. My mother died when I was two years old—suddenly—and my father slipped south of the border into that endless cavern of mystery known as Mexico. I grew up in foster homes, in East LA, got luckier than most with the foster parents I drew, paid attention in school, and now I'm a highly trained agent for the

Criminal Investigation Division of the 8th US Army in the Republic of Korea.

Beats low-riding Whittier Boulevard.

My partner, Ernie Bascom, had a stable youth and an adventurous adolescence, and then ran into the brick wall of Vietnam. After two tours in Chu Lai he acquired a number of bad habits. The breakable ones, like heroin, were behind him now. The unbreakable ones, like the United States Army and mouthing off, were probably going to stay with him for the rest of his life.

So when we received the order to go to Camp Edwards we both saw it as an opportunity to screw off for a while. Get away from the flagpole. Run the village. We would go through the motions, but if we arrested somebody for black marketing army-owned building supplies, they would have to be trying to get caught.

Of course, a lot of people were.

After a couple of days at the "Repo Depot," the 2nd Infantry Division's Replacement Company, I had gotten the shortest haircut of my life, sewn two dozen Indianhead patches on the sleeves of all my uniforms, and stood about a million useless formations. When the bus marked "Western Corridor" pulled out of Camp Casey and wound through the snow-covered hills, I took a deep breath and watched the smoke curl from straw-thatched farmhouses. We passed the occasional cart pulled by an ox snorting through wet nostrils, hot breath billowing toward the gray Asian sky.

Camp Edwards was a large compound. It sprawled for half a mile along the Main Supply Route leading north to the Demilitarized Zone and was composed mainly of boxy concrete buildings, curved roof Quonset huts, and barbed-wire-enclosed storage areas. Everything that didn't move, plus some things that did, was painted the army's favorite shade of green: olive drab.

I processed in through the orderly room of the Headquarters Company of the Seven-Oh-Deuce Maintenance and Supply

Battalion. I received grunts from the company clerk and indifference from the supply sergeant, and then picked up a small pile of linen and blankets. An old Korean man in slippers, cutoff fatigue pants, and a black pullover sweater led me to my bunk. He told me it would be twenty-five bucks a month for him to do my laundry and shine my shoes. I paid him in advance and then we shook hands. Of all the people I'd met that day, he was the first to give me a personal greeting.

Another warm welcome from the United States Army.

The setup was that I'd process into Headquarters Company just like any other new trooper and set about working every day, keeping my eyes and ears open until I found out who was diverting the supplies into the black market. Ernie would be my control, and we had set up predetermined times for me to call him or, if possible, meet him at the Recreation Center 4 Snack Bar, about four miles to the north, to give him my reports. I also had a number where I could reach him at night in case of emergency: the RC4 Enlisted Club.

The Camp Edwards supply point filled the basin that sat in the center of an asphalt loop. I squatted on a raggedy patch of grass behind the barracks overlooking the basin and watched.

A trash collection truck painted bright blue pulled through the gate in the chain link fence that surrounded the supply point. A bunch of Korean workmen in faded and soiled fatigues jumped off the bed of the truck, pulled off some empty metal drums, and replaced them with those that were filled with trash. The truck pulled out of the supply point and continued on its rounds, picking up trash behind the mess hall and the NCO Club and the dispensary.

At the main gate, before the trash truck left the compound, an MP climbed up on the bed and used a long wooden pole to rummage through the trash drums, checking for any sort of contraband the workmen might be trying to smuggle off post.

While I was watching the trash collectors, a two-and-a-half-ton army truck rolled into the supply point. A group of slick-sleeve privates loaded the bed of the truck with something that from this distance looked like lumber and cement. When they were finished, the bed of the deuce-and-a-half sat low on its tires. Then everything was covered with a canvas tarp and tied up neatly.

Later I wandered down the hill toward the supply point and, when I got close enough, jotted down the bumper number of the truck. It was hard to read. Everything's done in dark letters—camouflage—so in case the North Koreans ever invade again, maybe they'll just sort of overlook us.

Except for the cooks in the kitchen, the NCO Club was deserted this time of day. I found a phone at the bar and dialed the number of the RC4 Snack Bar. The Korean who answered told me she didn't know anybody named Ernie Bascom.

"He's the guy with the round glasses," I said. "Chewing gum and playing the pinball machine."

"Oh." She set the phone down, and after a couple of minutes, Ernie came on the line.

"How's it hanging, pal?"

"Loosely. I got a bumper number for you. Ready to write?"

"Shoot."

"Seven-oh-two MB on the left side and then SP fourteen-twenty-three on the right."

"A truck?"

"Yeah. I don't think they'll be going anywhere tonight. They'd be too conspicuous out after curfew. Probably leave first thing in the morning."

"I'll be there." Ernie sipped on something. Coffee, I figured. "What're you gonna do tonight?"

"Run the ville."

"That little pissant village right outside the gate?"

"No. The one where the officers and senior NCOs hang out. Kumchon. About a mile and a half down the road. Tomorrow night, I'll meet you at the club there at RC4 about six, so you can tell me about the truck tomorrow morning."

After retreat formation I went to the chow hall and ate supper and then over to the orderly room and signed out on pass. The pass stipulated that I had to be back on compound before the beginning of the midnight-to-four A.M. curfew. I wouldn't get my overnight pass until after I received my venereal disease orientation from the first sergeant. They'd already given us one at the Repo Depot, but no matter how many times GIs are warned about the dangers, they still end up poking around in places where they shouldn't.

I flashed my pass and ID to the MP at the gate. There were a few paltry bars in a village across the MSR, that's where most of the GIs went, and a lot of them were shacked up in the hooches that sprawled off into the surrounding rice paddies. The senior NCOs and officers frequented Kumchon—a real town, not just a GI village. I figured that the number of supplies being diverted indicated more than just a little low-level pilfering, so I flagged down a Kimchi Cab and told the driver to take me to Kumchon.

When we arrived, he asked me where I wanted to get out. I didn't know, but after about two blocks, downtown Kumchon petered out and we were winding through frozen rice paddies again. I told him to stop, paid him, and wandered back toward the bright lights. The road through town was only two lanes, and the shops on either side were pushed right up against the narrow sidewalks. Kumchon had what all towns have: pharmacies, restaurants, a place for milling rice, a stationery store, and a few bars. I peeked through the windows of the bars but saw only ROK soldiers in uniform, toasting one another and laughing too loud. Finally, at the other end of town, I saw a bar with a little more neon than the others. The sign in Korean said KUM GOM—golden dream. The smaller English lettering beneath it said GOLDEN NIGHT CLUB.

There's a difference between a golden dream and the golden

nightclub, but it looked like the Koreans who worked there weren't going to let the GIs in on it.

I walked in. It was a big club, bigger than the others, and there were already a few GIs in small clusters sitting at the tables. Korean waitresses—young, pretty girls all—served them, and a few sat at the tables, slapping the groping GI hands and laughing. The music was loud, but not so loud that you couldn't talk, and it tended to be a little more sedate than what I figured I'd find in the clubs across the street from Camp Edwards.

Two grizzled old NCO types sat at one end of the bar, talking to a smiling barmaid. I sat at the other end of the bar, and when she stood up and walked toward me, I saw that she was a big woman. Broad shouldered. Ample dimensions everywhere. Gorgeous.

I ordered my beer in Korean and that made her smile and then she came back to see how well I could really speak the language. After a while, she told me that she was twenty-four, divorced with a daughter, and had originally come south with her family when she was an infant during the Korean War. Her hometown was Hamhung, far to the north in that area of the world that the Cold War mapmakers were still painting in red.

The guys at the other end of the bar grew antsy at the lack of attention and she had other orders to fill, but as soon as she had everybody smiling again she came back to me. I had a couple more liters of beer and we talked as if we were old friends. Her eyes lit up when I told her that I had just arrived in country, on my second tour in Korea. Opportunity for both of us. Her name was Miss Ma.

Someone kicked the door in. A group of shouting, hooting Americans trundled inside the Golden Nightclub. Officers. Even in civilian clothes they were practically wearing signs around their necks. First of all, they were acting like jerks. Also, they had whitewall haircuts and blue jeans and sport shirts that, although wrinkled, had been neatly pressed before they left the compound. They acted like they owned the place.

They pulled a couple of tables together and started ordering and grabbing at the waitresses, and one of them peeled away from the group and lumbered toward the bar. Miss Ma moved away from me quickly.

He didn't order anything. Instead, he leaned over and whispered something in Miss Ma's ear. At first she didn't move, but then she spoke to him and he seemed to become angry and she spoke again and then she had him convinced of something and they were both nodding and finally he walked away. She got busy filling orders from the waitresses, and it was another ten minutes before she returned to me.

"You go back compound tonight?"

"Yes. I won't have an overnight until tomorrow."

She exhaled slightly—relieved—and then her shoulders rose and she smiled. "Maybe I will see you then?"

Playing hard to get is a ploy that has never entered my repertoire.

"You will," I said.

After a couple more beers and a few dirty looks from the officer who had talked to Miss Ma, I stumbled out the door and made it back to Camp Edwards. Once I jumped in the rack, visions of her smiling face danced before me. Later that night I tried to struggle free from miles of unraveling copper wire, spinning off its spool, entrapping me in an ever-shrinking web of shimmering metal.

After watching the overloaded deuce-and-a-half pull out just before dawn, I spent the day trying to adjust to the routine of my new job as the assistant company clerk. The first sergeant was a little young, as first sergeants go, and seemed to be in over his head. The company clerk, Specialist 5 Flourey, didn't seem overly efficient, either. Basically the whole place was a mess. I did what I could, straightening out some files, typing some supply requests for the first sergeant, but mainly I concentrated on finding out who was who. After work I showered and shaved, signed out on my new overnight pass, and took a cab north to the RC4 Enlisted Club.

I pulled Ernie away from the bar, and we sat at the most isolated table we could find, which is sort of difficult in a one-room Quonset hut.

"The guy who drove the truck," I said, "was Sergeant First Class Rawlings, NCO-in-charge of the supply point."

"That's a lot of stripes for driving a truck."

"Depends on where he was going."

"And what he was carrying."

Ernie stopped the waitress and ordered us a couple of Falstaffs. "He went up north to the DMZ, Camp Kitty Hawk. A group of GIs unloaded the truck, and after he left I checked out the supplies."

"Find anything?"

"Nothing but lumber and cement," Ernie said. "I lead-footed it down the MSR and caught up with him."

"No other stops?"

"None."

"They must be getting the wire off post some other way."

We sipped on our beer for a while.

"They must be covering for him back at Camp Edwards," I said. "That amount of supplies couldn't be disappearing without somebody higher up noticing it."

"Who's the logistics officer?"

"Captain Calloway. All I have is a name so far. I'll match it to a face tomorrow."

"You need to get into the supply point and check their invoices."

"I think I can manage it," I said. "But not tonight."

"Why?"

"We might as well make this all-expenses-paid trip last for a while."

Ernie nodded.

"And besides, I have a date tonight."

The waitress brought our beers, smiling at Ernie. "So do I," he said. "With the entire village of Sonyu-ri."

A couple of hours later, Ernie wandered out into the village and I caught a cab and made it back to Kumchon. Ten minutes before the midnight curfew, Miss Ma took me by the hand and led me down long rows of narrow, dark alleys until we arrived at her hooch. Lying on the warm floor I discovered that she was more wonderful than I had imagined.

Her five-year-old daughter slept on the mat beside us.

In the middle of the afternoon a neatly uniformed officer stormed into the orderly room and chewed out the first sergeant for putting his supply point people on the duty roster. The first sergeant patiently explained that he was only trying to comply with army regulations, but the captain didn't appear at all satisfied. When he stomped out of the office, he shot a quick glance at me, and I realized that he was Miss Ma's paramour from the Golden Night Club. The one who had leaned across the bar and whispered in her ear. I also saw his nametag. Captain Calloway. The logistics officer.

I wedged the crowbar into the back window of the big Quonset hut, and after I pried in three different spots, it slammed open. I crawled through the window and closed it behind me. The place was typical GI issue. Rows of gray desks, filing cabinets, and a disbursing counter in the middle of the big cylindrical barn. I pulled out the flashlight I had bought at the PX and rifled through some of the files.

I pulled out my list of invoices, trying to match them to what was in the files, but the pertinent ones weren't where they were supposed to be. They'd been removed. We would have to go back to the issuing point at Camp Casey and retrieve copies of the original invoices, which were sequentially numbered, to prove that Camp Edwards had received the stuff. If they'd also been removed there, we'd have to go back to Seoul. It would be a lot of work, but eventually the accountability would be established.

I checked some of the desks. Nothing. Then I checked the desk with SFC Rawlings's name plate perched on the front edge. I found them in the bottom drawer, wadded up under a half-empty bottle of Old Overholt. I spread them out on the desk, took a shot of the whiskey straight from the bottle, and shone my flashlight on them.

About thirty invoices altogether. The ones I had on my list and a whole bunch more. Enough to put these guys away. I still didn't have the link, though. Captain Calloway, the logistics officer, would certainly be found guilty of dereliction of duty for not checking on them, but I would need more proof to nail him for actual collusion in the scheme. It could even go up beyond him. Maybe to the post commander.

Farfetched, perhaps. But it wouldn't be the first time.

Behind one of the file cabinets was a wall locker with a non-army padlock. I looked through Sergeant Rawlings's desk until I found a key. It worked. The locker was filled with some of your more valuable supplies: a brand new buffer with a pad, a few field jackets, a case full of Coleman lanterns. Under the shelves I found two large metal disks, about three feet across. They were rusted and soiled. Next to them lay a metal pole about four feet long. It had a narrow, flattened hook on the end.

I thought about it for a while, relocked the closet, and then went back and had another shot of Old Overholt.

I put the bottle of whiskey back where I'd found it, stuffed the invoices in my shirt, and climbed out the window. I stumbled in the snow for a minute, regaining my footing. Footsteps.

Before I could turn around, the back of my head exploded through my skull. My brains splattered against the olive drab walls of the sheet metal Quonset hut.

Or at least that's what it felt like.

I came to after a few minutes, and when my eyes focused, I

checked my watch. Almost nine. I'd been lying there for an hour. I stood up and inspected the various parts of my body. There was a big knot on the back of my head, but otherwise I was okay. The invoices, of course, were gone.

I almost climbed back into the Quonset hut to retrieve the bottle of Old Overholt, but then I remembered that the NCO Club was open. I could see the lights from there, and as I slogged up the hill I heard the music. I dusted the dirty ice off my jacket and gingerly combed my hair.

When I reached the bar I ordered a double shot of bourbon, straight up, and a Falstaff back.

Nothing had ever tasted sweeter.

I got drunk that night. Very drunk. And when they closed the club I wandered out into the darkness thinking about Miss Ma, but I never made it farther than the barracks, where I hit my bunk and passed out.

In the morning I took off my clothes, showered, shaved, and went directly to the dispensary. They gave me aspirin.

Ernie called me at the orderly room. It was a serious break in cover.

"What the hell is it?"

"There's been a murder. Outside. In Kumchon. What'd you tell me her name was?"

"The girl I was seeing?"

"Yeah."

"Miss Ma."

"That's her."

I clutched the receiver. The throbbing in my head seemed about to explode. I spoke carefully.

"How soon can you pick me up at the front gate?"

"Twenty minutes."

"I'll be there."

I told the first sergeant I had to go. He didn't like it, but I told him it would all be explained to him later. He said it had better.

I ran back to the barracks, changed into my blue jeans and sneakers, and was waiting at the front gate when Ernie's jeep pulled up in a burst of slush.

She looked like she was asleep until you noticed the indentation in her neck. And the copper wire.

The Korean police asked me how I knew her. Ernie had returned my CID identification to me, and I flashed it at them. I told them we had been working on a case on the compound—the pilfering of supplies—and we believed this murder might be related.

The landlady had discovered the body early that morning. She hadn't seen who had spent the night with Miss Ma, but whoever he was, he'd paid to have the old woman take care of the child for the evening.

Somebody who was flush. And wanted to get rid of witnesses.

After the police were finished in the room, they left her there. The landlady was supposed to be trying to notify Miss Ma's relatives, but so far she wasn't having any luck. I didn't hear the little girl. When I looked in the landlady's room she was just sitting there, her head down. No tears.

On the way back to Camp Edwards, I told Ernie about getting beaned last night. I also told him about the invoices, and the metal disks, and the long slender hook. He saw it right away.

"They were smuggling out the spools of wire under a false bottom in the trash drums."

"Right. And since they had that down to a science, no sense going after the more awkward stuff like lumber and cement and steel bars."

"And whoever followed you last night knew he had to get his hands on those invoices."

"Yes," I said. "But he also knew that eventually we'd follow the chain of paperwork until we nailed both the NCO-in-charge and the logistics officer. With a good lawyer they might be able to avoid getting charged with direct culpability, but no matter how you look at it, that much thievery on their watch would ruin their careers."

"The young captain would be out on his ass, and the old sarge would be lucky to hang on until retirement." Ernie popped another stick of gum into his mouth. "So why the girl?"

"Whoever it was that popped me on the head thought it over later and decided that he should have killed me. Aware of Miss Ma's charms, he decided that even with a bump on the head I'd make it out to her hooch last night."

"But you didn't?"

"No. So he was sitting there waiting for me, staring at her, and he realized that all she'd have to do is open her mouth once and I'd know who was behind the whole scene."

"So he killed her?"

"Exactly."

Ernie shook his head. "The guy should have taken the rap for the copper wire. Let it go at that."

We flashed our identification to the MPs at the main gate, and Ernie stared up the hill.

"Who do we see first? Sergeant Rawlings or Captain Calloway?"

I thought about it. Captain Calloway was a young officer, the kind who cherished his army career maybe more than he cherished his left testicle. But still he was young. And he had a college degree. If he got kicked out with a bad discharge, he could get up, dust himself off, and continue with his life. Sergeant Rawlings, on the other hand, didn't even have a high school diploma. And the skills he'd learned in the army—chewing out privates and pilfering supplies—don't pay a lot on the outside. He'd probably end up driving a hack and working on systematically demolishing his liver.

I decided to go with the more desperate of the two.

"Sergeant Rawlings first," I said.

▪ ▪ ▪

We found Rawlings at the NCO Club, on his favorite barstool, having a shot of bourbon with his lunch. It looked like the Chef's Special was pretzels.

He was a burly guy with wrists as thick as my biceps, so we didn't bother with any formalities. Ernie slammed his head down on the bar, I pulled his left wrist back and cuffed it, and then we both wrestled him off the stool until his arms were cuffed behind his back. Ernie took his knee off his spine long enough to read him his rights.

"Why'd you kill the girl, Rawlings?"

"What girl?"

"Miss Ma. Out at the Golden Night Club."

"Stuff it."

He clammed up and said he would tell us nothing until he talked to a lawyer. That's what I like about old NCOs. They always take a common sense approach to problem solving.

Captain Calloway's neatly painted jeep sat in front of the logistics office. I checked the odometer, yanked the trip ticket off its clipboard, and compared the readings.

Everything clicked, like a bunch of zeros lining up at a hundred thousand miles.

When we went in, he was talking on the phone and thumbing through paperwork, acting way too busy to talk to us.

When he finally hung up, he said, "Who the hell are you?"

I showed him my badge. He smirked.

"Undercover, huh? Well, you won't find anything missing here at Supply Point Fourteen. And all that copper wire, that can be explained."

Like I said, some people just want to get caught.

Ernie spoke first. "We're not here about the wire."

Captain Calloway flinched but quickly straightened his face. I held up the trip ticket.

"Your driver closed out the jeep's log last night at twelve thousand four hundred sixty-three miles, but now the odometer reading is twelve thousand four hundred sixty-six miles. Three miles. It's a mile and a half to Kumchon, so the jeep has traveled the equivalent of one round trip."

Captain Calloway's neck muscles worked up and down his throat, and his right hand crawled toward the telephone receiver, as if he were going to call for help.

I continued. "You started watching me when you noticed I was speaking Korean to Miss Ma at the Golden Night Club. Not your typical GI on his first tour in the Orient. That's why you were raising hell in the orderly room. An excuse to check me out. And then you followed me when I broke into the warehouse last night and clubbed me over the head when I came out.

"You've probably already destroyed the invoices, but you knew that with a little homework we'll uncover the whole scheme. You could deny any accusation Rawlings might make against you, just accuse him of trying to bargain his way out of trouble, but in the end you'll be charged with dereliction of duty; with letting your subordinates get away with pilfering hundreds of dollars' worth of supplies. That, at least. Even if you're found innocent, it will mean the end of your army career.

"Hitting me over the head and destroying the invoices was only meant to give yourself a little more time. A little time to go out to Kumchon and take your revenge on Miss Ma for finding a new boyfriend. Or maybe take your revenge on the new boyfriend and stop him from blowing the whistle on your little black market scheme. What you didn't expect is that I wouldn't go out there. And when I didn't show up, you took it out on her."

Calloway stared directly at me, but for him I wasn't there.

Ernie clicked his gum a couple of times.

"We can check with the MPs on duty last night," I said. "They'll remember you driving your jeep off post."

Calloway stood up slowly. "There's no need." He bowed his head for a moment, and then he looked up at us. "It was Rawlings's idea. He said he'd sold copper wire before, on previous tours over here. It was easy money. I used the money at first to spend weekends down in Seoul. In first class hotels. But then I met Miss Ma, and instead I spent all my time in Kumchon. I tried to get her to quit her job, stay with me, but she wouldn't do it."

His eyes widened, as if he were amazed at something.

"I'm an officer, with a good future, and I was getting rich, but she still turned me down. Can you believe it? But *you*! You with no money, just here for a few days . . . "

He shook his head, angry at the tears that were squeezing themselves out of his knotted face.

Ernie's gum clicked faster. He didn't like this kind of thing. He twisted Calloway around and made him assume the position up against the wall. Then he cuffed him and read him his rights. All the while Calloway cried, and when Ernie was finished, he had to unwrap two more sticks of gum and pop them nervously into his mouth.

We stayed at RC4 for a couple more days, wrapping things up, trying to enjoy the freedom of being away from the flagpole, but it didn't work.

Someone from Miss Ma's family came and took her body away. And the little girl.

We went back to Seoul.

On cold winter nights I still think of the woman from Hamhung, with her big warm smile, and the little girl who refused to cry.

THE DRAGON'S TAIL

Strange asked us to meet him at the Snatch Bar.

Its official title was the Snack Bar, but Strange liked to call it the Snatch Bar because he claimed he always found some "strange" there. That is, lonely female dependents of officers and NCOs who were unable to resist his charms. What charms those were, though, was beyond me. He was overweight and balding, always wore wrap-around dark glasses and sucked on a greasy plastic cigarette holder that never left his lips. His real name was Harvey and he was the non-commissioned officer in charge of classified documents at headquarters, working directly with the Commander of 8th United States Army and the Chief of Staff and everyone who made the most important decisions for the United States forces in the Republic of Korea. So my partner, Ernie Bascom, and I put up with Strange. We listened patiently to his fantasies, no matter how perverted, and, as a quid pro quo, we fed him fantasies of our own. The information he provided was just too good to ignore.

At the stainless steel serving line, I purchased a thick porcelain mug of steaming hot black coffee, carried it through the crowded cafeteria, and plopped it down on the table in front of Strange.

"Nothing for me?" he asked.

"Not until we hear what you have to say."

"I'll take hot chocolate," he replied, "with two marshmallows."

Ernie joined us at the table. As he sat down, he flicked Strange's cigarette holder with his forefinger. "How's it hanging, Strange?"

"The name's Harvey."

"Yeah, I forgot. *Harvey*. What've you got for us?"

Strange frowned at my cup of coffee. "I want hot chocolate," Strange repeated, "with two marshmallows."

"Talk first," Ernie said, "then the reward."

Strange glanced between us. "You guys going cheap on me?"

"Not 'going,'" Ernie replied. "We've always been cheap."

Strange shoved a new cigarette into his holder, tossing away the one Ernie had bent. He never lit them, just kept them dangling. He said he was trying to quit. As far as I knew, he'd never started. The sunglasses, the slicked-back hair, the cigarette holder were all part of the apparatus that he thought made him look intriguing. Actually, it just made him look like what he was, a pervert gone to fat.

Ernie and I waited. Strange surveyed the busy snack bar, making sure no one was listening, and then he leaned forward, whispering.

"You CID assholes have your butts in a wringer," he said.

"We always have our butts in a wringer," Ernie replied.

"This time it's different." Strange leaned in even closer. I could smell some sort of cologne or aftershave, like musk. It made me want to throw up. I jolted back some of the hot coffee. It didn't help much.

"This time," Strange continued, "they've got you dead to rights."

"Who's 'they'?" Ernie asked.

Strange leaned back, startled. "The Officers' Wives' Club. Who else? They've been pissed off at you for years for letting all those *yobos* into the Commissary and PX."

Yobo was GI slang for a Korean girlfriend.

"They're not *yobos*, they're wives," Ernie said. "They have dependent ID cards and we have no choice but to let them into the Commissary and PX."

"Maybe so. But the honchos at the OWC think you're letting them off easy on the black marketing. You should be busting each one of those sweet little Korean dollies, one by one, and taking away their privileges."

The US military in Korea meticulously controls the amount of goods a GI or his dependents can purchase each month out of the PX or Commissary. The official reason is twofold: to protect fledgling Korean industries from being swamped by duty-free US goods and to save the US taxpayer the expense of shipping excess consumer items across the Pacific. The real reason—the visceral impulse behind the mania to enforce ration control regulations—was because most Americans didn't like seeing a bunch of Korean female dependents, the wives of lower ranking GIs, in "their" Commissary or "their" PX. Racism is a cleaner word for it.

"You know how many black marketers there are," Ernie asked, "buying and selling every day? And do you know how many there are of *us*?" With his left hand Ernie indicated me and him.

"*Mox nix*," Strange replied. "The OWC thinks that if you weren't wasting your time on other assignments, you'd be able to do your job and clear the Commissary and PX of all those *yobos*."

The "other assignments" Strange was referring to were cases involving murder, rape, kidnapping, torture, extortion and various and sundry other acts of mayhem. The Officers' Wives' Club, however, thought that having to compete with three Korean women for the last bunch of bananas was more important than dealing with felonies. We'd heard this criticism before. But the 8th Army CID was spread thin. Most of the other agents were assigned to chores like investigating the pilfering of supplies from transshipment points or breaches in internal security involving Top Secret documents. That type of work meant dealing with the 8th Army hierarchy and required a certain amount of tact, which left me and Ernie out. We went after crime and to hell with kowtowing to someone's rank. Naturally, any shit detail—like the black market detail—devolved onto us.

Working crime out in the ville, which was GI-on-Korean crime mostly, took up most of our time: rapes, robberies, burglaries. Since I was the only CID member in the country who could speak Korean and since Ernie Bascom could blend in with the lowest dregs of any society, it was usually me and Ernie who were assigned to those cases. Therefore, fighting black market crime in the Commissary and the PX was left to twist slowly in the wind.

"Okay," Ernie said. "The OWC has a case of the jaws. So what? They've had it before. What are they going to do about it?"

Strange leaned back and puffed on his cigarette holder as if he were actually smoking, which he wasn't. "How about a little hot chocolate?"

Ernie glared at him, sighed, and pushed himself up from the table. As he stalked away, Strange said, "Don't forget the marshmallows."

I studied Strange. He was pleased with himself for having commanded our attention. A GI's life is controlled, from the moment he wakes up in the morning until the moment he goes to sleep at night, by the officers appointed over him. They can leave him alone if they want to—leave him alone to do his job, leave him alone to live his personal life—or they can mess with him constantly. Having been in the Army for the better part of a decade, Ernie and I had each experienced both levels of control and there was no question about it, being left alone was better. This is why we were listening to Strange so intently, out of respect for the heat that the OWC could bring down on us.

Ernie returned with the hot chocolate. Strange frowned at the steaming concoction, picked up the little metal spoon and bounced the two marshmallows in the hot liquid, making sure they both became completely soaked. Then he levered one out of the mug, stuck out his tongue, and slid it wriggling into his mouth. Ernie and I grimaced. Strange had the odd talent of being able to make the most mundane action appear obscene.

The marshmallow muscled its way down his throat. Burping

slightly, he turned and smiled. "What the Officers' Wives' Club is going to do," he said, "is bust you two down."

"Bust us down? For what?"

"For not busting enough *yobos*. But not right away," he added. "They'll give you a chance to get off your butts and start enforcing the ration control regulations."

Ernie groaned.

"Who's the OWC point man?" I asked.

Strange stirred his chocolate, watching the last marshmallow start to sink. "Who else?" he asked. "The Chief of Staff."

"Colonel Wrypointe?"

"Bingo. His wife just got elected president of the OWC."

Millicent Wrypointe. I'd run into her before. When she shopped she actually wore her husband's rank insignia on the lapel of her blouse. One day, when I was in the Commissary's accounting department checking purchase records, she'd barged through the big double-doored "Employees Only" entrance and asked, "Are you CID?"

When I'd nodded, she literally pulled me out onto the Commissary floor. In aisle number seven she pointed at a gaggle of Korean women loading up on a shipment of frozen ox-tail. The Commissary manager had taken the ration limit off. Usually, the shopper was limited to two packets of any given meat item per day. This batch of sliced ox-tail, however, had arrived from the States late because of a power outage on the refrigerated transport ship. If the Commissary didn't sell it quickly, the meat would spoil.

Mrs. Wrypointe pointed at the women loading up their shopping carts. "You have to *do* something!"

When I explained why the ration limit had been lifted, she exploded. "Nobody can eat that much meat. They're going to sell it on the black market."

I nodded. "Probably."

"That's a crime. You're a law enforcement officer. Do something!"

"I'd have to follow them off compound and catch them in the

act of making the sale," I told her. "Right now, I'm working on another case."

"Then send someone else."

"I'll notify the Provost Marshal," I told her.

She studied my face. "But you don't think he'll do anything, do you?"

I shrugged. "We're short on manpower."

She pointed to the silver eagle rank insignia on her lapel. "Do you know who I am?"

"Yes, ma'am," I replied.

Her face reddened. When I made no further comment, she said, "My husband's going to hear about this. There's no excuse for this. None whatsoever!"

She'd stormed away, marching resolutely down the aisle, bumping into two Korean women who were so busy fumbling through the frozen ox-tail that they hardly noticed. As it turned out, I never heard about the incident again. Nor did I hear from Mrs. Wrypointe. Not, that is, until today.

"Has Colonel Wrypointe discussed this with the Provost Marshal?" I asked.

"Not yet. He's getting his ducks in a row. Two clerks in his office are working overtime putting charts and graphs together, all pointing to the fact that black marketing has been exploding. He's going to brief the Commander, explain the OWC concern, and put the pressure on the Provost Marshal to allocate more manpower to the black market detail."

"Thereby giving us less time to investigate real crime."

"They don't care about real crime," Strange said, "unless it happens to them."

"When is this briefing going to be held?" I asked.

"Tomorrow. Zero eight hundred. Prepare for heavy swells."

After devouring the second marshmallow, Strange seemed to be finished with his hot chocolate. He turned to Ernie, waiting patiently for his dirty story. Ernie told him one, making it up as he went along.

I stood up, walked back to the serving line, and pulled myself another mug of hot coffee. All I could think about was the rape case we'd been working on. Sunny, an innocent business girl out in the ville, beat up, tortured, and then raped by three American GIs who were still at large. And so far we had no leads.

When I returned to the table, Strange was gone.

"Where'd he go?" I asked Ernie.

"Who the hell knows? He thinks I screw half the women on Yongsan Compound."

"Don't you?"

"Not yet."

That night, Ernie and I ran the ville.

We strolled past neon and the open doors of nightclubs where mini-skirted young women cooed with pouting lips and crooked painted fingers, beckoning us to enter. At the top of Hooker Hill we hung a right and then a left until we were strolling through a dark alley lined on either side with ten-foot-high walls made of brick and cement. At one opening we paused and Ernie pounded on the double wooden gate. Rusty hasps rattled.

"*Nugu seiyo?*" someone said from inside. Who is it?

"*Na ya,*" Ernie replied. It's me.

His Korean was getting better. The door opened.

We stepped into a floodlit courtyard of flagstone circling a garden of scraggly rose bushes. An old woman closed the door behind us and then padded on plastic sandals up to the raised wooden porch that led into the complex of hooches. We slipped off our shoes, stepped up onto creaking wood, and walked down the dimly lit hallway. The place was quiet. Most of the young women who lived here had already left for the night, for their jobs as waitresses or hostesses in the dozens of bars and night-clubs and dance halls that comprised the red light district of Itaewon. The sliding paper door of the third room shone with golden light. The old woman slid it open.

Like a cloud, the odor of urine and rubbing alcohol rolled

out of the room. On the floor, amidst a rumpled comforter, lay Son Hei-suk, or Sunny, as the GIs called her. She was a young woman, maybe eighteen, but she seemed younger because of her open smile and her naïve way of laughing at anything a GI said. Most of the American soldiers treated her gently, teasing her like a younger sister, but two nights ago while she was pulling a shift as a hostess at the Lucky Seven Club, three Americans who nobody recognized coaxed her outside the club, apparently to help them buy some souvenirs at the local Itaewon Market, supposedly to send back to their families in the States.

Sunny never returned.

A farmer pushing a cart full of turnips found her the next day before dawn, near the Han River, unconscious, bleeding, barely alive. The Korean National Police were called, a surgeon at the Beikgang Hospital reset her broken left arm, shot her full of antibiotics, and used twenty-three stitches to sew up tears in her vaginal and anal areas. The waitresses and hostesses and whores who lived in this hooch had chipped in to pay her hospital bill and have her carted back here by taxi. No family members had been notified. Sunny, when she regained consciousness, begged that they not be.

Ernie set the PX bag full of painkillers and antibiotic cream and an electric heating pad on the floor. The old woman said she'd take care of it for us. We sat on the warm vinyl floor and watched Sunny. She snored softly. Gently, the old woman poked her shoulder. Slowly, Sunny roused herself awake. Groaning, she rolled over. Big brown eyes popped opened. She focused on us and raised her head slightly. A pink tongue licked soft lips and then she said, "You catch?"

Ernie shook his head. "Not yet, Sunny."

"I told you," she said, "one GI big, curly brown hair. 'Nother GI skinny, short white hair . . ."

"Shush, Sunny," Ernie said. "Don't get excited again. We have your description. We wrote it all down."

"Then why you not catch?"

Ernie looked down. "It's not that easy."

Her eyes widened. She looked at me and then back at Ernie.

"But they GI. You GI. You supposed to *catch*."

"We're trying," I said. When she continued to stare at me, I said, "They're new here in Itaewon. Nobody we talked to at the Lucky Seven recognized them. Not the Korean women working, not the GIs we found who'd been there that night. Everybody agrees on one thing, they're not stationed in Seoul. One girl said one of them had a jacket with 'Second Division, Second to None' embroidered on the back. So far, that's all we have to go on."

Ernie spread his hands. "There are twenty-seven compounds and thirty thousand GIs in the Second Infantry Division," Ernie said. "We're looking but we thought maybe you'd remember something more."

Sunny's stared at the ceiling, not at us, as if seeing something far beyond this little room. Although her facial features didn't move, moisture, like water welling up from a spring, started to ball in her eyes. One by one, the tears fell.

We waited a little longer. The old woman brought in some seaweed soup and tried to coax Sunny to eat. She refused.

Ernie and I rose to leave. As we stepped out onto the porch, Sunny called after us.

"Smoke."

We turned.

"One GI call 'nother one," she said. "'Smoke.'"

"Anything else, Sunny?" I asked.

She shook her head. And then the tears were flowing again. The old woman scowled at us and slid shut the door.

The next morning, Colonel Brace, the 8th Army Provost Marshal, called us into his office. He let us stand, completely ignoring us, while he puffed on his pipe and studied the folder in front of him—an old ploy that lifers use to let you know that, compared to them, you're lower than dog shit. Finally, he looked up at us.

"Your black market statistics are abysmal," he said.

"A lot of crime out in the ville, sir," Ernie said. "It's been taking up most of our time."

"I know what you've been working on," Colonel Brace said. "And I know how much time you've spent on the black market detail and it hasn't been enough. From today forward, you drop all other investigations and concentrate on black market activities."

"We've got a woman out in the ville who was raped and beaten," Ernie replied, "by a gang of Division GIs who we haven't been able to identify yet."

"A prostitute, isn't she?" the Colonel asked.

"A hostess," Ernie replied.

Colonel Brace raised one eyebrow. "There's a difference?"

"If you met her, sir, you'd realize there is. She's an innocent kid with no family to speak of who came to Itaewon because she had no other choice."

Colonel Brace shrugged. "Probably," he said, "this 'innocent kid' believed she hadn't been paid enough and started a hassle with our servicemen."

"They broke her arm, sir. And she received twenty-three stitches for her trouble."

Colonel Brace glared at Ernie and then at me. He wanted to say something but instead he puffed on his pipe, not happy with us contradicting him. Most of the other CID agents would never dare. "I appreciate your concern," he said finally. "I'll have Staff Sergeant Riley forward your report up to Division MPI."

Ernie sighed. We both knew that the 2nd Infantry Division Military Police Investigators hated criticism of their troops, especially when it came from rear echelon pukes like the 8th Army CID. They'd see the rape of an Itaewon "business girl" as nothing more than their self-sacrificing soldiers letting off a little steam. The case would not only be ignored but probably suppressed.

"Meanwhile," Colonel Brace continued, "Eighth Army has other priorities, especially with these black market stats spiraling out of control. Now listen to me, the both of you. From this moment forward, you are assigned to the black market detail and the black market detail only. You're both capable of increasing your arrest rate. I know you are because I've seen you do it before."

He was waiting for us to say "Yes, sir!" or shout something gung-ho or at least nod. Neither of us did.

Colonel Brace frowned and stood up, leaning across his desk. He said, "I want you to put the fear of God into those *yobos* in the PX. I want them to be afraid to even think about black marketing. Do you understand me?"

This time we both nodded. He asked if we had any questions.

"How about an increase in our petty cash allowance?" Ernie asked.

To my surprise, Colonel Brace didn't flat out turn the idea down. Instead, he said, "What is it now?"

"Fifty dollars a month."

"Tell Sergeant Riley to increase it to a hundred."

"Yes, sir."

With that, we were dismissed.

On the way out the door, Colonel Brace said, "I'll be monitoring your results."

Staff Sergeant Riley sat behind his desk. "How'd it go?" he asked.

Neither one of us answered. Ernie told Riley about the increase in the petty cash allowance and then headed for the coffee urn. I plopped down in the gray vinyl chair in front of Riley's desk.

"Smoke," I said.

"What?"

"That's the nickname of one of the GIs who raped Sunny."

"That business girl out at the Lucky Seven Club?"

"She's not a business girl, she's a hostess."

Riley shrugged. "Same difference." He shuffled through paperwork and then paused. "Smoke. Isn't that a term that's used by the field artillery?"

That's when I remembered. Each company-sized unit in the field artillery has an NCO who's in charge of laying and firing the guns. His official title is Chief of Firing Battery but what GIs usually call him is Chief of Smoke—or just "Smoke."

When Ernie returned with his coffee I ran the idea by him. He frowned. "But according to Sunny, these guys were young. A Chief of Smoke is usually an older guy."

"All Americans look the same to a Korean," Riley said. "They can't tell our ages."

Miss Kim, the statuesque administrative secretary, glanced up from her typing, a prim frown on her lips. When she noticed me watching, she turned away and resumed her typing.

"Maybe Sunny's wrong about their ages," Ernie said, "of at least one of them, this guy called Smoke. Or maybe he's just a baby-faced guy who got promoted fast."

"None of the faces Sunny told us about," I said, "could be described as babies. They're all monsters to her."

"Still, it's worth checking out," Riley said. "There are four artillery battalions in the Second Division, with three batteries each." He lifted the phone and dialed. Within seconds he was chatting with a buddy of his at 8th Army personnel, asking for a print out of every GI assigned to Division artillery. Riley said, "Thanks," and slammed down the phone. "I'll have the printout before close of business today."

"Good. Another thing you can get for us."

"What's that?"

"The blotter report from the MPs up at Division."

"Why would you need that?"

"Once GIs start raping women and kicking ass, they have a tendency to keep doing it."

"Okay," Riley said. "I'll get that too. Meanwhile, you guys better get some black market arrests."

"Screw that," Ernie said.

"Don't piss off the Provost Marshal," Riley warned. "He's serious about this. The shit's rolling downhill big time."

Ernie sipped again on his coffee, left the half-empty mug on Riley's desk, and rose to his feet. Together, we headed outside.

Ernie and I sat in his jeep, sipping PX coffee we'd bought in the snack stand in front of the commissary. It was hot and tasted about as acidic as your average quart of battery fluid. We were watching customers, mostly Korean women, flow out of the commissary, trotting behind male baggers who pushed huge carts laden with freeze-dried coffee, soluble creamer, mayonnaise, concentrated orange drink, bottled maraschino cherries, and just about anything else that was imported and therefore highly prized on the black market. After the groceries were loaded into the trunk of one of the big black Ford Granada PX taxis, the women tipped the baggers and climbed into the back seat.

"Which one should we bust?" I asked.

"Let's finish our coffee first."

"Okay by me."

We sipped on our coffee for a while and then Ernie said, "Whoa!"

I glanced up and realized immediately what had gotten his attention.

She was a tall Asian woman, with a willowy figure and raven hair piled high atop her head. She wore a long blue dress that clung to her curves like wet tissue paper moistened by a tongue. Silver earrings dangled from the side of her heart-shaped face and her slender arms were lined with bracelets.

"Who's *she*?" Ernie asked.

"I don't know," I replied. "Never seen her before."

Ernie poured his remaining coffee out the door of the jeep and tossed the empty cup into the back seat. He started the ignition.

"I think we've just found our culprit," he said.

"I think we have."

He slammed the jeep in gear, jolting forward. Coffee splashed on the front of my shirt.

■ ■ ■

The PX cab containing the tall woman didn't leave Yongsan Compound right away. Instead, it crossed the Main Supply Route, heading for Main Post and came to a halt in front of the Class VI Store. "Class Six" is the old army supply designation for items such as beer, wine, and hard liquor. The cab waited while the tall woman went inside. A few minutes later she reemerged with a man in a gray smock following her, pulling a flat cart laden with two cases of American beer, two cases of soda, and a large paper bag containing what appeared to be bottled liquor.

"Max purchase," Ernie said. "Four bottles of hooch, two cases each of beer and pop."

Under 8th Army ration control regulations, that's all a GI was allowed to buy in one day and four bottles of liquor was all that he, or his dependent, were allowed for a month. When everything was safely stored in the trunk, the woman tipped the man with the cart and climbed back into the cab. We followed her out Gate Number Five. Ernie swerved into honking traffic. She continued east along the Main Supply Route heading toward Itaewon but before she got there, the driver hooked a quick left toward the Namsan Tunnel.

"Where the hell's she going?" Ernie asked.

"She's a downtown woman," I said.

"Downtown woman with a figure like a lingerie model."

"But not skinny."

"No," Ernie agreed. "Not skinny."

The cab slowed at the booth to pay the toll for going through the tunnel and Ernie hung back, swerving toward the extreme right lane reserved for military and government vehicles. When the PX taxi entered the tunnel, we followed.

Namsan tunnel stretches about a mile through Namsan Mountain in the southern section of Seoul and, along with the Pusan-to-Seoul Expressway, it is the pride of the country. Both projects had been completed just a few months ago and high-rise buildings were popping up throughout downtown Seoul. President Pak Chung-hee had recently proclaimed that the Seventies would be the decade when Korea would begin to take its rightful place amongst the great economic powers of the world. After the devastation of the Korean War a little more than twenty years ago, the country had gotten off its back and was now rising. On paper, things looked better. Unfortunately, this new economic prosperity hadn't spread to everybody. In fact, in the red light district of Itaewon it had spread, as far as I could tell, to exactly nobody.

When we emerged from the tunnel, I spotted the cab. "There," I said, "she's taking the Myong-dong turnoff."

Honking and bulling his way through the tightly packed traffic, Ernie stayed with her. Then we were in narrow downtown streets. Myong-dong was the area of Seoul famous for the Cosmos Department store, chic boutiques and, at night, upscale nightclubs and Scotch Corners, the fashionable term for barrooms.

The PX taxi seemed bulky down here, surrounded by all the smaller Hyundai sedans. Ernie had no trouble following. We passed through the fashionable area and entered a section of town that had not yet been selected for gentrification. Most of the buildings were the brick and cement slab three- and four-story buildings that had been slapped together haphazardly after the war. Sandwiched between them were tin-roofed shops and eateries supported by walls of rotted wood. Finally, the cab veered into a narrow lane that rose upwards at a slight incline and after about a hundred yards ended in a cul-de-sac at the top of a hill. Ernie didn't turn into the lane but came to a stop just past it. As the cabs behind us honked, he said, "I'll circle around the block."

"Okay." I hopped out.

We'd done this before, plenty of times. Once we were close, Ernie would either find a place to park or circle the area while I followed on foot. The pedestrian traffic was practically wall-to-wall but composed mainly of working people hustling to and from small factories or hauling loads of charcoal briquettes or hemp sacks on wooden A-frames strapped to their backs. Vendors with large carts lined the walkway, shouting for passersby to stop and enjoy some fried meat dumplings or a nice warm bowl of cuttlefish soup.

At the mouth of the alley, I peered at the PX cab parked on a slant in front of a double iron gate in a stone wall. There was a small courtyard and beyond that a brick building that loomed above the others in the area, three stories high. A huge sign, faded now, had once been painted in bright red letters on the highest floor on all four sides. I could still make it out: Tiger Kang's.

No wonder this woman looked so elegant. She was a *kisaeng*. I'd heard of the place before. Tiger Kang's had once been the most famous *kisaeng* house in Seoul, a playground for the rich and powerful.

Kisaeng are female entertainers and their tradition is at least as old, and probably older, than the ancient geisha tradition in Japan. But the polished skills of plucking the twelve-stringed *kayagum* or performing the swirling drum dance or composing *sijo* poetry are reserved now for specially trained students. The so-called *kisaeng* of Tiger Kang's—and of the other joints that were popping up all over the city—were reduced to pouring scotch and lighting cigarettes and laughing at rich men's jokes. Still, it was work. Maybe not the most honest work, but it paid well.

Ernie came running up behind me.

"Where the hell'd you park the jeep?" I asked.

He shrugged. "I pushed one of the carts out of the way."

"That will make friends and influence people."

"That's what I'm here for," he said. "An international ambassador for peace."

The iron gate was open and apparently the tall woman had gone inside. The white-gloved PX cab driver was busy hauling the grocery bags out of the trunk and handing them inside.

"Tiger Kang's?" Ernie asked.

"That's right."

He whistled softly. "An upscale bust for once."

"We haven't made the arrest yet," I said. "We have to sneak inside somehow and witness the money exchange."

"Don't sweat the small stuff, Sueño. You worry too much. She brought the stuff here, that's enough. The sale is implied."

"What if she lives here?"

Ernie paused. "You mean maybe she's a *kisaeng* herself?"

"Right. She could claim that she brought the stuff here for her personal use. Not to sell."

"Hell with that. If she knocked back all that beer and liquor, she'd be as fat as the kitchen god. We bust her anyway. Let the JAG office figure it out."

He was right. We'd come this far, might as well get credit for the arrest. If JAG dropped the charges, that was on them. Mrs. Wrypointe could fuss at the Judge Advocate General and leave us alone. Still, it would be better if we waited awhile, to give them a chance to unpack and start exchanging money.

The last of the grocery bags were passed through and the iron door clanged shut. Ernie went back to check on the jeep.

At the bottom of the incline, I waved the PX cab driver to a halt. He blanched. Actually, it wasn't his fault. All he did was transport a passenger to her destination. Still, in a society totally controlled by the military and the police, any run-in with a cop was enough to worry a Korean. Especially when he held one of the few unionized jobs in the country—working for the American PX—and a compensation package with decent benefits. I wrote down the driver's name and cab number and chatted with him a while. No, he didn't know the passenger, he'd never seen her before. And no, he'd never driven a fare to Tiger Kang's before either. In fact, she'd had to direct him here or he would've had trouble finding it. I asked him how much his tip was. He reached in his pocket and showed me. A crisp, US five dollar bill. Exorbitant. He thought so too. I thanked him for his cooperation and told him he could leave.

Five minutes later, Ernie returned.

"Everything all right?" I asked.

"I gave the cart lady a thousand *won*." Two bucks US. "She was all smiles."

"Everybody's a big spender," I said.

"Except you," Ernie said.

He always accused me of being cheap but I didn't think I was. Thrifty, yes. But that was because I knew what it was like to be poor, and hungry.

We climbed up the hill and approached the iron gate of Tiger Kang's. Ernie stood with his back against it. "Ready?" he asked. I shoved my notebook into my jacket pocket and said, "Ready."

At first there was no answer but Ernie kept pounding. Finally, we heard footsteps on the other side of the wall and the door creaked open. The chubby face of a Korean man peered out. Without asking permission, Ernie shoved his way in.

"*Weikurei?*" the man said. Why this way?

Ernie ignored him and crossed the small courtyard. A rusty bicycle leaned against a cement brick wall. No outhouse, I noticed, so they had indoor plumbing. And no garden. This area was strictly used for storage. Two to three dozen wooden crates were piled against the back wall filled with empty brown OB Beer bottles. Next to that were smaller crates of crystalline Jinro Soju bottles, bereft now of their fiery rice liquor. A metal pail held a few empty bottles of imported scotch.

Ernie scampered up cement steps that led into the back door of the building.

The little man ran after Ernie, his face reddening now. "*Weikurei!*" he shouted again, clenching and unclenching his fingers. I stayed close behind him.

We entered another storage area, this one filled with more crates of beer and *soju*, these bottles unopened, and then into a large tile-floored kitchen.

It looked like something out of a historical magazine. Heavy iron pans hung from thick metal hooks, an ancient gas stove was covered with a gleaming metal canopy, and two geriatric refrigerators were hooked to rusted transformers, buzzing and wheezing like old men on life support.

"The place is clean, anyway," Ernie said.

It was that. Old but clean.

A dozen oddly shaped appliances lined a wooden counter, the functions of which I couldn't fathom, and beyond that, like stout soldiers, a short row of rice cookers. In the next room a huge mahogany dining table was covered with lace doilies. Slanting sunlight revealed swirling mites from a recent dusting. The tall, elegant woman was nowhere in sight.

The enraged man was still sputtering so Ernie stopped and pulled out his badge. This halted him. As he studied the shiny brass in the open leather folder, I spoke to him in Korean.

"*Kiga ko-nun yoja*," I said. The tall woman. "Where'd she go?"

He seemed to have trouble speaking, and at the same time he was struggling to swallow. Without answering, he glanced at the doorway leading out of the dining room. I showed him my badge and, speaking softly, I pointed back toward the kitchen.

"*Chogi kiddariyo.*" Wait there.

When he didn't move, Ernie shoved him back into the kitchen and slid shut the wooden door.

We headed deeper into the plush environs of Tiger Kang's.

The place smelled of must and cigarette smoke and spilled liquor. Ernie inhaled deeply, a smile suffusing his lips. He felt exactly the way I did; an old dive, dark, quiet, comfortable and filled with expensive liquor and cheap women. Exactly the type of place we both loved.

I stepped into the entrance foyer. The front door was locked from the inside. A cloak room was filled with thick wooden hangers but otherwise empty. Down the hallway, we ran into a dividing wall of fish tanks bubbling with blue water. Elaborate coral reefs and sunken pirate ships loomed beyond the murk and exotic sea creatures gaped at us in goggle-eyed amazement. On the far side of the tanks, a cocktail lounge opened before us, lit by soft red light and lined on one side with plush leather booths and on the other by a polished mahogany bar. The odor of cigarette smoke was overpowering now and seemed to emanate from every padded barstool and from every brass fixture lining the wall. A few tables in the middle were covered with white linen.

"Have we gone back in time?" Ernie asked.

I didn't answer. The murmur of soft voices drifted downward from upstairs. We climbed thickly carpeted steps.

"Up here must be where the action is," Ernie said.

A wrought-iron railing circled the entire second floor and opposite it, every few yards, dim sunlight projected through double sliding doors covered with embroidered silk. The elaborate designs depicted silver dragons and flaming orange tigers and pale blue flowers and bubbling green waterfalls; all elegant scenes of ancient Asia. One of the doors was slid open. That's where the talking was coming from. We padded down the carpet.

Ernie stood at the edge of the door and nodded to me. I'd go in first. I entered the room, pulling my badge out as I did so, and stuck it forward like a shield.

"Eighth Army CID," I said. "Black market violation. Nobody move."

A group of about a half-dozen Korean women sat around a low table, all of them leaning over metal bowls of steaming soup. Mouths hung open. Chopsticks clattered against porcelain.

"Where's the tall woman?" I asked in English. "The one who just came from the PX?"

Two or three of the women were young and the others not so young, but trying to look that way. Their hair was in disarray and their eyes sleepy but they were all attractive. Very attractive. Ernie entered the room, grinning.

"*Yoboseiyo*," he said. "Where's the stuff from the commissary? Come on. *Bali, bali.*" Quickly.

None of the women seemed to understand him although I knew that if they were hired as hostesses to the rich and famous, they must speak English, and probably Japanese. I scanned the room. No sign of the contraband.

"Come on, Ernie," I said. "Let's keep looking."

Before he followed me out of the room, he stopped and waved at them. "Goodbye, girls."

We slid open every paneled door but each room was filled only with flat cushions for sitting and low mother-of-pearl inlaid tables. Downstairs, I lifted the countertop on the end of the bar and searched back there. Nothing. Ernie found a storage room and managed to pry it open. Fumbling around in the darkness, he finally located a light and switched it on.

"Here it is," he said.

The walls were lined with wooden cupboards holding neatly arranged bottles of liquor, wine, champagne and various decanters filled with liqueurs and aperitifs the names of which I couldn't pronounce. Some of the containers had the Korean customs import stamp on them, some didn't.

Atop a raised wooden pallet sat the two cases of soda, the two cases of American beer and about a half-dozen paper bags. I rummaged inside the bags. Stuck between four bottles of Johnny Walker Black Label, I found the receipt from the Class VI Store, dated today, time-stamped less than an hour ago. I lifted it out and shoved it into my pocket.

"Where'd she go?" I asked.

"Hell if I know," Ernie replied.

We stepped out of the storeroom and back into the cocktail lounge. Someone was waiting for us. A middle-aged Korean woman, tall, full-figured, with an elaborately coiffed black hairdo, her body wrapped in a flower-patterned blue silk dressing robe. She stared at us for a moment, her face dour, the brow wrinkled.

"*Koma-ya!*" she said. Boy!

A slender young man appeared out of the shadows, wearing black trousers, a pressed white shirt, and a black bow tie. He bowed to the woman.

"*Kopi, seigei*," she said. Coffee, three.

He bowed again and backed away.

Then she motioned toward the largest linen covered tables in the center of the room, her eyes never wavering from ours. "Sit," she said.

"No time to sit, mama-san," Ernie said. "Where's the tall woman? The one who brought you the Johnny Walker Black?"

"She go," she said.

"Where?"

"Not your business."

"It is our business," Ernie said, pulling out his badge. "We're from Eighth Army CID and you're in violation of Korean import restrictions. We can call the Korean National Police and we will, if you don't tell us where to find the tall woman with the dependent ID card."

"Sit!" she said, pointing a polished nail at two upholstered wooden chairs.

Ernie walked forward. "Why the hell should we?"

"Because," she said, "I am Tiger Kang. I know every honcho at Eighth Army and every Eighth Army honcho know Tiger Kang!" She pointed her red-tipped forefinger at Ernie's nose. "And you two are in deep kimchi."

"We been there before," Ernie replied.

The boy reappeared, this time holding a tray with a silver pot of coffee and three saucers and cups. He placed them atop the immaculate tablecloth, along with tiny silver spoons, a container of cream and a bowl of sugar. He bowed once again to Tiger Kang and departed. The coffee smelled good. I sat down. So did Tiger Kang. Finally, reluctantly, so did Ernie.

In the Army, when you break a regulation, even a foolish black market regulation, it is tantamount to disobeying a direct order—and, therefore, under the Uniform Code of Military Justice, serious stuff. Abusing one's Commissary and PX privileges by either reselling purchased items or giving a gift of more than twenty-five dollars value to an unauthorized person was a breach of United States Forces Korea Regulation 190-2 and a violation of the Republic of Korea's customs laws.

On small black market cases, people would be adjudicated guilty on the preponderance of evidence, which sometimes came down to nothing more than the word of me and Ernie. In addition, American GIs were deemed by the military to be responsible for the activities of their dependents. More than one GI had been denied promotion because his wife had been caught black marketing. A few were even busted down in rank. A small handful, depending on the extent of the black marketing operation, were court-martialed, spending weeks or even months in the Army Support Command stockade.

Ernie and I wielded a lot of power in this regard. Usually, we were reluctant to use it and sometimes we gave people a break. But we both figured that anyone making good money at the oldest *kisaeng* house in Seoul could afford a little inconvenience. Besides, Mrs. Wrypointe was breathing down our necks. Even from where I sat, in the middle of Tiger Kang's *kisaeng* house, I could still feel the hot breath of the President of the Officers' Wives' Club. We needed a bust and we needed a bust soon. To get Mrs. Wrypointe off our backs, to get the Provost Marshal off our backs, but more importantly to free up some time so we could hunt for the men who had raped and brutalized the innocent Itaewon bar hostess known as Sunny, we needed to proceed with this arrest—despite Tiger Kang's threats.

"Where is she," Ernie asked, "the woman who bought that stuff out of the Class Six?"

Tiger Kang glowered at him. "Why you bother her? She good woman."

"She works for you?" I asked.

"Sometimes. Sometimes we have big party. Need more girls. I call. Sometimes she come. Sometimes she no come."

"What's her husband think about this line of work?" Ernie asked.

Tiger Kang shrugged again. "Not my business."

"We want to talk to her," I said.

"She go."

"So quickly?"

"She think you follow her, so she go."

That was pretty brazen. She could've taken the stuff home, wherever that was, and then we'd have no case against her. Instead, she'd brought it here to Tiger Kang's, as if to taunt us into making the arrest; figuring we wouldn't because of Tiger Kang's connections.

"Wherever she's gone," Ernie said, "we'll find her."

I had the receipt. That and the ration control record at the Class VI would be enough to trace her.

"Maybe," Tiger Kang said.

"No maybe about it," I replied. "We'll find her. And we're going to confiscate that stuff in the storeroom."

"No," Tiger Kang said. "You no take." Tiger Kang poured cream and ladled sugar into her coffee. "You no take," she repeated.

"Why the hell not?" Ernie asked.

"Honchos get angry. Your honcho, Eighth Army, they all the time come here."

"They drink your black market scotch?" I asked.

"Of course," she said. "Anything they drink. They all the time want American beer. That's why I buy."

Ernie sipped on his coffee. "Not bad," he said.

"Tiger Kang no use Folgers," she said. "I buy from Colombia."

"Nice," Ernie replied. "You must have some rich dudes coming in here."

"Yes." She nodded. "Many rich dudes."

Ernie glugged down the last of his coffee and stood up. "Let's get that stuff, Sueño, and load it into the jeep. We still have time to make a couple more black market busts today and get old Mrs. Wrypointe off our butts."

Tiger Kang was studying him as he spoke.

"You leave here," she said, "then you don't have to take to MP Station, get hand receipt. Save you time."

Ernie eyed her suspiciously. "You know a lot about how this works."

"Tiger Kang know," she said, pointing at her nose. "All the time I talk to honchos."

It actually wasn't going to make any difference if we confiscated the commissary and Class VI items. We already had the receipt and even without that, through the ration control records, we'd soon know the name of the woman who'd purchased them, and the name of her husband. As far as proof of the fact that she'd delivered them to Tiger Kang's, our testimony was good enough. Usually we took both the woman and the black market items back to the MP Station—mainly just as a show to humiliate her more than anything else—but since she was gone, it was too late for that.

We could've contacted the Korean National Police liaison and turned Tiger Kang in for a customs violation but that would've been a waste of time. The KNPs wouldn't do anything to someone who hobnobbed with the rich and powerful. Mrs. Wrypointe and the 8th Army Provost Marshal wanted volume, a lot of black market arrests. If the details of the police work were a little sloppy, that was besides the point. The purpose was to scare the hell out of the *yobo*s and thin out their ranks in the commissary and PX. Ernie and I knew the game. We'd played it before.

Ernie turned to Tiger Kang. "What's her name?" he asked.

"Who?"

"The woman who brought the liquor and beer."

"*Kokktari*," Tiger Kang replied. Long Legs.

"That's it?" Ernie asked. Even he knew that wasn't a proper Korean name.

Tiger Kang shrugged. "That's what we call her."

"Where does she live?"

Tiger Kang shrugged her silk-clad shoulders. "*Moolah* me." I don't know.

"All right," Ernie said. "No name, no address, no Johnny Walker Black."

He rose from the table and we walked back to the storage room. We left the two cases of pop but Ernie hoisted the beer and I hoisted the liquor and we carried it out past Tiger Kang, through the kitchen, and out to the jeep. All the while, I kept thinking Tiger Kang would jump us and try to scratch our eyes out, or at least have her boys do it. Other black market mama-sans had attacked us before in attempt to protect their ill-gotten contraband. But Tiger Kang did nothing. She just crossed her arms and glared at us.

I kept thinking of her curse. Maybe that's why she didn't lift a finger to stop us. Maybe somebody else would. Maybe some-body in our own chain of command. And maybe Tiger Kang was right. Maybe we truly were in deep kimchi now.

But like Ernie said, we'd been there before.

Back at the Class VI Store I made the Korean manager come out and unlock the green metal ammo can that held the ration control punch cards. With him watching, I shuffled through the thick stack and compared each one of the cards to the purchase receipt I held in my hands. Finally I found it: two cases of soda, two cases of beer and four bottles of Johnny Walker Black.

The name imprinted on the punch card was Mei-lan Burke-walder, dependent wife of Captain Irwin Burkewalder, US Army. Her first name didn't sound Korean to me. Maybe Chinese. Since Red China was our avowed enemy and therefore no-man's land for American GIs, I figured she must be from somewhere else. Hong Kong or Singapore, maybe. More likely Taiwan. Back at the CID office, I asked Staff Sergeant Riley, the Admin NCO, to use his contacts at 8th Army personnel to find out more about the Burkewalders.

Later that afternoon, Ernie and I made two more black

market busts, these out in Itaewon, and we figured that would take the pressure off of us, at least temporarily.

Early the next morning, Ernie gassed up his jeep at the Twenty-one T (Car) motor pool, picked me up at the barracks, and we wound our way off compound, through the still-quiet streets of Seoul, past carts being pushed and glimmering piles of cabbage being unloaded, and headed north on the Main Supply Route. At the outskirts of the city, the sign said UIJONGBU, 15 KM. What we were looking for was a lead on the GIs who'd gang raped Sunny.

Fallow rice paddies lined the road. Ernie stiff-armed the big steering wheel around broad curves. Off to the east, the sun was just beginning to peek over distant hills.

"It feels good," he said, "to be investigating real crime for once."

I inhaled the crisp autumn air. Wisps of smoke rose through metal tubes atop tile-roofed farmhouses. Men in straw hats and women huddled in linen hoods balanced wooden hoes and scythes across their backs as they trudged toward distant fields.

"What'd Riley find out about that *kisaeng* we busted yesterday?" Ernie asked.

"She's a third country national," I told him, "from Taiwan. Mother's Korean, father's Chinese. They fled mainland China with the Kuomintang to Taiwan a couple of years before she was born. Somehow she met this Captain Burkewalder. They got married."

"Where's he stationed?"

"Vietnam. MAC-V advisory group."

Ernie whistled. "Lucky dog," he said.

Ernie'd spent two tours in Vietnam, loving every minute of it. The first tour he drove big trucks up and down Highway One and spent his off-duty hours smoking pungent hashish in his sand-bagged bunker. By the time he returned on his second tour, things had changed. No hashish available. The only way for a GI to get high was to buy pure China White from snot-nosed kids through the concertina wire.

"Uncle Ho used it as a weapon," he always said, "and it worked."

For Americans, the war had wound down. Richard Nixon's Vietnamization program had succeeded and the few thousand American GIs still left in-country were mostly advisors to ARVN troops. Still, it was a dangerous job, maybe more dangerous than being part of an American combat unit, and I didn't envy the assignment.

"So you think they'll notify Captain Burkewalder about his wife having her PX privileges revoked?"

"They have to," Ernie replied. "He's her sponsor, theoretically responsible for everything she does. Helluva thing to have to worry about when you're concentrating on staying alive."

We reached the outskirts of the city of Uijongbu and Ernie downshifted the jeep.

"Where to?" he asked.

"Turn right up there, toward Songsan-dong."

We were headed to Camp Stanley, headquarters of the Division Artillery.

I riffled through the printout Staff Sergeant Riley had collated for me yesterday: the names and ranks and DEROS (date of estimated return from overseas) of every Chief of Firing Battery in the Second Infantry Division. Two battalions of artillery were stationed at Camp Stanley, another battalion of 155mm howitzers nearby at Camp Essayons, and a final battalion closer to the DMZ up at Camp Pelham, about thirty miles northwest of here in the Western Corridor. There were three batteries per battalion so that made a dozen NCOs who held the official designation of Chief of Firing Battery or, in GI jargon, Chief of Smoke.

If taking these guys down involved violence, that would be fine with us. Ernie'd brought his brass knuckles. I'd brought my .45.

"Smoke?" the young GI asked. "You want to talk to the Chief of Smoke?"

"That's right."

"Hold on."

He trotted away.

We were on Camp Stanley, in the motor pool of Bravo Battery, 1st of the 38th Field Artillery. Six 105mm howitzers were aligned in a neat row, leather-sheathed barrels pointing toward a crisp blue sky. Next to them, in geometrical counterpoint, sat six square equipment lockers; everything air mobile, everything ready to be airlifted by chopper into a combat zone at a moment's notice.

Ernie unwrapped a stick of ginseng gum and popped it into his mouth. "This is man's work," he said. "Not all that sissy paper-pushing like back at Eighth Army."

"Nothing sissy about Eighth Army," I said. "You think it's easy busting housewives who purchase too many packages of sanitary napkins?"

"No, I guess not," Ernie replied. "I've got the scars to show for it."

A man wearing the three-stripes-up and two-down insignia of a Sergeant First Class strode toward us. Using a red cloth, he cleaned grease off his hands.

"You looking for me?"

I showed him my badge. "You're the Chief of Firing Battery," I said.

"Chief of Smoke," he corrected.

He didn't bother to shake hands because he was still cleaning them, which was okay with us. His nametag said Farmington. We asked about leave policy and if a senior NCO had to sign out on pass.

"No," he replied. "In the Division if you're E-6 or above, your ID card is your pass. What's this all about?"

"Where were you this past weekend? On Saturday night to be exact."

He crinkled his eyes. "Why do you want to know?"

We told him about Sunny, and how she'd been brutally raped.

"The guys who did it," he asked, "they were in this unit?"

"We don't know yet," Ernie said. "That's what we're trying to find out."

Sergeant Farmington told us that he had a steady *yobo* out in the village of Songsan-dong and that was where he'd been. "I don't see the point of taking the bus all the way down to Seoul and then paying too much for pussy. I'd rather stay up here where things are cheap."

"Can you prove that you were here?"

Farmington thought about it. "Yeah, I suppose I can. First, I bought a case of beer at the Class VI on Friday night, that should be in their records. And Saturday morning I checked in with the CQ about two of my soldiers who were assigned to weapons cleaning duty."

"The Charge of Quarters put that in his log, you suppose?"

"I suppose."

"What about Saturday night?" Ernie asked.

"My *yobo* can vouch that I was there. And by Sunday night all the beer was gone."

Farmington grinned.

I took notes and knew that if we had to, every step of Sergeant Farmington's alibi could be checked out, but I also knew that, for the moment, we wouldn't bother. Farmington's long record in the service and his easy-going attitude left little doubt that he was telling the truth. Time was everything. We'd move on to the other names on the list.

"Anyone else from your unit went to Seoul recently? Maybe a group of three guys?"

"Not that I know of. Nobody was bragging about anything. And they usually do when they come back from Seoul."

When we told him more about Sunny, and what had happened to her, his face clouded with concern. He volunteered to go into the Bravo Battery Orderly Room and check the sign-out register. This was a big help because we didn't need any hassles from some Battery Commander suspicious of 8th Army investigators from Seoul.

After about ten minutes, Farmington returned. "Nobody in the unit went to Seoul last weekend."

"At least not that they admitted to," Ernie replied.

"Right, at least not that they wrote in the pass register. But I'd be surprised if anybody did. We were out in the field last week, came in late Friday. There was still a lot of maintenance to do Saturday morning. So they wouldn't have been able to get away until mid-afternoon Saturday at the earliest."

"How long does the bus to Seoul take?"

Farmington shrugged. "Maybe an hour. Hour and a half when the traffic's bad."

"So still possible."

"Yeah," he agreed. "Definitely possible."

Ernie and I conducted the same type of interviews at Alpha Battery and then Charlie Battery and then at the other three batteries on the far side of Camp Stanley and then three more 155mm howitzer batteries at Camp Essayons. Each one of the Chiefs of Firing Battery was suspicious at first but then cooperative when we described what had been done to Sunny.

It was mid-afternoon by the time we were finished.

"A lot of alibis," Ernie said.

"One for each Chief of Smoke."

"We have to check them out."

"No time," I replied. "The Provost Marshal will be busting a gut by now." I checked my watch. Our whole trip up here had been a long shot. We thought maybe, with the knowledge that one of the rapists had been called "Smoke," that we might be able to stumble on a Chief of Firing Battery without an alibi. Of course, things are not usually that easy. "If we leave now," I said, "we'll still have three or four more hours to bust people at the commissary."

"Screw the commissary," Ernie said. "Let's go direct to the source."

I knew what he meant. We could get a couple of easy busts by working with a man we knew in Itaewon. A man by the name of Haggler Lee.

We hopped in the jeep and headed toward the MSR.

▪ ▪ ▪

"They owe me money," Haggler Lee said.

Haggler Lee was substantially older than us, maybe forty, but in some ways he seemed younger. He had a baby face, kept his black hair neatly coiffed, and he wore the sky blue silk tunic and white cotton pantaloons of the traditional outfit of the ancient *yangban* class who ruled Korea during the Chosun Dynasty. He seemed soft, patient, averse to violence. A hell of a thing for the man who ruled the Itaewon black market operation with an iron fist.

When we entered his warehouse, he sat on a flat square cushion in the middle of a raised floor heated by charcoal gas flowing through subterranean *ondol* heating ducts. Swirling mother-of-pearl phoenixes and snarling dragons were inlaid into the black lacquered table in front of him. As we approached, he lay a horsehair writing brush on an inkstone and looked up at us.

"*Anyonghaseiyo?*" he asked. Are you at peace?

We lied and told him that we were, slipped off our shoes, and stepped up on the warm *ondol* floor. We grabbed a couple of cushions and sat. Out of the darkness, a young woman, wearing a full, flowing *chima-chogori* traditional gown, appeared and, using two hands, poured steaming hot water into porcelain cups. She hefted a small tray onto the table that was laden with sugar, soluble creamer, Lipton tea bags and a jar of Maxim instant crystals. Ernie and I both stuck with the coffee. We ladled it into the hot water and swirled it around. It tasted good after our long drive back from Division.

"It has been too long since I've seen my good friends," Haggler Lee told us, sipping on a handle-less cup of hot green tea.

"You know why we're here, Lee," Ernie said. "Eighth Army's going nuts on the black market statistics again."

Haggler Lee nodded and set his cup down. "Mrs. Wrypointe," he said.

"You know her?"

"Oh, yes." He smiled his pleasant smile. "A fine lady."

"You like her?" I asked.

"Yes, very much."

"But if she gets her way, she'll kick every Korean woman out of the commissary and the PX. That would be the end of your business."

"*If* she gets her way. Right now, she's merely driving up prices, which of course is good for my business."

"But she hates Koreans," Ernie said. "That's why she wants them all out of her commissary and her PX."

"That's one way to look at it," Haggler Lee said. "Another way to look at it is that she's a woman of principle. She actually believes that black marketeering is bad. One has to admire such a steadfast attitude."

"You admire that old witch?" Ernie asked.

"Oh, yes. An admirable lady."

"Where did you meet her?" I asked.

"At Hannam House. She's quite taken by traditional Korean music and dance."

Hannam House was a cultural center sponsored by the Korean Ministry of Education. Foreign dignitaries, even American soldiers, were invited to periodic performances in order to better introduce them to the world to Korean culture. Of course, most GIs avoided the place like a bad case of the clap.

We told him that we needed to make a couple of black market busts and we needed to make them fast. The quid pro quo, of course, was that generally speaking, when 8th Army wasn't putting too much pressure on us, we'd leave his operation alone. Mostly we did anyway. Black marketing, compared to rape and assault and theft and extortion and even the occasional murder, was not high on our personal priority list. Haggler Lee hated violent crime as much, if not more, than we did. And his contacts throughout Itaewon were extensive. He knew every mama-san, every business girl, every bar owner, every chop house proprietor and every Korean National cop in the entire red-light district.

As such, he was a great source of information and, more often than not, we cooperated with him.

Of course, 8th Army and especially the Provost Marshal knew nothing about this cozy relationship and if we had anything to say about it, they never would.

Haggler Lee told us about the two women who owed him money.

"They can pay," he said, "but they keep doing business with me, keep saying they will pay next time. I know their plan. When they and their husbands pack up to return to the States, they will leave me with a fat bill. Many have tried this before. Many fail."

"If we bust them," I said, "they'll lose their ration control privileges and no one will make any money. Not them. Not you."

"Yes," Haggler Lee replied. "But if more women believe they don't have to pay me, then more won't pay me. I must punish these two women to set an example."

The women in question were black marketing and that was against 8th Army regulations. It was our duty to bust them for it. If it happened to coincide with Haggler Lee's business model, so be it. He gave us their names and addresses.

On the way out, Haggler Lee escorted us to the door. The plan was that his pick-up man, Grandfather Han, would peddle his bicycle over to the homes of the two women who were our marks, pretending to make his weekly pickup. He'd find some excuse for arriving earlier than scheduled. Normally what he did was enter the home, box up the PX goods, and strap the cardboard load to the heavy-duty rack on his bicycle. This time, as he made the transaction, Ernie and I would follow him in and make the arrest.

The entire operation went off without a hitch and by early evening Ernie and I had two more black market busts.

"Where do you two get off," Riley said, "nosing around Camp Stanley after the Provost Marshal told you to lay off?"

We were back in the CID office. The cannon for

close-of-business had been fired and the flags of the United States, the Republic of Korea, and the United Nations Command ceremoniously lowered. We returned to the office thinking we'd be congratulated on our black market arrests. Instead we were being reamed out because of a phone call the DivArty Adjutant made to the 8th Army Provost Marshal. Apparently, someone in the 2nd Infantry Division chain of command found out that we'd been interviewing soldiers in their area of operations and had pitched a bitch.

"Colonel Brace had to *apologize* to the man," Riley said, his face red. "Do you understand what that means?"

"Yeah," Ernie replied. "It means he doesn't have the balls to back us up."

Miss Kim, the admin secretary, plucked some tissue out of a box, held it to her slender nose, and rose from her desk. She didn't like it when voices were raised or when American vulgarisms were used. She once told me that when she started work here she hadn't understood any of our four-letter words. As she learned them, looking them up one by one in a Korean-English dictionary, they often made her cry; especially when GIs accused one another of doing horrible things to their mothers. As she clicked in her high heels across the office and turned out into the hallway, all of our eyes were riveted to her gorgeous posterior.

Riley started in on us again. "The Provost Marshal says you are not to return to the Division area until he has a chance to talk to you, personally."

"Where is he now?" I asked.

"On the Eighth Army golf course."

"Oh, Christ," Ernie said.

"He left a half hour ago," Riley said. "His foursome includes the Chief of Staff."

"Sure," Ernie said. "Just because three GI gang rapists are on the loose is no reason to delay your tee time."

"Can it, Bascom," Riley told him. "The Provost Marshal gets a lot of mileage out of these golf dates."

"Like what?"

"Like briefing the Chief of Staff on your excellent increase in black market arrests."

"Two days' worth," Ernie said.

"You'll get more."

"Not today," I interjected.

Riley glanced at his watch. "The commissary doesn't close for another hour. You still have time."

I stood up. "Black marketing isn't the only crime we have to investigate."

Riley said, "You're not dumb enough to go back to Camp Stanley, are you?"

"No," I said. "You can count on that."

Ernie and I started out the door.

"Where are you going?" Riley shouted after us.

Neither of us answered.

The Western Corridor is sometimes called the bowling alley.

It is a natural invasion corridor running up and down the spine of the Korean Peninsula, mountains on either side divided by a long lush valley. Armies have trod down it since ancient times: Chinese infantry, Mongol hordes, Manchurian cavalry and, heading the other way, Japanese samurai warriors. Most recently Communist North Korean armored battalions backed up by two hundred thousand of Mao Tse-tung's "volunteers" streamed down the Western Corridor until the ROK Army and American GIs managed to stop them and push them back at least as far as the Demilitarized Zone, some thirty miles north of Seoul. All in all, the Western Corridor has a colorful history, a history soaked in blood.

There are checkpoints along the Main Supply Route. American GIs and ROK Army soldiers, all holding rifles propped against their hips, all waving with gloved hands for the motorist to slow and then stop, peering into the jeep, checking ID cards, examining vehicle dispatches, then waving us on into the deepening fog-shrouded night. After passing the third Western Corridor checkpoint, there was nothing but countryside surrounding us. In the lowering gloom, I spotted it, a little white sign with an arrow pointing to the right.

"There," I said. "Sonyu-ri."

Ernie turned right. A half-mile in, we passed a VD clinic. I knew we were close. Three quarters of a mile further, floodlights shone atop the chain link fence surrounding the small American compound known as RC-4, Recreation Center Four. Beyond that, a neon strip lined the narrow two-lane road: the Sexy Lady Club, the Black Cat Club, the Kimchi Rose Club, the Playgirl Club, the Sonyu River Teahouse. The bars and nightclubs were interspersed with legitimate businesses: Mr. Cho's Tailor Shop, Aimee's Brassware Emporium, Fatty Pang's Chop House. Business girls in short skirts and tight halter tops peered through beaded curtains. Rock and roll blared from tin speakers. Gaggles of GIs wearing blue jeans and sneakers and nylon jackets prowled from bar to bar, sniffing the air like small packs of jackals.

"My kind of village," Ernie said.

After a quarter mile of non-stop debauchery, a well-lit wooden arch rose into the sky standing like a rainbow above a chain-link fence and a wooden guard shack. The arch was painted white with black lettering that said WELCOME TO CAMP PELHAM, HOME OF THE 2ND OF THE 17TH FIELD ARTILLERY, SECOND TO NONE.

We pulled up to the MP at the guard shack and showed him our dispatch. After checking our identification, he pulled the gate back, creaking on iron rollers, and we coasted into the dimly lit field of Quonset huts known as Camp Pelham.

We'd been here on an earlier case so Ernie knew exactly where to find the Battalion Ops Center. It was a big tin Quonset hut painted olive-drab like all the rest of the buildings on the compound. A fire light shone over the main entrance. Ernie parked on gravel and we climbed out of the jeep. The Staff Duty Officer was Lieutenant Orting. As we explained why we were here, he at first seemed concerned and then proved to be cooperative. Two of the Chiefs of Firing Battery were easily located. One was in his quarters, the other having a few beers with his buddies in the NCO Club. The interviews went smoothly and both seemed to have alibis that would preclude them from having been in Seoul on Saturday night. Once again, we didn't have time to check out the details of their alibis but, for the moment, we'd take them at face value.

The final Chief of Smoke was from Charlie Battery. His name was Singletary and according to everyone we talked to, he lived off compound with his *yobo*. They had a couple of kids, we were told.

"A homesteader," Lieutenant Orting told us. "He's been here over five years."

"Five years?" Ernie said. "I thought that was the max."

Army regulation doesn't allow any soldier to stay in Korea for more than one year at a time and if you want to stay longer a request for extension must be submitted and approved annually. Five years is the max.

"Singletary is an outstanding soldier," Lieutenant Orting said. "His sixth year was approved by the Division Commander himself."

And probably by 8th Army, I thought, but I didn't say so. These Division soldiers think that God Himself has set up shop in the Division head shed and there's no higher authority than Headquarters 2nd ID.

He didn't have the address of Singletary's hooch. Instead, Lieutenant Orting called the CQ runner, a young Spec 4, and told him to alert Singletary. Before we could object, the young man hatted up and trotted out the door. Lieutenant Orting grabbed a paper and pencil, drew us a map, and handed it to us.

"Singletary lives right off compound," Orting explained. "He's always the first in on an alert."

Ernie studied the map. "It's right outside the main gate."

"Hang a left," Orting said, "a few yards down past the Crazy Mama Club and then follow the path toward Shit River."

Actually, it was called Sonyu River, but I didn't correct him.

I stuffed the map into my pocket and we shook Lieutenant Orting's hand. Ernie and I left the jeep on compound and walked back toward the main gate. Outside, as we walked along the strip, the rock and roll and the shouts of laughter and the cooing of the business girls assaulted our ears. A hint of marijuana smoke wafted on the air.

Ernie gazed admiringly at the long, glittering row of neon. "Everything a GI's greedy little heart could desire."

Before we left 8th Army we'd changed into our running-the-ville outfits: blue jeans, sneakers, nylon jackets with fire-breathing dragons on the back. Still, we didn't blend in with this crowd. Everyone up here knew everyone else. The fact that we were strangers escaped no one's attention. From deep inside the open doors of the barrooms I felt eyes assessing us, both GI and Korean.

Ernie studied the map. "It's back here," he said, pointing.

Behind the bright neon that lined the strip, the night was pitch black. No street lamps, not even any single bulbs that I could see. Only tightly packed tile roofs jumbled on top of one another, gently descending toward the river below.

We found a muddy path. It was only wide enough for us to walk single file. We entered the darkness. Walls made of rotted wood lined the alley. Through cracks, candlelight glimmered, and now I could make out an occasional single light bulb glimmering through oil-papered doors. The pathway veered to the right and then sharply back to the left.

That's when we saw them, a herd of apes lurking in a jungle. There was no mistaking their height and bulk. GIs. A small squad. Whether they were black or white or Hispanic or Asian was impossible to tell. Like a dying comet, a flaming ember arced toward the mud, sizzled briefly, and died. The stench of burnt marijuana permeated the air.

One of the shadows growled. "Rear echelon mother fuckers."

Another voice said, "Come to mess with us." In the distance, yellow bulbs glimmered atop the concertina wire-topped fence that surrounded Camp Pelham.

Then one of them stepped forward and shouted, "Don't mess with my *people!*"

In the darkness, I bumped into Ernie. If I'd thought fast enough, I could've grabbed him and told him not to say anything. But I wasn't fast enough.

Instead, Ernie stepped forward and said, "*Fuck* your people."

And then something flew at us from out of the dark.

Ernie dodged and launched himself at the pack of men, as if he were born to assault vermin. One by one, the GIs stepped back, shadowed faces registering surprise, resentment. I hurried after Ernie down the alley, scowling, my shoulders hunched, my fists clenched but luckily none of the men reacted. They were too startled by Ernie's bold action. We scurried toward where the alley opened on the pedestrian walkway and then turned to parallel the narrow channel of the Sonyu River. It wasn't much of a river, nothing more than a creek really, running about knee-deep through clay. We were clear of danger, or so it seemed.

Ernie marched down the path, whispering over his shoulder to me, "pussies." Just as he said that something clattered out of the darkness—a chunk of plaster, or a brick. It tumbled through the air and landed ineffectually in the stream, splashing against pebbles.

They hurtled down the alley, the entire pack of them, emerging out of darkness into moonlight. Some of them held what looked like clubs in their hands. Ernie swiveled and crouched, scrabbling in the creek bed until found what he wanted—a rock the size of his head, which he tossed at them. I scrambled toward a chunk of driftwood.

"Use your forty-five," Ernie said, pulling out his brass knuckles, slipping them on splayed fingers. The GIs kept running toward us, screaming like banshees.

"Not yet," I said.

One of them plowed into me. I absorbed the shock,

sidestepped, swung my driftwood bat and clunked him on the head. He went down. Another came at me and I swung again, missing. And then he was inside my defenses, clawing at my face. I warded him off and popped him with a left jab and then a sharp right. As he staggered, another GI flung himself on me. We grunted and wrestled and struggled, ankle-deep into the muddy creek, until finally a voice bellowed out of the darkness.

"*At ease!*"

Reflexively, I froze, holding my fist cocked in mid-air, my left hand still clutching the ripped shreds of somebody's shirt. Everyone else froze also. In the middle of a fight, in the middle of a blood ritual familiar to every young man, we froze. Why? It was our training. Each one of us had spent hours responding to shouted orders—on the parade field, during physical training, as part of combat simulations—and when a command was bellowed at us with enough conviction, enough un-self-questioning authority suffusing the voice, all of us—me, Ernie, and the nameless GIs hassling us—immediately responded to the order.

A pair of combat boots tromped rhythmically through the mud.

"Who's that?" the same voice shouted. "Is that you, Quigley?" When there was no answer the voice said, "Is that you, Conworth? What the hell you doing back here? Smoking that shit again? Let me see your face."

A flashlight shone. The pale, beard-stubbled face of the GI called Conworth stood illuminated in the light. Hairy nostrils. Blood-shot eyes.

"What'd I tell you about that shit?" the man holding the flashlight asked. "Didn't I tell you about getting burned in the next piss test?" Thick black fingers gently slapped the white face. "Didn't I?"

"You told me, Sarge."

"And still you come out here smoking that reefer." The light lowered and then rose back to the face. "You taking any other kinda shit?"

"Nothing, Sarge."

The light switched to the next GI, this one with a longish face the color of swirled milk chocolate.

"And you, Quigley? You out here thinking you're going to kick some rear echelon ass? What I tell you about fighting? Come on, what I tell you?"

"You said to take it to the gym, Sarge."

"That's right. They got gloves down there. You practice hard enough maybe you get out of the artillery into one of those Special Service units. Didn't I tell you that?"

"You told me, Sarge."

"All right." The light lowered to the mud. "Now apologize to these two gentlemen." No one said anything. "They come all the way up here from Seoul just to do something good and you treat them like this. Come on, now. Apologize."

A few surly voices mumbled something that sounded vaguely like the word "Sorry."

"Anybody hurt? Anybody need to go to the aid station?" When no one responded, the man with the flashlight said, "All right now. Nobody has an overnight pass. I know that. Get your butts out of here and back to the barracks. And put down that reefer. You hear me?"

Again, a few more mumbles. Something like, "We hear you."

Their heads down, hands shoved deep into their pockets, the GIs filed past us. Five of them, I counted. There were a few cuts and bruises and at least one of them would wake up tomorrow with a serious knot on his head, but apparently there were no serious injuries.

When they were out of sight, the man with the flashlight said, "How about you two? Either one of you hurt?"

"Not a chance," Ernie said. "Lucky for them you stopped us when you did. "

In the reflected light, a large black face smiled wryly. "Yeah, they lucky. Come on then, follow me."

He turned and, fanning the beam of the flashlight in front

of him, tromped off down the pathway. Ernie and I followed. The narrow walkway rounded a bend and the floodlights from Camp Pelham suddenly illuminated our way. The man in front switched off his flashlight and kept walking, head down.

"Lucky you came along," Ernie told him, repeating himself, still angry. "I was about to kick me some serious ass."

The man didn't respond. He was thick-shouldered and broad-hipped and walked with a pronounced bow-leggedness; it would be impossible to knock him off his center of gravity. He wore fatigue pants and combat boots but no headgear and only a green t-shirt covering his upper torso.

At a wooden gate facing the river, he stopped and knocked and shouted out, "Rodney *Ohma*." Rodney's Mother.

Footsteps pounded on earth. A small door in the gate creaked open. The man motioned with his flashlight for us to enter.

"Who the hell are you?" Ernie asked.

The man seemed surprised. "I'm Singletery. The CQ runner told me you was looking for me."

"That's why you came looking for us?" I asked.

"Dangerous town," Singletery said. His face kept its flat, earnest expression as he spoke. There was no hint of irony in his voice. Immediately, I understood why the officer corps thought so highly of Sergeant First Class Singletery and why his tour in Korea had been extended beyond five years. He knew how to handle the troops, which was more than most of the officer corps could say, and he got the job done without the customary smirk of superiority or taunting tone of voice that many NCOs used to mask their resentment of authority.

Ernie crouched through the small door first. I followed.

It was a surprisingly large courtyard for the crowded village of Sonyu-ri. The wall on the left was lined with earthenware kimchi pots and the wall on the right featured two cement-walled *byonso*, outdoor toilets. One wooden door was slashed with black paint spelling *yo*, woman, and the other *nam*, man.

In the center of the courtyard was a small swing set, rusty

but sturdy with shiny new bolts at the metal joints. In front of us were two hooches forming an L shape and running along their front was a low, varnished wooden porch. In the awning overhead, bright bulbs shone, illuminating the entire scene. Behind the porch some of the oil-papered doors had been slid open. A small pack of children squatted on a warm *ondol* floor watching cartoons with various anthropomorphic creatures squawking and growling in high-pitched Korean.

A woman emerged from one of the hooches. She was Korean, wearing a thick woolen housedress, long, unkempt hair sweeping back from a high forehead. She was a big woman for a Korean, husky. She flashed us a crooked smile that moved only the lower half of her long face and then she bowed slightly, motioning for us to enter the hooch opposite the one where the children were watching television.

"That's my wife," Singletery said, but he didn't attempt any more formal introductions.

We slipped off our shoes and stepped up on the porch and Mrs. Singletery dealt flat cushions out on the floor. The room had sleeping mats rolled against one wall and a large inlaid mother-of-pearl armoire against the other. She folded down the legs of a small table, set it in front of us, and hurried out toward the kitchen. Singletery, after slipping off his combat boots, sat down opposite us. With moist brown eyes he stared at us, his legs comfortably crossed, his big hands relaxed in his lap. He didn't say anything. Neither did we. We just listened to the bang, slap, roar of the cartoon next door. The children were enraptured but they weren't laughing.

Finally, Singletery's wife brought a brass pot of hot water and we helped ourselves to Folgers instant coffee. Ernie took sugar in his, I took mine black. Singletery sipped on a strawberry soda.

The cartoons ended. The children filed out of the room, slipped on their shoes, and bowed to Singletery's wife, who stood on the porch to see them off. In a small pack they trotted across the courtyard, pushed through the gate, and tumbled shouting out into the street. A little boy of about four came over and sat in Singletery's lap. He was obviously his son, with both the dark skin and curly hair of his father and the smooth Korean features of his mother.

"The wife likes the kids to play here," Singletery said. "That's why she lets 'em watch TV."

Many of the poor families in Sonyu-ri, and throughout the country, could not afford televisions.

"That's nice of her," I said.

Singletery didn't answer. He held the bottle of pop while his son drank from it. His wife didn't join us. A pot clanged in the kitchen.

Ernie and I already figured we were in the wrong place. The likelihood of this guy, a lifer with well over ten years in the Army, traveling to Seoul with a couple of buddies and raping a business girl on the banks of the Han River were slim to non-existent. Still, we were here. Might as well ask some questions.

"Your boys seem a little over-exuberant," I said.

Singletery stared at me blankly.

"They're anxious to kick some REMF ass," Ernie translated.

Singletery smiled, brown eyes shining. "They some tough boys."

"In your platoon?"

"In my *battery*," he corrected.

"Right. Your battery. Do you get down to Seoul much?"

"Every payday," he said proudly.

"Get a kitchen pass?" Ernie said, smiling. "So you can run the ville down in Itaewon?"

Somberly, Singletery shook his head. His son was growing bored with our adult conversation, his eyes drooping. He snuggled up closer to his dad. "No," Singletery replied. "Every payday me and the wife and the boy jump on the bus out of RC-Four. Go to the commissary."

He was referring to 8th Army's big Yongsan Commissary in Seoul. Whole families from the Division area mob the place shortly after end-of-month payday, and mob the free military buses going back and forth. Most of them carry empty Army-issue duffel bags down with them, then load them up with imported merchandize and lug the heavy load all the way back up north.

"How about last weekend?" Ernie asked. "Did you or anybody in your unit go to Seoul?"

Singletery shook his head. "We was out on alert."

"Where?"

"Nightmare Range."

I knew where it was. A military reservation set aside for war games, at the top of the Eastern Corridor, sandwiched between the Imjin River and the Demilitarized Zone.

"The whole battalion?" I asked.

Singletery nodded his head.

That was that. We'd checked on every Chief of Firing Battery in the entire 2nd Infantry Division, every NCO who could conceivably be called "Smoke," and we'd come up with nothing. Still, Singletery had been living and working in the Division area for over five years. I decided to level with him.

"There was a rape," I said, "down in Seoul. A business girl named Sunny was hurt badly."

Singletery patted his son on the butt and told him to run off to his mother. The sleepy boy did. Singletery sipped on his strawberry soda and studied me with his brown eyes. I filled him in on the details and told him that we were up here because one of Sunny's attackers had been referred to as "Smoke."

"Smoke," Singletery repeated.

"So we thought," Ernie said, "that the guy might be a Chief of Firing Battery."

"Have you heard anything?" I asked. "About three guys going to Seoul last weekend, maybe one of them coming back with some scratches on his face or on his arms? Maybe bragging about the women they'd met? Something like that?"

Slowly, Singletery shook his head. He set down his soda. "That's fucked up," he said.

"Yes," I replied. "Very fucked up."

He shoved his soda away, as if it had turned sour. His wife returned and offered us more coffee. We declined. Singletery continued to think about what we'd said, as if we'd upset him deeply. When he offered no further information, we thanked him and his wife for their hospitality, went to the porch, slipped on our shoes, and escaped into the cold night.

A thousand lights reflected off the rotating glass disc. Rock and roll blared out of the juke box and I had to lean close to Ernie to make myself heard.

"We should drive back tonight," I shouted. "Make some more black market arrests in the morning."

"Why?" Ernie asked. "Five arrests in two days. That's enough to hold 'em for a while."

"Not with Mrs. Wrypointe on the warpath."

"Screw Mrs. Wrypointe."

"Not with your dick," I told him, although my heart wasn't in it. Ernie'd glommed onto a buxom young woman wearing hot pants and a halter top. Her name was Miss Kim or Miss Lee or Miss Pak, I don't remember which, and when the midnight curfew approached Ernie told me that he'd be staying with her at her hooch and he'd meet me in the morning.

"Where?" I asked.

"At the jeep. There's a PX snack stand in front of the Battalion Ops Center. Zero eight hundred."

"That late?"

"You worry too much, Sueño."

Patting Miss Kim or Miss Lee or Miss Pak on her tight butt, he strode out the back door of the Kit Kat Club and entered the dark maze of alleys that pulsed through the village of Sonyu-ri like purple veins through a heart.

I finished my beer and wandered out into the street. Standing in shadow, I watched GIs, many of them arm-in-arm with business girls, scattering toward refuge before the oncoming midnight-to-four curfew. Lights in many of the shops had already been turned off, metal shutters rolled into place. Up and down the strip, neon flickered, buzzed, and then shut down.

A woman stood next to me. "We go, GI?"

She was older than me. In her thirties, maybe forty. I couldn't stand here all night. I asked her how much. She told me. It seemed reasonable.

She was surprised, I suppose, that I didn't bargain. Most GIs would. But I didn't believe in bargaining with business girls. They were desperate and only did what they did because of poverty. I knew about desperation and I knew about poverty. But these days I had money coming in every month, whether I needed it or not. And I had no wife to spend it on, and no son. Not that I could find, anyway.

She took me by the hand and her flesh was warm. I held on tight as she led me into the night.

In the morning, I was up with the PT formations. PT—that's the army's acronym for physical training. Or, as drill sergeants love to say, "physical torture." Before dawn, each unit falls out in the company (or battery) street and does the daily dozen. Calisthenics, civilians call them. Jumping jacks, squat benders, leg thrusts, push-ups, sit-ups, the usual. When done with that, the next order of business is the morning run. Years ago, a mile was deemed to be an appropriate distance. But these days, longer distances are in vogue and no self-respecting firing battery would bother with a run of less than two miles. Each of the three Camp Pelham firing batteries exploded, in formation, yelling their lungs out, from beneath the arched main gate. An NCO led them, shouting out cadence, the men chanting in response, and the unit wound like a very noisy caterpillar down the main street of Sonyu-ri. "Wake up! Sonyu-ri! Wake up! Sonyu-ri!"

No unit in the States could get away with running past a residential area and making that much noise. The civilians would complain. In Korea, the local populace doesn't even think about

complaining. Who would they complain to? The military dictatorship that runs the country? The local police who take orders
from that dictatorship? The Commander of Camp Pelham? All
futile. Instead, they put up with the shouting and the pounding
of feet and when the sound fades away they roll over and go back
to sleep.

When the last battery exited Camp Pelham, it made its way,
like the others, down the main drag of Sonyu-ri. About two hundred yards on the other end of the strip, another unit emerged
from the compound called RC-4, Recreation Center Four. In
addition to their regular sweatpants and sweatshirts, each member of this unit wore a red pullover cap. The lead runner carried
a guidon, a pennant fluttering atop a pole that identified them as
combat engineers. As the two units approached each other they
both started the same chant, even louder than the chants before:
"On your left! On your left! Sick call! Sick call!"

The ultimate insult. Instead of doing your job, you spend
your time running to the dispensary, claiming to be one of the
"sick, lame, and lazy."

The units passed each other, trading barbs and descriptive
hand gestures, and continued on their runs. I strode to the Camp
Pelham gate. An American MP stared at me with a bored expression. I flashed my identification and passed through the narrow
pedestrian entrance. A few yards inside, I found our jeep still
parked in front of the Battalion Ops Center. I sat in the passenger seat, crossing my arms across my chest for warmth, waiting
for Ernie. About half an hour later, the snack stand across the
street opened for business. I bought a Styrofoam cup filled with
acidic coffee and a cinnamon roll made of dough that had the
consistency of chewing gum. Still, the breakfast warmed me and
filled my empty stomach.

I thought of the woman I'd spent the night with. Already, I
could hardly remember her face. What I did remember is how
deferential the landlady had been to her because she'd landed
a customer. She brought us a metal pan of hot water and hand

towels and soap and asked us to play the radio low so we wouldn't disturb the children sleeping in the hooch next door. The landlady bowed to her when she brought the pan of hot water and called her "*ajjima*." Aunt. It may sound crazy but I thought I'd helped the old business girl in more ways than one. I'd given her money, of course, which she clearly needed, and maybe just as importantly I'd given her face. It may not seem like much but in a lifetime filled with hardship and a constant gnawing sense of desperation, it's something.

Ernie always told me I was a nut case. "You can't save the whole *freaking* world," he used to tell me. I knew he was right but that didn't make things any easier.

I was about to purchase another cup of coffee when Ernie showed up, right at zero eight hundred like he'd promised. He jumped behind the steering wheel and started the engine.

"You get your ashes hauled last night?" he asked.

I shrugged.

"Okay," he said. "Be that way."

He backed the jeep out into the battalion street, jammed the gearshift into first, and a few seconds later we were outside the main gate of Camp Pelhem. Across the street stood a boxy whitewashed building with the flag of the Republic of Korea fluttering in front.

"Pull over," I said.

"Why?" Ernie asked.

"I want to talk to them. They might have something for us."

He groaned but pulled over and came to a screeching halt.

I climbed out of the jeep and walked into the Sonyu-ri Korean National Police Station. Once the desk sergeant saw my badge, he became cooperative. I asked him if there'd been any incidents involving GIs this weekend, particularly on Sunday afternoon or evening. He thumbed through a ledger and finally pointed to an entry written in the neat *hangul* script. He read it to me. I occasionally slowed him down while I translated and made notes. When we were through, I thanked him and asked if there'd been anything else.

Nothing, he replied, other than that one incident. It had been a quiet night. I thanked him and returned to the jeep.

"What'd they have?" Ernie asked.

"GIs ripping off a cab driver."

Ernie grunted. "So what else is new?"

"Apparently they were local GIs," I said. "They had the driver let them off in the middle of the Sonyu-ri strip and then they ran into the alleyways, disappearing before the driver could catch them."

"They knew their way around."

"Right. The driver was from Seoul," I said. "Picked them up in Itaewon."

"That doesn't mean they're our boys," Ernie said.

"No," I agreed. "It doesn't. All three of them were Caucasian. At least the driver thought they were." Sometimes Koreans aren't so sure about race. For many of them there are only two races. You're either Korean or you're not.

"Descriptions?" Ernie asked.

"Big. Wearing blue jeans and sneakers and nylon jackets. They smoked a lot and were very noisy."

"That narrows it down."

"Right."

Ernie shoved the jeep in gear and we pulled away from the police station and started rolling through the main drag of Sonyu-ri. At the Kit Kat Club Ernie downshifted, gunned the engine, and honked his horn. The front door was open. Through a beaded curtain, three pairs of manicured hands waved gaily, brightly colored bracelets dangling from slender wrists.

Ernie grinned and waved back. "My fan club," he said.

And then we were on the Main Supply Route, heading south toward Seoul. I shivered and wrapped my arms tighter across my heart, sheltering myself as best I could from the cold wind of the Western Corridor.

■ ■ ■

When we returned to the 8th Army CID office, Miss Kim looked up from her typewriter and smiled. Staff Sergeant Riley was just finishing up a phone call.

"All right," he said. "Got it." He slammed down the receiver and looked up at us. "You're here," he said. "Officers' Wives' Club. Disturbance. The Provost Marshal wants you two over there immediately, if not sooner."

"A disturbance at the OWC?" Ernie said.

"That's right."

"What happened? Somebody stole the knitting fund?"

"I don't know what the hell happened," Riley growled. "Other than that the MP patrol says there's an ambulance sitting outside and Mrs. Wrypointe is hysterical. Now get the hell over there."

Ernie set his empty coffee cup on the edge of Riley's desk and we ran outside toward the jeep.

MP Sergeant Unsworth stood next to his MP jeep in front of the big green Quonset hut set aside for the Officers' Wives' Club. A green army ambulance was parked behind him. Both Ernie and I have worked with Unsworth before. He's a grown man and a responsible adult and a hell of a good Military Policeman, so seeing tears welling up in his eyes was downright terrifying. Ernie and I strode up to him.

"What the hell happened?" Ernie asked.

Unsworth jammed his thumb over his should. "Mrs. Wrypointe. I just can't talk to her."

His hand was shaking.

"Why?" Ernie asked. "She hurt?"

"No," he answered. "I mean, yes. She says she is." The tears were already running down his face. "She threatened me," he said.

"With what?" I asked.

"Demotion." Then his eyes widened and he stared at us as if begging. "I can't take the cut in pay. My wife and my kids back in the States are barely getting by as it is."

I patted him on the shoulder. "Don't worry about demotion,"

I said, not sure if I believed it. We realized we weren't going to gather much more information here so we left him and ran to the open door. Above the entranceway an engraved wooden sign was bolted: EIGHTH UNITED STATES ARMY OFFICERS' WIVES' CLUB, YONGSAN BRANCH.

Ernie and I entered.

Mrs. Wrypointe sat on a metal chair, covering her eyes with her left hand, the right being held by another American woman, who was comforting her. A half-dozen women swiveled to stare at Ernie and me as we entered. I pulled out my CID badge.

"Agent Sueño," I said, "and Agent Bascom."

They all started talking at once. Out of the hubbub the name that kept getting repeated was "Burkewalder."

The convoy left the compound about twenty-two hundred hours that evening, or 10 P.M. civilian time. Colonel Brace, the 8th Army Provost Marshal, was at the lead, riding in his green army sedan with his Korean civilian driver. Two jeeps full of MPs came next, followed by me and Ernie. We emerged from Namsan Tunnel and gazed down at the bright lights of downtown Seoul. Colonel Brace's driver took the familiar turnoff toward Myong-dong.

"So she popped her a good one," Ernie said.

"So they claim," I replied. "Mei-lan Burkewalder interrupts the meeting of the OWC and reads off Mrs. Wrypointe for being behind the crackdown on black marketing and now her husband's been notified and he's in the middle of combat operations as part of the remaining US military advisory group in South Vietnam."

"So Mrs. Wrypointe calls her a black marketing whore and Mei-lan karate chops her in the nose."

"What Mrs. Wrypointe called her is in dispute," I said, "but everybody agrees about the punch. Not a karate chop, a straight right. Knocked off Mrs. Wrypointe's glasses and bloodied her nose."

"So now we're going to bust Tiger Kang for black marketing."

"Mrs. Wrypointe insisted."

What worried me were the people riding up front in Colonel Brace's sedan. Lieutenant Pong, the Korean National Police Liaison Officer to 8th Army, I could understand. He was a law-enforcement professional and his presence was required to coordinate the arrests of any Korean civilians. The other person was along for the ride strictly because of who she was married to and because of her proven ability to intimidate: Mrs. Millicent Wrypointe.

"Colonel Brace might as well turn over the authority of his office to the OWC," Ernie said.

"Might as well," I agreed.

Colonel Brace's driver took a wrong turn and Ernie and I waited at the intersection for them to figure it out. Ten minutes later they were back, the two jeeps full of MPs trailing behind, and they pulled up next to us. Colonel Brace rolled down his window.

"Where is this damn place?" he shouted.

"Follow us," Ernie said and without further discussion we took off. Once again, we parked at the foot of the hill leading up to Tiger Kang's. It took some time for the MPs and Colonel Brace's driver to find safe places to park. When the entire party was assembled, Ernie said, "We have to approach on foot."

Colonel Brace, wearing a starched set of fatigues, nodded. "So they won't have time to destroy the contraband."

Mrs. Wrypointe wore pressed slacks and sneakers and a warm pullover sweater. Her nose was bandaged with white gauze. "Come on then," she said. "The more time we give all these Koreans to gawk at us, the more time they have to warn this Tiger Kang."

Apparently, she thought all Koreans worked together.

With Ernie at the lead, we trudged up the hill. As we passed each streetlamp, I fell back further and further. Something told me not to get too involved in this; it wasn't going to turn out right, and if things went wrong, Mrs. Wrypointe would love nothing more than to blame me and Ernie.

But Ernie couldn't resist the excitement. I believe he'd fallen in love with Tiger Kang's *kisaeng* house, and maybe with Tiger Kang herself. And he certainly had a crush on Mei-lan Burke-walder. The hand-carved front door was lit by a floodlight and Ernie pressed the buzzer and in seconds the door popped open. Reflexively, two beautiful young women in tradition *chima-chogori* Korean gowns held their hands clasped in front of them and bowed so deeply they exposed the jade pins knotting their ebony hair. Ernie bowed back but as he did so Lieutenant Pong pushed past the women, followed immediately by Colonel Brace and Mrs. Wrypointe. The MPs milled around outside, thumbs hooked over their web belts. I told two of them to watch out back and two more to wait here at the front entrance. The other four followed me into Tiger Kang's.

Ernie was already upstairs. That's where the parties were going on, the noise and the laughter, and that's where Lieutenant Pong, Colonel Brace and Mrs. Wrypointe headed first. When I reached the top of the stairs, I saw a startled group of Korean businessmen, seated next to beautiful young Korean hostesses inside one of the raised-floor party rooms, faces flushed by imported scotch. Lieutenant Pong looked inside, then proceeded down the row. All the rooms were empty until he reached the party room at the end of the hall. Lieutenant Pong slid open the oiled-paper door and stood there as if he'd been turned to stone. Colonel Brace and then Mrs. Wrypointe were following on his heels so closely that they practically bumped into him.

Ernie studied the expressions on their faces and then turned and grinned at me.

Mrs. Wrypointe screamed.

"What the hell did they expect to find?" Ernie asked. We were back in his jeep, winding our way through the brightly lit district of Myong-dong. "Eighth Army honchos out for a night on the town, where the hell else are they going to go? Tiger Kang's."

"She didn't expect to find her husband," I said, "with his tongue down the throat of Mei-lan Burkewalder."

"Mei-lan probably made sure that he picked her for the evening."

"Out of revenge?"

"What else?"

"Maybe they'd been an item for a while," I said. "Maybe that's why she wasn't worried about us busting her for black market."

"Maybe." Ernie zipped up onto the expressway and half a mile later we entered Namsan tunnel. "Anyway, they got their black market arrest. And a historic moment it was. Tiger Kang arrested and taken down to the local KNP station."

"They'll treat her like a queen."

"You can count on that."

When we emerged from the tunnel, Ernie turned left on the MSR. After zigging and zagging through a quarter mile of heavy traffic, he turned down a dark lane and parked the jeep in one of the back alleys of Itaewon. We should've gone back to the MP station to file our report but somehow I needed to cleanse myself of 8th Army for a while. What better place than Itaewon, the greatest red-light district in Northeast Asia?

We found two empty barstools at the Lucky Seven Club. Sunny still hadn't returned to work. We asked about her and the barmaid said she was improving. She didn't sound too convincing. We ordered two cold OBs and two shots of black market bourbon. Within seconds we'd jolted them down and ordered two more.

"What the hell happened to you?" Riley growled.

"What do you mean?" I asked.

"You look like dog shit."

It was zero eight hundred. At some point last night I'd staggered back to the compound, made it up the hill to the barracks and collapsed in my bunk. The houseboy, Mr. Yim, shook me awake in time for me to shower and shave before dragging myself to the CID office, but I'd made it. I touched my face. "I look all right."

"Except for your eyeballs spurting blood."

"They're not bleeding."

"No. They just look that way."

I made my way to the counter and poured myself a cup of coffee.

"Where's your partner in crime?"

"I don't know."

"You better find out."

"Why?"

He tossed a pink phone message on the front of his desk. "This came in for you last night, to the MP desk officer."

After sipping my coffee, I staggered back to his desk, grabbed the message and sat down heavily in a gray Army-issue vinyl chair. I stared at the message but couldn't focus.

"Some guy named Singletery," Riley said. "The desk sergeant said the connection was bad but Singletery seems to think that you need to get up there real quick. He has a lead for you."

I studied the note. It was garbled, written in pencil in a childish script. I willed the pounding in my head to subside and tried to concentrate. It was a long message, filling up the entire pink square, finally trailing off at the end, but I got the gist of it. I set the note down on Riley's desk

"He's in danger," I said.

"Who?"

"Singletery."

For once, Riley didn't make a smart remark. "Where's Ernie?" he asked.

"Not in the barracks."

"Out in the ville?"

I nodded.

"I'll call the MP duty patrol to take you out there."

I nodded again.

■ ■ ■

I found Ernie with one of the Lucky Seven waitresses who lived in the same complex of hooches as Sunny. He came wide awake when he saw me.

"What is it?"

"Singletery. He identified the guy called Smoke."

Ernie shoved back the silk comforter. "That's good, isn't it?"

"Very good. But according to his phone message, the guy called Smoke has identified him too."

"He knows Singletery's our snitch."

"You got it."

Ernie sprang to his feet and started searching for his pants. The waitress sleeping on the mat next to him pulled the comforter over her head and groaned. In about a minute, Ernie was dressed and we were outside and striding through the narrow lanes of Itaewon.

"You bring your forty-five?" Ernie asked.

"Got it," I said, patting the shoulder holster beneath my nylon jacket.

"Do we have time to get mine?"

"I don't think so."

"Okay." He reached in his pocket and pulled out his brass knuckles. "At least I got these."

Camp Pelham looked deserted. The MP at the gate emerged from the guard shack and said, "They're on move-out alert."

"Where'd they go?" Ernie asked.

The MP frowned. I pulled out my CID badge. "We're on a case," I said, "involving one of the guys in Charlie Battery."

"Across Freedom Bridge," the MP said. "That's all I know."

We thanked him and Ernie turned the jeep around. The village of Sonyu-ri looked deserted too, as did the compound at RC-4. No GIs to spend money, no business, no activity.

■ ■ ■

At the approach to Freedom Bridge we were waved to halt by another MP. This one wore a heavy parka with a fur-lined hood. The wind blew cold off the Imjin River. I showed him my identification.

"We're looking for the Second of the Seventeenth Field Artillery," I told him, "particularly Charlie Battery."

"They're all together," he told us. "Turn right after Camp Greaves and follow the road back to the river. You'll find them about four klicks upstream at Dragon Tail Canyon. That's where they're conducting the bridge-crossing exercise." We started to roll away and he shouted, "Better hurry or they'll be south of the river before you get there."

We veered onto the wooden roadway, gigantic iron struts looming above us. Every few yards an armed American MP, wearing gloves and winter gear, stood guard watching the vehicles rolling slowly past him and searching below for any attempt at sabotage. The churning Imjin flowed rapidly, an occasional chunk of mountain ice crashing into the huge cement stanchions below.

On the far side, a long line of military vehicles, both Korean and US, waited to cross the river. We sped past them on the two-lane highway and soon Camp Greaves was on our right. Then the road divided. If we went left we'd continue north to Camp Kitty Hawk and the truce village of Panmunjom, which sat smack dab in the middle of the Demilitarized Zone. Instead we turned right, as the MP had advised. After about ten minutes the road swerved south and once again we could see the rapidly flowing waters of the Imjin.

The river was narrower here at Dragon Tail Canyon and therefore moving faster. The banks on this side were low and sandy, like a beach, but on the far side loomed three- or four-story high red bluffs. Already, the river crossing exercise had begun. Huge pontoons held flat wooden barges, large enough to hold two deuce-and-a-half ton trucks along with two 105mm howitzers. The guns and their crews were aboard the low-lying craft and being propelled forward by huge outboard engines. As powerful as the engines were and as much smoke as they were giving off, they still could not propel the barge straight across the river. The current was so strong that the barges were being swept about a half-mile downriver, where they abutted a wooden quay. They hit there with a heavy bump, then were tied up by another crew so the guns and the trucks could drive off onto dry land.

"Combat engineers," Ernie said.

The same unit I'd seen running PT outside of their compound on RC-4. Upstream a thick bank of fog was rolling in like a huge cloud of mist.

"Our visibility won't last long," I said. "Do you see Charlie Battery?"

"Over there. They're about to load up."

"Come on."

Ernie drove the jeep down a narrow dirt road that led to the beach. He pulled up in a cloud of dust. I spotted Sergeant Singletery's huge hunched shoulders and his bow legs. "Over there."

We climbed out of the jeep and trotted toward Singletery. He was supervising the loading of the last of Charlie Battery's howitzers onto the last barge.

"Chief of Smoke," I said.

He turned, startled. "About time," he said, grinning.

"We came as soon as I got your message."

He stood with his hands on his hips, facing us. "I was thinking about what you said. About three guys, about one of them called 'Smoke,' about them maybe wanting to brag about what they did and maybe wanting to do it again. I asked around. It ain't just Chiefs of Firing Batteries."

"What isn't?"

"They ain't the only ones called 'Smoke.'"

"Who else?"

Singletery turned and nodded toward the barge. A crewman had thrown off the last heavy line. "Them," Singletery said. "Come on."

We didn't have time to discuss it further. It was the last barge and it was leaving. Signletery trotted onto the quay and we followed. When the barge was about a yard from the end and floating free, the three of us leapt aboard.

The fog upstream was even closer, engulfing us like a giant nightmare.

"So who else is called 'Smoke'?" I asked.

Singletery turned and, as if to answer my question, stared down at the far end of the barge. Three men stood there, three combat engineers. Next to them was a huge contraption that looked like an electrical generator with some sort of tubing attached, like a short-barreled mortar. As we stared at the men, one of them aimed the tubing at us.

"Is he gonna fire that thing?" Ernie asked.

"It don't fire," Singletery said.

"Then what the hell is it?"

Before he could answer, the full force of the bank of fog slid silently over the barge. Within seconds it swallowed up the wooden planking and the canvas-covered trucks and the glistening metal barrels of the 105mm howitzers. We were enveloped in darkness.

"We better get 'em," Singletery said, "before they start that thing up."

"What is it?" I asked but already he was moving away from us, just a dark shadow in the mist. I grabbed Ernie's elbow and pulled him forward and together we followed Sergeant Singletery and then, before we could reach the end of the barge, we heard an engine coughing, choking, and then starting to life— and then roaring.

"Shit," Singletery said. He stopped abruptly and we bumped into him.

"Gas!" he shouted.

All around us we could hear artillerymen popping open canvas holders and scrambling to pull out rubber protective masks, yanking them over their heads, adjusting the straps, blowing out forcefully to clear the air inside, and then lowering the protective rubber hood over their shoulders.

And then we saw it, dark and black and menacing. Smoke. Tons of it, roiling out of that metal tubing we'd seen a few seconds ago. CS—better known to the civilian world as tear gas.

"Come on."

Ernie and I ran to the upstream side of the barge, toward the thickening fog, groping blindly. At least most of the tear gas was being swept south by the prevailing winds, which whistled loudly out of North Korea, following the southerly flow of the current.

"If that shit gets in our eyes," Ernie said, "we'll be helpless."

"Blind, maybe," I said, "but not helpless." I pulled out my .45.

We'd both experienced CS gas before. It's part of every soldier's basic training; to step into a gas filled tent, take off your protective mask, recite your service number backward, and be shoved outside coughing and spitting by your Drill Sergeant.

We stood in the fog behind the lead truck on the barge. Ernie whispered in my ear, "They're on the far side of the truck, next to that thing spitting out the gas. As soon as we hit land, they'll skedaddle."

"So we wait here," I said. "When we land and this freaking gas clears, Singletery tells us who they are and we make the arrest."

Ernie was about to say something when we heard a scream, then cursing, men grunting and the sound of bodies flailing against metal.

"Singletery," I said.

We rushed around the front bumper of the truck. As soon as we stepped past the truck, the gas hit us. I kept my eyes closed, popping them open briefly and trying not to breathe. Amidst the fog and the pumping CS gas, I could see only shadows. Ernie surged forward, swinging at phantoms with his brass knuckles. I tried to aim my .45. A hunch-shouldered figure that I took to be Singletery was struggling with two of the combat engineers, the men I suspected had raped Sunny. Ernie had found the third and was holding him in a headlock and punching his face with the brass knuckles. Singletery staggered backward. It looked to me as if someone had ripped off his protective mask. I saw the hood go flying off the edge of the barge.

My eyes burned with pain. Tears flooded out of them, so fast I couldn't see. I knew the worst thing you could do when under assault by CS gas is to wipe your eyes because that just makes them burn worse. But if I couldn't see, I couldn't fire. Using my sleeve I bent and wiped moisture from by eyes. Then, with an act of will, I opened them as wide as I could and through the fog and the gas I took aim with the .45 and fired at the two men assaulting Sergeant Singletery.

I didn't mean to hit them, I only wanted to scare them, but it was too late. They'd finally managed to shove the huge man off his center of gravity. As I fired, he reeled, waving his arms in the air, and tilted backward. He fell away, tumbling off the end of the barge. The sickening sound of a splash hit my ears.

I fired again, this time aiming to kill. I hit something and the two men went down.

"Don't move," I shouted. "I'll blow your heads off!"

The man wrestling with Ernie lay flat on the deck. Ernie backed away, staggering toward the two-and-a-half ton truck. When he was next to me, he knelt on the wooden deck. Down the barge I heard men shouting, their voices muffled by their protective masks. "Man overboard!"

There was no rescue craft that I knew of, and no Coast Guard to notify. What I did know was that the waters of the Imjin were freezing and the current not only flowed quickly but was also known for its treacherous undertows.

Ernie crawled toward the machine spewing out the gas and pawed at the controls. Somehow, he managed to get it turned off. A couple of minutes later we bumped against the quay on the opposite bank and the air started to clear, the gas and the fog flowing swiftly downriver. Although my eyes were watering way too much for me to read it, I managed to recite from memory a prisoner's rights from the Uniform Code of Military Justice to the three men lying motionless on the deck.

A search was launched for Singletery. They spent two days looking for him. His body was never recovered. At 8th Army JAG, murder was added to the long list of charges against the three combat engineers.

Two months later Ernie drove his jeep and I rode shotgun, literally. I held an M-16 rifle across my chest while in the back seat sat a representative from 8th Army Finance. He carried a leather briefcase with a combination lock on it.

Mei-lan Burkewalder had long since lost her ration control privileges and her command sponsorship. This meant that she no longer received the cost-of-living housing allowance, which was apparent as Ernie drove us down bumpy lanes, splashing through mud, honking his horn at the crowds of taffy vendors and trash dealers and old ladies holding huge bundles of laundry atop their heads. Finally, we found the address: painted on a grease stained board: 21 bon-ji, 37 ho, in the Mapo district of Seoul. Ernie parked the jeep against a moss covered brick wall and we climbed out and tromped through the mud toward the splintered wooden gate. I pounded and we waited.

Mei-lan Burkewalder opened the gate herself. Her face was wan and gray, with no hint of makeup. The bracelets that used to dangle from her forearms were also gone. She didn't bother to invite us into her hooch. She just let us into the courtyard and sat on the narrow wooden porch that ran in front of the sliding oil-papered doors. The guy from 8th Army Finance sat next to her. He unlocked the briefcase, pulled out a sheaf of paperwork, read it to her and asked if she understood. She nodded.

"Would you say that out loud please," he said, "in front of these witnesses."

He nodded toward Ernie and me.

"I understand," she said.

Then he handed her a pen and she signed the paperwork. He

kept the top white copy and the yellow copy, which was for her husband's pay and earnings folder, and handed her the bottom pink copy.

Captain Irwin Burkewalder had been killed in action while on combat operations in a support role with the 2nd Ranger Group near Pleiku. Word had come down about a week ago. Mrs. Mei-lan Burkewalder had been notified and now, as spousal beneficiary, she was receiving her ten thousand dollar payout from Serviceman's Group Life Insurance. The finance guy pulled the money out of the briefcase and counted the twenty dollar notes out in front of her. They made an impressive pile. Then he handed her some paper bands and let her bundle them up. She fumbled the job. He helped her finish.

When he was done, he shoved his signed paperwork into the briefcase and clicked it shut. He stood and nodded to her.

As he walked back to the gate, Mei-lan Burkewalder looked at Ernie and then at me. Her eyes were dry. Too dry. The eyes you see when there are no tears left.

We backed out of the hooch and returned to Ernie's jeep.

THE GRAY ASIAN SKY

Puffed bruises spotted the young faces, and their black hair stuck out in disarray. The girls were still angry. The boys just frightened.

In the States a police station full of student demonstrators would have been a madhouse of noise and activity. Here there was an eerie silence. Two of the Korean policemen chatted quietly while another dialed the telephone.

Order. That's what you can count on in a police state. Law if you're lucky.

Ernie and I waded through the crowd to the desk sergeant. He stared up at us, mouth slightly open. I spoke to him in Korean.

"We're here to see the body."

"Of the American?" he said.

"Who else?" Ernie whispered in English.

I nodded.

"Just a moment," the policeman said. He got up and strutted into the back room.

The glaring eyes of the students sitting around us were like forty pairs of laser beams burning into my body. America. That's what they saw in Ernie and me. The country that had allowed thinly veiled dictatorships to rule on this peninsula since we liberated them from the Japanese at the end of World War II. Ernie and I were almost as disliked in our own military bureaucracy;

a couple of flakes, they called us. Here we represented the power and influence of the mightiest country the world has ever seen.

You can't win.

The policeman reappeared and waved for us to follow. Forty sets of eyes swiveled as we walked out the back door.

A couple of policemen and a white-clad ambulance driver stopped their mumbling as we walked into the room. Batons, riot control shields, padded vests, and gas masks hung from pegs lining the walls. Lumpy linen draped a stretcher on the floor.

The desk sergeant stepped forward and ripped back the sheet.

His chest has been crushed, and his face was so purple and distorted that even if he were my brother I wouldn't have been able to recognize him. I kept my face straight. The desk sergeant watched us, a greedy gleam in his eye.

"Did he have any identification?" I said.

The desk sergeant pulled the sheet back over the corpse, then walked over to a metal cabinet and retrieved a plastic sack filled with keys, some US coins, and a wallet. We went back to the front desk where he had us sign a receipt for the personal effects.

The GI's name was Ralph Whitcomb. He had a weapons card that showed he was assigned to Headquarters Company, 8th United States Army. The photo on his green military ID was more revealing than the anguished distortion we had just seen. I showed it to Ernie.

"Seen him around," he said.

His wallet contained four thousand *won*, twenty-three dollars in wrinkled Military Payment Certificates, and seventy-five cents in change. The desk sergeant accounted for everything on the receipt. I signed it, fitting my long horizontal signature into the little vertical box on the form. He gave me a copy.

"Did any of these students know him, or see what happened?"

"No. Not that they've told us yet."

I handed him my card, inked by the 8th US Army printing plant in Bupyong.

"If they tell you anything, will you call us?"

He clenched his fist. "They will tell us something."

We walked out of the Sodaemun Police Station, glad to be away from the little room so filled with hatred.

Ernie and I had been the only two agents at the 8th Army CID Detachment headquarters when the report came in.

"I want you guys to get over to Chungang University," the first sergeant said. "Fast. There's been an American hurt, maybe killed, in one of their demonstrations."

Ernie was still rubbing his sore arm. The reason we had stopped in the administration office, instead of staying out in the field and pretending to search for some black market arrests, was that it was autumn and time for our annual mandatory flu shots. The army has a thing about flu shots. Every year. And they check to make sure each unit attains one hundred percent compliance. We were bringing our freshly stamped shot records back to Reilly, the NCO in charge of the CID Detachment's administrative section. A new vaccine has to be developed every year to ward off whatever brand of flu might have mutated into existence in the last twelve months, and the army's a great place to test it. If it kills a few GIs, you make a few adjustments and try again.

Mine felt as if it were going to kill me. I get sick every year after the flu shot. I'm not sure if it's from the vaccine or from the forced penetration.

"Get his name and service number," the first sergeant said. "And if he's hurt, make sure they hold him until one of our ambulances arrives. I'll wait until you call because I don't want to send a US Army ambulance into that part of town with all those students milling around."

"What about us?"

"You're expendable. Get going."

We studied the big map of Seoul on the wall of the admin office until Ernie was sure of the directions. Then we hopped in his jeep and made it over to the Sodaemun, Great West Gate, Police Station.

The one thing we had going for us on this foray into enemy territory was that our jeep was unmarked. There are a lot of jeeps operating in this country, all part of the generous US government military aid. And as Criminal Investigation Division agents we were required to wear coats and ties rather than our uniforms.

Of course, with our short hair the bad guys still spotted us for what we were. Might as well hang a neon sign around our necks.

The narrow lane in front of the big stone archway that led into Chungang University still glistened with the water from the fire hoses. The sky was overcast and spotted with dark patches of rolling gray. I breathed deeply of the damp air and inhaled the scent of flowers mingled with the diesel fumes of the just departed military vehicles.

Ernie found a spot in a back alley for the jeep and padlocked the steering wheel to the chain welded to the floor.

"What do you expect to find here?" Ernie asked.

"I don't know. Maybe a witness."

"And maybe a lot of angry shopkeepers. The Korean National Police aren't going to like it; it's their jurisdiction."

"Yeah, but it's our GI."

Ernie parked the jeep, and we walked down the roadway. The street was lined with shops, the type you'd expect in front of a college: a florist, a few stationery stores, bookstores with titles in English, French, and German, a couple of dress boutiques, and a whole bunch of teahouses. Not the type of teahouses that serve crumpets in mid-afternoon but the type that serve espresso and apple wine and sponsor poetry readings and political rallies.

A few remaining blossoms on a large treelike shrub still splashed the lane with purple. *Mukung-hua*, the Korean national flower, prized more for its sturdiness and beauty than for its rarity. Ahead, beyond the archway, a vast lawn unfolded around stately old trees. The campus of Chungang University.

It was an exciting neighborhood, and suddenly I was overwhelmed with the desire to have parents who could afford to send me to school. Hell, it would be nice to have parents even if they couldn't afford to send me to school.

I shook it off.

There were a few riot police in padded vests and huge caged helmets still hanging around. Mopping up.

Actually, it was incorrect to call them riot police. They are a branch of the armed services, and most of the so-called riot "police" are actually conscripts. The children of rice farmers who are drafted and sent to a few weeks of basic training, then deployed to college campuses to knock the heads of their peers who happen to come from wealthier families and can afford to attend university. Class warfare, controlled by the state.

When they saw two Americans approaching, an officer in a fatigue uniform was summoned. Ernie and I both flashed our identification.

"Where was the American killed?"

The officer gestured with his hands toward one of the tea shops. "This way."

The shop was located at a curve where the narrow road crooked like an elbow toward the university gate. A portly Korean woman, her hair done in a little round permanent and her body wrapped in a long white apron, rustled out of the shop. Her face was wrinkled in worry. I spoke to her in Korean.

"Did you see what happened, Aunt?"

"You mean the American?"

"Yes."

"I saw him. After he was hurt. It was horrible. One of their big war vehicles rolled right over him. Both sets of tires, they say, the front and the back. Blood was everywhere." She pointed toward the gutter. "They've washed it with their fire hoses, but it was everywhere."

Tears sprang into her eyes, and she shook her head. A gray-haired man, probably her husband, hustled out of the shop and pulled her back in. Other merchants came out into the street when they saw the two Americans with the Korean officer. They gathered around us, and I didn't have to ask any more questions, just strained to understand what they were saying.

"They ran over him and killed him. They ran over anything in their path."

"I saw it, I saw it all. They don't care what they do to these young people. They don't care."

"It's their fault, the army's fault. No one would have gotten hurt if they hadn't attacked."

I found an opening in the hubbub and shouted my question.

"Did anyone see the American fall?"

There was a silence and then mumbling as they looked around at one another. A trim man with jet black hair and a full-length blue apron stepped forward. I figured him to be about forty.

"I am the florist," he said. "I saw the American fall. He was with a small group of Korean students, two girls, two boys. I remember them because the American stopped in my shop to buy one of the girls a flower for her hair. When the armored vehicles charged up the lane, spewing water, I ran out of the shop. The American and the girl were right here, along the sidewalk at the curve. One of the vehicles took the curve too sharply and went up over it, and as the students jumped out of the way, I saw the American fall forward, very abruptly, as if he'd been pushed. He landed face first in the gutter. When the armored vehicle dropped back to the road, it landed right on top of him. Everyone was running my way and another vehicle was closing in, so I had to run back into my shop."

"Did you see who pushed the American?"

"No. I couldn't. I was too far away, and there were too many people."

A siren wailed and then got louder as it turned down the lane toward us from the main road a block away. The merchants began to disperse, and when the young officer saw that it was a police car he said goodbye to us and trotted back to his unit. Another police vehicle followed, and khaki-clad men jumped out and began to cordon off the neighborhood with white tape. One of the policemen came toward us.

"May I be of assistance?" he said.

Ernie answered. "We were just leaving."

We walked up the road to the florist's shop and went inside. The proprietor braced himself against the counter.

"What type of flower did the American buy?"

"A chrysanthemum." He went to a vase full of them and caressed the petals. "A foreign flower. But very beautiful. And very expensive this time of year."

I thanked him and went back to the jeep. Then we drove back to the police station and found a parking space across the street where we could see in through the big front windows. Ernie waited in the jeep while I went in. I spoke to the desk sergeant.

"Did you get any information from the students about the American's death?"

He nodded. "It appears to have been accidental. From a taxi cab trying to clear the area too quickly. We're looking for him now. When we find him, we'll let you know."

Back outside, I told Ernie what he had said. He snorted. "They don't want to admit that one of their army vehicles killed an American. It's an international incident. All hell could break loose."

"I'd hate to be the cab driver they accuse of hit and run."

"He'll be somebody on their shit list."

I found a pay phone and called the first sergeant.

"Who's the dead American?"

"A GI." I gave him the name, service number, and unit.

"What the hell was he doing out there during a demonstration?"

"What else? Trying to make it with one of the coeds."

I held the phone away from my ear while the first sergeant expressed his opinions. Colorfully. "The meat wagon's on its way. Make sure they pick up the body and all his personal effects."

"Sure. It might take awhile. You know how the Koreans are with paperwork."

"You and Bascom stay away from those demonstrators, you

understand me, Sueño? And get back here as soon as the body's been transferred to our custody."

"You got it, Top."

He hung up without even asking how Corporal Ralph Whitcomb had died.

We watched a parade of well-dressed, middle-aged Korean men and women walk into the Sodaemun Police Station. They stood at the front desk, did a lot of bowing, filled out some paperwork, and then, one by one, they were ushered into back rooms.

"Payoff time," Ernie said.

When they emerged, their young wards were delivered to them and they left the station. Usually the guardian was scowling and the student stared at the ground.

The girl with the chrysanthemum in her hair didn't have to wait too long. A dapper young Korean man who seemed more like a lawyer than a parent escorted her outside. Clinging to her arm was another college-age girl with short hair and a plain round face. Tagging along behind them were two boys, one of them thin and good-looking with short curly hair, the other slightly stout, wearing glasses. Studious looking.

"That dude liberated a whole pack of them," Ernie sad. "Must have cost him a bundle."

"Our young lady of the chrysanthemum has money and plenty of friends."

"The two go together," Ernie said.

The three other students said goodbye, and the lawyer and the flower girl climbed into a chauffeured Rekord Royale sedan. He sat in front. She sat in back. I copied the license number on my little notepad, and when they pulled away from the curb, Ernie followed, two car lengths behind in the rushing Seoul traffic.

They turned left at the ancient edifice of the West Gate and traveled northeast toward the heart of Seoul. After about a mile and a half of weaving through traffic, they took a left up a road that wound through a residential area and stopped at a big house on a hill overlooking the downtown business district. Stone walls and iron gates.

"This gal is rich," Ernie said. "Why does she want to overthrow the system?"

"She'll change her mind later."

Autumn is the usual time for demonstrations. School starts up again, and all the students are excited about being reunited with their friends and confident about getting the good grades this year that they didn't work hard enough for last year. And normally—if the government feels up to it—elections are held in the fall. The opposition parties had been growing stronger the last few years. One of their leaders received international recognition after he fled the country rather than allowing himself to be jailed for the offense of having more popular support than the president. Therefore, the ruling party had taken a wise step. They were going to allow elections, but a certain percentage of the seats in the legislature were going to be reserved exclusively for the ruling party. For some reason the students took umbrage at this and had taken to the streets.

When demonstrations are imminent, there's usually a reminder in the 8th Army Bulletin about political rallies being off-limits to military personnel. In fact, the only political activity GIs are allowed to participate in is the absentee ballot—if you remember to fill out the postcard and mail it to your home state. Other than that, forget it. And Corporal Ralph Whitcomb had made the foolish mistake of getting himself killed in the midst of an unauthorized activity.

The army doesn't mind you getting killed charging a machine gun nest—as a matter of fact they sort of like it—but don't meet the grim reaper at a political rally. That's frowned upon.

Whitcomb wasn't worried about it any more. And the only thing that bothered me was not where he died, but how he died. Someone had pushed him into the path of that charging armored vehicle, and I was going to find out who, even if nobody else really wanted to know.

Ernie drifted to a stop and parked out of sight. I jumped out of the jeep and peeked around the corner. The lawyer climbed out of the Rekord Royale, unlocked a metal grating in the stone wall, and rolled it up using a hand crank on the side. Then he got back into the car and they pulled into the narrow garage. The metal grating ground down and clanked shut.

I walked over to the front gate and copied the family's name and address from the engraved marble plaque embedded in the stone wall: Shin, 201-26 *bonji*, 34 *ho*, Hyonjo-dong, Seoul, Republic of Korea.

I walked back to the jeep.

"I'm going to try to talk to her," I said. "If I'm not back in thirty minutes, send in the Eighty-Second Airborne."

"If you're not back in thirty minutes, I'll be gone."

I returned to the front gate and rang the bell. An old woman shuffled out of the house and crossed the garden. When she saw my face, she started calling for someone named Lawyer Hong. He appeared at the door, speaking English.

"Can I help you?"

"I want to speak to Miss Shin. About what happened at the demonstration." I showed him my identification.

"Just a moment." He closed the gate in my face and walked quickly back into the house. After a few minutes, he reappeared. "Miss Shin will be unable to talk to anyone for a few days."

"But it's about the man who was killed . . . "

The door slammed in my face again.

As I walked away, I saw a baggy-faced old man glowering at me from a second-story window. I hated to drop a dime on little Miss Shin like that. American boyfriends aren't exactly good news to the ears of Korean parents. But it could have been worse. She could have been the one under those tires this afternoon.

I ducked back in the jeep and plopped into the passenger seat.

"No luck?"

"None."

"Where to?"

"Let's go find out a little bit more about the unfortunate Corporal Ralph Whitcomb."

The Charge of Quarters at Headquarters Company, 8th Army, was unsure if he should let us into Whitcomb's room.

"We showed you our identification," Ernie said. "What more do you want?"

"You need a warrant or something, don't you?"

"This is government property." Ernie waved his arms, taking in the entire three-story building. "People inspect it inside and out all the time. Who needs a warrant?"

The little guy brushed his brown hair back and reached for the ring of keys on his hip. "I guess you're right. The first sergeant came through this morning tearing down FTA signs, and last week the dogs came through sniffing for dope."

"If anybody wants privacy," Ernie said, "they better rent a hooch out in the village."

We walked down the hallway and the CQ opened Whitcomb's door. The cement block walls of the rectangular room had been painted a pale yellow. Bunks sat in three of the corners with big double-door wall lockers strategically placed to give each soldier a modicum of privacy. A row of shoes, starting with a highly spit-shined pair of combat boots, sat under each tightly made bunk. A bikinied Korean beauty beckoned from the OB Beer calendar on an otherwise naked wall.

There was no question about which bunk was Whitcomb's. The wall behind was plastered with photographs, many showing him robust and alive. He had been about five foot ten and seemed to be always smiling. A shock of blond hair waved over a pair of army-issue horn-rimmed glasses. There were photos of him posing in front of pagodas and shrines and ancient ruins, all places that I'd heard about but never had the gumption to visit.

In some of the photos Whitcomb was accompanied by young Korean women. In those, the backdrop was usually what appeared to be college campuses.

"This guy didn't waste his time or money on the girls out in the village," Ernie said.

"No. Looks like he went after the good ones."

Ernie checked some of the photos more closely. "Nice," he said. "But these good ones can be more dangerous."

"You're talking about getting trapped into marriage."

"That, too," he said.

There were more photos in an album and a packet of new photographs in a cloudy transparent wrapper.

Miss Shin, without her chrysanthemum, stood next to Whitcomb on the campus of what looked like Chungang University. The plain, round-faced girl and the two young men we had seen at the police station were also smiling broadly at the lens. I turned it over. Their first names were penciled in, from left to right. Miss Shin's first name was Myong-hui.

I stuck the photograph in my pocket.

"Time to visit a few dormitories," I said.

"You're just hoping we'll run into a panty raid."

"They have those here?"

"They have them everywhere," Ernie said.

We didn't bother with the administrative offices, just asked a young woman, strolling through the campus, where we could find the women's dormitories. She pointed, surprised to see two big Caucasian men on campus. She wasn't carrying any books. Classes had been cancelled for the day.

When we arrived at the row of dormitory buildings, we started asking young women if they knew the whereabouts of Shin Myong-hui or her friend. I showed them the photograph. Ernie kept picking out the best looking girls to question until we found one who was willing to answer. She also pointed, this time to a two-story brick building, and we trudged up cement steps until a middle-aged Korean woman barred our way. I spoke to her in Korean, showed her the photograph, and she ushered us toward a waiting room with a sitting area, a couple of card tables, and a pot of hot water on a charcoal-burning space heater.

Ernie wandered over to the game room next door and fumbled with the foosball machine.

The girl from the picture was short and her complexion was about the color of a cup of coffee lightened by an ounce of cream. She wore a plain beige skirt and blouse, kept wringing her hands in front of her flat belly, and bobbed her glasses beneath her crinkled brow. I asked her to sit down. The middle-aged woman made sure I caught her long hard look and then turned and marched out of the room.

The young woman pulled a handkerchief out of a pocket and started worrying it.

"We're here about the American who was killed today," I said.

Ernie padded into the room, pulled over a straight-backed chair, and sat down facing both of us.

I continued. "You're a good friend of Miss Shin Myong-hui?"

"Yes."

"The American, Ralph, he bought her a chrysanthemum today."

The crinkles on her forehead softened for a moment, and she almost smiled.

"It was very nice," she said.

"Were they lovers?"

"No. Not yet. But I think they would have been."

She looked back down at the floor, and the handkerchief waggled.

"Tell me about them."

Her sentences rolled out in precisely pronounced English, and I could see her editing her grammar as she went along.

"I was with Myong-hui when she met Ralph. He was taking photographs, here on campus, and he asked us to take a snapshot of him next to the fountain. Then he asked us, one by one, to pose with him. Later we went to a teahouse and talked, and before he went back to the compound, he had exchanged phone number with Myong-hui.

"At the time she didn't think she'd ever hear from him again. Mainly she was curious—about Americans. He was the first she'd ever met. And the first I'd ever met. He seemed nice. I warned her about Hei-sok, her boyfriend, but she wouldn't listen. She was always so open about everything. When he found out, he was upset, but he did his best to hide it. He tried to act . . . " She searched for a word. " . . . sophisticated about the whole thing. But I know he was very hurt and very angry. We met Ralph again about a week later, and he took us to see an American movie."

"On Eighth Army compound?"

"Yes. In Yongsan. And after the movie we went to your snack bar and ate some ice cream. It was very delicious."

"Thank you."

"You're welcome. When Hei-sok heard that we had gone to an American compound, he was furious, but he was smart enough not to scold Myong-hui. He knew that she would be sure to do whatever he told her not to do. Today was the fourth time we had seen Ralph, and the second time the four of us had gone together."

"Who was the fourth person?"

"Pak Un-sil. Hei-sok's friend. He is a very good student and wants to start a Department of Confucian Studies here at the university."

"Confucian studies?"

"Yes. He is very upset that the old proprieties are not being observed."

Ernie lifted his eyebrows. I changed the subject before he became too fidgety.

"Wasn't Myong-hui concerned that her parents would become upset when she received a phone call from an American?"

"Ralph called Myong-hui at the dormitory."

"I thought she lived in Hyonjo-dong with her parents."

"No. She doesn't like it there. She forced them to pay for a room in the dormitory here. She didn't go home very often. Only when she was in trouble."

"What kinds of trouble did she get into?"

"Well, her grades aren't very good. And she's had a lot of boyfriends." Her voice trailed off. "But today is the biggest trouble yet."

I asked it softly. "Why?"

She looked up and her eyes widened. "Because now everyone will know she had a date with an American."

I nodded. Made sense to me. Ernie opened a new package of gum but didn't offer her any.

"When did Ralph call her?"

"Two days ago. He said he was off today, Friday, and he wanted to meet us and go to one of the teahouses near here. Our teahouses at Chungang University are very famous. Many young people come here for the music and the artwork."

"If there was going to be a demonstration, why did you meet him here?'

"We didn't know there was going to be a demonstration. We found out about that later, but we didn't think it would be so big. And we didn't think that the army would come."

"Why did Hei-sok and his friend come along?"

"I think he wanted to keep an eye on his rival."

"How did Myong-hui feel about that?"

"She didn't mind. I think she liked the idea of men competing for her."

I pulled the photograph out of my pocket. "Is this Hei-sok?"

"Yes."

"And this is his friend, Pak Un-sil?"

"Yes. They go everywhere together."

"Is Pak Un-sil your boyfriend?"

"Oh, no." She dropped her handkerchief and turned a bright red. I waited for her to bend over and pick up the handkerchief.

"It must have been awkward," I said. "Ralph here to see Myong-hui and yet all five of you together?"

"Yes. It was awkward." She sat up a little straighter, her normal color gradually returning. "The only reason I stayed was to support Myong-hui against Hei-sok. But it turned out that Hei-sok's friend was the one who kept making mean remarks. About Americans. Ralph couldn't understand, of course."

"What sort of remarks?"

"About your impoliteness." She looked at me and almost smiled. "Things like that. Myong-hui didn't like it at all."

"What happened after you met Ralph?"

"First we went to a teahouse. We all had coffee, except for Myong-hui. She had cola. Hei-sok tried to act as if he were very rich and insisted on paying for everything. After about an hour the demonstration was starting and some students were making speeches over loudspeakers, so we went outside to see what was happening. Everything was fine until the army moved in. It was funny at first, their taking it so seriously. It was only a few speeches, about politics. I really didn't pay much attention. That's when Ralph stopped in the shop and bought the flower for Myong-hui."

"What did Hei-sok think?"

"He was angry, but he didn't say anything. Myong-hui loved the flower. Instead of spending so much money in the teahouse, Hei-sok should have done something like that. Since his money was all gone, all he did was pluck a withered old blossom for her hair. I think that's what gave Ralph the idea, but she threw the blossom away when Ralph gave her the more beautiful flower he bought in the shop."

"Was the blossom a *mukung-hua*?"

"Yes. You know about our national flower?"

She seemed impressed, which is why I said it. I had paid close attention during my Korean language classes. Might as well get some credit.

"What about Hei-sok's friend?" I said. "How did he react?"

"I didn't see because that's when everyone started yelling when they noticed the riot police moving in behind us. We couldn't get out. It was strange, really. They kept telling us to leave the area, but there was no way out. I wasn't too worried then, there were so many of us, and everyone had been peaceful. But of course the speakers had said so many impolite things about our president. I think that must have made the soldiers angry."

"What did you do when the armored vehicles moved forward?"

"We tried to move out of the way. Students climbed over fences and ran down alleys. The vehicle moved very slowly. I'm sure the driver didn't intend to run over anyone."

"Did you see Ralph go down?"

"No. There was too much confusion."

"Where was Hei-sok?"

"I don't know. Myong-hui and I were holding on to one another, trying to get out of the way. We didn't see what happened to Ralph. It was only later that we heard about it."

"Does Hei-sok live on campus?"

"Yes. In the first men's dormitory."

I put my hand in the right pocket of my coat, Ernie's cue to take over the interrogation.

"Young lady," he said, "do you love Myong-hui?"

She seemed to be surprised that Ernie could speak. "She is my best friend."

"And you'd want to protect her, wouldn't you, from ruining her life by becoming involved with a foreigner?"

"I think it would be best to marry a Korean," she said, and then her mouth fell open. "You think that I . . . "

"Where were you when Whitcomb went down?"

"I told you. We were trying to get away. It was an accident. He must have fallen."

"This Hei-sok, does he study *tae kwon do*?"

"No. He is very frail. He could not have done anything like that."

And then she dropped her head into her lap and she was crying.

■ ■ ■

My face felt feverish by now, the flu shot was getting to me, but I took a breath of the garden-scented air and the dizziness subsided.

We had to ask directions a couple of times, but gradually we made our way to the boy's dormitory on the other side of campus. The boys in the waiting room looked at us suspiciously, but soon shouts were ringing up the big cement hallways for Li Hei-sok. He looked thin and frightened, and there were still scratches on his neck from where a policeman must have collared him. We walked with him into the game room, getting as far away as possible from a pair of students slamming a small white globe at one another in a vicious round of Ping-Pong.

Ernie backed him into a corner.

"You pushed him," he said. "You pushed Whitcomb, he fell, and then the armored vehicle ran over him. And we're here to take you in."

He looked at me, confused. I translated what Ernie had said into Korean.

"No," he said. "It didn't happen that way. I didn't do it. You don't understand."

He fell back against the wall, clutched his stomach, and looked about him for support. The Ping-Pong ball careened back and forth.

Some of the other young men noticed Hei-sok's frantic face and wandered over. Just curiosity so far, but I wondered if the hot emotions of the morning would carry over into the dismal afternoon. My fever was coming back.

When I heard the slam, I almost jumped out of my suit.

The word *propriety* flashed through my mind, and I remembered my Korean language teacher slamming his pointer down on the desk, explaining the cardinal rules of Confucian propriety. I cursed myself for not seeing it earlier.

It was a baseball bat, coming down flush on the Ping-Pong table. The little guy with glasses in the photograph, the one Myong-hui's friend had said was named Pak Un-sil, stood before us. His breath came hard, and he wore a white bandana tied around his forehead. Indecipherable Chinese characters were slashed in red ink across the bandana. He spit as he screamed, but I could pick up most of what he was saying.

"Don't touch him, you fornicating foreign dogs! You've ruined enough here in our country. Whitcomb deserved what happened to him. I pushed him, and I'd push him again!"

He slammed the baseball bat back down on the Ping-Pong table for effect. It was certainly getting that. I was dizzy and feverish, only from the flu shot, I hoped.

"Whitcomb was trying to get Myong-hui, even though he knew that she was Hei-sok's girlfriend. He bought her a flower and presented it to her right in front of all of us. He didn't care who was embarrassed. He didn't care about his own face, and he didn't care about any of us. He just wanted her. To use her and then throw her away, like he threw away our national flower. I would not let him insult Koreans like that."

Ernie backed away from the cowering Li Hei-sok, and we both took a couple of steps from each other so if Pak Un-sil went for one of us, the other would be able to get him from behind. I saw Ernie glance at a chair he could grab if the kid lunged. I was ready to turn over the Ping-Pong table.

A crowd gathered, at a respectful distance. Nobody wanted to get too near a loony with a baseball bat.

The young man slammed his bat onto the top of the Ping-Pong table again. It rattled. He slammed the bat again, and the table gave up and caved in. Splinters flew everywhere. Ernie lifted the chair, like a lion tamer, and charged. The kid swung and almost knocked the chair out of Ernie's hands. I pounced on the kid's back, grabbing for his arms, and then Ernie gripped the bat. The three of us waltzed around the room a couple of times, sweating and cursing, until Ernie ripped the bat from the young man's hands.

He was still cursing, frothing at the mouth, and he tried to bite me. I let go and then the other kids were around us, everyone pushing and shouting, and the stocky kid broke away and darted upstairs.

Ernie and I wrestled ourselves free and ran after him.

I heard his footsteps pounding up past the second floor landing and on up to the third floor. Wood rattled, and when we arrived at the top I saw his sneakers disappearing through a trapdoor in the ceiling. Ernie went first. He pushed the door up carefully, ready to drop back quickly if the kid had found another bat. The coast was clear, and when he was up, I scrambled up after him.

On the roof of the big dorm, eternity loomed above us, domed by a vast gray sky. No sign of the kid. Ernie pointed toward the stone spire. He was climbing up, over gargoyles, like a crazed Korean Quasimodo. We ran over and started shouting at him to come down. Wasting our breath.

"I'm not going up there," Ernie said. "No way."

More students came up on the roof and stood around gawking. They cupped their hands around their mouths and shouted. The kid kept climbing.

When he reached the top of the spire, he straddled the pinnacle and stood straight up, his arms outstretched. He looked fragile up there, against the gray Asian sky.

A wave of nausea ran through me. Whether it was from the flu shot or from the heights or from the desperate young man wavering above me, I couldn't be sure. I have never been sure.

More students gathered down below in front of the dormitory, and I heard their distant cries.

I decided I had to try, and I walked toward the spire. I found a handhold, braced myself, and looked up.

The young man's arms were outstretched, and his eyes closed for a moment as if he were praying. Then his knees flexed and he pushed himself forward, and for a few brief seconds he was flying.

I can still hear the crunch. And then the screams.

■ ■ ■

The line-of-duty investigation determined that since Corporal Ralph Whitcomb had died as a result of unauthorized activities, his parents were ineligible to draw his serviceman's group life insurance. Eighth Army put out a special bulletin reminding everyone to stay away from political rallies of any sort—especially student demonstrations.

Whitcomb was, however, authorized a headstone by the Veteran's Administration.

It took two days' worth of brandy to rid myself of the flu.

SEOUL STORY

The early morning Seoul traffic swept us along like a rushing river of metal. Ernie managed to pull over, and we climbed out of the jeep. The boy was still there.

"Looks like he fell from a ten-story building," Ernie said.

This would have been plausible except that there was nothing around but a shrub-filled lot and a long sidewalk leading to the intersection between the district of Itaewon and the 8th United States Army headquarters on Yongsan Compound.

Bare feet stuck out of ragged cuffs, and the boy's pullover sweater was as soiled and greasy as his skin. A crusty, transparent film oozed out of his tightly shut eyes, and blood bubbled and caked on his puffy, cracked lips.

Ernie knelt down and felt for a pulse.

"He's alive," he said.

We tossed him in the back of the jeep. He weighed nothing. Ernie revved up the engine, let out the clutch, and bulled his way into the traffic.

"Now that we got him," he said, "what the hell are we going to do with him?"

"Feed him," I said. "Get him cleaned up. And then find out how he ended up face down on the pavement of Seoul."

■　▦　▨

I have a room on the compound, but in the early morning you'll most often find me walking back from Itaewon, the nightclub district the Korean government has set aside for GIs. It's a long walk, but usually I'm too numb to feel it. Rats scurry out of the way, stacks of drained OB beer bottles sway in the cold wind, and zombie-like Americans head for the warmth and comfort of military barracks. Normally I shower, shave, slip into the suit and tie required of all CID agents, and stumble over to the 8th Army snack bar for a cup of coffee and a copy of the daily *Stars & Stripes*. But today, on the way in, I almost stepped on something: a boy lying face down on the pavement.

Korea may not have a whole lot of excess wealth, but you don't often see beggars. Most of the panhandlers are kids, and they're healthy and full of spunk, put up to it by some Fagin lurking in the alleyways.

So to see a boy like this, passed out, drenched in grime, his dirty cheek scrunched up against the cold cement—it wasn't an everyday occurrence.

I'd heard about people in New York who just walk around someone in trouble. In East LA, where I'm from, we aren't exactly known for our neighborliness either. But I always figured that if I ran into a helpless waif I would stop, see if I could help.

Except I was on the last empty stretch of sidewalk that led to the compound, and there were no other pedestrians, and if I stopped to help the boy what would I do for him? Back in Itaewon you can catch a cab without too much problem, but no driver ventures out on this long empty stretch unless he already has a fare, and you can bet he's not going to stop for some six-foot-four American with a filthy urchin draped over his shoulder. If I carried him to the compound, I'd get hassled at the gate. All guests have to be signed in and their Korean National ID card numbers entered on the MPs sign-in roster.

All these complications flashed through my mind in the few seconds it took to stride toward the body lying on the cold cement.

As I said, I had always thought of myself as the exception—the guy who would leap out of the crowd to assist. But when I tried to imagine myself trudging down a road on a bustling Seoul morning with a lifeless mendicant draped over my shoulder, I just stepped over him, lengthened my stride, and plowed ahead toward the compound.

By the time I changed clothes and met Ernie at the snack bar, regret had overcome me. I described the situation. He gulped the last of his coffee, stood up, and said, "Let's go." I followed him out to the jeep. When we reached the long empty stretch of sidewalk, the boy was still there.

I was relieved. A chance for redemption.

We took him back to the barracks, and under the pulsing warm water in the shower room, he came to. He was frightened at first but then realized that he was no longer cold and he was getting a bath, so he accepted the soap from my hands and in short order had himself pretty well cleaned up. After he dried off, Ernie gave him some of his underwear, which was very baggy on the boy but at least was clean and helped him resemble a human being more than he had all morning. Back in the room he wolfed down a can of beans and made quick work of the soda Ernie bought him out of the vending machine.

After a brief chat in Korean I told him to lie down and rest and we'd be back to see him after work. Mr. Yim, the houseboy, wasn't too keen on the idea of having this stranger lurking about his wing of the barracks, but the boy went to sleep immediately. Anyway, he didn't have any clothes, since we had thrown his rags away—after I had determined that he was indeed as poor as he seemed.

On the way back to the CID detachment headquarters I was filled with that warm glow a good deed can give you, but I was puzzled about what the boy had told me. About his aunt, the one who had been murdered.

■ ■ ■

We were late for work, and the first sergeant didn't particularly want to hear that we were helping a boy passed out on the sidewalk.

"You guys have a job to do," he said. "There are agencies to take care of orphans. I want you to contact one of them and have him turned over today, but first you have some black market arrests you owe me."

We hadn't busted as many people as we should have in the last couple of weeks, and the provost marshal had been embarrassed when he'd briefed the commanding general.

"Who has their finger in the dike, colonel?" the CG asked. "Or are we allowing the whole country to be flooded with scotch whiskey and American cigarettes?"

Actually, it wasn't the damage the black marketing did to the Korean economy that bothered him, it was the Korean wives of GIs shopping in the commissary and getting in his wife's way. That was what bothered him. That and the hell he caught when he went home.

The first sergeant told us he wanted three arrests, minimum, before the close of business. No sweat. We had two of them before noon. Then we took the rest of the day off.

No sense spoiling him.

The St. Francis orphanage was an austere little cluster of shoebox-like buildings. It reminded me of boot camp except it was filled with smiling faces bursting with happiness. Father Art was a burly man with thick forearms, a pug nose, and a bald spot shaped like a heart atop his head.

"This must be the little fellow you called about," he said.

"Yes, sir." The boy was dressed in the smallest set of gym clothes we could find in the PX. "We brought him here as soon as we could get off work."

Father Art knelt and spoke in rapid Korean. Soon the boy was nodding to Father Art and had taken his hand. They spoke for almost ten minutes, and at times I thought the boy was going to cry. I could follow most of the conversation but a little of it was beyond me. Father Art's mastery of the Korean language, to me, seemed as good as any Korean's.

Father Art stood up and looked at us. "Did you follow any of that?"

"A little."

"He say that his aunt was murdered, after he'd only been living with her for about two weeks. Prior to that he had lived with his father, a tenant farmer out in the country near Anyang. When his father died, he inherited his life's savings: two hundred thousand *won* and a gold watch, an heirloom from his grandfather. He wrapped it all up and tied it around his waist and then took the train to Seoul to find his aunt."

"What happened to the boy's mother?"

"She died in childbirth, having him. The boy's name is Yun Chil-bok. His aunt's name is Ahn Chong-ai."

"And he says she was murdered?"

"Yes. She owned a *pochang ma-cha*, a vending cart, in downtown Seoul. In Myongdong. Do you know the area?"

Ernie and I looked at each other. "Yeah. We know it."

It was the biggest nightclub district in Seoul. GIs mostly stayed down in their own little set-aside, Itaewon, near the 8th Army headquarters, but some of the more adventurous amongst us prowled the streets of Myongdong from time to time.

I knelt down and asked the boy to tell me where his aunt set up her *pochang ma-cha* each night. He said it was always in the same place, in Myongdong near the Oriental Brewery Draft Beer Hall. Myongdong is a big district. I asked him to narrow it down a little more, but the best he could do was to tell us that it was about a five-minute walk from the Cosmos department store.

The boy said that he had helped his aunt in preparing the food, serving the customers, and replacing the perforated charcoal briquette that fired the little stove. At night they slept under the draped cart, on wooden boards, or when it got particularly cold and his aunt could afford it, they stayed in the common room of a *yoinsuk*, a Korean inn.

"Did you have any friends or relatives in the area?"

"No relatives, but everyone who came into her *pochang macha* was her friend."

"How old was your aunt?"

"Very old. Maybe thirty."

"Did she have a boyfriend?"

"Maybe. One man used to come around and bother her all the time. She would be very upset after he left. I'm not sure why."

"What was his name?"

"Cruncher Chong."

"Cruncher?"

"Yes."

"Why did they call him that?"

"Because he was always chewing on something."

"What happened to your aunt?"

"One morning I woke up, and there was only the board beneath me. The cart was gone, and so was my aunt."

"Somebody had rolled the cart away while you slept?"

The boy hung his head. "Yes."

"And your aunt was gone?"

"Yes. I checked with everyone in the neighborhood, but no one had seen her leave and no one knew where she had gone. I waited there five days. Finally I was just too hungry, and I wandered off."

"How long did you roam around Seoul until we found you?"

"I'm not sure. Two or three weeks."

"What makes you so sure that your aunt was murdered?"

"She wouldn't have given up her cart without a fight, and I knew she wouldn't have allowed us to be separated, for any reason, unless she was dead."

"What happened to your two hundred thousand *won*?"

"She has it. I gave it to her when I arrived, as my father had told me to."

"And the gold watch?"

"Yes. And the gold watch too."

We thanked Father Art and left a package of goodies from the PX that we hoped the kids could use: soap, powdered milk, cookies. Then we said goodbye to Yun Chil-bok. I told him to listen to Father Art and we'd return to visit him this weekend. He thrust his shoulders back and looked me straight in the eye.

"You are policemen," he said. "Will you find out who killed my aunt?"

"We will talk to the Korean police about it," I said.

"But I don't know them. I only know you."

Ernie shuffled his feet. He often surprised me with how much Korean he could understand.

"We'll look into it for you," I said.

"I will be waiting."

As we climbed into Ernie's jeep, I looked back at the boy. Father Art held his hand, but Yun Chil-bok stared straight at us, as if he were trying to evaluate our trustworthiness.

He didn't seem grateful for what we had done. But maybe he felt that at the age of eight years he had a right to be picked up off the pavement and fed and taken care of.

I agreed with him.

Lieutenant Pei, liaison officer for the Korean National Police at the 8th Army provost marshal's office, didn't hold out much hope.

"I spoke to the captain of the Myongdong Police Station. He said that the woman who ran the *pochang ma-cha* in the area you describe has indeed disappeared, and her cart along with her. But there's no reason to believe that she was murdered. If she had an unwanted nephew on her hands, maybe she decided that just packing up and leaving would be the best of all concerned. After all, he did end up in an orphanage."

"But the boy says she was murdered."

"We have no reports of any killings in the Myongdong area in many months. The captain was insistent on that."

We thanked him and walked out of his office. Ernie surprised me by bringing up the subject first.

"We haven't been to Myongdong in a while. Wouldn't hurt to stop by the OB Beer Hall tonight and have a few wet ones."

I looked at him. "You're right about that. It couldn't hurt nothing. Nothing but our livers."

The OB Beer Hall hummed with customers, most of them Korean businessmen just off work, standing at the counters chatting with friends. Blue-suited girls with jet black hair tied snugly under white bandanas ran back and forth to the tap, refilling huge mugs of beer. The hefty young woman behind the stick wore a red and white nameplate with the OB Beer logo pinned above her breasts.

After our second refill I spoke to her in Korean.

"Miss Kim, do you ever get a customer in here known as Cruncher Chong?"

"Cruncher? Oh, yes. He comes in here often."

"Is he here now?"

The young lady scanned the room. "No. I haven't seen him. *You* know him?"

"No. Not yet. But we're looking for him on behalf of a boy named Yun Chil-bok."

The girls looked at us blankly. "Well, if Cruncher Chong is not here, he is usually at the Black Dragon nightclub."

"Where's that?"

She pointed. "Two blocks down and turn right past the Teahouse of the Seven Virgins."

Two more uniformed young women popped through swinging doors carrying freshly washed mugs and more snacks to put on display. Ernie stared at them, and for a moment I thought he was going to drool. Over the mugs or the girls, I wasn't sure which. I said thank you to Miss Kim and pulled Ernie out of there.

■　■　■

The Black Dragon nightclub had a long bar with upholstered bar stools and cocktail tables peeking out from behind planters and aquariums full of tropical fish. When our eyes adjusted, I saw that the joint was only about half full. The crowd was younger than at the OB Beer Hall. And full of hustle.

A tall, slender man with a heavily greased pompadour stood at the bar. He was talking, and the bow-tied bartender kept smiling and nodding. He stared at us when we walked in, as most of the people in the place did, and then he reached in his pocket and pulled out something long and gnarled. He stuck the tip of it into his mouth. At first I thought it was a carrot, but as my eyes refocused I realized it was a piece of ginseng root.

They say that true ginseng grows only in the soil of the Korean peninsula. It has been known since ancient time for its medicinal powers, but most men saw it as an aphrodisiac.

As I passed him, I could almost see my reflection in his big white teeth. I fought off the urge to say, "What's up, doc?"

Only Ernie would have gotten away with it.

We took a seat at a table, and after a while a heavily made-up waitress in a tightly wrapped dress came over to serve us. We ordered two beers and a plate of dried cuttlefish. When she delivered the wets, Ernie smiled and made her promise to come back and talk after taking care of a few more orders.

The tall man at the bar continued to drink, but I didn't see him forking over any money. Four more sleazy types paraded into the Black Dragon and joined him. They laughed at his jokes and backed off when he playfully poked them with his ginseng root.

When the waitress came back, we discovered that her name was Miss Min and that she had been working there for six months. When we asked her if she had a boyfriend, she laughed.

"Do you know Cruncher Chong?" I asked.

Her head turned involuntarily toward the bar. "Oh, yes. Everyone knows him."

"Is he a gangster?"

She dropped her head slightly and shook it so her short, curly black hair bounced and shimmered. "I don't know."

"Did you know Ahn Chong-ai, the woman who owned the *pochang ma-cha* on the street here?"

"No. I don't know her." Her smile had disappeared. She picked up her cocktail tray. "I must go now."

Ernie grabbed her by the wrist. "Don't speak to anyone about our conversation," he said. I translated what he said to Korean. She glared at us and left.

I took a sip of my beer. "We're not making many friends."

"Not yet," Ernie said.

We ate the dried cuttlefish and nursed our beers until they were just suds. Cruncher Chong and his cronies, waving and making much noise, said their goodbyes and paraded out the door.

We paid our bill. It was about twice as expensive as in Itaewon.

The tail was easy. They weren't expecting to be followed, especially by a couple of foreigners.

Seven or eight customers sat around the cart on wooden stools. Steam billowed from a vat of soup, and the reddened faces of the revelers glistened in the glare of the naked bulb overhead.

Cruncher Chong and his buddies monopolized the attention of both the customers and the rotund woman who poured shots of *soju* into small cups. The men toasted the company and drank heartily of the potent rice liquor.

The crowds of Myongdong streamed past the little *pochang ma-cha*. Blue and white canvas flaps were draped over iron ribs, protecting the customers from the elements and the curious stares of passersby.

"If this is the cart that belonged to the boy's aunt," Ernie said, "they only moved it about ten blocks."

"Enough to confuse an eight-year-old who'd never been in the city before."

We waited around the corner until Cruncher Chong and his buddies got up and left. Then we joined the revelers at the open-air cart. There were three Korean men and two women, all middle-aged working-class people who were surprised to see us. We ordered a couple of shots of *soju*, and the proprietress threw in some unhusked peanuts, gratis, in honor of our being the first foreigners to be seen in these parts.

On the pole next to me I noticed a red document. A license of some sort, or a health inspection certificate. I stood up halfway to take a better look. I couldn't read all the officialese, but I could make out that the current owner's last name was Chong. The beginning date of the certificate was two weeks ago. The certificate was in a plastic holder, and there was something else behind it. I flipped it forward and saw the name Ahn Chong-ai.

The revelers called to me. Everyone had raised their cups. To friendship between Korea and America. I joined in.

A thick-bladed hatchet sat on the cutting board next to the kettle of soup. I asked the round smiling woman if I could take a good look at her cart, since I was an Amerian and we didn't have such things where I came from. Her face crinkled into a huge round smile, and she nodded. Behind where she stood was a double panel in the side of the cart. The interior was hollow for carrying the big kettle and the cooking utensils and the canvas cover when the cart was wheeled away on its oversized bicycle wheels. I rubbed the bottom of the wood. It was splintery, not smooth, and a reddish-brown stain spread across more than half of the flat board.

I figured I could climb inside the cart and no one would know I was there.

I stood up and flamboyantly told the crowd how cleverly the cart was arranged and how resourceful were the Korean people. They cheered, and we all drank a little more *soju*.

I sat back down and watched the woman hack a helpless turnip to smithereens and dump it in the boiling cauldron.

The Myongdong night was in full swing now, and the streets were bustling with people on their way to restaurants or bars or just gawking at the sights. We headed back to the Black Dragon.

"You don't just dispose of the body of a grown woman in this part of Seoul," Ernie said, "without somebody's noticing."

"The boy said Cruncher Chong had spent some nights with his aunt," I said. "Maybe he took care of her while they were alone and then got rid of the body."

"How?"

"The cart. It's the perfect hearse for transporting a stiff through town."

"And then he had the nerve to reopen the car for business under his own name?"

"Maybe he forced her to sign a bill of sale or something."

"Or bribed the government inspector into not checking too close."

"Maybe."

"And maybe we've been drinking too much *soju*," Ernie said.

I couldn't argue with that.

We had just turned down an alley, to cut from one main street to another, when I heard the footsteps behind us. I swiveled on the balls of my feet.

Cruncher Chong and two of his boys.

The light from the other end of the alley faded. I glanced backward. Three more guys were behind us. We took a couple of steps toward Chong.

"You have been following us," he said. "And asking questions."

The streets of LA had taught me that there is only one real advantage in a fight—the first strike. I kept walking toward Chong, casually, as if I were going to join in the conversation. When I was a few steps from him, I hopped forward and snapped a kick into his groin. He doubled over and I slammed his partner in the face and kept moving, past them, down the alley. Ernie was right behind me, but one of the guys grabbed him. I turned and kicked him in the side and he let go long enough for Ernie to break free and then we were running.

Once we reached the main street it was a breathless three blocks until we found a policeman. He pointed us toward the Myongdong Police Station.

Lieutenant Lee, night commander of the Myongdong Police Station, was somewhat skeptical of our explanation of a murder that had taken place in the middle of his precinct. But we were Americans, and CID agents, so he brought a couple of uniformed patrolmen with him and followed us to Cruncher Chong's *pochang ma-cha*.

We showed him the recent change of certificate, and he nodded and lifted out the old certificate behind it. He showed me that the deed had been legally transferred, with both a beginning and ending date for the ownership of Miss Ahn Chong-ai.

As I was about to take him around behind the cart, the rotund woman pulled a bloody, newspaper-wrapped piece of meat, which must have just been delivered, from beneath her cart. She sliced off a piece, pulverized it, and dropped it into the cauldron. Pork. She re-wrapped the large chunk and put it back down inside the cart. When Lieutenant Lee and I looked into the base of the cart, fresh blood had been added to the stain I had seen before.

Lieutenant Lee's jaw bulged as he stared at me, trying to figure what to do with us. Finally he spoke.

"What you say about Cruncher Chong carting this Miss Ahn's body off in the cart is, of course, possible. The evidence, however, is slim as yet. We will locate Cruncher Chong and have a talk with him."

I nodded and thanked him.

Ernie's lips were clamped tight and his head rotated slightly on his neck, as if it sat atop a greased ball bearing.

A couple of dumb Americans, meddling where we shouldn't. I was starting to worry that Cruncher Chong might bring up assault charges.

■ ■ ■

After about thirty minutes Lieutenant Lee walked out of the back room, tugging off his fingerless leather glove.

"Cruncher Chong has confessed to everything," he said.

He shrugged, loosening his shoulders. A sheen of perspiration glistened atop his high brown forehead.

"And we know where to find Miss Ahn Chong-ai. Tomorrow morning I will take you there."

We met him at the compound and followed his police sedan in our army jeep. It was a crisp, bright blue morning. After we left the outskirts of Seoul I breathed deeply of the clean air and had no doubt about why the ancients called Korea the Land of the Morning Calm.

Suwon is a small town in the country, surrounded by green rice paddies and groves of apple trees. It has little of the hustle and bustle of Seoul. Lieutenant Lee's driver asked directions one time and after a couple of turns parked in front of the Paris Beauty Shop.

There wasn't much family resemblance, but of the three beauticians on duty it was easy to figure out who was Miss Ahn Chong-ai. When she saw two Americans and the uniformed Korean police lieutenant, her eyes grew as big as two hairdryers.

A couple of days later I called Father Art, and Ernie and I drove out to the orphanage.

Miss Ahn had sold her cart and Chil-bok's gold watch to her boyfriend, Cruncher Chong. That, along with the two hundred thousand *won* she stole from the boy, had allowed her to invest in the business of her dreams, a little beauty shop in Suwon. She was single, and maybe she thought an eight-year-old boy tagging along would hurt her chances for marriage, or maybe she just didn't deem family ties to be as sacred as did most Koreans.

I thought of Father Art's words when I explained the situation. "The greatest shame," he said, "that could scar a Korean's soul is not honoring their family."

Lieutenant Lee's treatment of her had not been gentle. If she'd robbed a bank instead of abandoning her only nephew, he probably wouldn't have been so offended.

When Miss Ahn sold the shop and refunded the money, Lieutenant Lee turned the proceeds over to the KNP Liaison Office at the 8th Army provost marshal's office. It was all in one Korean bank note totaling four hundred and sixty-five thousand *won*, made out to Yun Chil-bok. I signed the receipt and we went to the orphanage.

Father Art and Chil-bok were waiting for us. I knelt down and gave him the envelope.

"What of my aunt?" he asked.

I patted him on the shoulder. "Keep her memory well," I said.

"And the man who killed her?"

I thought of the hardness in Lieutenant Lee's eyes as he glowered at the petty criminal, Cruncher Chong.

"He will be punished," I said, "many times over before his life is through."

"Thank you," the little boy said. Then he bowed.

ASCOM CITY

The breath of hungover GIs steamed the windows of the rickety army bus as it swerved around potholes on the road to ASCOM City. Things couldn't have been better. Except that we weren't going there to run the village, we were going there to look at a corpse.

When Ernie and I received the assignment from the first sergeant, we thought it was harassment.

"GIs turn up dead in business girls' hooches all the time," Ernie said. "Carbon monoxide poisoning. Routine."

"Maybe so," the first sergeant said. "But this time the girl wasn't lying next to him. She cleaned out the room, and she's gone."

Ernie shrugged. "She probably got scared. The Korean National Police will find her."

"Or you will." The first sergeant looked at his watch. "A bus leaves for the Army Support Command every other hour. I expect you two guys to be on the next one."

Ernie started to say something, but I slapped him on the elbow. He looked at me, I jerked my head toward the door, and we rose to our feet and walked out. We didn't speak until we were halfway down the hallway.

"The team from the inspector general is going to be here tomorrow," Ernie said. "That's why he wants us out of the way."

"Maybe. Or maybe his cop's sense of propriety is offended when a GI wakes up in the morning dead."

"Yeah. Maybe." Ernie slammed through the big double doors of the red brick CID building. "At least it'll give us a chance to run the ville in ASCOM City."

"Yeah," I said. "Maybe."

We flashed our identification to the desk sergeant at the ASCOM MP station.

"Lieutenant Crane has been waiting for you," he said. "Straight down the hallway. Third room on the left."

Lieutenant Crane was a gangly man in his early twenties with fatigue pants covering the length of his stilt-like legs. When we walked in, he looked up from a scattering of paperwork and ran a hand through his hair.

"I don't know why they sent you down here. The KNPs are still looking for the girl, but other than that it's nothing more than a carbon monoxide poisoning."

Erne let me do the talking. He usually did when we talked to officers.

"Let's go see the hooch anyway, Lieutenant. You never know."

His face went through suspicious contortions, but then he came to the conclusion that since we were from 8th Army headquarters, and since we were on an official investigation, it would be best to cooperate. In our business those thought processes are familiar.

He strapped on his .45, perched his shiny MP helmet liner atop his head, and ambled out into the hallway. As we went through a doorway, the top of his narrow shoulders hunched forward and stayed that way. "I'll be in the ville," he told the desk sergeant, "on the VonEric case. Send a patrol for me if you need me."

The desk sergeant nodded.

At the gate, armed MPs carded Ernie and me but just saluted the lieutenant and let him by.

The ville started right across the street: Lee's Tailor Shop, the Brass Emporium, Chosun Souvenirs. Farther down the road came a few nightclubs: the Hideaway, the Lotus Blossom, the UN Club. And then the alleys. Narrow. Mud-filled. More nightclubs, more neon, and more rock and roll blared out of darkened doorways. Little eateries were interspersed throughout the maze, advertising fried chicken and *yakimandu*, fried dumplings. Old women carried bundles of laundry atop their heads. Young girls scurried back and forth from bathhouses, flat sandals slapping against the balls of their feet.

Ernie took a deep breath.

"Nice place they got here," he said.

We wound down another couple of alleys, Lieutenant Crane leading, until he turned down an opening that was nothing more than a gap between cement block walls. As we passed through, I turned slightly sideways to keep the arms of my leather coat from getting scuffed. A quick jog to the left and then he pounded on a high wooden gate.

"*Ajjima*," Crane said. "*Honbyong!*"

I was impressed. He announced himself in a polite way as being a representative of the military police. And his pronunciation was good.

An old woman opened the gate and let us in.

The hooch was typical. A small dirt-floored courtyard surrounded by a tile-roofed building divided into four or five rooms. Without bothering to speak to the woman, Lieutenant Crane stepped up on the wooden porch in front of the nearest hooch and slid back the wood frame door.

"It was here," he said. "We found Specialist VonEric dead about zero seven hundred this morning. This old lady called the Korean National Police, and they relayed the message to us."

I talked to the old woman. She was surprised at first that I spoke Korean, but she went on to explain that she had heard nothing with the possible exception of the front gate slamming some time before dawn. Of course she might've been dreaming it, she said. I liked the old woman. She had a fat oval face that broke into concentric circles when she smiled, which she often did. The smile disappeared when I asked her about the body.

It was late, the sun was already up, and she knew the GI who was staying in the first hooch should have been on his way to work, but she had heard no noise. She called to the woman who lived there—her name was Yu Kyong-hui—and when there was no answer, she rapped on the rice-papered door and slid it open.

She couldn't smell the carbon monoxide, of course, because it's an odorless gas, but she saw the gray pallor on the GI's face and smelled the evidence of the loosening of his bowels. She opened all the windows and called the police, but it was too late.

Ernie wandered around the courtyard, restless. A few young Korean women were playing flower cards in their room and had slid back the door when we came in. Ernie winked at them. They giggled.

The old woman said she recognized the GI. He had lived with Miss Yu in the past but hadn't been around for over a month. Who had Miss Yu been seeing during that time? No one. She kept talking about an old boyfriend who would be coming back to Korea. The old woman didn't know who he was. She had never seen him, that had all happened before Miss Yu ever moved here. The old woman also had no idea where Miss Yu had gone, and there had been no indication that she was planning to leave but, yes, most of her clothing had been taken with her. It didn't look like she was planning on coming back. She'd left a deposit on the room, the old woman said, but it didn't cover the back rent she owed.

Ernie and I slipped off our shoes before we stepped into the hooch. A large western-style bed filled most of the space. There was a beat-up old hi-fi set, a few scattered jars of makeup, some loose scraps of clothing, and a jumble of naked coat hangers in the small plastic wardrobe.

"The KNPs have already searched the room," Lieutenant Crane said. "They're very thorough."

"I know that," I said.

Just for drill I lifted the mattress, and Ernie poked around behind the wardrobe.

After a little searching Ernie said, "This must have been where the gas came out."

There was a crack in the cement floor. Most Korean homes are heated by charcoal gas that is pushed through ducts beneath the floor. When the floor is covered with vinyl and a soft mat is laid down, it makes a comfortable place to sleep during the cold Korean winters.

Ernie lifted his fingers. They were dusted with powdered cement from the edges of the crack. "The hole opens directly into the gas duct," he said.

We stood up and straightened our clothes. On the way out I noticed something white and pointed peeking out of a crack in the wallpaper. It was flat against the wall, and I had a little trouble prying my fingernail under it to pull it out.

It was a wallet-sized photograph of a GI. His smiling face beamed out at the world over his neatly pressed dress green uniform. Blue infantry piping draped his arm.

The morgue was in the basement of a thick-walled cement building that was so heavily fortified it must have been an ammunition storage building at one time. I shivered when the white-smocked attendant slid the body out of the refrigerated cabinet.

"The remains of Specialist Four Rodney VonEric," Crane said. "Former stalwart employee of the ASCOM Repo Depot."

I compared the pasty gray face of the corpse to the bright suntanned face in the photograph. Not even close.

Lieutenant Crane decided he had pretty well wrapped up the case for us, so he left us and went back to his office. A small army compound is always nervous when somebody from 8th Army comes poking around, but Crane figured that the case was so clearly an accident he'd be able to tell the ASCOM provost marshal that there was nothing to worry about from us.

Probably he was right.

After he left, we wandered around the compound. Neatly clipped patches of lawn had been bleached yellow by the cold breath of autumn. A few crinkled leaves hadn't given up for some reason and clung stupidly to skeleton branches.

'Should we catch the last bus to Seoul?" Ernie asked.

"I keep wondering why that girl disappeared."

"The KNPs will find her. That's not for us."

"Yeah."

We wandered past the façade of the post theater. A fantasy was playing, with the half-naked daughter of some movie star in the lead. Nothing I wanted to see.

"Anyway, let's check out the Repo Depot," I said. "Give us some more notes for our report. Then we can spend the night here in ASCOM City. Go back to work late tomorrow."

Ernie shrugged. "The ville looks pretty good, but I don't know."

"Don't worry," I said. "It looks even better at night."

What was commonly called the Repo Depot was more properly known as the Army Support Command Replacement Detachment. After a GI lands at Kimpo Army Airfield, he is hustled through a maze of inoculations and customs procedures and then bused to the Repo Depot here at ASCOM. A day or two later, the unit he will be assigned to is decided upon.

This is a crucial moment in a GI's life. He could be assigned to the sunny beaches of Pusan in the south of the country, or he could be banished to freezing night patrols along the Demilitarized Zone between North and South Korea.

When we strode into the Replacement Detachment area, Ernie grunted.

"They kept me here for four days. Couldn't decide what to do with me."

"It's those lousy efficiency ratings you got," I said.

"Yeah. Sure. That's why they sent me to Eighth Army headquarters."

"To keep an eye on you."

He shrugged. "Fuck up and move up."

A wall-sized map of Korea greeted us as we walked through the entranceway. The US Army compounds scattered throughout the peninsula were marked in red, and a chubby hand pointed to Pupyong over the stenciled message YOU ARE HERE. The map had been there during my first tour in Korea, and it had probably been there for years before that. A geographical anchor for disoriented troops.

There was some traffic in and out of the Replacement Detachment. Unusual for a sleepy compound on a Sunday afternoon, but not so unusual if they just got a flight in full of replacements. We sought out the Charge of Quarters.

The nameplate said Buck Sergeant Freddy R. Waitz. He had just sent some men away from his desk and was rummaging through a stack of paperwork, checking off blocks with a pencil. He looked up when we approached.

"Spec Four VonEric used to work for you?"

Waitz was not a tall man, about five seven or five eight, with a husky build and a flat, hooked-nose face that would have looked Indian if he hadn't been fair-skinned, blond, and blue-eyed. He spoke with an Alabama drawl. On a small compound like this, he didn't have to ask if we were CID. He knew.

"That's right."

"Where's his desk?'

"There." He pointed past some filing cabinets and a stencil machine on the other side of the room. "I was gonna have it cleaned out today, but we got a flight in."

The desk was standard army issue. Gray. Metal. Boxlike. There was an in and out box on top of it and a few manuals but no pictures of relatives. I riffled through the paperwork and then checked the drawers. Ernie wandered over to the water cooler and became interested in the pure spring refreshment from Mount Sorak.

It was the bottom right drawer where I found them. Stacks

of neatly folded newspapers. The last few weeks' worth of the sports page of the *Pacific Stars & Stripes*. On each page penciled figures surrounded the pro football betting line.

Waitz looked over at me as I rummaged through them.

"He bet football?" I asked.

Waitz shrugged. "I don't know."

I stoop up and stepped closer to him. "Come on, Waitz. Betting football is a petty offense. Not nearly as serious as getting yourself dead out in the ville. Now, who did he bet with?"

Waitz turned his face. The profile would have looked at home on the flip side of a buffalo head nickel.

"He bet with Phil Austin. I don't know much about it, but it was just innocent stuff. You know, to have a little money down on the games so he could look forward to the Tuesday issue of *Stripes*, so he could see who won."

"Who was his favorite team?"

"Huh?"

"Didn't he have a favorite team?"

"Not that I know of."

"Where was he from?"

"Somewhere up north. Indianapolis, I think."

"They don't even have a pro team there."

"We don't have one in Birmingham, either."

Waitz reached in his pocket and pulled out a cigarette. He lit it with a match from a brightly colored box.

"Do you know the girl VonEric was staying with?"

"No. I've seen her around, but I never paid much attention. He's been moping around because they broke up a few weeks ago."

"Broke up? Did you see them together last night?"

"Not out in the ville. At the EM Club. I stopped there to get something to eat and I saw him all smiles, leaving with her."

"What time was that?"

"About ten."

"You eat late."

"Flight in yesterday."

Waitz fiddled with the matchbox in his hand. It bore the logo of the Olympos Hotel and Casino in Inchon.

"Do you go to the ville often?"

"I stay away from that dump. I have a section to run here. I don't want my men to see me out there."

"What do you do for recreation?"

"Work."

His blue eyes squinted at the smoke curling up from his nostrils.

"Where can I find this Phil Austin?"

"I don't know where he is today. He works at the printing plant."

I searched through the remaining drawers of the desk and found nothing except army issue office supplies and a few notes concerning the assignments of GIs to various bases throughout the country.

A group of sergeants entered for processing, and Waitz got busy handing out forms and explaining how to fill them out. When he wasn't looking, I slipped a couple of things into my pocket and then we left, without saying goodbye.

"Zilch," Ernie said. "It's time to hat up."

"Why are you in such a hurry to get back? Is the nurse waiting for you?"

"Yeah. You know how she is. Freaks when I stay out overnight on a case."

"With good reason."

Ernie snorted.

"But you've never run the ville of ASCOM City," I said. "You don't want to miss your chance. And tomorrow we can sleep in late before we catch the bus back to Seoul. Before we do, we'll check in with this guy Austin at the printing plant, just to wrap things up."

"How many clubs you figure they have out there?"

"More than we can hit in one night."

Ernie's pale green eyes focused on some distant vision.

We stopped at the ASCOM NCO Club, had the pork cutlet special with a big bottle of chilled red wine, and then ID'd our way through the heavily fortified gate. After trotting across the traffic of the Main Supply Route, we strolled into the neon night of ASCOM City.

The Pupyong Police Station, Western Area, was a small cement block building painted yellow with a winged flower over the entranceway. We showed our identification to the sergeant on duty and told him we were here to investigate the death of Rodney VonEric.

He immediately knew which case we were talking about—GIs don't die every day in ASCOM City—but his English was poor and he was relieved to find out that I could speak Korean.

"Have you found the girl yet?"

"No." He thumbed through a notebook in front of him. "The police in her hometown have been contacted. They talked to her mother, but she claims that they have not seen or heard from her for many months now."

"Where is her hometown?"

"Pankyo. A country village north of Taejon."

"Was she registered here as an entertainer?"

"Yes."

He took us over to a large booklet with the names of nightclubs stenciled neatly on top and dozens of small photographs pasted beneath. Blank female stares winked at us as he thumbed through the book.

"Here she is," he said. "She worked at the Blue Dragon Club and her name is Yu Kyong-hui."

I thanked him, and we walked out of the police station. He didn't have an extra copy of the photograph, but even considering the poor quality of the black and white snapshot, I wasn't likely to forget that face.

No matter how many years I spent in Asia I would never get used to the number of gorgeous women who were forced to work in dumps like ASCOM City.

We rolled through the alleys. Rock and roll blared from darkened nightclubs, brightly manicured fingers clutched at us as we passed. Finally we found the Blue Dragon. From the outside it appeared to be one of the larger clubs, and it sat in one of the most crowded and brightly lit alleys. I figured we were approximately in the center of the red-light district known as ASCOM City.

We pushed through the beaded curtain, and thirty set of blinking eyelashes followed us as we stepped carefully through the multicolored darkness to the bar. The place was mostly empty, just a few GIs at tables in desultory conversation with a couple of the girls. An old woman approached and brought us a couple of cold beers, and then a pair of mini-skirted girls materialized out of the darkness. They became a little standoffish when I mentioned Miss Yu Kyong-hui, but they swore they hadn't seen her for two nights. "Two nights?"

"Yes," one of the girls said. "She wasn't here last night. And the night before that she went out early with a GI, but she never came back."

"Did Miss Yu have a boyfriend?"

"Yes. But she finished with him about a month ago."

"Why?"

The girl shrugged her slim bare shoulders. Ebony hair cascaded around them and glistened in the gyrating light.

"Maybe not enough money. I don't know."

"This GI who took her out night before last, do you know him?"

"No."

"What did he look like?"

She conferred with the other girl, they chatted, and soon some of the other girls had gathered around and were offering their opinions. Finally, the girl I had been talking to turned back to me and said in English, "We don't know what he looked like. Just GI, that's all."

The old woman brought another couple of wets, and Ernie gave one of the girls some money and sent her out to buy dried squid and peanuts. The girl I had been talking to was named Miss Kwon, she was from Taegu, and she had high hopes of becoming a secretary some day. For the rest of the night we drank and feasted, and when curfew came, I put away all thought of going back to Seoul.

After pounding on a small wooden door for five minutes, I managed to wake up Ernie. It took him about thirty more seconds to get his clothes on, and we promised the girls we'd be back and bundled out the door into the cold Korean morning.

Ernie looked up at the sky. "Oh, good," he said. "It's cloudy."

A sharp wind whipped particles of grit into my face.

"What time is it?"

Ernie checked his watch. "Ten thirty."

I groaned.

We showered at the post gymnasium and then paid for shaves at the PX barber shop. By then it was almost noon, so we went over to the NCO Club and ate lunch. By the time we arrived at the 8th Army Printing Plant it was already past one o'clock.

"Maybe we ought to call the first sergeant," Ernie said.

"With no news? Let's wait a little longer."

The 8th Army Printing Plant was a huge, thick-walled building, so brightly whitewashed that it hurt my eyes. The Japanese Imperial Army had built the compound that we call ASCOM and they must've kept a lot of valuables on hand because the whole place was like a fortress.

We walked into the admin office and flashed our identification, and it wasn't long before we had the plant manager, an American civilian, buzzing around us.

"Corporal Austin is one of our most reliable employees," he said. "I can't imagine what could be wrong."

"Maybe nothing," I said. "We just want to talk to him."

Austin was at his printing press, ink smeared on his fingers and a folded newspaper covering his head.

He was almost as tall as me, but lanky, and muscles stood out on his arms, pulsating in almost as steady a rhythm as the machinery behind him. He stared at us with intelligent brown eyes.

"It's about your bookmaking operation," I said.

He said nothing.

"How much was Rodney VonEric into you for?"

He didn't move. The only change in his face was moisture that appeared in his eyes. Finally, he made his decision. He answered.

"Over fifteen hundred dollars," he said.

Ernie whistled.

"But I didn't kill him."

"Where were you Saturday night?"

"Out."

"Where?"

"I go hiking sometimes. Through the Korean countryside." He waved an ink-stained hand. "It's very peaceful out there, once you get away from the city."

"Where did you stay?"

"In a grove of trees."

I stared at him.

"I take my rucksack and a few C rations. When it's cold enough I take my sleeping bag."

"Was anybody with you?"

"No."

"Did anybody see you leave?"

"I doubt it. Most of the guys in the barracks were already out in the ville. You know how they are."

"Yeah," I said. "I know."

Apparently the civilian manager had taken it upon himself

to call the MP station because just then he walked in with Lieutenant Crane at his side. Crane started snapping questions, and Austin told him the same story. Crane turned to me.

"Why didn't you notify me?" he said. "This case belongs under our jurisdiction."

Ernie piped up. "You weren't doing nothing."

Crane glared at him and then turned back to Austin. He took a green walkie-talkie off his belt and fiddled with it until it beeped. Thirty seconds later, two MPs came into the printing plant at a brisk walk.

Crane looked at Austin. "You're under arrest. Clean off your hands and step over here against the wall."

Austin did as he was told, and soon the MPs had him trussed up and Crane entered into a feverish conversation with the plant manager.

We left. I was happy to be outside in the fresh air and away from the noise of the churning machinery.

Back at the Blue Dragon Club we sat at a table nursing a couple of wets, waiting for Miss Kwon and her girlfriends to come back from the bathhouse. When they came in, they were wearing only T-shirts and short pants and had towels wrapped around their hair, and their clean, fresh faces bubbled with laughter. When they saw us, they surrounded our table.

Miss Kwon said, "You come back."

"Sure," Ernie said. "We're not number ten GIs. We came back to say goodbye."

They went upstairs to change, we ordered another round of beers, and Miss Kwon was the first one back.

I fiddled with my wallet, looking for the first sergeant's number, thinking of calling him so we wouldn't get in too much trouble. The photograph of the GI I had found in Yu Kyong-hui's hooch fell out. Miss Kwon snatched it up.

"Where you get this?"

"From Miss Yu's hooch."

"She *taaksan* crazy about this GI. He's infantry, but he was stationed here before. He almost married Miss Yu, but he ran out of time to get an extension and had to go back to the States."

"Well, she kept his picture for a long time."

"Not so long. Maybe two years. She still gets letters from him, and she told everybody that he got orders and he will be coming back soon."

"If she was waiting for him to come back to Korea, why would she leave here so suddenly?"

Miss Kwon shrugged. "I don't know."

Then it clicked. The whole thing. I slammed my palm on the table. Ernie jumped.

"What the . . . "

"We've been idiots, Ernie. If VonEric needed money to pay off gambling debts, where would he get it?"

"Well . . . "

"Sure. I'm going to call the first sergeant right now and let him know that we're going to be here a while longer. We have some paperwork to do."

Ernie frowned. While I was on the phone behind the bar trying to get through to Seoul, he made sure to finish all the beer.

Word of our snooping would spread quickly, so I waited until Waitz was off duty to start going through the records of the Army Support Command Replacement Detachment. I compared some of the entries to the notes I had pilfered from VonEric's desk. As we went over the assignments for the last few months, Ernie started to see the pattern.

"Waitz has been diverting guys to posts in Korea where their specialty is not required."

"Right." I stood up and reached for my coat. "Let's get off base and find a taxi."

"Where are we going?"

"To Inchon."

"What the hell do you want to go there for?"

"They have a nice place there I want to visit. The Olympos Hotel . . ."

"You don't need a room. Miss Kwon will put you up."

"I don't want a room. It's the other half of the title I'm interested in."

"What's that?"

"The Olympos Hotel and Casino."

The cab driver swerved rapidly through the countryside, and I kept telling him to slow down so we wouldn't slide off the slick roads. When we came over the crest of the hills surrounding Inchon, the huge harbor spread out below us like rippling green glass. Rusty merchant ships nodded lazily on the gentle waves like drunken sailors sleeping against lampposts. At the edge of the water, on a slight hill above the rest of the city, stood the Olympos Hotel. Half of its square eyes twinkled in the sunset.

Chandeliers, plush red carpet, beautiful women flashing brightly colored cards across green felt tables.

"Let's get out of this dump," Ernie said.

"I just want to see if he's here."

"Who?"

"Waitz."

There was not much of a crowd, since it was Monday night. A few Japanese tourists, a couple of high-rollers from Hong Kong at the baccarat table, and a smattering of bewhiskered merchant marines. Although there wasn't much foliage for camouflage, I didn't have to take any extra precautions to conceal myself from Waitz. He was humped over one of the blackjack tables, jabbing his finger into the green felt when he wanted a hit, waving his hand from side to side when he wanted to stay. His small pile of chips dwindled and then disappeared before our eyes. Without looking up from his cards, he reached back into his wallet and pulled out another short stack of twenty dollar bills. The dealer arrayed them like a fan on the table, counted them quickly, and then made a pencil calculation converting them to *won*. She pushed two small stacks of chips out to him, and Waitz dropped almost half of them into the betting circle.

We waited outside the hotel. I figured it wouldn't take long.

He walked through the lobby rubbing his face, and the red-coated attendant opened the door for him. I couldn't see his face, but his shoulders were still hunched and he stumbled as he walked. We put down the beers we had been drinking in the small garden overlooking the bay and followed.

His cab pulled up in front of Whiskey Mary's, one of the oldest establishments in Inchon's nightclub district. I told our driver to cruise by, and we watched Waitz walk in.

By the time Ernie and I peeped through the beaded doorway, Waitz was already too busy arguing with a Korean woman to notice us.

"Who is she?" Ernie asked.

"Miss Yu Kyong-hui."

"How did you know?"

"Waitz and VonEric were both gambling. One out here at the casino, the other on football, placing bets with Austin. When Waitz got in too deep, he started taking bribes to give GIs choice assignments."

"If VonEric was in on it," Ernie said, "how did he get in so deep to Austin?"

"From checking the records, it looks like he wasn't taking bribes. Maybe he figured he'd rather be in trouble with an illegal bookmaker than get caught by the army for abusing his official position and thereby face a court-martial. But he worked in the same room with Waitz, so eventually he must have realized what Waitz was doing, or maybe Waitz told him, figured to enlist him as a collaborator. Who knows? Then when VonEric wouldn't go along with the program, it made Waitz nervous. Maybe real nervous. And maybe VonEric even threatened to turn him in. The records were there, the ones we saw this afternoon. Enough to convict him, or at least build a hell of a case against him. If anybody knew about it."

"So Waitz decided to kill VonEric."

"Right." I jerked my thumb toward the entranceway to Whiskey Mary's. "And he knew that Miss Yu Kyong-hui had jilted him, so he talked to her. It turned out they had something in common. Miss Yu's old boyfriend was infantry. He had probably just gotten lucky on his last tour to Korea and been assigned down here, maybe to the Special Forces detachment on the ASCOM compound. But he wouldn't be so lucky again. It would be the DMZ for him. Miss Yu might not be able to see him for weeks on end."

"And Division isn't real big on helping GIs get their marriage paperwork through."

"Right. So Waitz made a proposition to Miss Yu. Just take VonEric home with her, loosen a crack in her floor that was already there, and her boyfriend would receive a choice assignment away from the DMZ."

A shriek rippled through the beaded entranceway to the club. Ernie was first in. I pushed my way through a gaggle of sweet-smelling business girls and found Ernie wrestling a bloodied knife away from Miss Yu.

Waitz was already pushing through the back door. I ran toward him but had to dodge sloshing beer and broken bottles from the cocktail tables he'd turned over behind him. When I made it outside, I spotted him down the street hopping into a taxi. There were no others around, so I couldn't follow him. I returned to the club.

Miss Yu was screeching and clawing at Ernie's face, like some great warrior bird.

"He's got to fix the assignment!" she said. "I don't care about MPs. I don't care about CID. I did what he want me to do, now he must help me!"

"What is it you did for him?" I asked.

Miss Yu glanced around at the business girls and the handful of merchant sailors. They all stared at her. Suddenly, she realized that she'd said too much.

"Nothing," she replied. "I did nothing."

It took us half an hour to get her booked into the Inchon Korean National Police Station. I briefly explained what the charge was but told them that Ernie and I had to leave in order to arrest the American who'd been her accessory.

When we reached the main gate of the Army Support Command, red lights flashed. We piled out of our jeep and showed our badges to the first MP we saw.

"What happened?"

"He opened up with a weapon."

"Who?"

"Waitz, that's what everybody's saying. The guy at the Repo Depot."

"A rifle?" Ernie asked. "A forty-five? What?"

"A forty-five. Johnson tried to card him, check his ID and pass, but instead Waitz shot him."

"Is he dead?"

"They say it's just a wound to his leg, no arterial bleeding. The MedEvac chopper is on the way."

"Where'd Waitz go?"

The MP pointed toward the flashing neon of ASCOM City.

Ernie and I trotted through the narrow alleys.

"Where would he go?" Ernie asked. "He can't get away."

"I think he knows that."

"Then what the hell is he doing?"

"He's toast and he knows it. Unless he destroys the evidence and finds a way to silence Miss Yu."

"How's he going to do that?"

As if in answer to Ernie's question, a tongue of flame shot over the tiled rooftops. When we reached Miss Yu's hooch, it was already engulfed in flame.

"He can't get away with this," Ernie said.

"He's panicked," I replied. "Not thinking clearly."

"Which makes him dangerous."

"Very."

"Where to now?" Ernie asked.

"Back to the next thing he needs to eliminate."

"Miss Yu?"

"Right."

During the five-mile drive to Inchon, Ernie broke every speed limit in the books. At Whiskey Mary's the girls were hysterical. I convinced one of them to calm down and she told us that Waitz had returned, this time with a gun, and he'd threatened to kill them all if they didn't tell him where he could find Miss Yu. They told him she'd been arrested.

Minutes later, we screeched up in front of the Inchon Police Station, just as a GI in civvies trudged up the stone steps, a pistol hanging at his side. Ernie didn't even slow down. He slammed the jeep into low gear and the vehicle thumped up the steps. Waitz turned in horror but before he could bring his weapon into play, the front bumper of Ernie's jeep sent him flying.

A dozen Korean cops streamed out of the building, some of them with their weapons drawn. Ernie and I stood with our hands straight up in the air and I started shouting that we were American MPs and here to arrest the man who lay injured on the steps. When everyone calmed down, I turned Waitz over and clamped the cuffs on him. His left leg had suffered a compound fracture so Ernie pulled off his belt and used it as a tourniquet. Waitz screamed when Ernie pulled it tight.

"You ran me over," Waitz said. "On purpose."

"I should've stepped on the gas," Ernie replied.

"Why'd you kill VonEric?" I asked.

Waitz stared at me, his eyes wide with glazed panic. "I didn't kill *nobody.*"

Ernie slapped him, and then slapped him again. Finally, I had to make him stop. We tossed Waitz in the back of the jeep and drove him, howling all the way, back to ASCOM City. It wasn't easy but I managed to keep the MPs there from killing him before we even had a chance to book him for murder.

The MP Johnson survived. While she rotted in jail, Miss Yu's case made its slow and painful way through the intricacies of the Korean judicial system. At Waitz's preliminary court-martial hearing, there was so much evidence piled up against him that he and his military attorney copped a plea. The result: twenty years' hard labor at Fort Leavonworth, Kansas. He'd probably be out in five.

NIGHT OF THE MOON GODDESS

Outside the main gate of Osan Air Force Base the narrow lanes of Songtan-up wind off in three directions. Each alleyway is crammed with brightly painted signs touting the best in leather goods or the tastiest in beer or guarantees as to which bar offers the greatest prospects for romance. At night the place is lit up as brightly as the spangled posterior of an overage stripper. In the morning it looks quiet and sad, especially when a low-lying mist crawls through the damp cobbled streets.

"How we ever going to find this joint?" Ernie asked.

I pulled the note I had made out of my pocket. "Kim's Tailor Shop and Brassware. It should be easy. I even have the address."

Ernie snorted. "Addresses don't mean nothing in this mess."

It turned out that he was right. It wasn't so easy. Each little number hand-brushed in white paint over a doorway was covered with tote bags and running shoes and jogging outfits hanging from every available rafter. While we were searching, an old woman approached us and offered herself as a guide to that particular nirvana that all young GIs seek. I shooed her away and held Ernie back, reminding him that we had a job to do. He stared straight ahead and chomped more viciously on his clicking wad of gum.

Ernie and I had jumped at this case because it gave us a chance to get out of Seoul. Osan is the largest US air base in the country, situated about thirty miles south of the capital city of Seoul and about fifty miles from the Demilitarized Zone that slashes like a knife through the heart of the Korean Peninsula.

We were on what's called a "SOFA case," a claim made against the US government by Korean civilians under a treaty known as the Status of Forces Agreement. A young woman, Miss Won Hei-suk, had committed suicide. The family contended that she had been driven to it by an American serviceman who had taken advantage of her youth and gullibility and promised her— among other things—marriage. The monetary figure they came up with included not only her projected productivity and value to the family in the future but also the price of their emotional suffering. How they figured that one I didn't know.

The US Army pays out millions of dollars in claims each year. In Germany it might be the price of an apple tree mowed down by a tank on maneuvers, in the Philippines income lost from rice churned up by the navy construction battalions. In Korea, it's the loss of a daughter.

Of course, the army didn't want to pay, so it was our job to find out if the story of this sordid little love affair was valid or bogus. A copy of Miss Won's family register had been submitted to 8th Army along with the claim, and it proved that she was clearly underage. One way out for the military was to find the GI, court-martial him for statutory rape, and force him to pay the claim. But finding him could be a problem. Not only were there a couple of thousand airmen stationed on Osan itself but the place was also a popular vacation spot for Marines from Okinawa and Japan. They caught military flights over here—at government expense—and they stayed in billeting facilities on post for four or five dollars a day. While here, they shopped for the cheap brassware and leather goods and textile products that the village offered in abundance and shipped tons of junk back to the States. They also enjoyed the more ephemeral charms of Songtan-up, when the sun went down and the neon began to sparkle.

We found Kim's Tailor Shop and Brassware in a side alley. The sign was painted in English with the small Korean translation below. The back walls were hung with drapes of gray and blue material. The front of the shop was lined with brass vases, urns, and sculptures, the most prominent of which was a fist displaying a stiff upward-thrust index finger.

When we walked in, a man rose from a small leather sofa.

"Welcome," he said. "If you want suits, Kim's Tailor number one in Songtan Village."

He was a sturdy looking Korean man, a few years older than us, maybe thirty, with short cropped black hair brushed neatly back along the geometric lines of his big square head. His leathery brown face was trying to smile, but it couldn't get past the lines of concern folded just beneath his eyes. When I pulled out my badge, he sighed and deflated, as if he had been expecting customers rather than cops.

"Are you Mr. Kim?"

"Yes. I'm Mr. Kim. I already tell everything to Korean police."

He plopped back down on the sofa and folded his short, bulging forearms across his knees. I sat down in a wooden chair across from him. Ernie wandered around the shop, running his fingers lightly over the contours of a brass female nude.

"The Korean police didn't find out much," I said. "Not even the name of the GI."

"Sure. I show them."

He reached across the coffee table, grabbed a large dog-eared book covered with red cardboard, and thumbed through the onionskin sheets. After flicking the pages back and forth a few times he jabbed a stubby finger at one of the receipts and turned it toward me.

"Here. These are the names."

"There were more than one?"

"Sure. GI never come from Okinawa alone. They all come in here buy some brassware. Two of them bought suits."

I stared at him for a moment.

"Only one of them went out with Miss Won," he said. "This guy here. The Cheap Charlie."

"He's the one who didn't buy a suit?"

"Yes."

The names were scribbled in *hangul*, the Korean script, and I sounded them out haltingly.

"Tom-son. Jo-dan. Pok-no."

"That's him. Pok-no. He's the one who went out with Miss Won."

The first two names were easy enough—Thompson and Jordan—although there must be a few hundred Marines on Okinawa with those last names. The last name, Pok-no, I couldn't figure. Mr. Kim had no idea how to spell it in English.

Could it be phony? It didn't seem likely that he would have passed off a false name with his buddies hanging around. Unless they were all in on some sort of plan. I figured it was more a translation problem than anything else. Some of the sounds of English don't work all that well in Korean.

Mr. Kim offered us cigarettes. I refused, as did Ernie. Kim wrinkled his eyes shut as he lit up, and with the free side of his mouth he started to talk.

"They were three happy GIs, always talk too much and play around, and they made Miss Won laugh. I told her not to go out with GI. I told her many times, but you know young girl. They no listen nobody."

"Had she been out with GIs before?"

"Never. He first one. Maybe I should've fired her." He blew a smoke ring toward the wall-papered ceiling. "If I told her I fire her, then maybe she don't go out with GI. She was a good girl. Send all her money home to her family."

"What was her job here?"

"Help with receipts, clean up shop, wrap orders for GIs who want to mail things back Stateside. Not much. Everything I can do myself, but shop must have flower if shop want to bring in bees."

During the Korean War, the country was completely flattened.

In the twenty years since, the economy had improved, but not much. Attractive young women are an expendable commodity. Their main job is to work in factories or shops and save money for a dowry so they can get married. A woman doesn't have any real status until she's old and has a slew of grandchildren running around.

"How often did she go out with Pok-no?"

"Only once."

"Once?"

"Yes. He was here from Okinawa for only a few days, but every day he come here and talk to Miss Won and after second day I let him take her to lunch. On third day he took her to dinner, but she come back after eat to work night shift."

"What time did she get off?"

Kim's eyes widened. "She don't get off. After work she sleep here. Someone must protect shop from slicky boys. Me, I go home."

"But you said she only went with Pok-no once."

"I wasn't counting lunch or dinner. I give her one day vacation each month. She was like little girl, very excited each time her day off come. She always go to country to visit her parents or to visit her sister at temple. She's a . . ." He snapped his fingers. "How you say? *Suknyo?*"

He said the word in Korean, but I didn't know it either. We looked it up in his Korean-English dictionary.

"Nun," I said.

It wasn't vocabulary that was often used in Songtan-up.

Ernie quit fiddling with the brassware, grabbed a folding chair, straddled it, and leaned forward at Mr. Kim.

"Let me get this straight," he said. "On their one date this Miss Won takes some Marine from Okinawa with her to her family in the countryside or to visit her sister who is a nun and then she comes back here the next day alone and that night kills herself?"

"Yes." Mr. Kim nodded somberly. "She worked all day and that night. After I left, she locked up the shop and went out."

"And the next morning the police found her body on the railroad tracks." Ernie leaned back on his chair.

Kim nodded and smoke drifted out of his nostrils toward the soot-stained paper above.

Before we left, I jotted down an address, and Ernie bought one of the brass fists. Kim wrapped it up awkwardly with the paper wadded too tightly around the hard, pugnacious digit.

The jeep purred along the ribbon of asphalt that wound through the acres of wavering green rice paddies. Straw-hatted farmers, their pant legs rolled up past their knees, bobbed through rows of sprouting shoots. Long-billed white cranes lifted gently from the muck and mire and flapped serenely into an endless blue sky.

"Don't they have any bars out here?" Ernie asked.

"Not for GIs," I said. "Besides, you're driving."

"I won't be for long if I don't get a cool one."

After we slowed to read the signs at a crossroads, I motioned for him to turn right, and three kilometers later the village of Chunhua loomed ahead of us. The cluster of straw-thatched huts sat on a rocky promontory like a crown of thorns amidst the spreading wet fields.

Ernie jammed the jeep into low as we chugged up the one dirt road that led into the village. Pantless toddlers and flapping-winged chickens scurried out of our way. We stopped in the center of the cluster of huts and stepped out of the jeep. Old men in hemp cloth tunics and women cowled in white linen stared at us curiously.

As I turned my back on the dying roar of the engine, I felt for a moment as if we'd stepped back in time. Bright eyes peered at us from within mud brick walls. Then I spotted a rusty Coca-Cola sign and I snapped out of it. I flashed my badge to the proprietor of the open-stalled store and told him who I was looking for, and he yelled at a boy who went scurrying off toward the fields. While we waited by the jeep, a crowd of children too young for school surrounded us, and Ernie horsed around with them and broke apart his last few sticks of gum trying to make sure that no one was left out.

A thick-legged man trudged up the hill, his dark face hidden between his straw cap and his broad shoulders. He approached and spoke to me in Korean.

"I am Won Man-yuk. Hei-suk's father."

He nodded but kept his grip on the short scythe in his right hand and made no motion for us to move toward his home or out of the sun. If he could be direct, so could I. I spoke Korean.

"We are here to find out why your daughter killed herself."

"The lawyer said he took care of all that."

"He is taking half of what you receive for his troubles, is he not?"

"We are farmers. If it wasn't for him, we'd get nothing."

"Maybe your daughter killed herself for some other reason. Not because of the American."

"She was a happy girl. She would never have killed herself if she hadn't been involved with foreigners. It was our mistake for letting her work in the city. But we have other children. Other mouths to feed."

"Did she ever bring the American here?"

"She didn't ask."

"Would you have allowed it if she had?"

"No."

"She had only known the American for a few days. During that time you never saw her—or saw him. You have no way of knowing why she killed herself."

"It had to be that. There could be no other reason."

"The claim is for a lot of money. Would you move away from Chunhua?"

"No. I would buy more land."

"Does your oldest daughter also send you money?"

His face hardened. "Don't speak of my oldest daughter. She wastes her life as a hermit on White Cloud Mountain, tending to some old temple that no one ever visits."

His knuckles bulged around the hilt of the scythe. I took a half step backward. Ernie moved around the jeep, but I waved him off.

"We believe that Hei-suk spent her last day with your oldest daughter."

"Then she wasted her last day of life. Better if I'd kept them both in the fields."

His dark face turned up at me, and in the shadow of his broad-brimmed hat, his black eyes burned like fire in a pit. The cracked flesh of the cheeks quavered and for a moment I thought it would break, but then his face set itself back into stone, like the granite outcroppings that form the foundations of the ancient village of Chunhua.

I didn't know what else to ask him, and I wondered why we had even bothered to come. A claim like this was a family's only chance to pull themselves out of poverty, and they'd try to get it no matter what the facts of the case. Still, I had a job to do.

As gently as I could, I nodded and thanked him. We climbed into the jeep and rode away, the crowd of children running after us and the sturdy old farmer standing like a rock amidst the swirling dust.

The steep cobbled lanes of the village of Ok-dong had been carefully washed and festooned with bright blossoms and hanging paper lanterns in anticipation of the coming Festival of the Spring Flower. The aroma of boiling beef and onions wafted out of open-fronted noodle shops. Freshly scrubbed, lacquered wooden table of *soju* houses that serve rice wine beckoned with their smiling, silk-bedecked hostesses and the warbling sounds of female crooners crackling out of small wooden speakers.

"This place ain't half bad," Ernie said.

"Maybe we can stop on the way back," I said, "but first we have to climb halfway up White Cloud Mountain."

We had stopped at the police station, and then told us that a Taoist nun by the name of Won Un-suk did indeed live on the mountain. Her official occupation was listed as the tender of the Temple of the Jade Emperor.

The crisp-suited young police officer could barley contain his mirth when we asked about her. Most of the inhabitants of Ok-dong considered her eccentric at best, but they tolerated her because her little temple sometimes caught the overflow of tourists who came to Ok-dong to visit the much larger Buddhist temple farther up the mountain.

"Did you see the American who visited her last week?" I asked.

"Of course. We always notice such things. Now some more Americans only a few days later. Ok-dong is becoming an international attraction."

He gave us directions to the nun's hooch, and we walked out of the station.

"Real wise-ass," Ernie said.

"Everybody's gotta have some fun."

As we climbed up the steep mountain path, the chatter and the clanging of pots in the village of Ok-dong below gradually gave way to the rustling of wind through pine trees and the scurrying of squirrels through brush. Ernie wiped the first beads of sweat from his brow.

"Why don't we just write up the report that it was a suicide brought on by statutory rape and let that farmer have his claim? Why go to all this trouble?"

"I want him to have the claim, too. But remember, there's a Marine who could get burned."

"He deserves it, going after the innocent stuff when there's all those business girls in Song-tan willing to give him what he wants for a few bucks."

"Besides," I said, "this case doesn't seem right. Why would she take it so hard so quickly? For all we know, he hadn't even left Korea when she killed herself."

"Eyewitnesses say she walked onto the tracks and nobody else was around."

"So it wasn't murder. Still, before you kill yourself, you at least brood about it for a while."

"How do you know?"

"Some of us brood all our lives and never work up the courage."

"Jesus," Ernie said. "We really do need to stop in one of those *soju* houses. If the rice wine doesn't perk you up, the girls will."

"All right. On the way back, I promise."

At a bend in the pathway a sign pointed up toward a plateau above the pines. We followed it, and when we crested the ridge, we came upon a small wooden hut surrounded by a carefully tended garden of sprouting turnips. I shouted as we approached.

"*Yoboseiyo!* Won Un-suk *keiseiyo?*"

A tall, thin Korean woman with a scraggly bobbed hairdo and loose blue cotton skirt and tunic emerged from the hut. Her full lips worked hard to cover her big front teeth but slid back into a broad grin when she saw us. Her eyes sparkled and she seemed to be having trouble keeping from breaking into a laugh. I saw the resemblance to the stern farmer we had met at the village of Chunhua, but she was like an inverted image of him, one that saw the gaiety of life rather than just its grimness.

"Are you Won Un-suk?"

She nodded. I showed her my badge, but she waved it away, still smiling up at us.

"You're here about my sister," she said.

"Yes."

"Come in. Come in."

The floor of her little hut was immaculately clean and covered with a smooth thick layer of oil paper. We took of our shoes and entered and sat down cross-legged while she happily buzzed about preparing some Black Dragon tea. A brass pot of water was already hot, as if she had been expecting visitors. As she worked, she talked.

"My sister came here to visit me on her last day of life." She turned and flashed a quick, toothy smile. "For this I am very pleased. She brought an American. He had less hair than you do and was very lean and strong. My sister, I think, was in love with this man, which is a very happy thing but also a very dangerous thing. Don't you agree?"

I nodded. Ernie just stared at her, slightly dumfounded by her bright manner, although he couldn't understand the rapid Korean that she spoke.

She unfolded the legs of a small oak table, set it in front of our knees, and poured cups of warm tea. I didn't bother to interrupt her. She seemed happy to have visitors and happy to talk about her sister.

"Many people visit me. The Temple of the Jade Emperor is very popular. Of course, sometimes people expect something a little more elaborate."

She waved to a small hand-carved shrine in the corner. In it sat a statuette made of jade. A somber old gentleman in thick robes, his eyes closed, was apparently meditating.

"The Jade Emperor. What you Americans would call the god of the universe. Of course we Taoists realize that even the gods are subject to the whims of the Tao."

She flashed one of her gleaming smiles.

I noticed another shrine on the opposite wall. Made of inlaid stone, it was a type of mosaic of a beautiful woman floating above the clouds, her long silken garments trailing gracefully behind her. The nun continued her monologue.

"They stayed for a while and had tea. My sister was very proud of her young man." She smiled again. "Pride is a very dangerous thing, don't you agree? After tea they left because he was anxious to get down to all the excitement of Ok-dong. She was very disappointed by this because we don't get to visit too often and of course we will get to visit even less often now."

I began to understand why the young policeman in Ok-dong found it so humorous that a couple of American investigators were planning to visit this hermit of White Cloud Mountain. She turned her smiling eyes on Ernie, who wasn't paying any attention to her chatter but merely sipped contentedly on his tea. She looked at me.

"He is a student of the Tao."

I glanced at him. "Yes. I think he is."

Ernie looked up, realizing we were taking about him, but turned back to his tea.

"A very advanced student," the nun said. For once her face turned solemn and she nodded slowly. "You must be wondering why my sister would kill herself. Of course, the answer is obvious. Love with a man will only lead to pain, and the sooner you get the pain over with, the sooner you will be able to resume your journey toward the eternal principles of the Tao. The great sage Lao-tze would have nothing to do with love, he was much beyond that, and eventually he found the Jade Elixir of Immortality."

She thrust her finger into the air and waved it like a baton, her wide mouth sparkling below.

Ernie set down his tea. "Don't you give a damn that your sister's dead?"

She turned to me, puzzled. I translated. She smiled back at Ernie. "She's much better off now. She escaped the illusion of love. Quite an accomplishment for one so young."

Ernie swiveled his head. "What'd she say?"

"Never mind, Ernie. This broad's crazy. I'll just ask one more question and we'll get out of here and down to that *soju* house."

"Good idea."

I turned back to the nun and spoke again in Korean. "When did you last see your sister?"

"When she walked down the mountain with the American."

I nodded. "Thanks for the tea." I pulled out some Korean money, a thousand *won* note, and slid it under the teapot. Laughing, she pushed it back at me.

"Oh no. Only devotees have to make contributions. You came as guests. This isn't necessary."

I picked up the wrinkled bill and shoved it back into my

pocket. On the way across the turnip garden she smiled and bowed to us like a woodpecker after termites.

We went back to the *soju* house in the center of Ok-dong, and soon a bevy of giggling hostesses were sitting around us. "We had another American here," one of them said, "just a few days ago."

"Did he have short hair?" I asked. They nodded. "And a Korean woman with him?" They nodded again.

"She became very upset and left after only about an hour."

"He stayed here alone?"

"Not alone!" They all laughed at this. "He had us to keep him company."

"He spent the whole night?"

"Not the whole night. After a while he left with the Moon Goddess."

I asked her what she meant by that, but they all giggled. Ernie was horsing around with the other girls and making them laugh and somebody turned the music up louder so I couldn't talk anyway. After a few more shots of rice wine I figured it must be one of those obscure Korean literary allusions. I tried to forget about the investigation. It was clear what had happened. The boyfriend, like any red-blooded Marine, had forgotten his little girlfriend from Songtan when he'd encountered the beautiful courtesans of White Cloud Mountain. She had lost much face and left on her own. Maybe she was crazy, like her sister, or intense to the point of madness, like her father. For whatever reason, she couldn't take her first amorous rejection, and she returned to Songtan and did her job like the well-trained child of Confucius that she was, and when the night closed around her, she went to the railroad tracks and waited for the train and walked out in front of the whistle and the clanging and the barreling light.

I tried to put these thoughts out of my mind and laugh along with Ernie and the girls. At first I couldn't, but after a few more shots of *soju* I managed.

One of the girls slipped something into my hand. It was a temporary ration card issued by the Osan Ration Control Office. She pouted.

"He said he would give me more money later, when he comes back, and he gave me this." The temporary card was only good for a month, and on his next trip to Korea he'd easily be able to get another. I shook my head.

"It's not worth much."

She sighed. "You keep it then. Are all GIs big liars?"

I nodded somberly and put the card in my pocket. The name on it was typed neatly. Faulkner, Robert R.

Korean has no letter for *F*, so a hard *P* is usually substituted. The letters *L* and *R* are interchangeable and sometimes dropped. "Pok-no" was a reasonable good transliteration of the name Faulkner.

More food and more rice wine were brought out. Korean men entered the shop, and some of the girls drifted off toward them. Everyone seemed quite happy to see Americans in such an out of the way place, as if we confirmed that White Cloud Mountain was a spot well worth visiting. The night turned out to be a great success, Ernie was in a rage of blissfulness, and the ladies of Ok-dong were all they promised they'd be.

We didn't leave until morning.

At the Osan provost marshal's office the next day we had the teletype operation transmit a message to Iwakuni Air Force Base in Okinawa with the names of the three Marines. While we waited for the response, we went to the snack bar and loaded up on fried eggs and bacon and hash browns.

"Could you believe those chicks last night?" Ernie asked.

"They've never talked to Americans before," I said. "We were a novelty."

"Damn. If it'd been any more of a novelty, they would've killed me." He sipped on his coffee. "So we recommend approval of the claim, huh?"

"I don't see why not. Another case of a GI's gonads guiding his common sense."

"Understandable."

"Yeah."

After breakfast, we still had more time to kill, so we stopped at the base library. I found a book on Taoist cosmology and found out that the Jade Emperor was indeed considered to be the supreme god of the universe. His powers were somewhat limited, however, since the Tao itself, the inexplicable principles that rule existence, cannot be broken but only followed, even by gods of immense power.

His-wang-mo, the Goddess of the Moon and the dispenser of the elixir of immortality, was a little more to my liking. A beautiful woman, she was changeable like the moon itself, and as such she was the goddess of the seasons and the weather and of all things that were always in flux—which seemed like everything to me. An engraving in the book looked much like the second shrine we had seen in the little hut on White Cloud Mountain.

In a book on Korean rhetoric, I couldn't find any reference to a saying like "leaving with the Moon Goddess." I asked the Korean librarian, but she had never heard of it. I wrote it off as just the mutterings of a bunch of party girls.

When we returned to the Osan PMO, the transmission was waiting for us. Jordan and Thompson had been located easily. The problem was that Lance Corporal Robert R. Faulkner had not yet returned to Okinawa and was being carried by his unit as absent without leave. They told us that if we found him we should arrest him—and send him back under armed guard.

The evidence was too thin to involve the Korean police, so Ernie and I strode resolutely past the police station through the main street of Ok-dong without stopping and, even though the shadows of the pines were growing longer, hiked up the side of White Cloud Mountain.

When we crossed the crest that led to the Temple of the Jade

Emperor, I shouted, but no one emerged from the rickety hut. We checked inside. Empty.

Ernie kicked around in the turnip patch until he came upon a rectangular clump of fresh black soil. He searched behind the hut and found a shovel, and we started to dig.

The Temple of the Jade Emperor was also a shrine to the Moon Goddess, and it wasn't too surprising that the girls of the Ok-dong *soju* house called the crazy woman who tended the shrine the Moon Goddess. After her humiliation, it was only natural that Miss Won would've returned up here to her sister's hut and told her about the betrayal by her American boyfriend.

Won Un-suk had told us that after her sister left with her boyfriend that night she had never seen her again. Maybe she was lying. Or maybe she meant it in a spiritual sense: she had never again seen the innocent person who had once been her sister.

The concerned nun might've gone into the village herself to talk to the wayward young man. Had she brought him back up here? Maybe they'd talked. What had happened then I didn't know, but I did know that Faulkner had never made it back to Osan in time to catch his flight to Okinawa.

The jolt in Ernie's shovel answered the question.

We bent down and scraped away the dirt. As flesh came into view, we did our best to hold our breath to protect ourselves from the rotten odor.

We cleared away more of the earth. In the fading light of sunset his skin seemed to have a green pallor, but it was the stomach that startled us most. Ernie jumped back, and we peered down into the pit.

"Looks like he swallowed a damned bowling ball," Ernie said. "I've never seen a stomach so distended."

"What could it have been?"

"I don't have any idea."

We threw a couple of feet of dirt back on the body and went into the hut to wait. Ernie watched out the window on one side, I watched out the other. Three hours later large black clouds rolled in but scurried away, as if anxious to flee the neighborhood.

"I'm not going to sit up here all night," Ernie said. "What we do is we go back down the mountain, report it, get a team up here to exhume the body, and we're through."

"But she might slip away."

"She's already gone."

I sighed. "You're probably right."

We walked outside the hut. Another cloud rolled away and the face of the full moon glimmered down on the turnip patch.

"The Moon Goddess is watching," I said.

"Knock that crap off," Ernie replied.

We started down the path.

At the first bend in the trail the moonlight lit up a granite cliff in front of us almost as brightly as the white screen of a drive-in movie. I hadn't noticed it on the way up because our backs were to it, and in the light of day it would just be another rock. Something darted across the cliff. I grabbed Ernie's arm.

"Look! Up there. On a ledge on the granite cliff."

Ernie squinted.

"I'll be damned."

"It looks like her."

"Yeah."

We scrambled toward the cliff and found a pathway leading up. Soon we were climbing above the pines. The moonlight beat down on us, and with the reflection off the smooth granite the sky around us seemed almost as bright as day. The valley below crouched like some dark creature.

The ledge narrowed, and when we rounded a corner, we saw her, sitting atop a large boulder that leaned out into the open air above the abyss.

"Welcome," she said, "to the realm of the Goddess of the Moon."

She waved her hand at us.

"No. Don't come any closer. You will be severely punished if you do." She held a jade tumbler no larger than a small wine carafe up into the moonlight. "I will deny you the Elixir of Immortality."

She lowered the tumbler into her lap and laughed softly.

"It's the same formula Lao-tze took before passing beyond the Gates of the Western Mountains into the land of the immortals. It has taken me years to perfect it. I wanted my sister to take it but she was of small mind, so instead I challenged her boyfriend, the young American, to try it. He was very bold. Or maybe it was the rice wine he had consumed with the brazen ladies of Ok-dong. But whatever the reason, he grabbed it out of my hand and poured it straight down his throat."

She lowered her eyes. "I suppose he wasn't ready for it." She glanced back up at us and laughed. "To follow the path of the Tao takes years of preparation. I saw you consulting with him in the turnip patch. I'm afraid he's not too talkative now. My sister couldn't get him to say a word, and when she couldn't, she seemed frightened of him and ran away down the mountain. I was happy when I learned that she had found a way of transcending her troubles. Maybe she was, after all, wiser than I thought."

She held the tumbler out toward Ernie.

"Will you have some? You seem like one who is wise enough in the ways of the Tao to sample the Jade Elixir. You will have immortality! No? No matter."

She raised the tumbler high above her head.

"To the Goddess of the Moon!"

As she opened her mouth and started to pour I ran forward, but the boulder was slippery and my leather shoes found no traction. Ernie was behind me and cupped his hands for my feet, and I slid up and over the curved surface. As I reached for her, she poured the last of the green fluid into her mouth. A violent eruption convulsed her stomach. I expected vomit to explode out of her mouth but instead she seemed to choke and then she dropped the tumbler and clenched her throat and the jade container clattered along the side of the cliff until it crashed into the rocks below.

Ernie pushed again, but this time I found a handhold and resisted. I didn't want to go sliding over the far edge of the rock.

The nun stood and looked down at me, her face green, her throat shriveled up like a dried stick of bamboo, her eyes wide in terror. A croaking noise erupted from her open mouth and she stepped backward and her foot slipped. As I reached out, her hand slapped mine and slid off my fingers, and she vaulted into the black night, twirling end over end until her skull smashed into the rock below, cracking like a moist melon.

I lay still, clinging to the rock for a long time until Ernie pulled me off the precipice.

On the way back to Ok-dong long clouds skittered in front of the silver face of the moon, wavering in the wind, like silk streamers trailing after the Moon Goddess.

SEOUL MOURNING

Staff Sergeant Riley, the Admin NCO at the Criminal Investigation Detachment, plopped the big folder into my hands and somehow managed to smirk around buck teeth. Dark hair slicked back, so skinny he seemed to rattle inside his starched fatigue shirt, he pulled a pencil from behind his ear and tapped the eraser on the folder.

"SOFA case," he said. "Hot. For you and Ernie."

SOFA. A military acronym that stands for the Status of Forces Agreement. The treaty between Korea and the US that covers everything from criminal jurisdiction over military personnel to the prohibition on selling imported maraschino cherries down in the village.

"SOFA case?" I always have something clever to say when I'm getting screwed. "How'd me and Ernie get it?"

"Top figures you've been goofing off on the black market detail long enough. Besides, this thing is such a pile of manure that nobody else wants it."

He thumbed through the folder and pulled out a carbon-backed invoice. Five thousand bucks. To be delivered, in cash, to the family of Choi Un-suk, the little girl referred to in all the reports as "the victim."

Riley marched back to his desk and sat down, his gravelly voice rolling over a barricade of paper-clipped reports.

"The first sergeant wants it taken care of," he said. "Now!"

Tonight, after a couple of shots of bourbon, Riley'd be the sweetest guy in the world. At work he was a bear.

Arguing about an assignment once the decision had been made would be a waste of everybody's time. Instead, I found a corner, sat down in a gray military chair, and thumbed through the folder.

The title of the report was Serious Traffic Incident, which was a hell of an understatement. An American army jeep, traveling south on the Main Supply Route between Camp Red Cloud in Uijongbu and Yongsan Compound in Seoul, managed to kill a young girl, Choi Un-suk, age thirteen, a student at the Kuk-min Middle School.

It didn't run her over. According to one of the GI passengers, the driver, Private First Class Dwayne Ortfield, had been speeding and swerving through traffic the entire trip. The ten-foot antenna, bent forward from the radio in the back, hadn't been properly secured. The front portion whipped from side to side. When he and the other two passengers complained, PFC Ortfield ignored them and kept driving at a high rate of speed.

It was at a bus stop, crammed with black-suited children on their way to school, that PFC Ortfield tried to pass a taxicab on the right. One of the girls, the safety monitor, stood slightly off the curb. When she saw PFC Ortfield heading toward her, she turned, raised her white-gloved hand, and blew her whistle. Ortfield swerved away, but the antenna, obeying the immutable laws of physics, didn't follow.

The tip of the antenna jammed into the little girl's eyeball, pierced her brain, and splattered half her skull over her screaming schoolmates.

Private Ortfield didn't want to stop, but after being punched by his passengers, he went back, supposedly to do what he could to help.

They were forced to leave, however, because a mob formed

before the arrival of the Korean National Police and the GIs in the jeep would have been, in all probability, torn limb from limb.

Ortfield had a long history of traffic violations. But his MOS, his Military Occupational Specialty, was 64 Charlie, transportation. When he first joined up, he had been designated as a driver by the army, and despite the proofs of his incompetence, a driver he had remained. Until this.

The Korean National Police turned jurisdiction over to US military authorities. The theory was that since he was army, let the army take care of him. Besides, we give their government millions of dollars in assistance each year. No one wants to cause hard feelings. American GIs are only sent to Korean courts when public outrage demands it. This was a small case, not well covered by the press. No outrage. Not yet.

The court-martial was scheduled for this morning at the 8th Army judge advocate general's office.

Meanwhile, the family had filed a wrongful death claim with the United States government under the provisions of the Status of Forces Agreement. It had been approved. An easy way out of the mess for our side. Five thousand bucks. A tiny globule of wealth siphoned from a sea of taxpayer money.

The hard part was having to stand face to face with the family, and that dirty job had fallen on us. But there was no way out.

Ernie and I don't have much bargaining power with the first sergeant. Ever since an incident over a year ago when we arrested the 8th Army chief of staff, he saw us as a couple of lowlifes. I'd been punished by having to serve a stint with an artillery unit along the DMZ. Ernie'd been relegated the black market detail, making sure Korean dependent wives didn't buy too much coffee and mayonnaise out of the commissary and sell it for a profit in the ville.

I wasn't going to beg to get out of this. I'd do it and get it over with.

While I was reading the report, Ernie wandered in. Late

again. He sat next to Riley's desk, feet up, sipping a cup of snack-bar coffee. I strolled over and waved the folder under his nose.

"Did Riley tell you about this SOFA case?"

"Yeah," Ernie said. "Crap City."

Riley didn't look up from his paperwork. "I have every confidence that you two can handle it tactfully."

Ernie snorted, finished his coffee, and stood up. Ever since Vietnam, words like "tactful" have disappeared from Ernie's vocabulary.

Without looking back, we walked down the long hallway, pushed through the big double doors, and hopped down the stone steps of the CID building. We jumped into the jeep, and as Ernie started it up, he turned to me.

"Who is this guy Ortfield anyway?"

"A young driver who didn't take his responsibilities seriously."

"I want to see him."

There was plenty of time, and I wasn't in a hurry to face with this Korean family.

"The court-marital starts in ten minutes."

"Let's go."

He shoved the jeep in gear, and we rolled down the tree-lined streets of Yongsan Compound.

The 8th Army courthouse was a small brick building with red Korean tile on the roof turned up at the edges. Inside, a summary court-martial sat in session. The judges, a row of uniformed officers behind a high wooden panel, appeared properly somber. The prosecutor at one table shuffled paperwork. The defense lawyer, a young second lieutenant, conferred with the defendant, Private First Class Dwayne Ortfield.

Ortfield sat hunched over, elbows on the table, listening to his army-appointed lawyer. His hair was longish on top, greased, hanging over his eyes. His dress green uniform hadn't been properly pressed. With his monthly salary held in abeyance, he probably hadn't been able to pay his houseboy since the death of Miss Choi Un-suk.

Tough beans.

Ernie and I passed the armed MP at the door, walked down the carpeted steps, and took seats in the gallery. I looked around for Choi Heng-sok, the father of the deceased girl. Neither he nor his lawyer had made an appearance. Since this court-martial was considered to be an internal US military affair, they probably hadn't even been notified.

The colonel in charge of the proceedings banged his gavel.

Witnesses were called in rapid order. First, the MP on the scene, who confirmed what everybody already knew: he had found a dead girl surrounded by a lot of angry Koreans. He was followed by the Traffic Control Officer, who, although the milling crowds had pretty well messed up the evidence, managed to present the court with some well-done charts of what had happened. With a pointer he noted the position of the other cars, how Ortfield had swerved to his right, and where the antenna had swung out and pierced the thirteen-year-old girl through the eye.

It was Ortfield's passengers who did the most damage. They went over what they had written in their statements. That Ortfield was driving too fast, swerving around the road, cursing, not listening to reason.

The whole thing went fast. A little less than two hours. Military justice at its best. I figured Ortfield would be spending a lot of years licking cement.

When the defense lawyer went to work, he didn't even try to dispute the facts. He just said that they couldn't punish PFC Dwayne Ortfield because it would be detrimental to the mission of the 8th United States Army.

I really couldn't believe what he was saying. I wondered what it had to do with anything, and I kept waiting for the judge to cut him off, but they let him prattle on.

Road conditions were tough in Korea, the defense lawyer said. Snow, rain, sleet, mudslides, downed bridges, loose electrical lines, mountain roads, floods, you name it.

He had that right, anyway.

And GIs were being sent out into these conditions all the time. They didn't want to go, but the training mission of the 8th Army and the defense of the Republic of Korea required that they risk their lives in these hazardous conditions. Routinely.

That was true but I didn't understand what it had to do with the Ortfield case.

If you punish a GI, the lawyer said, for responding to difficult traffic conditions and trying to make time through the undisciplined maze of Seoul, you'd be sending a message to all the other drivers of US military vehicles in Korea. The message would be: don't take chances. If road conditions are rough, pull over. Or worse yet, refuse to haul the load. After all, one mistake and you end up with your career ruined, a criminal record, possibly with a sentence to the federal penitentiary in Leavenworth, Kansas.

PFC Ortfield was just doing his job, the lawyer said. Sure, the antenna should've been properly secured. He made a mistake. He admits that. But he shouldn't be punished for the unfortunate accident and for the unfortunate death of a civilian who happened to be standing one meter away from the curb.

To my surprise the judge ordered a ten-minute adjournment.

Ernie and I stood outside for a minute, away from all the people lighting up cigarettes and yapping about the case.

"He's gonna walk," Ernie said.

I swiveled my head. "You're kidding. He might as well have stuck a gun to that little girl's head and pulled the trigger."

"She was standing off the curb. He was doing his job."

"Everybody stands off the curb here. It's a Korean custom. Besides, she was the safety monitor, and she was supposed to be directing the other girls. And doing your job doesn't mean speeding through traffic with a loose antenna."

"Doesn't matter," Ernie said. "The defense lawyer was exactly right. Those officers on the panel think about mission first. And if burning Ortfield will hurt the mission of the Eighth Army, they won't burn him."

"No way. You've got to be wrong."

"Come on. You'll see."

Everyone doused their cigarettes and headed back into the courtroom. We followed and took our seats. The judges filed back in.

I heard the gavel and then the colonel's voice, but I still couldn't believe it.

Private First Class Dwayne Ortfield was restricted to compound, his driver's license suspended indefinitely, and 8th Army Personnel would be notified to review his current posting with respect to immediate reassignment.

They were sending him back to the States with a slap on the wrist.

I stood up and gripped the varnished wood railing. I wanted to scream. But when I saw the clean-shaven jaws of the judges and their crisply tailored jackets as they walked out, I knew it wouldn't do any good.

Ernie grabbed me by the arm and pulled me out into the cold winter air.

At 8th Army Finance, it took a while for them to count the money in Korean *won* and stuff it into a leather briefcase. There was already a handcuff on the handle and I attached it to my wrist. It was heavy. Still, it didn't seem like much to trade for a little girl's life.

Ernie slid the jeep between two kimchi cabs, honked his horn, found about three inches of open roadway, and hooked his fender in front of the cruising cabbie next to us. When the light turned green, he gunned the engine, swerved in front of the guy, and studied the madly swirling traffic ahead, prowling for his next opening.

All of this was done while slumped back in his canvas seat, fingertips hanging lightly on the bottom of the steering wheel, his face set in a completely bored expression. Occasionally he veered wildly to the right or left, stepped on the gas, tapped lightly on the brakes. Ernie's nervous system might've been seared by the war in Vietnam and the pure white horse he bought from the kids through the wire, but he was still one hell of a driver.

He leaned toward me. "What was that address again?"

I glanced at my clipboard. "One twenty-eight *bonji*, 533 *ho*, Kirum-dong."

He straightened his back. "Yeah. Kirum-dong. It's right over here."

We had left the skyscrapers of central Seoul and were now in the outskirts of the vast city, heading north on the road that lead to Uijongbu and beyond that the DMZ. The Demilitarized Zone. The barbed and mined gash that slices through the sweet center of the Korean peninsula like a butcher's knife through wurst.

After the Korean War ended, no peace treaty was signed. There was only a cease-fire. The Communists in the north have an army of seven hundred thousand. The republic in the south has only four hundred and fifty thousand men under arms supplemented by the US Second Infantry Division. With both sides tense and armed to the teeth and staring at each other across the line every day, there are regular violations of the cease-fire. The casualties, if they are American, are reported to the world press. If the slaughter involves a North Korean or a South Korean, it's kept quiet. They see it as a family affair. Nobody else's business.

Melted snow sprayed from the tires of the kimchi cabs in front of us as we sped through the gray overcast morning. I didn't feel comfortable about dumping all this cash on the Choi family. It was a bona fide claim under the Status of Forces Agreement, but it seemed disrespectful somehow. As if the US government was saying, yeah, your daughter was slaughtered, but here's the loot and don't bother us any more.

And Ernie and I were the messenger boys.

We sat in silence. Ernie turned off the main road and swerved down a narrow lane; I checked the addresses. They were engraved in Chinese script on metal placards embedded in the stone or brick walls and difficult to read. I spotted one: 436 *bonji*.

"Hang a left," I said.

Ernie turned the jeep uphill, and we passed shops on either side. Brightly colored stacks of preserved noodles and canned milk, stringy-limbed cuttlefish drying in the cold wind, corpses of skinned hogs hanging red and limp in a butcher's window. The numbers changed fast and I was losing track, but I knew we were in the right area.

"Pull over here."

Ernie parked the jeep snugly against a massive stone wall and chained and padlocked the steering wheel. We climbed out, bending our lower backs and stretching our legs.

A stone stairway ran up the hill, lined on either side by brick walls and the gates to houses until it wound off out of sight. I looked at the address again.

"Up there?" Ernie said.

"Yeah. I think so."

Nothing is precise about Korean addresses. The city is divided first into sections (*dong*), then into areas (*bonji*), and finally into individually numbered dwellings (*ho*). And the numbers can be a mad swirl, winding back onto each other like a dragon's tail. Still, the best way to find one was on foot. We trudged up the jagged staircase, stepping gingerly over the tenacious remnants of last week's snow. A cold drizzle started, slashing into our faces, and stopped just as suddenly.

When we rounded the corner, the alley widened, and in front of the open gateway stood a crowd of people. Schoolgirls for the most part. Silent. All wearing long black skirts and tight black waistcoats. Their shimmering ebony hair was capped with the neatly trimmed bangs, making them look like a flock of clipped ravens. They seemed to be praying. I realized that there was an even larger crowd inside the gate, and I saw the placard: 533 *ho*, Choi Heng-sok *juteik*, the residence of Mr. Choi, the father of the slain girl.

We pushed our way through the crowd, sullenly puffed faces turning as we passed. It was good to be surrounded by so much femininity, although they all seemed to hate me and they were all too young and our lives were lived worlds apart. Still, I liked them. The warmth of their massed bodies enveloped me and the freshness of their unscented skin filled my senses. I didn't blame them for how they felt about me.

Beyond the crowded courtyard, the paper-paneled doors of the main house had been slid back. Inside sat a group of elderly people, the men in baggy suits, the women in *hanbok*, flowing traditional Korean dresses. Towards the back of the room on some sort of wooden platform was a long, blanket-draped figure. The body.

On the narrow wooden porch that ran the length of the house, a shrine had been set up. The sharp tang of incense bit into my sinuses. Surrounded by flowers of all colors was a large black and white photo of a plain, round-faced Korean girl. The only expression on her blank features seemed to be surprise, as if she never expected to receive so much attention. We always treat people better in death than we treat them in life.

One by one, the schoolgirls filed forward and paid their respects. Some placed flowers on the growing bunches, others knelt and bowed their heads for a moment. A few crossed themselves. Most, however, raised their pressed palms to their forehead and lowered themselves in the Buddhist fashion.

Wrinkled eyes in the darkened room turned toward us. I stepped in front of the porch, placed my feet together, and bowed slightly from the waist.

"*Anyonghaseiyo,*" I said. "*Nei irum Geogi ieyo. Mipalkun.*"

Good afternoon. My name is George. Eighth US Army.

A slender woman in a western skirt and blouse rose and nodded and waved for us to enter.

"*Oso-oseiyo,*" she said. Come in.

She looked a little like the dead girl in the photograph, but I figured she was probably just an aunt. The two people next to the body, the ones with the tearstained faces and the disheveled hair, were unmistakably the parents. They looked as if their ears were still ringing from the explosion of an A-bomb.

Ernie and I slipped off our shoes, stepped up on the narrow porch in our stocking feet, and entered the room. The solemn-faced occupants shuffled around on the vinyl floor to make room and slid a couple of embroidered purple cushions over for us to sit on.

The body was covered not with a blanket but a light silk shroud. The girl still wore her black school uniform, although some spots were moist, as if someone had attempted to scrub off the bloodstains. The woman I assumed to be the mother crouched next to the body, and when I entered she leaned forward and pulled the shroud away from the face.

I recoiled slightly but caught myself. One side of her head was red and raw. Indented. Caked with blood. She looked as if some twenty-foot prehistoric lizard had bounded out of an alley and chomped his fangs into her skull. I thought about a speeding jeep and laughing, careless GIs. In some respects there wasn't much difference.

The mother leaned forward, touching the cold flesh with her lips, and whispered to the corpse.

"*Sonnim wayo. Musopjima.*" Guest have arrived. Don't be afraid.

Ernie looked at me, his pale eyebrows rising slightly. I widened my eyes and turned away from his gaze. We sat down on the cushions.

I busied myself with my clipboard. Nothing like paperwork to help you keep your bearings in a situation that's threatening to reel off into insanity.

The receipt for the money had to be filled out and verified by officials of the US government, namely me and Ernie. I cleared my throat and started asking questions.

"Who are the parents?"

All heads turned to the woman squatting next to the body and a man sitting cross-legged on the floor next to her. He was unbelievably thin, but he held his back perfectly straight. A white shirt and tie seemed incongruously bring beneath his weathered face. His cheekbones were high, like ridges of stone.

"You are Choi Heng-sok?"

He nodded.

"And the deceased is your daughter?"

He nodded again.

"May I see some identification?"

The words were written right there on the questionnaire, but as soon as I said them, I regretted them. An intake of breath rustled through the crowd. Even Ernie glanced over at me. Mr. Choi didn't seem to notice, however. He reached back in his wallet and pulled out a laminated card and handed it across to me with bony, leather-skinned fingers, as steady as his rock-like expression.

I took the card, placed it on my clipboard, and copied down the Korean National Identification number. When I was finished, I handed it back to him.

As I filled in the receipt, I sensed movement next to the body. Something rustled. Then something shrieked.

"She is my daughter!" the woman screamed. "My baby and you have killed her!"

Ernie started to stand up. A couple of the relatives slid across the floor toward her, getting between us. Soon she was enveloped in grasping hands and cooing words.

She was crying now, shaking her head violently, her lips and cheeks quivering, drool dripping from her mouth.

I filled out the last of the form. Mr. Choi had turned toward his wife but looked back at me when I thrust the clipboard toward him.

"Sign," I said. "It is necessary to receive your claim."

He nodded and took the board from my hand, and while I pointed at the signature block he scribbled three Chinese characters in a quick, sure hand. He started to give it back to me, but I wouldn't take it.

"Your wife must sign also."

He stared at me, confused. In Korea, a husband can sign for the entire family. He and his ancestors had a long acquaintance with the peculiarities of red tape, however, and he was dealing with foreigners, after all. Acceptance came to his face and he slid forward across the immaculately polished floor. He and the other relatives soothed the girl's mother. She kept mumbling about the beasts from across the sea, and her family laughed nervously, glancing at us, hoping Ernie and I wouldn't take offense.

Ernie couldn't understand much Korean, but he knew an insult when he heard it. Still, it didn't seem to bother him. After the initial shock of the scream, he had settled back on his cushion. The only concession he made to nervousness was a stick of gum that he pulled out of his pocket and resolutely chomped on. He hadn't offered gum to anyone else, which was unlike him. I knew he hadn't suddenly become stingy. He was just preoccupied. Worried about getting fragged.

Mr. Choi and the others finally convinced the girl's mother to sign the form. They handed it back to me. Her signature looked like the frenzied slashes of a sharp blade.

I slid the money to him. Ernie and I stood.

For a moment I thought of saying I'm sorry. It would be embarrassing, but it would probably do them a lot of good. But I hadn't killed their daughter. I wasn't Dwayne Ortfield. And I wasn't the US government that had brought him over here.

I tried to think of other times I'd heard apologies on behalf of the US government. I couldn't think of any.

Maybe there was a regulation against it.

The mother started to cry. Softly this time.

A solemn man who'd been sitting by himself in a corner leaned forward and riffled through the briefcase, stacking the money on the floor and counting it. At first I thought he was some sort of bodyguard. He was tall and lean and strong, watchful of everything. But then I realized he must be the lawyer. Taking charge of the finances. I wondered what his cut would be. Probably half.

We backed out of the room. To turn while leaving would've been a sign of disrespect. With things as tense as they were, even Ernie wouldn't risk delivering such a slap in the face.

The courtyard was empty. The girls must've finished their ceremony and left so quickly that I hadn't noticed. We shuffled across flat stone steps, but before we reached the gate, I heard footsteps behind me and someone grabbed me by the arm. I swiveled and stared into the stern face of the lawyer.

"What of Ortfield?" His English was heavily accented but understandable.

"The court-martial is finished," I said. "He will be sent back to the States."

"That is all? No jail? No punishment?"

I shook my head.

"Nothing?"

"He won't last long in the army," I said. "He will never be promoted again."

His narrow eyes hardened. "That will not be good enough for Mr. Choi."

I shrugged. "There is nothing I can do."

Ernie stepped forward, positioning himself to kick the lawyer in the groin. I waved him back with the flat of my palm.

The lawyer glanced at him, coldly evaluating his size and strength, and turned back to me. His grip on my arm was strong, and his confidence, facing men a head taller than him, was impressive.

"The parents demand justice," he said.

"It is too late for that. The Korean police gave up jurisdiction."

"When does Ortfield leave?"

"Soon."

"Not soon enough," he said. "He won't board an airplane without . . . " He searched for a word. "Without atonement." He waved his arm around the courtyard. "This may not seem like the home of a rich man, but Mr. Choi lived a hard life, and when he made money he saved it. There are many people who will do his bidding for the right price."

There was no question about that. The going rate for a murder in Seoul was about two hundred thousand *won*—three hundred dollars US.

Ernie'd had enough. He pushed his way in front of me. "Are you threatening me?"

The lawyer let go of my arm and backed off half a step. "Not you."

"Ortfield then?"

"Yes." The lawyer nodded. "He will pay."

I grabbed Ernie by the elbow. "Come on. Let's go."

He resisted, but I yanked him toward the wooden gate and pushed him outside. The lawyer didn't follow.

I started to say something. To tell Ernie that they were just upset and the threats didn't mean anything, but I gazed down the alleyway and my mouth slammed shut.

They were waiting for us. A hundred grim-faced girls lining either side of the narrow lane. Some were beautiful, some plain, some plagued by pock-marked faces or erupting complexions. But they all stared at us as we walked by.

Ernie strutted, twisting his head back and forth, disdainful of their hatred.

As we descended the long flight of steps, I felt the eyes of the girls on the back of my neck. Fire flushed through my skull until my face burned.

Back at the compound, Ernie was still angry and made the mistake of telling Riley about the threats to Ortfield's life. It wasn't long before the first sergeant heard about it and then the provost marshal.

Riley strutted into the admin office, the starch in his fatigues crinkling with each step.

"Straight from the first sergeant," he said. "New assignment for you guys."

"No more payoffs, I hope."

"Not this time. Guard duty. Ortfield's hold baggage is being picked up in the morning. He catches the first flight out of Kimpo tomorrow afternoon."

He slapped a plane ticket and a packet of orders into my hand.

"Until then you and Ernie watch him. Every minute. Day and night."

"Babysitting."

"You got it. And if he doesn't make it to that flight, the provost marshal is to send you both back to the DMZ."

I unfolded the tickets, checking the flight times, making sure the emergency orders were signed and sealed. Ernie's face flushed red. He looked as if he were about to bust somebody in the chops. I spoke before he had a chance. No sense bitching about it.

"Tell the provost marshal thanks for the vote of confidence."

"Be happy to," Riley said. "Enjoy your duty. And have a nice day."

We found Ortfield in the 21 T Car barracks—that's the 21st Transportation Company (Car). He was playing grab-ass with one of the houseboys, a man twice his age, who was trying to ignore him and get his work done.

Ernie decided to set Ortfield straight from the beginning. He grabbed him by his scrawny shoulders and slammed him up against a metal wall locker.

"Hey! What's the idea?"

Ernie shoved his forearm under Ortfield's chin. Cheeks bulged. "The idea is that you're a dirt-bag, and from this moment until you get on that plane you're going to do everything we say." Ortfield gurgled. "You got that?"

His voice came out choked and frightened. "Okay. Okay!"

Ernie let him go and told him to go back to his bunk and quit bothering the houseboy. We followed him over to his area and found that he hadn't even begun to pack. Ernie dug out his canvas duffel bag from the bottom of his footlocker, threw it at him, and told him to get busy. Ortfield grabbed it on the fly and, completely convinced of Ernie's sincerity, went to work.

Ernie walked over to me and whispered, "The maggot. Babysitting him all night means we miss Happy Hour."

"Tough duty," I said.

"I'll take the first shift. Put the fear of God into him. You come back after chow and take over for a while."

"Right," I said. "See you then."

The sun was setting red and fierce into the Yellow Sea when I strolled back to Ortfield's barracks. I went in the side door, down the hallway, and into the four-man room. Empty. No Ortfield. No Ernie.

I rushed out toward the front entrance and the office of the Charge of Quarters. An overweight staff sergeant in wrinkled khakis sat behind the desk reading a comic book.

"Have you seen Ernie?"

"The guy guarding Ortfield?"

"Yeah."

"He left about ten minutes ago to pick up some beer. Decided to give the kid a break, his last night in country and all."

And give himself a break, too.

"Did he take Ortfield with him?"

"No. Isn't he in his room?"

"No. I just came from there."

"Maybe he's in the latrine."

I sprinted down the hallway and checked the latrine, and when I didn't find him there, I ran upstairs and pounded on as many doors as I could. After five minutes of scurrying around the barracks it was clear. Ortfield had disappeared.

Whistling, a bag of cold cans in his arms, Ernie strolled toward the front of the barracks. I caught him at the entrance but before I could speak he saw it in my eyes.

"The little dirt-bag took off?"

"You got it."

"But I was being nice to him."

I turned back to the CQ. "Did any Koreans come into the barracks?"

"Not that I saw."

We checked around, but none of the GIs and none of the houseboys had seen any unauthorized Koreans in the barracks.

"We're going to have to track him," Ernie said.

We returned to Ortfield's bunk. Ernie popped me a beer and opened one for himself.

"No sense letting it go to waste," he said.

I sipped on mine, thought for a moment, and started looking through the junk in Ortfield's locker. I found it amongst the toiletries, behind a red and white striped can of shaving cream. A photograph. Ortfield sitting at a cocktail table with a Korean woman. I handed it to Ernie.

"Do you recognize her?"

Ernie squinted, slugging back his beer. "Yeah. A business girl. I've seen her around. Out in Itaewon."

I studied the façade behind them. "We're experts at every bar in the red light district, Ernie. Look hard. Which club is this?"

He thought about it, sorting the possibilities in his mind. "Colored light bulbs on the ceiling, plaster made to look like the walls of a cave. Round cocktail tables with plastic tablecloths. The Sloe-eyed Lady Club. It's got to be."

"You're right. That's what I thought." I stuffed the photograph in my shirt pocket. "Let's go."

Ernie glugged down the last of his beer and followed me out the door.

By the time we hit Itaewon, the sun was down and neon lights flashed lewd invitations to the few packs of GIs roaming the streets. Girls stood in doorways, half naked in the cold winter air, crooking their red-tipped fingernails, cooing siren songs of sensual delight.

We ignored them, heading like two hound dogs toward the top of the hill and the Sloe-eyed Lady Club. We pushed through the padded vinyl doors of the club and entered a world of blinking red bulbs and grinding rock music and the smell of stale beer. A sea of young women gyrated on the small dance floor. No men yet. Most GIs still hadn't left the compound.

As our eyes adjusted to the dim light, we scanned the room. No Ortfield. Ernie spotted her first. "There she is."

He waded out onto the dance floor, pushing girls out of his way like Moses crossing the Red Sea.

When he found her, he stood behind her, but she continued to dance. She still hadn't notice him. The girls dancing with her stopped. Ernie wrapped his arm around her slim body, pinning her arms to her sides, and escorted her quickly off the dance floor. I led the way to a table in the corner, and we sat her down. I leaned toward her.

"Where's Dwayne?"

"Who?"

"Ortfield." I showed her the picture.

"Oh, him. I don't know. I no see long time."

"Weren't you his steady *yobo*?"

"For two months. Maybe three." She waved her hand. "Anyway, he go. Catch another girl."

"Which girl?"

"I don't know. He butterfly honcho. Maybe catch many girls."

Ernie leaned in front of me and grabbed her wrist. Slowly, he began to twist.

"You *kojitmal* me?" he said, breathing into her face.

"Ok-hee no lie," she said.

They stared at one another. She seemed to enjoy the pain, and he enjoyed giving it. For a moment I thought they were going to clinch, but the music stopped and we heard a murmur coming from the girls on the dance floor. I glance back and saw angry faces and pointing fingers. Korean business girls protect one another. If they attacked, they'd rip us to shreds with their manicures.

I tapped Ernie on the elbow. "Come on, pal. Let's get out of here."

He let the girl go but continued to stare at her as we walked out the door.

There was nothing to do but search the clubs one at a time. When we saw business girls on the street, I stopped them and asked about Ortfield and showed them the photograph, but they all shook their long glistening black hair and said they hadn't seen him.

It was less than an hour before the midnight curfew. We took a break and ordered some onion rings at a stand outside the Lucky 7 Club. The GIs were out in force now, swirling from one joint to another in drunken abandon. We ordered two cold ones to wash down the greasy batter.

"We're screwed," Ernie said.

"Maybe he'll show up on his own."

"Maybe. And maybe he'll go AWOL, and you and I will both lose another stripe."

I shrugged. I'd lost them before. "That's not what worries me."

Ernie set down his brown bottle of Oriental Beer. "Then what does?"

"Mr. Choi."

"Who?"

"The dead girl's dad. He doesn't believe justice was done in our military court."

"He's right about that."

"I'm afraid he might administer justice on his own."

Ernie kept chomping on the onion rings. I heard footsteps behind me. I turned. It was the girl from the Sloe-eyed Lady Club, Ok-hee. Ortfield's old flame.

"I see him," she said.

"Where?"

"*Chogi,*" she said, pointing. Over there. "You come quick. Big trouble."

We set down our food and ran.

■ ■ ■

She led us down an alley that wound away from the lights of the bar district. We swerved past a dark movie house with an enormous billboard above the entrance painted with the faces of giant Korean actresses. A flight of broad cement steps led down to the main road.

At the bottom, next to a boxlike black sedan, stood two men. One of them was Ortfield. The other was a Korean taller than Ortfield, trying to force him into the car. Ortfield flailed wildly. That mad resistance of a drunk.

There were no crowds nearby. The buses had stopped, and most people had sense enough to find shelter before midnight when everyone had to be off the street. Only a few taxis, their yellow plastic lights bobbing above the flat roofs, sped by.

Ernie sized up the situation immediately and bounded down the steps, taking them two at a time. He yelled. "Hey! What are you doing there?"

The Korean man, still with a fierce grip on Ortfield's arm, turned and glanced up the steps. I recognized him. The lawyer. The same man who had confronted us at the home of Choi Unsuk's parents.

I started down after Ernie, taking the steps more cautiously. They were narrow and slick, and I didn't want to fall and bust something.

As Ernie approached, the lawyer seemed to evaluate his situation. He looked at Ernie, he looked at the squirming Ortfield, and he looked at the small back door of the black sedan. With a sigh of resignation, he let Ortfield go, opened the front door of the car, and climbed in.

Ernie hit the bottom of the stairs running. "Halt! You're under arrest."

We had no jurisdiction over Korean civilians, even ones caught red-handed trying to kidnap a drunken GI, but technicalities like the law never slow Ernie down.

The car pulled away. As oncoming headlights flashed through the cab, I saw that the lawyer sat in the front next to a driver. Neither one of them looked back.

Ernie grabbed Ortfield. "Who were those guys?"

Ortfield just babbled. He was so drunk—or stoned—that saliva dripped from his mouth.

When I reached the bottom of the steps, I watched the red taillights fade into the distance. What had they wanted? Why hadn't they killed him when they had the chance?

All the way back to the compound Ernie cuffed Ortfield on the head. Back at the barracks, I took the first shift. Ernie took the second. One of us was awake all night. Watching.

The next afternoon was a clear winter day with a sky so blue that it must've drifted over from the vast plains of Manchuria.

Ernie drove. Quiet. Pissed off that we had to babysit and upset that Ortfield was getting better treatment than most GIs. A civilian flight out of Kimpo International Airport. A chauffeured jeep instead of a cattle car loaded with smelly soldiers and duffel bags.

In the morning the movers had arrived and—without incident—boxed up what little baggage Ortfield had to be shipped: a stereo set, souvenirs of Korea, extra uniforms. After chow we loaded up the jeep and started out for the airport.

Ortfield was still hung over. Morose. Unapologetic for having run off by himself last night. Just one more romp through Itaewon, that's all he'd been after. He admitted to popping a few pills and drinking a bottle or two of Oscar, rotgut Korean sparkling burgundy. After that he remembered nothing. Not even the incident with the lawyer. All he remembered, he claimed, was the steady rap of Ernie's knuckles on his head as we marched him back to the compound. He rubbed his greasy skull resentfully.

The little jeep wound through the bustling life of Seoul, crossed the bridge over the crystal blue ribbon of the River Han, and sped past open rice paddies until we reached Kimpo International Airport.

In the parking lot Ernie padlocked the jeep. We watched as Ortfield shouldered his duffel bag and suitcase into the busy terminal.

I started to breathe a sigh of relief. The ordeal was almost over. At the check-in stand I handed the ticket and the military orders to a pretty Korean woman in a tight-fitting blue uniform. She checked and stamped everything quickly, asking for Ortfield's military identification. And then she handed everything back to us and we were on our way.

A flight of steps led upstairs to the departure gates, but just before we got there, a frail man stepped out of the restroom. He stood in front of us, blocking our way, and I realized who he was. Mr. Choi, the father of the dead girl, Choi Un-suk.

He didn't seem angry and he didn't have any weapons in his hand, he just stood in front of us, moving slightly every time we tried to step around him. I positioned myself between him and Ortfield.

"Ernie, take Ortfield up the steps. I'll deal with Mr. Choi."

I turned back to him ready to speak, but he ignored me, his eyes following Ortifeld and Ernie as they approached the stairway.

Another man appeared from behind a newsstand. With a start I recognized him. The lawyer.

Ernie saw him too, and bristled. The lawyer stepped forward. Ernie stuck his fist out to stop him but like a cobra striking a mouse, he grabbed Ernie's forearm and started to twist. Ernie was no novice. He went with the turn instead of resisting, and soon they were grappling with one another, banging up against the rattling newsstand.

Ortfield sized up the situation, re-hoisted his duffel bag, and started trotting up the stairs.

Good, I thought. Get to the flight. That's the main thing.

I hurried forward to help Ernie, but the lawyer had already

258 ■ MARTIN LIMÓN

backed off, his hands held up, palms open, making it clear he didn't want a fight.

Ernie's fists were clenched and his face red, and his nose pointed forward as if he were going to jab it into the lawyer's heart.

Mr. Choi started slowly up the stairs, his interest elsewhere. Ortfield was already out of sight.

That's when it hit me.

With the back of my hand, I slapped Ernie on the arm. "Come on!"

"What?"

"Ortfield. He's alone. These two guys were just trying to get us away from him."

Awareness came into Ernie's eyes. We'd been had. We ran toward the stairs and pushed through the steady flow of travelers descending from the upper deck.

The walkway opened into a long concourse that led to the various gates. No Ortfield. We ran to the end of the hall and turned but instead of another long passageway we were halted by a brick wall of people.

Everyone was agitated, trying to look forward over the heads in front of them. I saw braided black pigtails and white blouses and long blue skirts. Schoolgirls. Many of them. There were also men in white caps and slacks and blue sports coats and, toward the front, elderly women in long dresses. Everyone wore a white sash from shoulder to hip. The sign of mourning.

"Crap," Ernie said. We both knew what we were in for. A demonstration. One of the few acceptable ways in Korea to vent emotion in public. Once they get rolling, anything can happen.

We pushed through the crowd. In front was an open area and a platform, and a woman stood atop it trying to switch on a megaphone. It buzzed and crackled to life.

She was tall and thin and wore a long blue skirt and a blue vest and her black hair was pulled tightly back from her austere face. I recognized her. The aunt of Choi Un-suk we had seen when we delivered the money. She turned away from us, toward a small commotion in the crowd.

"*Wei nomu bali ka?*" she said. Why are you leaving so quickly? Everyone cheered.

Over the sea of heads I spotted Ortfield. Two men had grabbed his duffel bag and his suitcase, and he was struggling with them, trying to yank them out of their grasp. Between him and the woman on the platform was a huge shrine. A blown-up photograph of Choi Un-suk draped in black and bedecked in front with dozens of bouquets. Behind the flowers stood the family, her mother, her aunts, her uncles.

Ernie didn't like Ortfield, not at all, but he's a territorial kind of guy. Ortfield was our prisoner, and Ernie didn't want people messing with him or delaying him in boarding his plane. Before I could say anything, he shot forward like a Doberman freed from a leash.

He crashed into the two men holding Ortfield's bags and knocked them back into the arms of onlookers. A great roar went up from the crowd. Ernie tossed the bags to Ortfield and started shoving him forward, toward the boarding gate twenty yards away.

The woman with the megaphone shrieked.

I'm not sure what she said. Something about the life of a Korean woman. But whatever it was, it was enough. The crowd surged forward, me with it, and Ernie and Ortfield were enveloped by a sea of bodies.

Ortfield cursed and threw a punch, and Ernie jostled with three schoolgirls, and then they were down and there was more screaming and in the distance I heard the whistle of a policeman but I knew they wouldn't be able to make it through the melee.

So far, I had been left mostly alone, with nothing more happening to me than hands pushing on my back as everyone shoved forward to see what was happening. Shuffling sideways through the surging crowd, I made my way toward the platform.

The woman atop it was still screaming through the small megaphone. Now I could understand her.

"*Chukkijima!*" Don't kill them.

It didn't seem that anyone was listening.

I climbed up on the platform. She looked up at me, ready to swat me with the bullhorn. I bowed slightly.

"I want to speak to the people," I said.

She hesitated.

"Please," I said "I know why you are here. I know what needs to be done."

She gazed into my eyes. Maybe it was desperation she saw there. Maybe it was the fact that she knew she'd already lost control of the crowd. Reluctantly she handed me the megaphone.

Ernie had wrapped both arms around the duffel bag, like Ishmael clinging to Queequeg's coffin, and twisted and pushed his way through the crowd. Ortfield tried to fight, but half-a-dozen men had hold of him, one of them with a firm grip on his hair, yanking his head back. If someone had a knife, they could've sliced his neck clean.

Schoolgirls stepped out of the crowd, screaming curses at Ortfield. Some of them spit. Some of them threw weak punches.

In the distance a small group of policemen struggled forward at the edge of the crowd, blowing their whistles, making little headway. No one made a path for them.

I spoke into the megaphone, keeping my voice as calm as I could. "Ladies and gentlemen, may I have your attention?"

I used English. I wanted them to know that an American was speaking. Many heads looked up. I continued speaking soothing words. A murmur ran through the crowd and soon they started to quiet, like a sea calming after a storm. Finally, the only people struggling were Ernie and Ortfield.

I pulled the megaphone away from my mouth and hissed toward Ernie. "Don't let him move forward, Ernie. Hold him where he is."

All eyes were on me. Patient. Expectant. A class waiting for a schoolteacher to begin a presentation. Even the police were quiet. I knew what I had to do. I should've done it a long time ago. I pointed to Ortfield. This time I spoke Korean.

"Our young soldier is distraught. He has brought great shame upon himself and his family. They will wonder why he was sent home from the army so early and why none of his officers have anything good to say about him."

I looked at him, shaking my head, a pitying expression.

"But he has little education. See how he acts when you have been so kind to wait for him here. To give him a chance to do the right thing."

I covered the mouthpiece of the megaphone with my hand.

"Ernie! Take him in front of the shrine."

Ortfield looked up at me, nervous and afraid. Ernie wasn't sure what I was up to but we've been partners long enough for him not to question me. He grabbed Ortfield by the arm and when he pulled away, he twisted his wrist behind his back and shoved him forward in front of the flowers and the huge photograph of Choi Un-suk.

This time the crowd made way.

I spoke into the megaphone again, praying that Ernie would know what to do.

"We Eighth Army soldiers, we Americans, we who are responsible for Ortfield," I said, "*daedanhi choesong-hamnida.*" We are terribly sorry.

Right on cue, Ernie grabbed the back of Ortfield's head and forced it down. He struggled—choking, bent forward at the waist—but Ernie held him there for almost half a minute. I bowed at the same time.

Choe Un-suk's mother began to cry. Handkerchiefs fluttered in the trembling fingers of the elderly ladies. While Ortfield was down, the schoolgirls, Un-suk's classmates, bowed too, and the adults joined in, and like the ocean when the tide goes out, the crowd lowered.

When they rose again, there was much embracing and everyone turned their backs on Ortfield and Ernie and me.

I handed the megaphone to the sad-faced aunt, climbed off the platform, and as quietly as I could, pulled Ernie and Ortfield toward the departure gate.

When we arrived back at the CID office, Riley pulled a pencil from behind his ear and peered at us over the mountain of paperwork.

"'Bout time you guys got back. What the hell took you so long?"

"We had a couple of delays."

His eyes narrowed. "Goofing off again, eh?"

Ernie ignored him, sauntered over to the coffee urn, and poured himself the dregs of the day's java.

I stood in front of Riley's desk, studying him, wondering how much he'd understand. Wondering how much the army would understand. The explanation would be long and hard, and in the end it would be meaningless to them. No sense even starting.

I took of my coat and hung it on the gray metal rack. "Yeah, Sarge," I said. "You caught us. Goofing off again."

He nodded, grunted, and looked back down at his paperwork.

All was right with the world.

PAYDAY

The wrinkled sergeant cursed as he held the handkerchief to the knot on his head. Blood seeped through the white linen and trickled down his wrist.

"They were inside the jeep and pounding me before I could pull my weapon." An army-issue .45 was still holstered and buckled to his canvas web belt. "I don't know why she stopped. Probably just wanted to give them a ride."

Ernie and I were standing in the big black-top bus parking area next to the two-story red brick building that housed 8th Army Finance.

Ernie paced back and forth, watching the bleeding staff sergeant, studying him. "Let me get this straight, Holtbaker. You and this second lieutenant Burcshoff pick up the Aviation Detachment payroll here at Finance, you load the briefcase full of money into the jeep, you start to drive off, and she stops to pick up a couple of guys standing on the curb?"

"They waved us down."

"Then they jump in the jeep," Ernie continued, "club you on the head, shove you onto the sidewalk, and drive off with the jeep and the money and Second Lieutenant Burcshoff."

Holtbaker nodded. Blood puddled in the cuff of his green shirt.

"Did she put up any sort of a fight?" I asked.

"Yeah. I think she went for the pearl-handled pistol she carried, something passed down from her old man, she told me, a retired colonel. But these guys were ready. She didn't have a chance."

The sergeant described them. One tall and blond, the other average height, brown hair. The blond guy was somewhat thin. The brown-haired guy was average weight. No distinguishing characteristics. They were both wearing sneakers, blue jeans, and nylon jackets—what every off-duty GI in the country wears.

A typically miserable description from a witness.

"When they made their getaway," Ernie asked, "who drove? Second Lieutenant Burcshoff or one of the hijackers?"

"How the hell should I know? By then I was facedown on the sidewalk."

"How much money was in that briefcase?"

"The whole monthly payroll for the Aviation Detachment. Over ten thousand bucks."

Ernie and I canvassed the area for witnesses. At the Moyer Recreation Center, no one had seen anything. These thieves were quick and professional. Get in. Get the money and the jeep. Get out. Not your typical GIs pulling some caper.

"What's our next step?" Ernie asked.

"They have a jeep, they have a satchel full of money, and they have a female second lieutenant. What we do is put out an all-points-bulletin and wait for one of those items to turn up."

Ernie pulled out another stick of ginseng gum, unwrapped it, and popped it into his mouth. "Hopefully, it will be the second lieutenant."

I nodded in agreement. "And hopefully, she'll be alive."

"Always preferable to dead."

Ernie's wish came true. A half hour later we received a call from the Korean National Police in the city of Kimpo, about fifteen miles west of Seoul. They had Second Lieutenant Burcshoff. She was alive. She was on the phone. Shouting.

"They took everything! The money, the jeep. I can't believe it but the sons of bitches even took my goddamned .45!"

I held the phone away from my ear. She didn't sound frightened, she sounded angry as hell. I told her to remain calm. Ernie and I would be there in a few minutes. We drove to Kimpo.

Second Lieutenant Constance R. Burcshoff held herself as if she were constantly at attention. The Korean cops stared at her surreptitiously, appalled that a woman would be wearing a fatigue uniform and combat boots, but she ignored their amazement.

"The thieves kicked me out of the jeep about two miles from here," she said. "In the middle of a few acres of rice paddies. I caught a tractor into town."

"They didn't try to hide their identity?"

"They made me lie facedown in the back of the jeep. Still, I caught a glimpse of both of them."

The description she gave didn't match what Sergeant Holtbaker had told us. This time the blond guy wasn't as tall and not quite so thin. The brown-haired guy seemed a little chubbier in her description. None of it gave us much to go on.

We drove Lieutenant Burcshoff back to Seoul. She sat ramrod straight in the back seat of the jeep, staring straight ahead, occasionally touching the empty holster at her hip.

Ernie offered her a stick of ginseng gum. She refused. I tried to engage her in conversation, but she didn't want any part of it. I'd already checked her personnel records. She had earned her reserve commission from a Southern military-agricultural school, and she came from a long line of army officers. Her father had retired as a colonel and her grandfather had been a general in World War II. She even had ancestors who'd fought on both sides of the Civil War.

Lieutenant Burcshoff was the only female assigned to payroll officer duty and she was the only payroll officer who'd been robbed. I couldn't tell which was worse for her, the humiliation of being robbed or the humiliation of losing her grandfather's pearl-handled .45.

All the way back to Seoul she sat with her face set in stone.

That afternoon the stolen jeep turned up at the Seoul train station. Ernie and I hustled over there.

It was parked in front of the main red brick building next to other military vehicles belonging to the 8th Army Rail Transportation Office. There were many ways to leave the train station: by train, bus, subway, or taxi. Ernie and I interviewed a few of the ticket sellers and the security officers who controlled the taxi queue, but no one remembered two Americans in civilian clothes parking a jeep and walking away.

There were plenty of fingerprints on the jeep, none of which were likely to do us much good without the perpetrators.

Back at the CID office we were told that General Skulgrin, the commanding general of 8th Army, was hopping mad that someone would steal an army payroll. He wanted the thieves caught and he wanted them caught immediately, if not sooner.

Overseas, GIs are paid not in greenbacks but in Military Payment certificates. The theory is that Communist agents won't be able to hoard a bunch of US dollars and buy arms on the international market. Also, government officials fear that a few tons of US green in the local economy could lessen the value of the *won*, the Korean currency. Eighth Army has a press in Japan that prints up the MPC and each bill is assigned a serial number. Since GIs generally aren't big spenders, there are no denominations larger than a twenty.

At 8th Army Finance, Ernie and I obtained a list of the serial numbers issued to Lieutenant Burcshoff. We passed it up the chain of command to the provost marshal, who showed the 8th Army CG. The next thing we knew, 8th Army Finance had a task force formed to search all incoming MPC and report the appearance of any of the stolen bills.

We heard a lot of grumbling from the finance clerks. It was going to mean a lot of extra work for them.

Ernie and I had the easy job, waiting for one of the stolen bills to turn up.

About three days later, one did. Turned in at the bank on Yongsan, the headquarters compound for 8th Army. The problem was that it was part of the main PX cash deposit. No telling who had spent it there. Maybe one of the thieves. Maybe somebody they'd passed the bill off to. We were no closer than we had been.

It was a little disheartening, but Ernie and I took it philosophically. There was no way the crooks could leave the country with that much MPC. Every bag on every flight leaving Korea, whether military or civilian, is searched by a customs agent— one of the benefits of investigative work in a country that lives in constant fear of terrorism.

On the fourth morning after the robbery we caught a break.

The alert siren sounded, vehicles were prohibited from entering or leaving the compound, and the commanding general declared all Military Payment Certificates null and void. Everyone in 8th Army was instructed to turn in their old MPC to their unit commander in exchange for the new Military Payment Certificates. They were bright orange. The old bills had been blue.

At 5 P.M., close of duty day, all the old blue MPC would become worthless.

The change in MPC made the finance clerk's search a lot easier. Everyone who turned in the blue MPC had to produce military identification and sign a register that said how much they were exchanging and, if it was over a hundred dollars' worth, declare the source of the money.

A lot of lightbulbs burned at 8th Army Finance that night. Ernie and I paced the reception room, sipping coffee, waiting for something to break. Nothing did.

At about oh-dark-thirty, one of the clerks tapped my arm. "You Agent Sueño?"

I rubbed my eyes. "That's me."

"Here's the register with the stolen bills. A whole stack of them."

Ernie rose from a vinyl-cushioned couch, stretched, and leaned over me and the clerk as we studied the register. "MED-DAC," I said. The 8th Army Medical Command. "Six hundred bucks. Turned in by Specialist Four Crossnut, Reginald R."

A Spec 4 pulls down about two hundred and fifty dollars a month.

The clerk pointed to the remarks section of the register. "Claimed he made the money gambling."

"The old standby," Ernie said.

In the latrine, we splashed water on our faces and then ran outside. The first fingers of dawn crept over distant hills. On the wide cement porch we almost bowled over Lieutenant Burcshoff. She wore an immaculately pressed dress green uniform that clung to the curves of her lean body.

"You have a lead?" she asked.

Ernie grinned. "We got 'em nailed. Just a matter of time now. When you see those two thieves again, they'll be standing in a lineup."

A shadow of concern crossed the even features of her face.

We didn't have time to chat. Ernie and I ran to the jeep and drove to the barracks of the 8th Army Medical Command.

Specialist Four Reginald R. Crossnut wasn't tall and blond, and he wasn't short with brown hair. He was black. And pissed off when Ernie yanked on his mattress and rolled him out of his bunk. He hopped to his feet, swinging bony fists, cursing.

"Who the *hell* do you think you are?"

Ernie shoved him up against a wall locker.

"We're CID agents," Ernie told him. "And we've been up all night and we're pissed off and we don't like thieves. Where'd you get the six hundred dollars in MPC?"

Crossnut's eyes widened, realizing the trouble he was in. He glanced back and forth between us. Ernie and I looked as if we hadn't shaved in a week.

"The money is *mine!*" Crossnut said. He tried to wriggle out of Ernie's grasp, but it didn't work. "I won it in a poker game."

Ernie clicked steadily on his ginseng gum, breathing into Crossnut's face. "Gambling isn't legal in Korea, Crossnut. Not on compound. Not off compound."

Apparently Crossnut hadn't considered that. His brow wrinkled.

"You can tell us the story of where the six hundred bucks came from," Ernie continued, "and be on your way. Or we can arrest you right now for illegal gambling. Self-confessed."

He shoved Crossnut higher up against the wall locker. I stepped in closer. "Who's your black market mama-san, Cross-nut?" I asked.

"Ain't got no mama-san," he replied. Ernie knotted his fist and cocked it. He wasn't acting. I'd seen him rough up sus-pects before. Crossnut studied Ernie's face and apparently lost all doubts about his intentions. "I got a papa-san," Cross-nut said.

"Out in Itaewon?" I said.

Crossnut nodded slowly. "You going to bust me?"

"Only if you lie to us."

He studied our faces: tired, grim ready to punch out his lights if he didn't open up. "His name's Mr. Kang. Works out of the back of the Black Widow Club. He's a good dude. Knows how to treat the brothers. You mess with him, you'll have a lot of dudes down on you."

Kang wasn't much of a papa-san. Still in his twenties, he was too young for the role, as skinny as a broom handle, and wearing a red silk shirt and three gold chains around his neck. We were in the empty bar of the Black Widow Club. The place reeked of barf, beer, and disinfectant. All the chairs were turned up atop the cocktail tables, and an old woman sloshed suds on the floor with a dirty mop.

Kang chain-smoked between lips that were too thin. "Where I get MPC not your business," he said.

Ernie grabbed a handful of red silk and leaned into his face. "If you want, Kang, we'll call the Korean National Police. The commanding general of Eighth Army is pissed to the max about this stolen payroll. All it takes is one phone call from him to the KNP honcho and they'll have you locked in the monkey house for twenty years."

Ernie shoved him back. The cigarette flopped out of Kang's mouth and sizzled in the slick suds. His eyes narrowed as he straightened his shirt.

"A lot of GIs change money in Black Widow Club," Kang said. "How I know which one?"

"Six hundred dollars," I said. "You remember."

Kang shrugged, thinking it over. His black market and illicit currency exchange operation depended on the cooperation of the Korean National Police. He probably paid them a stipend each month to look the other way. But if a lot of grief rolled downhill from the 8th Army commander and the chief of police of the Yongsan precinct, the local KNPs would be embarrassed. And when corrupt cops get embarrassed, they also get angry. And they take it out on the crook who embarrassed them.

All these thoughts played themselves out on the features of Kang's shifty face. Finally, muscles stopped twitching. He'd made his decision.

"Maybe you no believe," Kang told us. "The guy with the six hundred, he not soul brother."

"Who was he?"

"Everybody surprise. Tall white dude walk in Black Widow Club, ask for me, want to do business. Later I check. He do business with a lot of black market mama-san. Change MPC in Itaewon."

"So you weren't his only stop?"

Kang shook his head.

It figured. With ten thousand dollars to exchange for Korean currency, the thief would have to use more than one fence. Later, he could take the *won* to a Korean bank and use them to buy international money orders in US dollars. Mail them home. Stuff them in a bank account somewhere.

"What was this dude's name?" Ernie asked.

"I don't know. Tall. White hair. That's all I know."

"You must know something more about him." Kang didn't answer. "Think hard, Kang, or your next interrogation will be conducted by the KNPs."

Ernie smiled. Civil liberties were about the last thing the local Korean cops were worried about.

Kang took his time lighting another cigarette. "He have black stuff on his fingers," he said. "Like maybe he work on car. Later I see him with other GIs."

"You know these GIs?"

Kang nodded.

"And they're all in the same unit?"

Kang nodded again.

"Which is?"

"Twenty-one T Car."

The 21st Transportation Company (Car). The main motor pool for 8th Army headquarters.

When Captain Turntwist, the commander of 21 T Car, saw two CID agents stride into his office, his narrow forehead crinkled like an accordion.

"What have they done this time?" he asked.

The troops of the motor pool weren't known for being sedate during their off-duty hours. They ran a neck-and-neck contest with the 8th Army Honor Guard for the number of times one of their members appeared on the MP blotter report.

I ignored his question. "I'd like to see a roster of duty assignments for your drivers."

Ernie pulled out another stick of gum and looked at me curiously. He had expected us to look through the personnel folders, searching the official photographs for two GIs who matched the descriptions give by Sergeant Holtbaker and Lieutenant Burcshoff. I had another idea.

Without argument, Captain Turntwist instructed his company clerk to provide me with the information. After ten minutes I came up with a list of names. I showed them to the captain. "Is one of these men tall, blond, and thin?" I asked.

Turntwist took the list out of my hands and studied it. "Yeah. Three of them," he said.

"Does one of those three have a best buddy who is average height with brown hair?

He stabbed his finger at a name. "Dartworth, Private First Class."

I found his name on the assignment list. "He's been driving a sedan for the Protocol Office."

"Right," Captain Turntwist said. "Shuttling officers to and from Eighth Army social functions."

"You need a personable guy for that."

"That's why we selected him."

"And his buddy's name?"

"Frankton."

"Where are they now?"

"The entire unit's in the auditorium. Mandatory winter driving class."

"We need to talk to both of them."

Captain Turntwist told the clerk to pull them out of training. While we waited, Ernie and I walked out onto the big cement entranceway.

"What made you look at their assignments?" Ernie asked.

"Something about this case has been bugging me. A few things."

"But Protocol," Ernie said. "Why would a couple of payroll thieves have anything to do with the Eighth Army Protocol Office?"

We heard the heavy tromp of combat boots down the hallway. "No time now," I said.

Dartworth was indeed tall and blond, and good looking enough to have a shot at doing Hollywood hair oil commercials. His short buddy, on the other hand, would've looked more at home modeling leopard skins. The tight muscles of Frankton's wide shoulders were knotted, as were his fists.

I decided to start with the formalities.

I pulled a copy of the Uniform Code of Military Justice from a bookshelf behind the clerk's desk and handed it to the commander of the 21st Transportation Company (Car). "Captain Turntwist," I said. "Would you do me a favor and read these two gentlemen their rights?"

We questioned them in separate rooms and it took only a few minutes for Frankton to confess. It was all his tall, good-looking buddy's idea, he said.

"Dartworth knew what time they'd be picking up the payroll, how much it would be, even the name of the sergeant who would accompany the payroll officer."

"How'd he know all this?" Ernie asked.

Frankton shrugged. "A friend told him."

"A friend?"

"For the last couple of months my good buddy Dartworth has been popping an officer and a lady."

We waited. I almost whispered the question. "Lieutenant Burcshoff?"

Frankton nodded. "That's right. Lieutenant Burcshoff."

While we searched their rooms, I explained to Ernie what had made me decide to look for a driver who might've had some chance of meeting Lieutenant Burcshoff prior to the robbery.

The first thing that seemed screwy was her stopping for a couple of GIs in civvies who stood on the curb and waved her down. Sharing rides is common in 8th Army but not when you have ten thousand dollars in military payroll in the back seat.

And the fact that she'd been vague in her description of the two thieves although she was a top graduate of her reserve officer class. Sergeant Holtbaker, who'd been bopped over the head, had noticed more detail than she had.

Also, when Ernie and I picked her up in Kimpo, she couldn't believe that the thieves had stolen her treasured family heirloom, the pearl-handled .45.

What had she expected from a couple of payroll hijackers? Normally they'll take anything of value. Her shock didn't make sense unless she knew more about these two particular thieves than she was willing to tell us.

And outside 8th Army Finance this morning, when Ernie told her that the arrest of the culprits was imminent, she seemed sad. Not elated.

In Dartworth's locker we found eight thousand dollars' worth of the old blue Military Payment Certificates.

An MP patrol arrived. They handcuffed Dartworth and Frankton and took them to the MP station to be booked.

It was then that something dawned on me.

"We've got trouble, Ernie."

"What trouble? We wrapped up the case."

"Not completely. What about her pearl-handled pistol?"

"You worry too much, George. Those two jerks probably sold it on the black market."

"Not a gun they didn't."

Korea has total gun control. Only the military and the police are allowed to possess firearms. Because of the threat of North Korean Communist spies, trafficking in guns has only one penalty: death. And it is enforced. Absolutely. Even the people who run the black market wouldn't be foolish enough to buy firearms.

Ernie nodded, seeing my point. "So what did Dartworth do with it?"

"Only one place that makes any sense."

"What's that?"

"He gave it back to Lieutenant Burcshoff."

"Good. She owns it. So what's the problem?"

"She's the problem."

I made a call to the Aviation Detachment headquarters and spoke to the commanding officer.

"Lieutenant Burcshoff? No. We've been looking for her, too. She disappeared about an hour ago. Not like her. Not like her at all."

I slammed down the phone. Ernie and I ran to the jeep.

We found her in the Women Officers' Quarters. Sitting in the recreation room, television off, small refrigerator humming in the corner. She seemed calm. Wearing cutoff blue jeans and a loose sweatshirt with the name of her alma mater blazoned across the front. She looked exactly like a hardworking young woman relaxing on her day off except for one thing. She pointed the barrel of her pearl-handled .45 right between my eyes.

Ernie lifted his hands slowly out to his sides. "It won't do any good, Lieutenant Burcshoff. Just tell the truth, and it will all be over soon. Maybe you were in on it with them, maybe you weren't."

She barked at him. "I *wasn't* in on it with them. It was the sonofabitch Dartworth." Her eyes started to glisten with tears. "I know it was wrong, an officer fraternizing with an enlisted man. But I met him while he was driving us to the Officers' club. He seemed so cheerful. So full of life."

With the back of her hand she wiped away the tears, still keeping the pistol trained on us.

"So it wasn't your fault," Ernie said. "You didn't know that Dartworth and his buddy were going to hit Sergeant Holtbaker over the head. You didn't know they were going to steal the payroll. All you did was stop when he waved you down."

She shook her head. "I did more than that."

Ernie and I waited. The silence grew long. Finally her eyes blazed with fury. "I didn't shoot the sonofabitch!"

Ernie and I flinched. I started to edge my way along the wall. If she had to swivel to take aim, she might not be able to plug both of us.

As quickly as it had come, the fury subsided. "It's a matter of honor," she said. "The money in that satchel was the hard-earned pay of soldiers in the Aviation Detachment. Soldiers under my command. Not receiving it when they were supposed to receive it caused a lot of hardship. Rents they couldn't pay, groceries they couldn't buy, money they couldn't send home to their families."

And booze they couldn't buy down in the red light district, I thought, but I didn't say anything.

She gazed at us, eyes wide, as if wondering if we'd understand. "It was my duty as an officer, as one sworn to obey the orders of those appointed above me, to protect that payroll. With my life, if need be. I should've pulled out this pistol and aimed it at Dartworth's blond head and blown his damn brains out!"

Ernie held out his hand, expecting the gun to go off. It didn't. She paid no attention to our discomfort but seemed wrapped in a world of her own misery. Ernie took a step to his left.

"Instead, what did I do?" she asked. "I took the soft way out. I thought of my own feelings, of my own failure to live as an officer first and as a woman second. I didn't live up to my responsibilities."

"Hey," Ernie said. "You liked the guy. Of course you didn't want to kill him. You're only human."

Coming from Ernie, the biggest woman-chasing, booze-guzzling ville rat in 8th Army, I almost laughed out loud at the remark. Lieutenant Burcshoff shook her head vehemently.

"My dad told me becoming an officer would be tough. My grandfather told me it would be tough. They told me if I couldn't handle the job, if my personal life was more important to me than doing my duty, then I should never put on the uniform of an officer of the United States Army."

Most of the officers I knew only talked a good game. The truth was that they *always* put their careers and their personal goals above their duty to God and country. I was about to tell Lieutenant Burcshoff this when a red light flashed outside the window. Ernie glanced over. "The commanding general," he said.

A line of staff cars led by an MP jeep pulled up in front of the Women Officers' Quarters. A blue flag spangled with four stars fluttered in front of the longest sedan. Someone at the MP station must've notified the CG, General Skulgrin, that we were on our way to arrest one of his officers.

When Lieutenant Burcshoff glanced outside, Ernie stole another step toward the humming refrigerator. "The CG is here for you," I told her. "Because he respects you and doesn't want anything to happen to you."

"You're lying," she said. "It's just more MPs come to arrest me."

The commanding general of 8th Army, tall and lean and craggy-faced, climbed out of the back seat of his sedan. "I'm not lying," I said. "He's come to help you."

"It's too late, she said. "I've humiliated my family. I've dishonored the officer corps."

With his back against the refrigerator Ernie could reach one of the plateglass windows. He rapped his fingers lightly and caught the attention of one of the MPs outside. As he turned and looked, Ernie flipped him the bird.

The MPs face crinkled in rage. "Screw you too, Bascom," he shouted.

That was enough for Lieutenant Burcshoff to swivel her head and the barrel of the pistol along with it. I took two running steps and leapt across the couch. Ernie charged at the same time.

Lieutenant Burcshoff, with the reflexes of a tennis pro, backed off at the last moment. Ernie and I crashed into one another. Still, I was able to fling out my right hand and grab hold of one of her wrists. With all my strength I wrenched her arm toward the ground. She screamed, jerked her arm away, and twisted the barrel of the .45 toward her mouth.

Ernie kicked and flailed beneath me. A shot rang out. The smell of gunpowder exploded up my nostrils.

Heavy boots pounded down the hallway, and a herd of elephants crashed through the door.

I kept grabbing and turning and twisting, hoping to keep her from firing again. Finally a pair of knees ground into my back. MPs knelt above me and handcuffed my hands. In the confusion no one knew who was friend or foe. They sat me up against a bookcase.

They dragged Ernie, kicking and screaming, behind the safety of the couch.

General Skulgrin, the 8th Army commander, marched into the room. He knelt next to Lieutenant Burcshoff, one khaki-covered knee sopping up a puddle of blood. He turned his head and bellowed an order. "Get an ambulance! *Now!*"

Ernie was till wrestling with the MP he'd given the finger to. I heard knuckles crack on bone, and then reinforcement held Ernie to the ground until he finally stopped struggling.

General Skulgrin stuck gnarled fingers into the base of Burcshoff's neck, feeling for a pulse. There wasn't much left of the top of her skull. Finally he spoke to the MP officer hovering nearby. "Cancel the ambulance. She's dead."

He started to reach for the pearl-handled .45. A voice erupted in the room. To my surprise I realized it was mine.

"Don't touch it! That pistol belongs to *her*! Not to her father. Not to her grandfather. Not to anyone else. It belongs to her!"

All eyes in the room stared at me, figuring I'd gone mad.

THE MYSTERIOUS MR. KIM

The old woman tugged so fiercely on my shirtsleeve that I almost toppled off of my barstool.

"You save my son!" she screamed.

Ernie set down his frothing brown bottle of Oriental Beer, swiveled, and grabbed the elderly woman by the worn cotton of her loose Korean tunic. I regained my balance and grappled with her for a moment, and soon Ernie and I wedged her between us, me waving my open palm in front of her nose and telling her, "*Choyong hei.*" Calm down.

Ernie and I were off duty, bar hopping through the red light district of Itaewon and, as we were wont to do, hoisting a few wets. About the last thing we expected was to be assaulted, for no apparent reason, by a hysterical old woman.

The out-of-tune rock band twanged their last note and then stopped playing, their mouths open, gawking at us. The GI customers also stared, as did the "business girls," their nightly work interrupted in mid-hustle.

The old woman stopped screeching long enough for Ernie and me to walk her over to a corner table. I sat down next to her, patting the back of her bony hand.

She had to be in at least her early sixties. Most of her teeth were missing. The strong brown eyes in the center of her face were enveloped by the burn wrinkles of someone who had spent the better part of her life toiling in muddy rice fields. When it seemed that she wouldn't start grabbing on me again, Ernie returned to the bar and brought over our drinks.

Now that she had our attention, she spoke in rapid Korean. Breathlessly, so fast that I had trouble following and asked her to repeat herself more than once. Finally, I managed to absorb the outlines of her story.

Her son had been arrested, tried, and convicted of that most horrible of crimes: murder.

The case wasn't exactly unknown to us. In fact, it was the biggest flap to hit 8th Army in years.

A US Army doctor, Captain Richard Everson, had been stabbed to death in one of the narrow back alleys behind the flashing neon of Itaewon. An ice pick was found at the scene, and smeared blood confirmed it as the murder weapon. The apparent motive? Robbery. Captain Everson's wristwatch, fraternity ring, and wallet were all missing.

Since the crime occurred outside of a military reservation, jurisdiction for the case fell squarely on the capable shoulders of the Korean National Police. With the international spotlight on them, the KNPs wasted no time. All known thugs in the Itaewon area were rounded up, and soon—after interrogations involving rubber hoses—a suspect was identified. Choi Yong-kuang was his name, the son of the woman sitting in front of us. He had accomplices. Three other young men who were members of his gang, according to the KNPs, but all three of the men had testified that it was Choi Yong-kuang who had actually done the stabbing of Captain Richard Everson.

Why had they killed Everson when they'd already had him outnumbered and disabled? Sheer meanness, according to Choi's former comrades. Choi Yong-kuang had just wanted to watch an American die.

Although Ernie and I had monitored the case—as had everyone else in 8th Army who worked in law enforcement—we hadn't actually worked on it. No Americans had.

I explained this to the old woman. She would have to talk to the KNPs.

Of course she already had.

"They told me to leave them alone, and when I refused, they did this to me." She pointed to a puffed blue welt on the side of her face.

I had been translating for Ernie as we went along. He turned to the old woman and said in English, "What the hell do you want us to do?"

She understood and answered in broken English. "My son rob American doctor," she said, "but he no kill American doctor. His friend, they all lie because Korean police beat them up. Somebody come later, after my son take money, go and stab doctor with ice pick. You Americans. Everybody in Itaewon say you CID. You can find out about American doctor. Find out who want kill him."

Ernie shook his head. "There's no reason in the world, Mama-san, to think that the killer was anyone besides your son."

"Yes. There's reason," she answered. "Korean police, they know. Ice pick come from drink place up top hill. The Silver Dragon."

The most expensive nightclub in the Itaewon bar district.

"How do they know that?"

"They know many things, but they no say."

"Why not?" Ernie asked.

"I don't know. You ask them. You find out."

Ernie shook his head again. "This isn't our case."

The old woman leaned forward and grabbed his wrist in a white-knuckled clench. "If I have money, I give you, but I no have money. Next week, they kill my son."

The Korean judicial system doesn't tolerate endless appeals or long waits on death row. Within a month or two of arrest, convicted murderers are on their way to the gallows.

"If my son die," she said, "then I die." She sliced her thumb across her throat.

Ernie glanced around at the swirling interior of the smoke-filled bar. The business girls had become bored with us and were back to hustling GIs. The rock band was blaring again. Waitresses were busy slamming down bubbling bottles of Oscar, a locally fermented sparkling burgundy.

Ernie crossed his arms. "No can do," he said.

With that, the old woman closed her eyes, fighting back tears. A moment later she started rocking back and forth, mumbling some Korean folk song.

Her singing grew louder, so loud that I could no longer hear the hubbub of the voices that surrounded me. I could only hear her ancient song of death.

Later that evening, after the old woman left, Ernie and I walked up the hill to the Silver Dragon Club.

"What the hell," Ernie said. "Won't hurt to look."

The joint was more elaborate than the other dives in Itaewon and the chairs even had upholstered seats. Also, club policy was to hire only waitresses with straight legs. With all these amenities the Silver Dragon Club was twice as expensive as the other local bars and as such was mostly patronized by civilian businessmen and American officers.

The bartender wore a white shirt with its sleeves rolled up and his collar held close by a black bow tie. I leaned over the counter. With a glistening metal pick, he chopped into a blue-white block of ice.

"What happened to the old ice pick?" I asked.

He looked up at me, as if he'd been shocked by electricity. "You policeman?" he asked.

I showed him my badge.

He pointed down the hall. "Then you go ask Korean policeman. They know everything about ice pick."

"Maybe you can explain it to me," I said. Ernie fondled a delicate glass goblet, tossing it up in the air, catching it, while keeping his eyes riveted on the bartender. The young man swallowed.

"Miss Tae, she took it."

"Who's Miss Tae?"

"A waitress. She used to work here. Same night GI doctor killed, she take ice pick go. Never come back."

"You told the Korean police this?" Ernie asked.

The bartender nodded.

"Did Miss Tae know Captain Everson?" I asked.

The bartender looked puzzled.

"The GI who was killed," I explained.

The bartender shrugged. "How I know? Miss Tae take ice pick, she go, she never come back. That's all I know."

"You saw her take it?"

"Yes. She told me she bring right back. So I say okay. She lie."

Ernie returned the bartender's goblet—unbroken. We walked down the hill toward the Itaewon district office of the Korean National Police.

Lieutenant Pak Un-pyong had handled the investigation into the homicide of Captain Richard Everson. He wasn't in at this time of night, but when I flashed my identification and told the desk sergeant what we wanted, he called Lieutenant Pak at home.

Fifteen minutes later Lieutanant Pak walked into the big concrete bunker of the Itaeown Police Station. He was a tall man, thin even by Asian standards, with a hooked nose and a no-nonsense cast to his sharp features. He waved to us, and without a word we followed him down the hallway to his office.

We sat on two metal chairs in front of his desk, pulled out a pack of Turtle Boat brand cigarettes and offered us each a smoke. When we turned him down, he struck a wooden match, lit up, and leaned back in his rusty swivel chair.

"We've been waiting for one of you Americans to ask this question," he said.

I hoped he'd explain, but instead Ernie spoke up. "This Miss Tae took an ice pick from the Silver Dragon Club," Ernie told Pak. "She disappears. Captain Everson turns up murdered by an ice pick. What's the connection?"

Lieutenant Pak let out a plume of smoke. "She's the girlfriend of Choi Yong-kuang."

The convicted killer and the son of the old woman who'd harangued us into looking into this case.

It came together quickly for Ernie.

"So Captain Everson is hanging out at the high-class Silver Dragon Club," Ernie said. "Spending plenty of money because doctors make more than regular officers. This Miss Tae spots him, fingers him to her boyfriend, and Choi Yong-kuang and his partners jump him and rob him. She delivers the ice pick so Choi can silence Everson for good."

"That's what we think," Pak said.

"But why kill Everson?" I asked. "He was down. They had his money and his watch and his ring. Why make things worse for themselves?"

Pak continued to puff for a moment and then finally spoke.

"Maybe they wanted to make sure that he couldn't identify them. Maybe they thought he would have more money on him than he did and they would all leave Seoul together, and they didn't want us following. Maybe Choi Yong-kuang hates Americans. Maybe he was jealous because Miss Tae had been having an affair with Everson. Maybe a thousand things. Who can say?"

"And Miss Tae disappeared?"

"We haven't been able to find her. Her mother lives alone in Masan. We checked. No sign of her daughter. The local police are keeping an eye out for her in case she shows up. So far, nothing."

The way Ernie was fidgeting, I could tell he didn't like Lieutenant Pak's explanation any more than I did.

"There has to be more to this case," I said.

Pak shrugged.

"If you don't find Miss Tae and if this guy Choi is executed, we'll never know for sure."

Pak shrugged again. "The government is happy."

I knew what he meant. The Korean government receives millions of dollars from the United States each year to help in their defense against the communist regime up north. When a Korean kills an American officer, that special relationship is at risk. The way to save grief is to have the case closed quickly. Hanging Choi Yong-kuang would make a lot of government bureaucrats breathe easier.

"What is Choi's story?" I asked.

"He says that he and Miss Tae had originally planned to murder Captain Everson. That's why she brought the ice pick. They thought he was going to be bringing a lot more money. Supposedly, so he could buy Miss Tae out of her contract with the Silver Dragon Club, so she'd be free to quit work and live with Everson. An old trick. But Everson didn't bring the money; he was using Miss Tae just as she was trying to use him. Choi say that when they realized Everson didn't have more than a few dollars, he was furious. His partners ran away, Choi claims, but finally he didn't have the heart to murder a helpless man. He dropped the ice pick and left while Everson was still breathing."

"Miss Tae had already left?" I asked. Pak nodded. "And a few minutes later, one of your officers found Everson's body."

"A routine patrol."

"How long had he been lying there?"

"Hard to say. It was a dark walkway, seldom traveled. Could've been as much as an hour."

"Plenty of time for someone else to come along, grab the ice pick, and murder Everson," Ernie said.

"That's what Choi told the judge. Nobody believed him."

"Plus," I said, "it's more convenient for the government not to believe him." Pak shrugged once again. I leaned across the desk and stared into Lieutenant Pak's dark eyes. "There's a reason you came out here at night to talk to us. You're not certain Choi is guilty."

Pak stubbed out his cigarette. "If I had jurisdiction, I would search further into Captain Everson's background. But I don't have jurisdiction on your American army compound, and besides, my superiors are satisfied with the resolution." He raised his open palms toward the ceiling. "What more can I do?"

"But we can do more," Ernie said.

Lieutenant Pak smiled at him like a teacher indulging a bright student.

"Yes," he answered. "You can do more. You can do much more."

The next day at the CID office, I looked over what records were available concerning the Everson case. Jake Burrows and Felix Slabem, two of our fellow CID agents, had been assigned liason duties. They'd studiously regurgitated the translated record of the Korean police version of events but had done no investigative work themselves.

Their reason for showing so little curiosity was simple. In the army, the less you know the safer your career prospects.

Ernie and I performed our routine black market detail duties that day, but when I found a spare moment, I made a few phone calls. What I was trying to determine was the identity of Captain Richard Everson's best friend. I found him: Bob Quincy, an engineering officer who had shared quarters with the late Captain Everson on 8th Army's South Post.

Early that evening Ernie and I paid Quincy a visit.

He was a portly man with a round face and round spectacles and a pugnacious air. He stared straight up at Ernie's pointed nose.

"You had to have some idea of what his social life was like," Ernie said.

"I don't believe in speaking ill of the dead."

"'Speaking ill?' What the hell are you talking about, Quincy?"

Quincy turned away and stalked down the long hallway of the Bachelor Officers' Quarters toward the dayroom. We followed. A green felt pool table and a TV sat unused. The room was empty. He plopped down heavily in a padded chair.

"I thought it was all over," Quincy said. "I thought no one would come around asking me questions."

I grabbed a three-legged stool and sat opposite Quincy. "A man's life depends on your truthfulness, Captain Quincy. Anything you say will be held in a file classified Secret."

He nodded, sighed, and let out a long burst of air. "Dick Everson jogged," he told me. "He was in good shape, and that's part of the reason he was popular with the ladies."

"What's the other reason?"

"He's a pediatrician. You know how women love pediatricians."

I didn't but I let him talk.

"So he gave a few speeches at the Officers' Wives Club. You know, on the welfare of children in the Command, on what the OWC could do to help, things like that."

Ernie pulled out a stick of ginseng gum and unwrapped it. "So Everson hooked up with a couple of the wives," he said.

Quincy swiveled his round head and frowned at Ernie. "Only one wife." We waited, the silence growing longer, hoping he'd tell us who. Finally he answered the unspoken question. "I don't know who she was. Dick Everson was a gentleman. He'd never talk. But every night when he put on his jogging suit and went out for a run, it always lasted a lot longer than it should have. At least an hour. More often two. And he came back smiling."

"How can you be sure he was meeting this woman?" I asked.

"He told me. I could tell something was up. I didn't pry, but he told me that she lived with her husband in quarters on post and he reassured me that this woman had no children."

"That was important to him?" Ernie asked.

"Very," Quincy replied. "He would have no part in traumatizing kids."

"Decent of him," Ernie said.

"But he didn't give you her name?" I asked.

"No. Like I said, Dick Everson was a gentleman."

"Boffing a fellow officer's wife," Ernie said. "Is that in the manual?"

Quincy's face flared red. "He broke up with her," he said. "She didn't want to, but he knew it had to be done."

"When?" I asked.

"Two months ago. Maybe three."

After that, Ernie shot some pool. I asked a few more questions, but they didn't go anywhere. When I finished with Quincy, we left.

Nothing else in Captain Richard Everson's military life seemed in any way unusual. Ernie and I weren't exactly sure where to take this unofficial investigation. At least we weren't sure until that night in Itaewon when we ran into Choi Yong-kung's mother again. She had been waiting for us on the road that leads from 8th Army headquarters to the nightclub district.

She grabbed my sleeve, pleading with me. Telling us she had someone she wanted us to talk to.

Miss Tae, the former waitress at the Silver Dragon Club, did indeed have long, straight, beautiful legs. She showed them off by keeping them crossed under her short skirt at the table in a Korean teahouse where we met.

After having escorted us to the teahouse, Yong-kuang's mother made a discreet departure.

"When I left Everson," Miss Tae said in Korean, "the ice pick was still on the ground, the GI doctor was alive, and Choi Yong-kuang had run away too."

"Why don't you tell this to the Korean police?"

"They would beat me. Make me tell them what they want to hear. So they don't lose face and have to admit that they were wrong."

I wasn't so sure if that was true. Not for Lieutenant Pak Un-pyong, anyway, the chief investigator in the this case. But it was probably true for the institution he represented.

"So who killed Everson?" I asked.

"I don't know."

"Then who does?"

Ernie couldn't take his eyes off Miss Tae's legs. I concentrated on her face. Too heavily made up for my taste, but I could still admire the darkly lidded narrow eyes and the gentle curve of the smooth white flesh beneath her high cheekbones.

She sipped on a porcelain cup of green tea, set it down, and then spoke. "To find out the truth, there is a man you must talk to. He paid us to murder Captain Everson."

I almost choked on my tea. When I recovered, I translated for Ernie.

"Paid you?" he asked.

She turned to him, speaking in English now. "Yes. But we no do. We no can do."

"Let me get this straight," I said. "Someone paid you and Choi Yong-kuang to kill Everson, but you couldn't go through with it?"

She nodded. "After we left, someone else kill Everson."

"Maybe this man who paid you," I said.

She nodded again.

"What is his name?"

"He called himself Mr. Kim."

I groaned inwardly. The most common name in Korea. More common than Smith or Jones in the United States. Miss Tae continued.

"Mr. Kim come in Silver Dragon Club. Quietly. Wearing hat and sunglasses. He watch me with Everson. When Everson leave, he talk to me. Find out I have boyfriend who is *kampei*." Gangster. She was talking about Choi. "Later he meet us both and offer us money to murder Everson."

"Did he say why?"

"No. He never say. But one thing . . ." Miss Tae ran her long fingers along the edge of her teacup. "He strange."

"Who?"

"Mr. Kim. I don't think he hate Everson. I don't think he even know Everson."

"Someone else wanted Everson killed?"

"I think so."

"But you don't know who," I said.

Miss Tae shook her head. I kept asking questions but was

unable to pull any further information from her. When his turn came, Ernie asked her questions having nothing to do with the Everson case. Before we left, Ernie had convinced her to go out with him. The date was set for next week, Tuesday. In her new job, in a nightclub downtown, Miss Tae wasn't off until then.

Ernie was willing to wait. "You think she's lying?" he asked.

We were walking down the brightly lit main drag of Itaewon.

"Probably," I answered. "This mysterious Mr. Kim is a convenient scapegoat. But if she's telling any part of the truth, it could mean that someone else actually did murder Captain Everson."

"Like who?"

I had an idea. But I didn't want to say anything yet. Not without proof.

The next morning I was on the phone again, identifying myself as a CID agent and asking questions. After about a dozen calls and a trip to the 8th Army housing office, I had the information I needed.

We sat at a table wedged against a side wall of the big Quonset hut that serves as the 8th Army snack bar. I sipped coffee. Ernie glanced at my notes. "Thorough," he said.

"Thanks."

What I had done was obtain a list from the Housing Officer of all the accompanied quarters on South Post along with the names of family members, and therefore I had a list of all the wives who lived on South Post. Almost two hundred names. First I crossed off all those who had children. The remaining list was about three dozen strong. I crossed off the enlisted families, and then I was down to twenty-six names.

"How'd you eliminate names after that?" Ernie asked.

"I made phone calls to their husbands' units. Found out what shifts they worked."

Ernie slapped his forehead with the palm of his hand. "Of course. Everson used to visit her at night. So her husband had to work nights. Probably a swing shift."

"Probably. That left us with three names."

"So we go talk to them?"

"No. I've narrowed the list down to one."

"One?"

"If I'm right, and if this woman were somehow involved in Everson's death, she would've had to be able to persuade a Korean man, this mysterious Mr. Kim, to take the risk of approaching Miss Tae and Choi Yong-kuang and paying them to commit murder."

"So she'd have to have a helluva a lot of influence over him."

"Right," I answered. "A helluva lot."

Ernie glanced again at the three names. "Two of these women don't work at all. What are they going to do? Offer their house-boys a pile of money to have somebody killed?"

I nodded. "But the third . . . "

Ernie whistled. "Big money," he said.

The third entry was Gladys Hackburn, the wife of Colonel Orin Hackburn. She had her own career, a good one. Her current position was contracting officer for the 8th Army Procurement and Facilities Office. She was a woman who made the final decision on the disbursement of millions of US taxpayer dollars to local construction contractors.

She was a woman with power.

Before we approached Gladys Hackburn, I made a few discreet inquiries at the 8th Army Procurement Office. The biggest contract currently under construction was a Top Secret Signal Intelligence Facility actually being built into the side of a mountain south of Seoul. The dollar figures involved were staggering, and the Korean contractor with the most at risk was a wealthy businessman named Roh Ji-yun. From his background security check folder, I pulled his black-and-white mug shot. That afternoon I made a phone call, and a few minutes later Ernie and I drove our Army jeep out to the same teahouse where we had met Miss Tae before. She was already waiting.

When I pulled out the photo of Roh Ji-yun, her eyes popped wide.

"That's him," she said. "Mr. Kim."

She was so impressed that Ernie almost convinced her to spend the rest of the afternoon with him at a nearby inn. I frustrated his plans.

"We have work to do," I told him.

Ernie pouted.

Miss Tae merely seemed amused.

We found Roh Ji-yun at one of his construction sites. He wore expensive slacks, a silk tie, and a white shirt with the sleeves rolled up. An orange hardhat balanced atop his big square head.

When I told him what we suspected, his face turned crimson and spittle erupted from fleshy lips.

The punch was a surprise. Most Koreans swear a lot when they're angry, but usually they don't hit.

I managed to dodge the blow, and then three of his assistants were on him, holding him back. He continued to curse in Korean, Ernie hurling epithets in English. It was obvious to me that we weren't going to coax much information out of him.

But for now we had enough.

At the 8th Army Procurement Office, Gladys Hackburn's secretary kept us cooling our heels for almost twenty minutes. Finally we were allowed to enter the inner sanctum.

She sat at a large teak desk, the flags of the United States and the Republic of Korea draped behind her. She wore a powder blue business suit, and her reddish hair was cut short and curled up in a wave that framed a youngish-looking oval face. When she stood to shake our hands, I could see that she maintained her figure at least as well as had the late Captain Richard Everson.

She smiled brightly.

An intelligent woman. A caring woman. A woman willing to help.

"What brings the CID to the Army Procurement Office?" she asked.

Instead of answering, I tossed the black-and-white glossy of

Roh Ji-yun onto her desk. A puzzled frown crossed her face. She glanced down at the photo but leaned back slightly as if she were afraid to touch it.

"You had him follow Captain Everson," I said. "To set him up for murder."

She stood perfectly still for a moment. Ernie and I both held our breath, wondering if she'd break down or tear the photo up or start screaming at us and call the MPs to escort us out of her office.

She did none of those things. Instead she sat down slowly and interlaced her well-manicured fingers atop the varnished surface of her desk as if composing herself to make a speech in front of the Parent-Teachers Association. She cleared her throat and then spoke.

"I loathed him," she said, "for what he did to me. The lies he told me. The promises he made about our future together." She shook her head as if trying to rid herself of a bad dream. "But we had no future together. He was just using me."

"So things didn't work out," I said. "And the plan to pay some-one to kill Everson slowly grew in your mind. But you weren't sure if it would work. So you followed, to make sure the job was completed. And when you saw him lying there in that alley and you were all alone and the ice pick was lying beside him . . ."

"Yes," she said calmly, staring directly into my eyes. "I killed him. I picked up the ice pick, and I stabbed it into his heart. And what's more," she said, her face as smooth as polished stone, "I'd do it again."

It took a while for the paperwork to be completed at 8th Army, translated, and then formally transmitted to the Korean National Police. It took even longer for the KNPs to send their report to the judge in charge of the Everson case. So long, in fact, that they almost hanged Choi Yong-kung for the murder of Cap-tain Richard Everson despite the fact that we had a confession from Ms. Gladys Hackburn.

Finally, though, a few hours before the sentence was to be

carried out, Choi was released from prison. His mother was there to greet him, of course, along with Miss Tae.

When the sun went down, Ernie and I made our way to Itaewon. We were ensconced on our usual barstools in our usual club in the heart of the nightclub district. The band had just taken their break when Choi Yong-kuang's mother tugged on my shirtsleeve.

This time she didn't pull me off the barstool, but I turned around anyway.

Everyone watched. The bartenders, the waitresses, the business girls and even the GIs, because they were aware of the man who'd been spared from hanging this morning.

Choi Yong-kuang's mother didn't speak. Head bowed, she held three sticks of burning incense in front of the billowing folds of her red silk Korean dress. She knelt to the floor, leaned forward, and lowered her head three times to the dirty tile.

It was sort of embarrassing. Ernie tried to laugh it off. I kept a straight face. For decorum's sake, mainly, but also so no one would notice the pressure building in my eyes.

THE FILIAL WIFE

Before dawn on the last day of her life, Mrs. Yi Won-suk rose from her sleeping mat beside her husband, washed her face, and slid back the oil-papered front door of her home. She stepped out into her plot of about one-half *pyong* in which she had been tending twelve rows of *peichu*, the thick-leafed cabbage that the people of Korea soak in brine and use as the prime ingredient in *kimchee*, their spicy national dish.

After her husband rose and trudged off to his fields, Mrs. Yi's daughter, Myong-son, wiped her sleepy four-year-old eyes and joined her mother in the field, making a pretense of holding a flickering candle so her mother could see more clearly as she slashed at the bases of the fat green cabbages.

As dawn broke behind Palgong Mountain, Mrs. Yi continued to work, tossing the heavy heads of *peichu* into her wooden cart. After she'd plucked all the ripe leafy vegetables from the earth, she took Myong-song by the hand and together they washed and changed into freshly pressed skirts and woolen blouses and bright red head scarves.

Myong-son climbed atop the pile of *peichu*, Mrs. Yi grabbed the handle of the cart, and together they walked through the first glimmerings of golden sunrise in the Land of the Morning Calm, heading for the produce market in the city of Taegu.

Today, mid-November by the Western calendar, marked the

beginning of *kimjang*, that time of year when Korean house-wives buy large piles of ripe *peichu* and prepare enough cabbage *kimchee* to last throughout the cold winter. Sales in Taegu were expected to be good. Mrs. Yi needed the money to supplement the earnings she and her husband made from the backbreaking work of tending their rented field of rice and soybean.

As Mrs. Yi and Myong-song entered the outskirts of Taegu, three-wheeled trucks and early morning taxicabs swished by on the narrow strip of blacktop that was the main road leading into the city from the west. Straddling the entranceway to the Taegu Market stood a huge wooden arch with fancy lettering welcoming one and all. Mrs. Yi pushed her cart past enormous glass tanks full of wriggling mackerel, past rows of snorting pigs and honking geese, and piled rolls of wool and cotton and silk. The entire market area was laid out like a giant squid in the center of the city of Taegu, with overhanging balconies and eaves and lean-tos made of canvas and bamboo blocking out the sun. Mrs. Yi finally jostled her way through the crowd until she reached the produce area and the stall of the mother-in-law of her husband's second cousin. The elderly woman smiled and greeted Mrs. Yi and hugged Myong-song and soon enough space was cleared on the raised plywood platform. Mrs. Yi piled her iridescent green cabbages alongside mounds of round pears and red persimmons and jumbled green beans and all the earthly bounty that the fertile southern valleys of Korea offer in such abundance.

Myong-song played, the women chatted, Mrs. Yi sold most of her cabbage at a good price, and for the last day of her life they tell me she was happy.

My partner, Ernie Bascom, held the photograph up toward fluorescent light. His lips were pursed and there was no apparent emotion on his face. Behind the round lenses of his wire-rimmed glasses, however, his green eyes glowed.

"Nice chest on her," Ernie said finally.

Mrs. Yi Won-suk, like many petite Korean women, was about as flat-chested as it is possible to be. Still, she was beautiful. The photo was taken at a resort area. She stood by the shore of the Naktong River, vamping with some of her girlfriends on an outing just before she was married some five years ago. Her face was calm and unblemished, with full lips and a smoothly rounded nose and eyes that were bright and cheerful. Her legs were straight and the calves, revealed by a short skirt, were full and round.

Ernie and I had been flown down to Taegu by chopper, mainly because the 8th Army provost marshal was worried that once the Korean newspapers got wind of what had happened to Mrs. Yi, the proverbial waste would be splattered all over the Korean tabloids.

I took the photograph out of Ernie's hand and slid it into the neat dossier that the Taegu detachment of the Korean National Police had prepared.

Our host was Lieutenant Rhee Han-yong. He'd picked us up at the military helipad and transported us over here in a police van, sirens blaring, until we reached this red brick police headquarters building in the heart of downtown Taegu.

Lieutenant Rhee pulled out a pack of cigarettes, Turtleboat brand, and offered one to me and then Ernie. We both declined. Lieutenant Rhee had the weathered face of a cop who'd spent many years standing on a round platform directing traffic. Now he directed a homicide squad. Smoke swirled past his flat nose, causing him to squint.

"GI," he told us. "Must be. Other foreigners live in Taegu we already check."

"They had alibis?" Ernie asked.

"Yes. Alibi. Good alibi. Very good."

"What kind of alibis?" I asked.

"Two Peace Corps workers. That day they take go mountain somewhere. Also five priests. How you say? *Chondu-kyo.*"

"Catholic," I said.

He nodded. "Yes. Catholic. Everybody say they inside church that day."

Taegu is a city of about a hundred thousand people. It sits in the central valley of South Korea and is responsible for more than half the country's output of exportable produce. Few foreigners live in Taegu because there are few business opportunities. The big industrialized capital of Seoul gobbles up most of those, along with the dynamic seaport of Pusan to the south.

That meant that the main source of foreigners living in Taegu was the US Army compound, Camp Henry, headquarters for the 19th Support Group. I'd already checked before Ernie and I left Seoul. Camp Henry was home to about fifteen hundred GIs. A decent-sized pond for a criminal to swim in.

Forensic science is not the most highly developed art in Korea. In fact, it has not developed very well here at all. Why? Because with the Park Chung-hee government firmly in power and the Cold War raging and President Nixon and now President Ford providing total backing to the Park regime, the Korean National Police enjoy the luxury of solving crimes with methods more traditional than forensic.

A judiciously employed rubber hose is one example. A sucker punch to the stomach another. But in this case those crude techniques wouldn't do much good.

No suspect was in custody.

Why were the KNPs so sure that the perpetrator had been a foreigner? Two pieces of evidence: the semen and the pubic hair. The semen showed a blood type of O positive, extremely rare amongst the ancient and largely homogenous tribe that occupies the Korean Peninsula. And the pubic hair was obviously Caucasian. Short, curly, light brown.

Because of this evidence, the Korean National Police had requested our presence to help them find the GI who had raped and murdered Mrs. Yi Won-suk.

When a married woman is violated and then strangled, right

in front of her four-year-old daughter, it is bad enough. When that unspeakably hideous crime is perpetrated by a foreigner, it becomes intolerable. The KNPs would go to any lengths to nab the killer. But their long arm didn't reach into the inviolable sanctuaries of US Army compounds.

That's where Ernie and I came in.

"I need to see the site," I told Lieutenant Rhee.

"You no go check compound?"

"We'll check the compound and we'll find the GI who did this. But first I see the site."

Ernie nodded his agreement.

Lieutenant Rhee glanced back and forth between us, not liking the idea. Finally, he sighed and stubbed out his cigarette. As he stood to his full height, he straightened his wrinkled khaki uniform and said, "*Kapshida*." Let's go.

Lieutenant Rhee, like most Korean cops, didn't want the 8th Army CID interfering in his operation. What he wanted us to do was the same thing the powers that be here in Korea wanted US military police to do. Control GIs. Slap them down when they became unruly and particularly when their wild ways caused grief to Korean civilians.

Not that the Korean government wanted us gone. Quite the contrary. Communists on the northern side of the Demilitarized Zone were massively equipped by the Soviet Bloc, fielding a standing army of over seven hundred thousand soldiers. South Korea's army could hold the northern troops off for a while, but in a prolonged conflict, the naval and air support of the US would prove indispensable.

The Koreans needed us here for their very survival.

But sometimes those of us assigned to defend their country—especially young GIs far away from home and far away from everything that made them civilized—could prove to be a royal pain in the butt. Like when they became drunk and unruly and brawled with whomever happened to be in their way. Or when they drove their tanks and their armored vehicles too fast through sleepy, straw-thatched-hut villages. Or when they treated Korean women as if they were dolls to be toyed with and then discarded.

We ducked through a rickety wooden gate and entered a small courtyard. Earthen jars, probably filled with winter *kimchee*, lined the wall to the right. On the left, chicken wire housed a skinny white rooster who was busy scratching the earth. Flagstone steps led to a raised wooden platform that served as the floor of the hooch. In front of the sliding door sat an old woman. The neighbor, Lieutenant Rhee told me, and the first person to hear the four-year-old Myong-song when she burnt her hand and started wailing.

I nodded to the old woman. With sad, wrinkled eyes, she nodded back.

Next to her, leaning against a pedestal, was a large photograph of Yi Won-suk bordered in black. In front of the photo stood a short bronze incense holder.

Cops at a murder site are not expected to participate in ritual behavior. I could tell by his body posture that Lieutenant Rhee wanted me to keep moving. But rules had been broken here. The KNPs had allowed this old woman to set up this shrine to the dead not more than a few feet from a police crime scene. The KNPs had let their own rules be broken not only out of respect for the dead but also because of the age of this mourner. Old grandpas with poor eyesight can totter across busy intersections in Seoul, against the red light, and cops with whistles will stop traffic and make sure that younger drivers swerve safely around the old man. To ticket a venerable elder for jaywalking would be considered the height of impropriety.

And no one had the heart to shoo away this old woman.

Ernie was already slipping off his loafers in front of the raised floor, but I didn't join him. Instead, I approached the old woman, bowed, and spoke in Korean. "I'm very sorry for your trouble, Grandmother."

She cackled. Surprised to hear a foreigner speak the tongue of the gods.

"No trouble for me," she answered. "Trouble for the young Mrs. Yi. And more trouble for her husband. And for their child, Myong-song."

"Yes. For my country's part in this, we are greatly ashamed."

"Good for you. But don't waste your breath on a foolish old woman."

"Did you see the man who did this, Grandmother?"

"No. I heard Mrs. Yi return from the market and push her cart through the gate, but after that nothing. Apparently Myong-song was asleep from the long ride home. All was quiet, so I went about my business until about an hour later. Then I heard Myong-song scream."

"And you came over here?"

"Yes. Myong-song was a quiet child. I'd never heard her scream before. I found her in the kitchen. Apparently her mother had taken a pot of warm water off the charcoal brazier, but she must've been interrupted because she left the flame exposed. Myong-song reached in and burnt her hand."

"And her mother?"

"In the back room." The old woman shook her head. "Don't ask me more. That young policeman knows everything."

I thanked the old woman, slipped off my shoes, and stepped into the silent home.

The front room was wallpapered but barely furnished. Only a small wooden chest with brass fittings and a stack of sleeping mats and folded blankets sat neatly against the wall. The floor beneath my feet was still warm. Apparently, the old neighbor woman had been good enough to change the charcoal for the heating flues that ran beneath the stone foundation. The late Mrs. Yi must've been a good housekeeper. The floor's vinyl covering was scrubbed immaculately clean.

We entered the kitchen. Pots and pans hung from the wooden rafters. No sign of struggle. Only an open charcoal brazier that had now died out. The metal lid had not been replaced. Surely the old woman was right. When Mrs. Yi Won-suk pulled the pan of hot water off the open charcoal flame, someone must've jumped her from behind. Someone huge. Overpowering. She wouldn't have had a chance to struggle. Yet someone who was stealthy enough to tiptoe past the sliding door and across the vinyl-floored front room without being heard. Or if she had heard him, maybe Mrs. Yi thought it was her husband returning early from the fields.

We entered the back room, where Mrs. Yi had been taken. Again, no sign of struggle. A small table in the corner with a mirror, bottles and jars of ointments and lotions, all undisturbed. Maybe the man had threatened Mrs. Yi with a knife. Or worse, threatened to hurt her daughter.

Lieutenant Rhee pointed to the center of the floor.

"The body was found here," he said in Korean. I translated for Ernie.

Then he told us that her skirt had been pulled up, her long underpants and leggings ripped off, and that the doctor who examined her corpse found enough tearing in her small body to conclude that she'd been violated forcibly by a powerful man.

Lieutenant Rhee pointed to his own neck. Bruises, he told us, had formed a line beneath the curve of Mrs. Yi's delicate jaw.

For the next two days, our work at Camp Henry was routine. After a while Ernie and I started to feel like a couple of personnel clerks. The officer corps was under orders to account for the whereabouts of every soldier in every unit under their command on the afternoon of the murder. Hundreds of soldiers were eliminated almost immediately because if there's one thing the army's good at it's keeping track of GIs. Support activities are what soldiers do on Camp Henry, so Ernie and I spent a lot of time making phone calls to ensure a truck convoy had actually reached its destination or that a piece of communications equipment had actually been repaired on the day in question.

Our progress was rapid. We were scratching off whole blocks of names and narrowing down our suspects to a short list. We didn't stop with the enlisted men, we also checked on the officers and even the three or four dozen US civilians employed on the base. The entire process became more and more exciting as each and every alibi was checked and the list grew smaller and smaller. Finally, at the end of the second day, Ernie and I compared notes. To our horror, we obtained the one result that neither of us had expected.

Everybody had an alibi.

We sat in stunned silence for a while, drinking the dregs of the overcooked coffee in the pot in the small office we'd been assigned.

Finally, Ernie spoke. "How the hell are we going to break this to Eighth Army?"

"I don't know," I said. "The Korean newspapers have been all over it."

The original thought that only the Korean tabloids would carry the story of the sordid murder of Mrs. Yi Won-suk had long since gone by the boards. Koreans have an affinity for the simple country life. Even though nowadays they work in high-rise office buildings or fly back and forth to Saudi Arabian oilfields or cut deals with Swiss bankers, they still think of themselves as the pure and virtuous agrarian people that their ancestors had once been. Mrs. Yi was so attractive, her surviving daughter Myong-song so charming, and her husband so stalwart and brave that the heart of the country had been drawn to their little family. The biggest newspapers in the country had run her photograph on the front page. Television reporters had produced specials on her, showing the craggy peaks and streams near her home. Some of them had even tried to talk to Ernie and me, but so far we'd managed to avoid them.

Finally, Ernie and I decided to do what we always do when we don't have a plan. We locked up the office, strode outside the gate of Camp Henry, and headed toward neon.

When I woke up, I didn't know where I was.

What I did know was that my stomach was churning and my head ached and my bladder was so full that I was afraid to move. Finally I did move. I threw a silk-lined comforter off my body, rolled over onto a warm *ondol* floor, and slowly rose to my feet. I was in a rectangular room not much bigger than a closet. I found my clothes and threw them on and pulled back the sliding door, stepped out onto a narrow wooden porch, and squatted down and put on my shoes. The courtyard wasn't much bigger than the room I'd been sleeping in. The sky was overcast and a light sheen of drizzle filled the sky. Quickly, I stepped across moist brick to the *byonso* on the other side of the tiny courtyard.

After I relieved myself, a woman with a pocked face, hair in mad disarray and a cotton robe wrapped tightly about her slim body, stood in the center of the courtyard waiting for me. I had no idea who she was.

She told me. I gave her the money that I had apparently promised her the night before, and I left.

Back at the temporary billets at Camp Henry, I showered, shaved, and changed into clean clothes. Still Ernie hadn't arrived. He was probably passed out somewhere in a hooch behind the bar district. I didn't have time to wait for him.

The night before, somewhere in our mad swirl from bar to bar, an idea had come to me. There was something I'd missed back at the murder site. I wasn't sure what it was but I had convinced myself that there had to be something.

Without bothering with breakfast, I strode over to the Camp Henry main gate, and once outside, I waved down a kimchee cab.

Three miles outside of Taegu, I told the driver to slow down. A few homes lined the right side of the road. Behind them were steeply sloping hills, spattered on the lower elevations with a few clumps of pear trees. On the other side of the road stretched many acres of rice and bean fields. Already, men wearing straw hats and with their pants rolled up to their knees were out there working, even in this foreboding overcast.

I saw the home of Mrs. Yi Won-suk and told the driver to slow down. We cruised past. I studied the home. Quiet. Next door, smoke rose from the narrow chimney of the old woman who had been the first to arrive on the murder scene.

I thought about what it would be like for an American in this area.

If he took a cab like I was doing now, he could cruise past the homes along the street and not be observed. Lieutenant Rhee and the Korean National Police had interviewed every cab driver in Taegu—Korean cabbies are used to providing information to the police—but no one had come forward and admitted to hauling a foreigner to this area on the afternoon of the murder. It was possible that someone was lying or had forgotten, but I doubted it. Koreans in general were upset about this case and wanted to solve it. That would include cab drivers.

The other possibility was that the foreigner had come here on foot. Or on bicycle. But either way he would've been noticed. Foreigners stay near the compound or in downtown Taegu. They have no reason to come out here to this agrarian suburb. And the road leading from town is lined with car washes, auto repair shops, noodle restaurants, and any number of curious proprietors who would've noticed a big-nosed foreigner walking or peddling by. The KNPs had interviewed them all and come up with nothing.

So how did a foreigner arrive in this neighborhood unobserved? And how had he managed to case the home which held Mrs. Yi Won-suk and her daughter? How had he known that she was alone? Surmise? Maybe. He would've guessed that her husband would be at work in the fields. Maybe taking that chance was part of the thrill.

That still didn't tell me how he'd arrived unobserved.

And then it hit me. The obvious: by POV.

POV. One of those cherished military acronyms. This one means Privately Owned Vehicle. Not a military vehicle. Most GIs aren't allowed to own a POV. You have to leave your car in the States when you're transferred to Korea. But some high-ranking NCOs and officers, mostly in Seoul, are authorized to have POVs. So are civilians.

But the whereabouts of the NCOs and officers and civilians at Camp Henry had already been accounted for. Of course there could be holes in those alibis. Someone might be lying or some-one might be covering up for a buddy. To expose that would take more digging. A lot more digging.

By now we'd traveled about a half mile beyond Mrs. Yi's home. The cab driver asked me where I wanted to go. I told him to turn around and drive slowly back toward town.

Were there possible suspects other than the foreigners sta-tioned at Camp Henry? Could someone have been driving out here in a POV and just by chance have spotted the attractive Mrs. Yi entering her home? After all, this road leads from Taegu up north to Taejon, the home of another US military base, Camp Ames.

But how would that work? Okay, so the guy's cruising along, he spots Mrs. Yi, maybe he slows down to follow her. He even turns around, and then he spots her entering her home, push-ing her cart through the gate with her daughter, Myong-song, inside. Nobody opening the gate for her. Nobody greeting her.

She's home alone.

But then what does he do? If he parks the car along this road he'd have been spotted. Somebody would've remembered him. Foreigners are a rarity in this area. Who knows? Somebody might've even gone outside and waited for him by his car so they could practice their conversational English. Koreans do that all the time. It's considered a friendly gesture. But nothing like that had happened. Lieutenant Rhee and his men had checked. Everyone along this road from here to Taegu had been interviewed.

They'd seen nothing.

So what had the guy done?

I told the cabbie to stop. Up above Mrs. Yi's home loomed a cliff covered with shrubs and tufts of long grass. I pointed and asked the cabbie if there was a way up there.

We'd have to follow the road we were on back into town, he told me, and then another road that led back to the top of that hill.

"Is it a seldom-used road?" I asked him. "One that's hard to find?"

He shrugged. "Anyone who drives around here knows about it."

I told him to show me.

Ten minutes later the cab pulled into an open area atop a hill. The space was used, he said, for parking on weekends when filial descendents paid homage to their dearly departed.

I paid him and climbed out of the taxi. More gently rolling hills spread behind me and away from the city of Taegu. Each was dotted with tombstones and small mounds.

A graveyard. Koreans bury their dead sitting upright, so they can maintain a view of the world around them. On weekends families come up here with picnic lunches, sit near the mounds, eat, talk, laugh, and try to make the dead person feel that the family hasn't forgotten them.

The cabbie asked me if I wanted him to wait. I told him no thanks. As he sped off I glanced down the hill in the direction of the city. Below spread a perfect view of the road we had been on and the home of Mrs. Yi Won-suk.

First I examined the parking lot. Nothing. Then I walked down the hill. It was an easy walk because a pathway had been cut by ten thousand footsteps. Soon I was behind the other homes in the area and no curious eyes peeked out to spy on me. A minute later, I stood in front of the open gate of the home of Mrs. Yi Won-suk.

That's how it must've happened. He'd cruised by on the main

road, seen Mrs. Yi entering the gate that led to her courtyard, driven up to park atop the hill, and then walked down here.

But who had the time during the middle of a workday? And who had a vehicle dispatched for his personal use? Not any GI at Camp Henry. The murderer had to be someone who owned a POV. Maybe he wasn't from Camp Henry at all. Maybe he'd been traveling. An inspection team from 8th Army? Not likely. They travel in groups.

Someone with his own POV, traveling the back roads of Korea. A happy wanderer.

That's when it hit me. A salesman. Insurance. That was it. They wandered from one military installation to another selling their wares. Like camp followers.

I walked back to the road in a state of excitement, dying to tell Ernie what I'd come up with. I had to wait twenty minutes until another cab cruised by.

You'd think that an unmarried GI with one hundred percent health insurance and free dental and a hundred thousand dollars' worth of cheap Serviceman's Group Life wouldn't need another insurance policy. And they don't. But life insurance salesmen somehow managed, every day, to convince young American GIs that they do. It's a legitimate product. In fact, before an insurance salesman is allowed access to one of 8th Army's compounds, he and his company have to be vetted by the Judge Advocate General's Office. Any policy they sell to a GI must contain a clause that his life insurance is still valid if he's unexpectedly shipped out to a combat zone. Most of the big companies have no problem with this. GIs are young and healthy and the odds are that not many of them are going to die soon.

So it's a profitable market.

Once Ernie and I returned to Seoul, I checked with JAG and was surprised to discover that there were over thirty certified life insurance agents operating amongst the fifty US military compounds in the Republic of Korea. Every one of them owned a POV.

Once we had a list, it was a matter of straight police work eliminating those with alibis. We didn't approach them directly but rather pretended to be potential customers and asked for the agents who served the Taegu area. Most of them didn't. Seoul and the area north to the Demilitarized Zone are where most young GIs can be found. Down south there are relatively slim pickings. None of the agents actually kept a home base there. But we found of the seven US insurance companies operating in-country, six of them had agents who traveled to Taegu periodically. We were able to establish that four of the agents had been in Seoul at the time of the murder of Mrs. Yi Won-suk. The other two had been traveling in the southern area of the country, covering the bases in Taejon, Waegwan, Taegu, and Pusan. Of those two, one insurance agent was a black man. The other was a Caucasian male with light brown hair and blood type O positive.

We had our man.

The bust was made with the assistance of the Korean National Police. Lieutenant Rhee from Taegu traveled all the way up here to Seoul for the honor of arresting the man who had caused such an uproar in the Korean media.

His name was Fred Ammerman. He lived in the outskirts of Seoul in a cement-block apartment complex in Bampo, just south of the Han River. His wife, a Korean national, was absolutely flabbergasted by the proceedings, but she knew enough not to interfere with the Korean National Police. Ammerman was a man of average height and average weight, except for the potbelly that protruded over the waistline of his tailored slacks. He remained calm while the Korean police handcuffed him and while Lieutenant Rhee told him in broken English that they were taking him in for questioning.

Ammerman did glance at us hopefully and say, "What about Eighth Army?"

"We have no jurisdiction over you, Ammerman," Ernie said. "This is between you and the ROKs."

As a civilian in country on a work visa, military law couldn't touch him.

After the KNPs took Ammerman away, I spoke to his wife for a few moments. She was a husky Korean woman, taller and stronger than Mrs. Yi Won-suk had been, but with attractive facial features that softened the pronounced bone structure beneath the flesh. She stared into the distance as she spoke.

"My children are both at school," she said. "For that I am happy."

"Did you know what he was doing on those trips?" I asked her.

"I knew he had women. That I know long time. But take woman like that. Punch her. Kill her. That I don't know."

But there seemed little doubt in Mrs. Ammerman's mind that the charges were true.

Already a crowd of neighbors was beginning to gather outside on the sidewalk. Mrs. Ammerman glanced toward them and, with a worried look, started clawing at her lower lip. After they'd arrested her foreign husband, the Korean cops had shown no concern about Mrs. Ammerman at all. They didn't question her because a wife is not expected to offer any evidence that might hurt her husband. And they certainly weren't concerned about her mental state. By now, Ernie was outside, leaning against his jeep, waiting for me, chewing gum.

"Is there anyone I can call?" I asked. "A friend or relative who can be with you?"

She glanced at me as if awakening from a dream. "Don't worry. Pretty soon they come. Everybody come. I no can stop them."

I left her and walked out to the jeep.

Once Ammerman was in custody, the evidence against him piled up fast. They tested his blood just to make sure that the medical records Ernie and I had checked earlier were correct. He was in fact O positive. And they matched his body hair by microscopic analysis with the pubic hairs found at the murder site of Mrs. Yi Won-suk. A perfect match. Also, Ammerman had no convincing alibi for his whereabouts on the day of the murder, but he took a hard line and chose not to speak to the Korean National Police. This was tough to do since they have their way of convincing you that it would be in your interest to answer their questions. But Ammerman gutted it out and kept mum.

His insurance company dropped him like a bad habit. But Ammerman did have savings and the word we received from the KNPs was that Ammerman was hiring some American lawyer from Honolulu who'd worked on foreign cases before. Not smart. The Koreans considered this move to be an insult to Korean lawyers and the Korean judicial system in general. The better move would've been to plead guilty and express great remorse and ask the court for leniency.

In fact, the Korean government would've been glad to give it. After a few months, a few years at the most, in a Korean jail, they would've shuffled him quietly out of the country. A face-saving gesture to assuage Korean public opinion. But if Ammerman fought them, they'd have to fight back to save face for the Korean judicial system and Korean pride and then they'd have to lay a sentence on him more commensurate with the enormity of his crime. Which was murder, after all, of an innocent woman. The Korean government didn't want to do this. They didn't want any publicity in the American press that would be adverse toward Korea and that might, in the long run, drive a wedge between the United States and Korea and jeopardize the long-standing security arrangements that held those seven hundred thousand Communist North Korean soldiers at bay. And even more importantly, the Korean government didn't dare damage the steady stream of American dollars that flowed from the US Treasury to the Korean government in the form of both economic and military assistance.

But not realizing this, Ammerman was taking a tough stance. He was refusing to cooperate with the Korean National Police, refusing to admit his guilt, and just in general pissing everybody off.

All of this would've been his problem if it hadn't been for the woman who appeared in the provost marshal's office two days before the scheduled start date of Ammerman's trial.

The woman was his wife, Mrs. Mi-hwa Ammerman.

Colonel Harkins, the current provost marshal of the 8th United States Army, didn't want to talk to her. However, he could recognize potential trouble when he saw it, so he let her into his office. Her English wasn't the greatest so I was called in for two reasons: I could speak enough Korean to translate and I was familiar with the case.

When I sat down, Mrs. Ammerman started in on me in rapid-fire Korean. I interrupted her and slowed her down several times and, as best I could, I translated for the colonel. The gist of her complaint was, the Korean National Police wouldn't allow her to talk to her husband.

Did her husband want to talk to her?

No. He had flatly refused and the KNPs wouldn't force him.

What she hoped to do was to convince her husband to plead guilty. Since the case had hit the newspapers and the television, everyone in the country had turned against her. That wasn't so bad, for herself she didn't care. But her children had been teased unmercifully at school and her oldest son, age twelve, had actually been beaten by a pack of older boys. So much disruption had been caused that the authorities at Seoul International School had asked Mrs. Ammerman to withdraw her children from the student body. With no money coming in, she would have to send her children to the Korean public schools. That would be a disaster. Not only were her children half-American, which was usually enough reason for harassment, but their father was a rapist and a murderer.

"I can't get a visa to go to the States," Mrs. Ammerman told me. "I am a Korean citizen, so are my children. My husband never had any interest in applying for US citizenship for us."

She leaned toward Colonel Harkins, still speaking Korean to him, with me translating.

"Even my older brother has had trouble. Everyone shuns him because of me, and now he's been fired from his job. No Korean company wants anyone whose sister was foolish enough to marry an American. Especially an American killer."

Then she started to cry.

I finished explaining everything she said to Colonel Harkins. He spread his hands and asked, "What does she want us to do?"

"What I want you to do," she said, "is force the Korean police to let me talk to my husband. I will convince him to plead guilty. Then my children's lives will be returned to them. We will have our face back. People will respect their father for at least having repented of his crimes. We will be pitied but we will be tolerated. And my brother, he will have a chance to beg for forgiveness for having such a foolish sister and he will have a chance to get his job back."

What she said made sense. In Korean society, once you plead guilty and ask for forgiveness, no matter how heinous your crime, you will usually receive at least some measure of leniency. When the criminal offers atonement, all is well again under Heaven and the King is secure on his throne. At that point, not to grant the request for forgiveness would mean that the person turning down the request is not a person of true Confucian virtue. As the Koreans would say, he wouldn't be showing a big heart.

Eighth Army would also be pleased if Ammerman pleaded guilty. Although he wasn't a soldier, we had sponsored his insurance company and his work visa, and his crime tainted the reputation of every American in Korea. A long, drawn-out criminal trial wouldn't help anyone.

The provost marshal was new in-country and the intricate dance of Korean justice he still found baffling. But he did know from every conversation he had over drinks at the Officers' Club that 8th Army wanted this prosecution iced. He turned to me. "What can we do, Sueño?"

I thought about it. "I'll talk to the KNP Liaison Officer. If you throw your weight behind it, we should be able to force our way in to talk to Ammerman."

The provost marshal nodded his consent.

Mrs. Mi-hwa Ammerman rose from her chair, her leather handbag clasped tightly in front of her black skirt. Then she bowed gracefully at the waist.

Colonel Harkins didn't know quite what to do so he just cleared his throat and nodded.

With ramparts of hewn rock and a roof of upturned tile shingles, Suwon Prison looks medieval. Built during the Yi Dyansty, it had later been used by the Japanese Imperial Army when they colonized Korea prior to World War II. After the surrender of Japan, the United States provisional government took over, and now the Republic of Korea runs the place with all the efficiency that a military-dominated government can bring to bear.

A uniformed guard led Mi-hwa Ammerman and me down cold stone steps. At the bottom of three flights, a light was switched on, and down a long corridor another guard waited in front of a thick wooden door. Our footsteps clattered on wet brick.

In front of the door, Mrs. Ammerman tiptoed to peek through the grated opening. I peered in from behind her. The guard clicked another switch and the cell was suffused with light.

Fred Ammerman stood a few feet from us, his beard long, his blue eyes bloodshot and wild.

"What do you want?" His voice rasped like the hinges of ancient doors.

At first his wife just cried. The guards and I stepped back to allow them some privacy. A few minutes went by. They whispered to one another through the rusted bars. I could make out some of what they were saying, but I tried to block it out. I didn't want to eavesdrop. All this was their personal business. Not mine. As a law enforcement officer, I wasn't officially involved.

The result we wanted, the conviction of Fred Ammerman for rape and murder, was a foregone conclusion. No Korean judge would dare set him free.

A voice began to rise—Fred Ammerman's, not his wife's. While he shouted, she stepped back against the stone wall. He kept up the tirade. Soon she knelt down, cowering, and made herself small. One of the guards had heard enough. He marched down the passageway and gruffly told Mrs. Ammerman that it was time to go.

As I walked her up the steps, her husband continued shouting.

"No way am I going to plead guilty," he said. And then he added a few epithets that, in my opinion, Mi-hwa Ammerman didn't deserve.

On the day of Fred Ammerman's trial for the rape and murder of Yi Won-suk, both Ernie and I wore our Class A green uniforms. We sat on polished wooden benches in the Hall of the Ministry of Justice in the heart of downtown Taegu. Mrs. Ammerman sat quietly in the first row directly behind her husband. Neither of her children was present.

The American lawyer Ammerman had hired was named Aaron Murakami. He was from Hawaii and when he spoke, a Korean translator hired for the occasion would interpret whatever he said.

How could Ammerman be so dumb? I had no reason to think that Murakami wasn't a good attorney, but he was Japanese-American. The Koreans are still chafing over what the Japanese Imperial Army had done to them during the thirty-five years leading up to the end of World War II. A foreign lawyer was bad enough, but a Japanese lawyer would cause the Koreans to dig in their heels. If Ammerman was toast before, he was burnt ashes now. Even Ernie realized the mistake. When Murakami walked into the hall, Ernie smiled smugly and crossed his arms.

"It's over already," he said.

In a Korean courtroom there's no jury. Only a grim-faced

judge who, in this case, stared on at us mere mortals through thick-lensed bifocals.

The judge droned on in Korean, something about the initial plea, but I could follow little of what was said. My facility with the Korean language started with the free classes that the Army offers on base, but after that most of it was picked up in barroom conversation. The legalese the judge spouted was beyond me.

Ernie and I didn't expect to be called to the stand until the trial was well underway. That would probably be late morning or mid-afternoon. Koreans don't believe in long, drawn-out proceedings. It's up to the police to capture the guilty party. After that, to spend a lot of time and effort and taxpayers' money just to find that same person innocent would be a great loss of face. Not only for the police but also for the entire Korean judicial system.

Ammerman would be tried—and almost certainly convicted —today.

Suddenly, I realized that the judge was speaking English. Even Ernie perked up. The language was halting, as if the judge didn't have too many chances to practice his conversational skills, but the syntax was precise. Not the bargirl talk I was used to.

Fred Ammerman, whose head had been hanging down, sat up and listened. So did his attorney.

"I want to be sure," the judge said, "that you fully understand what is being offered. You have a chance, before we go to trial, to plead guilty."

I understood the choice Ammerman had to make, even if he didn't. The Koreans don't plea bargain. You either plead guilty and have a chance of being shown mercy, or you plead innocent and face the full wrath of the law. The judge continued to talk, glancing sometimes at Aaron Murakami, sometimes at Fred Ammerman. He continued until he was sure that both men understood the gravity of the decision they were about to make.

When the judge finished, Murakami and Ammerman huddled and whispered fervently to one another.

Mi-hwa Ammerman, sitting in back of her husband, had previously kept her face lowered. No she looked up hopefully, as if she wanted to climb over the railing and insert herself between her husband and his attorney.

Fred Ammerman kept shaking his head.

His wife stared at him in despair. Her hand lifted from her mouth as if she wanted to reach out to him. Only by a plea of guilty would Fred Ammerman's family be allowed to reenter Korean society—not completely free of stigma but at least free of having to bear the burden of shame of being related to a killer and, even worse, of being related to an unrepentant killer. One who has not only defiled society but then proceeded to spit in society's eye.

Neither Fred Ammerman nor his attorney paid any attention to Mi-hwa. Aaron Murakami seemed to ask his client one final question. Vehemently, Ammerman shook his head. No.

Like a collapsing doll, Mi-hwa Ammerman sank back into her seat. I expected her to start crying again. Instead she stuffed her damp handkerchief into her open handbag.

Aaron Murakami rose to his feet. "Your Honor," he said in English, "my client has decided to plead not guilty."

A murmur of disapproval ran through the crowd. Dutifully, the translator repeated what Murakami had said but by then no one was listening.

Mi-hwa's face was set like stone and drained of color. She sat perfectly still, staring straight ahead, her small hand tucked inside her large leather handbag.

I elbowed Ernie. "She's taking it hard."

Ernie glanced over at Mi-hwa Ammerman. "Yeah," Ernie said, "but the woman Ammerman raped took it even harder."

The prosecutor, a dapper Korean man in a pin-striped suit, rose to his feet. He cleared his throat and started to drone on again in Korean legalese.

Since he'd been brought into the room, not once had Ammerman acknowledged the presence of his wife or even so much as glanced in her direction. Instead he glared at the prosecutor, as if he wanted to leap across the room and throttle his neck as he'd throttled the neck of Mrs. Yi Won-suk.

Ernie yawned and tried to make himself more comfortable on the wooden bench. We had already discussed which nightclubs we'd be hitting tonight. Before leaving Seoul, we'd changed a small pile of military payment certificates into *won*. The money would be put to its usual good use—cold beer and wild times, not necessarily in that order.

While I was pondering these soothing thoughts, a glint of metal flashed from the seating area behind Fred Ammerman. Without thinking, I rose to my feet.

Mi-hwa Ammerman, her face streaming tears, was standing now, her handbag dropped to the floor.

Without conscious thought, I lunged toward her. A long butcher knife appeared in her slender hand. She raised it. She stepped forward.

A shout bellowed through the hall.

I shoved people out of the way and stepped over benches, trying to reach her, knowing all the time that I wouldn't make it.

Fred Ammerman never turned fully around.

His attorney noticed that something was amiss and as he swiveled he instinctively held up his hands. A yell erupted from his belly but it was too late. Ammerman's bearded face was turning toward Mi-hwa as she leaned over the railing, raised the glistening blade, and brought it down full force into her husband's back.

Fred Ammerman let out a grunt of surprise. No more. I kept moving forward and was only a few feet from him now. Mi-hwa held onto the hilt of the blade, shoving it deeper into heaving flesh. Gore spurted from Fred Ammerman's back like the unraveling of a scarlet ribbon.

The confusion in Ammerman's eyes turned to dull knowledge. Then, a split second later, that knowledge turned to pain.

Aaron Murakami reached for Mi-hwa. I leapt forward and elbowed him out of the way. Uniformed police were now surging toward us. I folded myself over Mi-hwa, enveloping her in my arms. She let go of the butcher knife and leaned backward, allowing me to pull her away from the railing and protect her there, while other men hurtled toward us. Bodies thudded into bodies but I held on, not letting them have her.

She kept her eyes riveted on the back of her husband, as if mesmerized by the damage she had wrought.

Ernie grabbed hold of Ammerman. One of the Korean cops jerked the butcher knife out of the blood-soaked back. That's when Ammerman stood upright, supported by Ernie and Murakami, and then, as if someone had sucker punched him in the gut, he folded forward. Bright red blood spurted from his mouth.

Mi-hwa Ammerman didn't cry, she didn't struggle, she just let me hold her as she stared at her husband, as if amazed at what she'd just done.

And then someone jostled us and more men surrounded me, and despite my best efforts, Mi-hwa Ammerman was dragged from my arms. I followed her out of the main hall and down the corridor, but then she disappeared into the screaming, moving crowd. I returned to the courtroom.

Ernie grabbed me by the shoulders and stared into my face. "You still with me?"

I nodded.

He slapped me lightly on the cheek, making sure I was all right. Then he said, "That's one chick who knows how to save face."

On the floor, the thing that was once Fred Ammerman shuddered. Then his body convulsed and a whoosh of air exited his mouth, like a great bellows emptying itself in one final rush. The hot breath rose to the top of the stone rafters far above our heads, lingered for a while, and then was gone.

THE WIDOW PO

"Talking to dead people," Ernie said, "isn't exactly my idea of a good time."

Stone walls loomed above us as we wound our way through narrow cobbled lanes that led up the side of Namsan Mountain in a district of Seoul known as Huam-dong. Night shadows closed in on us, pressing down. A few dark clouds. No moon yet.

"You won't be talking to dead people," I told Ernie. "That's the job of the *mudang*." The female shaman.

Using the dim yellow light of an occasional street lamp, I glanced at the scrap of paper in my hand, checking the address against the engraved brass placards embedded into wooden gateways: 132 *bonji*, 16 *ho*. We were close.

The request had been a simple one, from Miss Choi Yong-kuang, my Korean language teacher: to come to a *kut*. I'd learn something about ancient Korean religious practices and I'd be able to observe a famous Korean *mudang* first hand. And I'd be able to hear from an American GI who'd been disrupting this *mudang*'s séances for the last few months. A GI who—so the *mudang* claimed—had been dead for twenty years.

"Bunch of bull, if you ask me," Ernie said.

"They'll have *soju*," I told Ernie. "And lots of women."

"Men don't attend these things?"

"Not unless invited."

Ernie gazed ahead into the growing gloom. "And you'll be able to get near your Korean language teacher. What's her name?"

"Choi," I told him.

Miss Choi was a tall young woman with a nice figure and a smile that could illuminate a hall. When she asked me to meet her after class, I would've said yes to just about anything. Even a séance. Ernie and I hadn't made this trip official. We were off duty now, carrying our badges but not our .45s. And we hadn't told anyone at 8th Army CID about our plans to attend a *kut*.

Who needed their laughter?

The lane turned sharply uphill and became so narrow that we had to proceed single file. Beneath our feet, sudsy water gurgled in a brick channel. The air reeked of waste and ammonia.

Finally, the lane opened into an open space in front of a huge red gate. Behind the gate a large house loomed. Upturned blue tile pointed toward the sky. Clay figurines of monkeys perched on the ridges of the roof, frightening away evil spirits.

At the heavy wooden door, I paused and listened. No sound. It appeared to be a huge house and there was no telling how far the grounds extended behind this gate.

Ernie admired the thick granite walls. "Not our normal hangout."

Once again, I checked the address against the embossed plate and then pressed the buzzer. A tinny voice responded.

"*Yoboseiyo?*"

In my most carefully pronounced Korean, I explained who I was and why I was here. The voice told me to wait. A few seconds later, footsteps. Then, like a secret panel, a small door hidden in the big gateway creaked open. An old woman stood behind, smiling and bowing. Ernie and I ducked through into a wide courtyard.

Neatly tended ferns, shrubs, small persimmon trees. In a pond beneath a tiny waterfall, goldfish splashed.

We followed the maid to the main entrance of the home and slipped off our footwear, leaving our big clunky leather oxfords amidst a sea of feminine shoes spangled with sequins and stars and golden tassels.

The maid led us down a long wood-slat floor corridor. Oil-papered doors lined either side. Finally, we heard murmuring—the sound of prayer. Women knelt on the floor of a large hall, praying. When we entered, they turned to look at us. I couldn't spot Miss Choi anywhere.

"They're all mama-sans," Ernie said.

"Hush."

Most of the women were middle-aged and matronly. And extremely well dressed. Expensive *chima-chogori*, the traditional Korean attire of short vest and high-waisted skirt, rustled as they moved. The dresses were made of silk dyed in bright colors and decorated with hand-embroidered dragons and cranes and silver-threaded lotus flowers.

The far wall was covered with a huge banner: the Goddess of the Underworld, wielding a sword and vanquishing evil.

"*Wasso*," one of the women said. They've arrived.

Then all the women rose to their feet and started rearranging their cushions into a semi-circle. Miss Choi Yong-kuang, smiling, appeared out of the milling throng. She wore a simple silk skirt and blouse of sky blue—less expensive than what most of the other women wore, but on her it looked smashing.

After bowing and shaking our hands, Miss Choi turned Ernie over to a small group of smiling women. They pulled him off to the right side of the hall. Miss Choi led me to the left side and sat me down cross-legged on a plump cushion. Low tables were brought out piled high with rice cakes and pears and sliced seaweed rolls. These were set in front of a long-eared god made of bronze who sat serenely on a raised dais in front of the banner of the Goddess of the Underworld. Incense in brass burners was lit and then an elderly woman dressed in exquisite red silk embroidered with gold danced slowly around the room, waving a small torch. Miss Choi whispered to me that she was the mistress of this home.

"Why's she waving the torch?"

"Chasing away ghosts." Embarrassed, Miss Choi covered her mouth with the back of her soft hand.

Gongs clanged, so loudly and with so little warning that I almost slipped off my cushion. Then sticks were beaten against thin drums. I glanced behind me and discovered that three musicians were hidden in shadows behind an embroidered screen.

The ambient light in the hallway was switched off and now the only illumination in the room was the red pinpoints of light from the smoldering incense and the flickering candles lining either side of the long-eared bronze god.

More drums and now clanging cymbals. Then silence. Breathlessly, we waited for what seemed to be a long time. Finally, the clanging resumed with renewed fervor. A woman dressed completely in white floated into the center of the kneeling and squatting spectators. A pointed hood kept her face hidden in shadows.

"Who's she?" I asked.

"The *mudang*," Miss Choi answered. "Her name is Widow Po. Very famous."

Miss Choi Yong-kuang is an educated and modern woman. Still, there was reverence in her voice when she spoke of the Widow Po.

Across the room, Ernie reached toward one of the rice cakes on the low table in front of him. A middle-aged woman slapped his hand.

The *mudang* continued her dance, eyes closed as if in a trance. The musicians handled the percussion instruments expertly, keeping the rhythm. Finally, when the first beads of perspiration appeared on the *mudang*'s brow, other women rose to their feet and began to dance. Soon about a half dozen of them were on the floor, swirling around like slightly overweight tops.

One of the women yanked on Ernie's wrist, trying to coax him to his feet. He hesitated, holding up his open palm, and then pointed to one of the open bottles of *soju* dispersed amongst the feast for the gods. She understood, grabbed the bottle, and poured a generous glug into Ernie's open mouth. Rice wine dribbled out the side of his mouth and onto his white shirt and gray jacket. Ernie didn't mind. He motioned for another shot and the woman obliged. Then he was on his feet, dancing as expertly as if he'd been attending ancient Korean séances all his life. Arms spread to his sides, gliding in smooth circles like some pointy-nosed, green-eyed bird of prey.

The Widow Po danced toward Ernie. When she was close enough, she grabbed his wrist and started twirling Ernie around faster. Soon the other women took their seats as my partner, Ernie Bascom, and the *mudang*, Widow Po, swirled around the entire floor. The rhythm of the cymbals and drums grew more frenzied. The Widow Po reached down, gracefully plucked up an open bottle of *soju*, and once again poured a healthy glug down Ernie's throat. One of the women in the crowd stood and pulled off his jacket. The Widow Po's hood fell back. She wasn't a bad looking woman, at least ten years older than Ernie but with a strong face and high cheekbones. The blemish was the pox. The flesh of her entire face was marked by the scars of some hideous childhood disease.

Ernie didn't seem to notice. Especially when the Widow Po started rubbing her body against his.

The matronly women in the crowd squealed with delight. Even the modest Miss Choi covered her face with both hands, attempting to hide her mirth.

Ernie motioned for more *soju* and the Widow Po obliged but then, after another glug had dribbled down Ernie's cheeks, the Widow Po suddenly stopped dancing. The music stopped. Ernie kept twirling for a few seconds and then stopped dancing himself. He glanced around, confused.

The Widow Po stood in the center of the floor, her head bowed, ignoring him. Sensing that his moment in the spotlight was over, Ernie grinned, grabbed the half-full bottle of *soju* off the low table, and resumed his seat on the far side of the hall.

No one moved for what seemed a long time—maybe five minutes. Finally, the Widow Po screamed.

The voice was high, banshee-like. The Korean was garbled, as if from a person who was ill or in great pain, and I could understand none of it. The attention turned to one of the women in the crowd. She was plump, holding a handkerchief to her face, crying profusely. The Widow Po approached her, still using the strange, falsetto voice. Finally, the crying woman burst out.

"*Hyong-ae! Wei domang kasso.*"

That I understood. Why did you leave me, Hyong-ae?

The Widow Po and the crying woman went back and forth, asking questions of one another, casting accusations, arguing. I leaned toward Miss Choi with a quizzical look on my face. She explained.

"Hyong-ae was her daughter. She died in a car accident last year. Now she's blaming her mother for buying her a car."

"The Widow Po is playing the part of her daughter?"

"Not playing. Hyung-ae's spirit has entered her body."

I stared at Miss Choi for a moment, wondering if she believed that. She blushed and turned away from me. I left it alone.

The crying matron and the Widow Po screamed back and forth at one another. The mom saying now that Hyung-ae, when she was alive, wouldn't let her rest until she bought her a car. Hyung-ae countering that a mother should know what is best for her child. They were bickering like any mother and willful young daughter and yet it was eerie. How did the Widow Po know so much about other people's lives? I didn't bother to ask Miss Choi about it. I knew her answer. The Widow Po was possessed by the spirit of Hyung-ae.

Suddenly, the Widow Po let out a screech of pain. She knelt to the floor, hugging herself, and remained perfectly still for a few minutes. Without a cue, the musicians started again and then the Widow Po was up and dancing and a few minutes later she yelled again. This time an old grandfather took possession of her body. Another woman in the crowd spoke to this ghostly presence, giving him a report on the welfare of the family. When she was finished, the old man scolded her for not forcing his grandchildren to study hard enough.

Then this grandfather was gone and a few minutes later another spirit took possession of the perspiring body of the Widow Po.

The *kut* continued like this for over an hour. Ernie was growing restless but the women surrounding him read him like a book and kept pouring him small glassfuls of *soju* and stuffing sweet pink rice cakes down his throat.

Ernie must've already polished off a liter and a half of *soju* by the time the Widow Po growled.

Her eyes were like a she-wolf. She stalked toward Ernie. He stared up at her, half a rice cake in his mouth, dumfounded.

"*Choryo!*" she shouted. Attention!

Ernie didn't understand but the women around him shoved him to his feet.

"*Apuroi ka!*" the Widow Po commanded. Forward march!

Again the women pushed Ernie forward and he marched to the center of the floor.

"*Chongji!*" the Widow Po told Ernie. Halt!

Ernie understood that one. "Halt" was the one Korean word that 8th Army GI's were taught, so they wouldn't be shot by nervous Korean sentries. Ernie stopped, standing almost at the position of attention, a half-empty bottle of *soju* loose in his hand.

Miss Choi leaned toward me. "The soldier," she said. "The one I told you about."

Ernie reached for the Widow Po, thinking she was going to start rubbing her body against his again, but she would have none of it. She slapped his hand away and stepped forward, her hands on her hips, screaming into Ernie's face. The words were coming out so fast and so furious—in a deep, garbled voice—that I could understand little of it. Miss Choi translated.

"He's angry. 'Why have you kept me waiting so long?' he says."

"Who's kept him waiting?"

"You," she said. "*Mi Pal Kun.*" The 8th United States Army.

"Waiting for what?"

"To talk to him. To let him explain."

"Who is he?"

Miss Choi listened to the rant for a few more seconds and then said, "I'm not sure. The name sounds like *mori di.*"

Mori means "hair" or "head" in the Korean language. *Di* meant nothing, unless the spirit was referring to the letter "d" as in the English alphabet.

Ernie was becoming impatient with being screamed at. He lifted the *soju* bottle and took a drink. The Widow Po slapped the bottle from his lips and it crashed against the belly of the bronze god. Then the Widow Po leapt at Ernie, throwing left hooks and then rights, punching like a man.

The matronly women bounded to their feet and grabbed the Widow Po and held her on the floor, writhing and spitting. Ernie wasn't damaged badly, just a bruise beneath his left eye.

The Widow Po kept shouting invective in garbled Korean, her burning eyes focused fiercely on Ernie.

"What's she saying?" I asked Miss Choi.

"He," she corrected. "*Mori Di*, the spirit who possesses her. He says that you must start your work immediately. There must be no further delay."

"What work?"

"I thought you understood."

"No. The Widow Po is speaking much too fast for me to follow."

"*Mori Di* was an American soldier," Miss Choi explained. "He died more than twenty years ago. He wants you to start an investigation and find the person who did this."

"Find the person who did what?"

"Find the person who murdered him."

The Widow Po let out one more guttural screech and her eyes

rolled up into her head until only the whites showed. Then she let out a huge blast of rancid air and passed out cold.

Ernie slapped dust mites away from his nose.

"This is bull," he said.

I tried to ignore him. Instead I continued down the row in the dimly lit warehouse, shining my flashlights on walls of stacked cardboard. We were looking for the box marked *SIRs, FY54*. Serious Incident Reports. Fiscal Year 1954.

Exactly twenty years ago.

The NCO in charge of 8th Army Records Storage hadn't been happy to see two CID agents barge in unannounced. He pulled his boots off his desk, hid his comic book, and had to pretend that he'd been working. When I told him what I wanted, he was incredulous.

"Nobody looks at that stuff."

But when we flashed our badges he complied and escorted us into the warehouse. After he showed us where to look, the phone rang in his office. He used that as an excuse to hand me the flashlight and return to the coziness of his cramped little empire.

When we were alone, I turned to Ernie. "You sort of liked that Widow Po, didn't you?"

"Yeah," Ernie responded. "Nice body."

"So we do her a favor. That's all. See if any GIs were murdered twenty years ago. Any GIs named *Mori Di*."

I stopped at a row of boxes. There, up at the top, Fiscal Year 1954. Grabbing a handhold, I started to climb on the boxes below. Ernie helped hoist me up.

"You don't believe any of that stuff, do you?" he asked. "Good show, but it's all an act."

I grabbed the box, blew dust off the top, and studied it. Bound with wire, no chance to check the contents up here.

"Pretty convincing act," I replied.

"But still nothing more than an act."

I slid the box down to Ernie. He broke its fall but it was still heavy enough to land on the cement floor with a thump.

"Wire cutters," I said.

Ernie returned to the office and brought back a pair.

"The Sarge says we'll have to rebind it ourselves."

"Screw him."

"That's exactly what I told him."

Ernie snipped the thick wire, pulled the top off, and then held the flashlight while I crouched down and thumbed through the manila folders.

I pulled a few out.

Fascinating stories. About GIs assaulting, robbing, and maiming other GIs. About GIs assaulting, robbing, and maiming Koreans. Very few about Koreans assaulting, robbing, or maiming GIs. The Korean War had ended only a few months before. The Koreans were flat on their back economically. GIs, comparatively, were as rich as Midas. Still, Confucian values dictated that the Koreans use their wiles, not their brawn, to obtain a share of US Army riches. I could've spent hours here studying these cases but we didn't have time. We were on the black market detail and this was our lunch break. The CID First Sergeant would be checking on us soon.

Then I spotted a thick manila folder.

"What is it?" Ernie asked.

I pointed.

There, typed neatly across the white label affixed to the folder was a name and a rank: Moretti, Charles A., Private First Class (Deceased).

We'd found *Mori Di.*

That evening, Ernie and I repaired to Itaewon, the red light district in southern Seoul that caters to GIs and other foreigners. But this time we didn't hit the nightclubs. Instead, we walked into the Itaewon Police Station. Captain Kim, the officer in charge of the Itaewon Police district, was waiting for us. I'd called him earlier that afternoon. Sitting behind his desk, he stared at us from beneath thick eyebrows. The square features of his face revealed nothing.

"No one remembers *Mori Di*," he told us. "Too long ago."

"Surely you have records."

"Most burn. Before Pak Chung-hee become President."

There were serious civil riots in Seoul and other major cities of South Korea when the corrupt Syngman Rhee government was overthrown in the early Sixties.

"Still," I said, "the murder happened only twenty years ago. There must be some cop somewhere who remembers the case." I glanced at the notes I'd taken while reading Moretti's case folder. "An officer named Kwang. A lieutenant. The given name Bung-lee. Most of the Korean National Police reports were attributed to him."

Captain Kim nodded. He already knew this. For him, keeping cards close to his vest was a lifetime habit.

"Why," he asked, "is the American army so interested in an old case?"

Ernie glanced at me but held his tongue. I hadn't told Captain Kim that our interest was unofficial. If I had, he wouldn't have cooperated at all.

"Long story," I said. "Are you going to tell us how to find Lieutenant Kwang or not?"

Captain Kim sighed, reached into his top drawer, and pulled out a slip of brown pulp paper folded neatly in half. He slid it toward us, his fingers still pressing it into the desk. "Before you make your report, will you talk to me?"

"Yes," I promised.

He handed me the slip of paper.

"You must be nuts," Ernie said.

He was driving the jeep and we were wearing civvies, faded blue jeans and sports shirts. It was Saturday.

"On our day off," Ernie continued, "chasing around the

Korean countryside after some murder case that happened twenty years ago all because you've got the hots for your Korean teacher."

"It's not just that," I said.

Ernie swerved around a wooden cart pulled by an ox. Rice paddies spread into the distance, fallow now after the autumn harvest.

"Then what is it?"

"You read Moretti's folder."

"No, I didn't."

"Well, I told you what was in it. His murder was never solved."

"He's been dead twenty years. What difference does it make now?"

"He was a GI, Ernie. One of us."

That shut him up for a while. After a few minutes, he resumed cursing softly beneath his breath.

The village of Three White Cranes sat in a bowl-shaped valley about halfway between Seoul and the Eastern Sea. Most of the world refers to the Eastern Sea as the Sea of Japan but the Koreans aren't particularly fond of that nomenclature.

After two hours of winding roads and narrow country highways, Ernie slowed the jeep and rolled past clapboard hovels that lined the main street of downtown Three White Cranes. The largest building was made of whitewashed cement and the flag of the Republic of Korea waved proudly from a thirty-foot-high pole out front. The Three White Cranes Police Station. Two cops inside had already been alerted by Captain Kim in Itaewon and they drew us a map to a pig farm about two clicks outside of town.

An old man stood in front of a straw-thatched hut. He wore a tattered khaki uniform of the Korean National Police that hung on him like a loose sack. When I climbed out of the jeep and approached him, he waved his bamboo cane in the air.

"*Kara*," he said. "*Bali kara!*" Get lost!

Ignoring rudeness is an important skill for any investigator. I approached the old man and started shooting questions at him in Korean about his involvement in the Moretti case.

Ernie stood by the jeep, staring over at a pen full of hogs. The fence was so rickety that he was worried some of them might break out.

"You go," the old man told me, using broken English now. "Long time ago. No use now. You go."

"Who murdered Moretti?" I asked the former Lieutenant Kwang.

"You go. No use now."

I kept at him, badgering him with questions, sometimes in English, sometimes in Korean.

"Why you cause trouble?" he asked me finally. A watery film covered the old man's eyes. "He dead now. Life hard in Korea that time. You no ask question."

"You know who killed Moretti," I said.

"No. I don't know. I don't want to know. Just like before. I don't want to know."

I started to ask more questions but the old man hobbled quickly toward the pigpen. Using his bamboo cane, he knocked loose two supporting beams and the rickety wooden fence collapsed. A herd of hogs charged out. I ran toward the jeep and jumped in. The huge animals swarmed around us, snorting and pawing and trying to climb into the vehicle.

Ernie started the jeep and backed down the dirt road. The hogs followed.

"If I had my forty-five," Ernie said, "I'd land us some pork chops."

Instead, he turned around, slammed the gear shift into first, and sped away.

When I looked back, the old man was still waving his bamboo cane.

An oil lamp guttered in the small office adjacent to Haggler Lee's warehouse.

Although he might've been the richest man in Itaewon, Haggler Lee had a habit of keeping expenses to a minimum. Electricity was seldom used in his place of business. He wore traditional Korean clothing, a green silk vest and white cotton pantaloons, and didn't believe in wasting money on haircuts. Instead he kept his black hair tied above his head and knotted with a short length of blue rope. We sat on the oil-papered floor in his office.

"Moretti," Haggler Lee said. "Nineteen fifty-four. Only one person I know of was in business back in those days."

"Who?" I asked.

Ernie sipped on the barley tea that Haggler Lee's servant had served shortly after we arrived. The entire room smelled of incense. A stick glowed softly in a bronze burner.

Haggler Lee rubbed his smooth chin. "Why would two famous CID agents be interested in a case so old?"

"What do you care?" Ernie said. "Your operation is safe. We're not after you."

"Thanks to my ancestors watching in Heaven," Lee replied. "Still, nineteen fifty-four. Unusual, is it not?"

"Unusual," I said. "Who was in operation then?"

"The black market was small in nineteen fifty-four. Koreans were so poor they could afford few of your imported American goods."

"Who is it, Lee?" Ernie asked.

"Whiskey Mary."

"Whiskey Mary? What's her Korean name?" I asked.

"I don't know. She's been called Whiskey Mary so long even we Koreans call her that."

"Where can we find her?"

"Last I heard she worked at a *yoguan* in Munsan-ni. An unsavory place."

Haggler Lee gave us the name of the inn, the Kaesong Yoguan. Ernie finished his tea and we left.

■ ■ ■

Munsan is a small city about thirty kilometers north of Seoul, near the DMZ. Ernie and I cruised through the narrow main road. This was Sunday morning so Korean soldiers were everywhere, elbowing their way past farmers pushing carts full of turnips and grandmothers balancing pans full of laundry atop their heads.

The Dragon Eye Yoguan sat in an alley just off the main drag. It was a ramshackle building, two stories high, made of old varnished slats of wood. When Ernie and I slipped off our shoes and stepped up into the musty foyer, a woman wearing a long wool skirt and wool sweater emerged from a sliding, oil-papered door.

"*Andei*," she said. No good. "*Migun yogi ei, andei*." American soldiers aren't allowed here.

Ernie didn't understand and I didn't bother to translate. It was understandable that the woman wouldn't want American GIs staying here. If her main clientele were Korean soldiers, that would be asking for trouble.

I ignored her remark, showed her my badge, and spoke to her in Korean. When I mentioned the name Whiskey Mary, her eyes widened.

"No trouble," I said quickly. "We just want to ask her some questions."

Shaking her head, the woman led us down a long narrow hallway. Sliding doors were spaced along the walls every few feet, some of them open, showing rumpled blankets and porcelain pots inside. The aroma of charcoal gas and urine filled the hallway. Occasionally Ernie and I had to duck to avoid bumping our heads on overhanging support beams.

Out back was a muddy courtyard with a few skinny chickens behind wire and two neatly spaced outdoor latrines made of cement blocks. The woman motioned with her open palm, turned, and left.

Ernie and I crossed the courtyard.

Whiskey Mary was bent over with her back to us, kneeling in one of the latrines, scrubbing with hot soapy water and a wire brush.

336 ■ MARTIN LIMÓN

"Whiskey Mary," I said.

She froze in mid-stroke.

When she turned around, I could see two teeth missing up front, the others blackened around the edges. Wiry gray hair, face full of wrinkles and a suspicious squint to her eyes.

"Why?" she asked.

"Moretti," I said.

She squeezed the wire brush, leaned on it, and began to cry.

In wine is truth, the Romans used to say, and maybe that's what happened to Ernie and me. When we returned to Itaewon that night we sat at the bar in the Seven Club and rehashed what we knew about the Moretti case.

Whiskey Mary had owned her own bar and run a success-ful black market operation out back. She wasn't worried about arrest because the US Army authorities had no jurisdiction over her and the Korean National Police were being paid off. She even showed us photographs of herself in those days. Sitting with the girls who were hostesses in Whiskey Mary's, all of them with new hairdos and makeup and wearing expensive silk *chima-cho-gori*. GIs brought in the PX-bought whiskey and cigarettes and instant coffee and Whiskey Mary turned it into cash and other favors from her hostesses. A sweet deal.

Until Moretti was killed.

He was one of her best customers. And went so far as to hus-tle other GIs, especially those new in-country, to use their ration cards to make a little money. And if they were worried about being caught by the MPs, Moretti would handle all transactions for them, taking half the profit for his efforts.

He was a good boy, Whiskey Mary told us. Most of the money he made, he mailed home by US Postal money order to his mother in Newark, New Jersey.

Then someone stabbed him to death.

Neither the KNPs nor the MPs had a clue as to who had mur-dered Moretti. But his body had been found in the middle of the street in Itaewon, apparently attacked just after curfew at four in the morning, stabbed in the solar plexus and left to bleed to death on a muddy road.

A senator from New Jersey raised hell and the Syngman Rhee government was under pressure to do something to insure the safety of American GIs. If the GIs left Korea, they'd take military and foreign aid money with them. The Rhee government couldn't tolerate anything like that so the pressure to charge someone with Moretti's murder was enormous.

Whiskey Mary was chosen.

"They wanted to take over my operation," she said. Her English was heavily accented but still understandable after all these years. "Somebody up high." She pointed toward Heaven. "In the government. The Americans were happy and the Korean big shots stole my business at the same time."

The charge was murder. She was arrested, tried, and sentenced to five years.

"Why only five years?" Ernie asked.

Whiskey Mary answered as if it were the most obvious thing in the world. "Because I wasn't guilty."

"But Eighth Army kept the case open," I said.

She waved her hand in the air. "They never happy with what Korean police do. American CID man, he know I no kill Moretti."

"How would he know that?"

She smiled her toothless smile. "Because he sleep with me that night."

When I asked her who did kill Moretti, she didn't know.

"*Mori Di*, he knew everybody," she said. "He have many friends and many girlfriends. I don't know why anybody want kill him."

When we finished our questions, I handed Whiskey Mary a few dollars. She stuffed them in her brassiere.

Probably an old habit.

The Seven Club's new all-Korean Country Western band clanged to life. Ernie and I sat through the yodeling and the twanging guitars patiently, both of us thinking about what we'd learned. When the Korean cowboys finished their first set, Ernie swiveled on his barstool and faced me.

"We both know who we have to talk to."

"We do?"

"Sure. We've been looking at this case in the wrong way from the beginning. All that *kut* mumbo jumbo bent our heads the wrong way."

I thought about that for a moment. Finally, I said, "I see what you mean."

"Tomorrow," Ernie said. "We wrap this damn case up."

We ordered two more draft OBs and drank to that proposition.

It was Monday now so we had to wait until after work. During the day, I called Miss Choi and tried to convince her to give me an address. When she figured out what I had in mind, she refused but promised to show us the way. Reluctantly, I agreed.

That night, driving through the crowded Seoul streets, Ernie and I didn't talk much. Miss Choi sat silently in the back of the jeep. At a park on the northeast side of downtown Seoul, she told us to pull over. A huge wooden gate painted bright red was slashed with Chinese Characters: *Kuksadang*. Altar for National Rites.

"We have to walk from here," Miss Choi said.

On the other side of the gate, stone steps led up a steep hill.

Miss Choi wasn't wearing her usual Western clothing. Instead, she wore a long white skirt and white blouse, very similar to what the Widow Po had worn during the *kut*. Also a large canvas bag was strapped over her shoulder.

"Why no blue jeans?" I asked.

She shook her head. "I must protect you."

"Protect us?" Ernie asked. "From what?"

"From the Widow Po."

When I asked her to explain she shook her head. We climbed

the long flights of steps in silence. Slowly, we wound our way toward the top of a line of steep hills—small mountains actually—guarding the northwestern flank of the capital city of Seoul. Square stone parapets lined the summit, built during the Yi Dynasty as protection against Manchurian raiders and Japanese pirates. Below, the glowing lights of the city sparkled in the darkening sky. To the east, a red moon started to rise.

While tossing back wets at the Seven Club, it had occurred to Ernie that the one person who knew more about the Moretti case than anyone in the world was the Widow Po. If you believed in ghosts, that would be because the spirit of Moretti took possession of her during a *kut*. If you don't believe in ghosts, that would mean that she had specific knowledge of the case.

Neither Ernie nor I believed in ghosts.

Behind the ancient battlements, a dirt pathway led through a small grove of quivering elms. Miss Choi marched in the lead, staring straight ahead. Ernie and I glanced at one another. She looked exactly as if she were going into battle.

Once past the grove of trees, we descended into a dry gully. On the other side a clearing held maybe a dozen hooches, all thatched with straw. Candles flickered in one of the windows. No street lamps or cars or electricity up here. Down below, the modern city of Seoul hummed vibrantly.

Miss Choi stopped and waited until we were close.

"Only I talk," she said. "Not you."

"We have to question her," Ernie said. "About Moretti."

"I do that. You listen."

Without waiting for further comment, Miss Choi Yongkuang turned and strode toward the one home with a light in the window. As she walked, she reached in her canvas bag and pulled out a small drum made of wood and leather. Using a short stick she banged the drum lightly, only once, and then in a steady rhythm. In front of the hooch, we waited.

Ernie grew impatient. "Why don't I just knock on the damn door?"

Miss Choi shushed him.

In the other hooches there didn't seem to be any life whatsoever. But someone must live here. Wash fluttered on lines behind the houses. A skinny rooster flapped its wings and scratched into soil. Were they all gone? Or were they sitting silently behind dark windows, watching us?

This afternoon on the phone, Miss Choi had told me that the entire village was reserved for mediums. Wealthy people from the city below climbed up here to have their fortunes told or to talk to dear departed loved ones. But there were no customers tonight.

The front door of the hooch creaked open. Miss Choi drummed a little faster. A figure in white stepped out onto the porch. Then she stepped off the porch, slipping into her plastic sandals, and followed a flagstone walkway until she stood just a few feet from us. Moonlight reflected off a pock-marked face: the Widow Po.

I expected her to smile at Ernie. After all, they'd practically been intimate during the *kut*. Instead, she ignored us and frowned at Miss Choi.

"You insult me," the Widow Po said in Korean.

"These are good men," Miss Choi retorted. "And you asked me to bring them to the *kut*. This is your doing."

"You expect I will hurt them?"

Miss Choi stopped drumming, slipped the instrument back into her bag, and pulled out a long red scarf embroidered with gold thread. I couldn't make out what it said but the embroidery was clearly stylized Chinese characters. She draped the scarf over her head.

The Widow Po took a step backward.

"You are *insolent*," she said. "Do you think I can't ward off evil spirits on my own?"

"Not evil spirits," Miss Choi said. "I want to ward off *you*. You must have some plan. It is not me who brought these men here tonight. It is you."

The Widow Po turned to me and then slowly turned to Ernie. She smiled.

"I should offer you tea," she said in English.

"Not necessary," Ernie replied. "We just want to ask you some questions."

"Will you be able to appease the troublesome spirit who has been haunting me?"

"That's up to you," I said. "How old are you?"

Her eyes widened. "A woman should never answer such a question."

"American women shouldn't," I said. "Korean women are proud of their age."

She smiled again. "I am older than you think."

"Old enough to have known Moretti?"

Miss Choi pulled a small prayer wheel out of her bag, started spinning it, closed her eyes, and chanted softly beneath her breath.

We waited.

Far below in Seoul, neon sparkled and an occasional horn honked. The orange moon was completely above the horizon now. Miss Choi's gentle chanting seemed to encourage its glow. Finally, the Widow Po spoke.

"I knew him," she said. "I was young then. And beautiful. Yes, beautiful," she repeated, as if I had challenged her. "Despite the marks on my face I was beautiful. We were never married in your Yankee way, what with all your military paperwork. It was only there to discourage American GIs from marrying Korean women. But we were married in the proper way, taking vows before the Goddess of the Underworld, swearing that our devotion would be eternal. That we would never part. Not like you Americans who change husbands and wives so often."

She was speaking Korean now. Ernie couldn't understand but he was following the intensity in her voice. I struggled to understand every word.

"But Moretti was like all you Americans, consorting with evil. With that woman called Whiskey Mary . . . "

Ernie understood that.

" . . . and with the girls who worked for her. And who knows who else? He wouldn't come home. He wouldn't perform the filial rights during the autumn harvest or visit the graves of my ancestors and introduce himself to them. He laughed at such things. Laughed!"

Now she was crying, her lips quivering in rage.

"When he was gone, I had to make a living. Not by finding another GI like so many women did but by honoring my ancestors. By doing this."

She waved her arms to indicate the totality of the little village of shamans and mediums.

"When he was gone," I said. "He was gone because you killed him."

The Widow Po stared into my eyes a long time. Miss Choi's chanting grew more rapid.

"Yes," the Widow Po said. "I killed him. I had no choice. He was dishonoring me. He was dishonoring the Goddess of the Underworld."

"And the Korean police left you alone."

The Widow Po smiled through her tears and thrust out her chest. "They were afraid of me."

"You allowed Whiskey Mary to go to prison."

Widow Po shook her head rapidly. "For a while. There was no choice. But I sent spirits to protect her."

I briefly translated everything that had been said to Ernie. He took a step toward the Widow Po. Miss Choi stopped chanting, alarmed.

"Why did you ask Miss Choi to bring us to the *kut*?"

"Because Moretti kept interrupting me," the Widow Po answered, looking surprised, as if it should be obvious. "Sometimes he took over the whole ceremony, upsetting everyone. Making my clients unhappy. How can they talk to their dead parents if some GI is always in the way?"

Miss Choi translated the answer for Ernie.

Ernie grabbed the Widow Po's elbow. Miss Choi gasped.

"Moretti won't be interrupting any more *kuts*," Ernie said. "Because you'll be in the monkey house. No *kuts* allowed."

The Widow Po understood the GI slang. Monkey house meant prison.

I was watching intently and as best I could tell, the Widow Po made no move. But maybe the light was bad, or maybe the glow from the orange moon and the candlelight in the hooch and the neon flashing from the city below caused me to miss something. But suddenly a rush of air escaped from Ernie's mouth and he doubled over as if punched by a two-by-four.

Miss Choi resumed her chanting, frantic now, garbling her words.

Ernie knelt in the dust. The Widow Po spoke once again in broken English.

"No monkey house. The Widow Po no go there. I show Moretti he can't beat me. That's why I called you. No one will ever know what I did to him. No one alive."

A glimmering butcher knife slipped out of the Widow Po's long sleeve.

Before I could move, Miss Choi shouted and leapt toward the Widow Po.

The knife was in the air but Miss Choi rammed head first into the body of the Widow Po. Amazingly, the *mudang* maintained her balance and hopped back a few steps, still holding the knife. I ran toward Ernie but he was in so much pain that he couldn't rise to his feet.

The Widow Po bounced nimbly on the balls of her feet, holding the butcher knife aloft, her long hair swaying loose in the mountain breeze, daring us to come at her.

I grabbed Miss Choi and held her. She bowed her head once again and started her chant. A different one this time, more guttural. Not Korean, I didn't think. As if she were speaking some ancient language of the dead.

The Widow Po stopped bouncing. The knife dropped from

her hand. She took a huge intake of breath, held it, and then a roar emitted from her frail frame. A roar of pain. Deep voiced. Thundering. The voice of a wounded man.

The Widow Po staggered, clutching her chest. She twisted, turned, knelt to the ground. She roared again in her deep-throated voice and then spat blood straight out into the air.

I rushed toward her but before I could reach her she crumpled to the ground. I turned her over. Still breathing. A pulse in her neck but she was out cold.

I rushed back to Ernie. He was on his feet, staring at me. "What happened?"

"She sucker punched you."

"How the hell did she manage that?"

I looked back at the Widow Po. She still hadn't moved. "I don't know."

Miss Choi was on her feet now, no longer chanting. She pulled off her white skirt and blouse, revealing blue jeans and a red T-shirt below. Carefully, she stuffed the white clothing in her canvas bag.

Lights flickered on throughout the village. Electric bulbs. A television chattered to life. The announcer spoke in rapid Korean: *Ilki yeibo.* The weather report.

People emerged from their hooches, completely ignoring Miss Choi and Ernie and me, except for three neighbor woman who approached and tried to help the moaning Widow Po to her feet. The exhausted *mudang* collapsed, the muscles in her legs like straw. I stepped forward to help but the women waved me back. Unbidden, two men emerged from a nearby home. Together the five of them carried the Widow Po back into her hooch.

Ernie and I looked at each other.

Miss Choi grabbed our hands and led us back down the dark pathway to the bottom of Kuksadang.

The next time I attended the classroom of Miss Choi Yong-kuang, I sat up a little straighter and paid a little more attention to her instruction. After the lesson, I waited behind until the other students had left. I didn't have to say anything. Miss Choi read my mind.

"The Widow Po is crippled," Miss Choi told me. "She hasn't moved from her hooch since the night we were up there."

"How will she live?"

"Rich people make offerings to her."

"They're still afraid of her."

Miss Choi nodded. I watched as she packed her lesson notes and her textbook into her leather briefcase.

"You knew what was going to happen," I said.

She shrugged.

"The Widow Po brought all this upon herself," I continued. "Because of a guilty conscience."

Miss Choi clicked the hasps on her briefcase and looked me in the eye. "The Widow Po is a brave woman."

I nodded in agreement.

"What about Moretti?" I asked.

"No need to do anything further. *Mori Di*'s taken his revenge."

I studied Miss Choi for a long moment. "You really believe that, don't you?"

"Yes," she said. "I do."

I helped her lock up the classroom and then walked her out the main gate of 8th Army Compound and escorted her to the bus stop. No muggers jumped out at us.

Neither did any evil spirits.

THE COLD YELLOW SEA

Freezing outside an Asian brothel in the middle of the night with a cold rain blowing in off the Yellow Sea is enough to make even the most dedicated investigator ponder the worth of a career in military law enforcement. Fabulous pay and benefits. Fun, travel and adventure. Three hots and a cot. And, if President Ford was to be believed, a raise that would bring my corporal's pay all the way up to $450 per month by the end of this fiscal year.

Wow.

The wet pellets slapping my face suddenly didn't sting so badly. Still, I shuffled deeper into the shadows beneath an overhanging eave.

Tonight, Ernie and I were after an MP gone bad. Last we heard, he was shacked up inside Building Number 36 in this maze of narrow alleys known as the Yellow House. Down the lane, light flickered out of large plate glass windows. Behind those windows sat groups of Korean women in flimsy negligees, waiting for the foreign sailors who periodically invade this port of Inchon on the western coast of Korea on the edge of the Yellow Sea. Merchant marines from all over the world—Greece, the Philippines, Japan, Holland, Sweden, and even the United States—are regular customers here.

The local US military contingent is not huge—just one transportation company, which trucks supplies from the Port of

Inchon to the capital city of Seoul, and one platoon of Military Police to provide security for the duty-free shipments.

A door slammed. A tall, dark figure emerged from the foot of the stairwell just outside the glow of the plate glass window. Then I saw someone behind him. A girl, bowing; telling him in a nice way: thanks for the money but now it's time for you to get lost. The tall man didn't acknowledge her farewell. He turned, shoved his hands into his pockets, and strode toward the alley.

As he passed the light of the big window I caught a glimpse of his face. Dark eyes, pug nose, heavy stubble of an eight-hour beard. Our quarry. The MP gone bad: Buck Sergeant Lenny Dubrovnik.

Ernie was on the other side of Building 36, making sure Dubrovnik didn't slip out the back. My .45 sat snugly in the shoulder holster beneath my armpit but I didn't expect to have to use it. Dubrovnik knew the deal. He was a GI in Korea. Once you're busted, there's nowhere to run. The peninsula is surrounded on three sides by choppy seas. The only land route is across the Demilitarized Zone. And all international ports of embarkation are monitored with a degree of efficiency that only a militarized police state can provide.

As Dubrovnik approached, I stepped out of the shadows, showing my badge.

"Hold it right there, Sarge," I said. "The game's up. Take your hands out of your pockets and assume the position."

Dubrovnik came to a halt on the flagstone steps, glanced at my badge and then at my face. His eyes seem baffled for a moment and then his lips began to curl.

"Alone?" he asked.

I should've told him I had a squad of MPs lurking right around the corner. The least I should've told him was that Ernie would be here in a matter of seconds. But Dubrovnik was an MP himself and cops always claim that we can make any bust by ourselves. Backup's not necessary. So instead of telling him what I should've told him, that he had nowhere to run and I could claim the entire weight of the 8th United States Army as my backup, I made my first mistake of the evening: I let pride take over.

I looked Dubrovnik straight in the eye and shrugged. As if to say: Go ahead, Charlie, try it if you've got the nerve.

My shoulders had barely lowered again when Dubrovnik turned and darted away.

I let out a yell—incoherent, but I knew it would be enough to alert Ernie. And then I was running down the narrow pathway. Past the three- and four-story buildings that lined either side of the lane. Past the women sitting in the well-lit rooms behind the large windows, gazing out at us, their mouths half open.

Dubrovnik turned a corner. I skidded after him. Dubrovnik turned another corner, winding away from Building 36. The district known as the Yellow House was actually about two acres square. The entire area was composed of one pedestrian alley turning into another, winding around like a maze, brothel upon brothel, no vehicles allowed.

Dubrovnik was fast and had the added incentive of knowing he was about to be locked up. Just when he was about to pull away from me, another figure leapt out of the darkness. Dubrovnik tried to dodge this new phantom but the shadow wrapped its arms around his shoulders.

Ernie.

How the hell had he gotten all the way over here? And then I remembered. Ernie knew the maze of the Yellow House probably as well as Dubrovnik did.

But Ernie's lunge was too high. Dubrovnik shoved it off and kept moving, turning and slapping at Ernie's grasping fingers. While they struggled I closed in but Dubrovnik was gaining distance and then Ernie and I were both panting down the alley, giving chase to the crooked MP.

Dubrovnik darted into an open door.

As we crashed in after him I noticed the number atop the opening: 47. Each brothel in the Yellow House area was licensed and therefore numbered. We sprinted up the first flight of cement block stairs into a foyer with varnished wood-slat flooring. Korean women stood around in various states of undress.

"*Odi*?" Ernie asked. Where?

One of them pointed toward a short flight of broad wooden steps that led down to the display area behind another plate glass window. Dubrovnik must be around the corner. Trapped.

Before we could consult on the best way to take him, Ernie leapt down the flight of stairs. Sitting and squatting women screamed and scooted out of his way but before I could react, Dubrovnik exploded from behind a mother-of-pearl inlaid chest and landed a punch solidly on the back of Ernie's head.

Ernie's knees buckled, he reached for his neck, but he didn't go down. Dubrovnik swiveled, realizing that the man he had just punched wasn't the first man who'd been chasing him. When he saw me standing at the top of the flight of steps, his shoulders sagged and for a moment a look of resignation spread across his swarthy features. I smiled and reached for my handcuffs. But then Dubrovnik seemed to brighten and before I could lunge forward he took a step backward, stiffened his body and leapt through the huge, gleaming, shimmering pane of glass.

Women screamed.

Amongst the hail of crystal shards that followed Dubrovnik into the alley, he somehow managed to roll upon impact. Like a circus acrobat he bounded immediately to his feet. Once again, he was off and running. By now Ernie had recovered and was already clawing his way toward the wicked looking glass blades sticking up from the edge of the window. He was disoriented and I knew he'd hurt himself so I grabbed his shoulders and held him.

"What the hell you doing? He's getting away."

"Out the door," I said, "so we don't get cut."

Ernie let me drag him back to the main foyer and brace him as we descended the cement stairwell. When we reached the brick-paved alleyway, Dubrovnik was nowhere to be found. A few yards past Building 47, we asked a few of the women huddling in open doorways if they'd seen him but they argued amongst themselves and pointed in four different directions.

We'd lost him.

Our next stop was the home of someone who we suspected of being Dubrovnik's accomplice, a clerk who worked at the US Army's Port of Inchon Transportation Office. His name was Lee Ok-pyong, a Korean National. Although he worked for 8th Army, Lee fell squarely under the jurisdiction of the Korean National Police. Technically, we shouldn't even have been talking to him. Our original plan was to arrest Dubrovnik, interrogate him on compound, gather all the information we could, and then, accompanied by the Korean National Police, arrest Clerk Lee and assist in the KNP's interrogation. The more information we could gather first, the more productive that interrogation would be. But now, with Dubrovnik on the fly, our plan had changed.

"We shouldn't even be doing this," I told Ernie.

"Screw it. If Dubrovnik makes it over here and him and this guy Lee compare notes, they'll be able to get their stories straight. We'll never bust anybody."

The crime was diversion of US Government property. PX property, to be exact.

The way the scam worked was that Clerk Lee Ok-pyong filled out two bills of lading. One with the actual amount of imported scotch and cigarettes and stereo equipment to be delivered and the other with a larger amount that would be actually loaded onto the truck. For security reasons, each truck was escorted by an armed American Military Policeman. But since both Dubrovnik and the Korean driver were in on the scam with Clerk Lee, there was nobody to complain about the phony paperwork.

Near the outskirts of Inchon, they would pull the truck into a secluded warehouse and unloaded the excess PX property. Then they'd continue on their merry way to the Main PX in Seoul. Before leaving the Port of Inchon, each truckload was padlocked and sealed with a numbered aluminum tag. If the tag was tampered with, the receiving clerk on the other end of the line could tell. Supposedly. I wasn't sure if the receiving clerk was in on the scam or whether Dubrovnik had somehow managed to figure a way to re-seal the load. That was one of the things we'd hoped to discover during Sergeant Dubrovnik's interrogation.

However they were doing it, the scam was working well and might have gone on forever if an audit in the States hadn't identified the discrepancy between what was being shipped to the Port of Inchon and what was actually arriving in the Main PX inventory. Once 8th Army CID was notified of the leakage, Ernie and I were given the assignment. A couple of days later we had figured out which MP and driver were in on it. Finding the clerk who supplied the phony paperwork took a little longer but now we had him. Everything would've gone smoothly if Dubrovnik hadn't eluded us at the Yellow House.

The lane leading to the home of Clerk Lee Ok-pyong was not as well-paved as the one leading to the Yellow House. A stone-lined gutter ran down the center of a muddy walkway. Brick and cement walls loomed over us on either side, most of them topped by barbed wire or shards of glass stuck into cement. If you don't protect yourself against thievery, the Koreans believe, you deserve to be robbed.

Using our flashlight, I found Clerk Lee's address etched into a wooden doorway: 175 *bonji*, 58 *ho*, in the Yonghyon District of the city of Inchon. A light glimmered behind the wall, flickering because of the still falling rain. Ernie rang the doorbell. Two minutes later a door creaked open behind the wall and someone padded out in plastic slippers across the small courtyard.

The gate opened and a face stared out at us. Ernie tilted the beam of the flashlight and then I could see that the face was beautiful.

She was a Korean woman in her late twenties. Her features were even and her skin was so smooth that I had to swallow before stammering out the lines I'd mentally rehearsed in Korean.

"Is Mr. Lee Ok-pyong in? We're here on official business."

"Who are you?" she asked.

As I answered I noticed that her hair was black and thickly luxurious, tied back by a red ribbon behind her oval-shaped face.

"We work on the American compound," I answered. "It's important."

She opened the door a little wider. Ernie pushed past her, sloshed over flagstone steps, and slid back the oil-papered door that led into the *sarang-bang*, the front room of the home. A thin man with thick-lensed glasses looked up at us. He wore only a T-shirt and pajama bottoms and had been studying a ledger. A lit cigarette dangled from his lips.

"Mr. Lee Ok-pyong?" Ernie asked.

"Yes."

"With all the money you made ripping off foreign hooch, seems you could afford a better place than this dump."

I'm not sure if Clerk Lee understood. Without being invited in, Ernie slipped off his shoes and stepped up onto the warm vinyl floor. I followed. The beautiful woman stood by the open doorway, not sure if she should run and notify the police or if she should stand here by her husband.

"Your wife is very beautiful," Ernie said.

Clerk Lee was fully alert now. He sat upright and stubbed out his cigarette. "What do you want?"

"We want you to tell us about Dubrovnik," Ernie said. "Have you seen him tonight?"

"Who?"

"Sergeant Two," I said. That's what the other MPs and the Koreans in the transportation unit called Dubrovnik rather than trying to pronounce his full name.

Clerk Lee's glasses started to cloud and the color drained from his face. His wife stepped into the room, knelt, and wrapped both arms around her husband's shoulders. She turned to us.

"Get out," she said in Korean. "No one wants you here. Get out!"

Ernie understood that. "Fine," he said. "We'll get out. Just make sure you don't let any other GIs in here tonight."

As we left, Mrs. Lee stared at us with the face of an ice goddess. Her husband looked as if he were about to vomit.

At this time of night, the local police station was a madhouse. The Korean National Police had arrested three prostitutes and two Greek sailors for drunk and disorderly. They also had taken into custody one pickpocket and two fellows who'd tried to break into an old brick warehouse near the port.

"Busy?" I asked the Korean cop.

He looked at me as if I were nuts. Ernie and I both flashed our badges. In a few minutes we were talking to the night shift desk officer. We explained that we wanted Clerk Lee Ok-pyong taken into custody immediately, so he wouldn't be able to talk to his cohort and thereby ruin our case against him. The khaki-clad officer listened patiently and when I was done he lifted his open palms off the top of his desk.

"Nobody," he said in English. "No cops."

Sure, he was short staffed, but the real reason he didn't want to help us was that he didn't want to bust a fellow Korean without orders from on high. Who knew who the man was connected to?

Ernie argued with the desk officer for a while but finally gave up. When the Korean National Police don't want to do something, they don't do it. I pulled him out of there.

Outside, the night was completely dark, and the rain drifting in off the Yellow Sea was colder than ever.

The next morning, Ernie and I rose early from the warm *ondol* floor in the room we'd rented in the Yong Param Yoguan, the Dragon Wind Inn. After we washed and dressed and pushed through the wooden double-doors, Ernie said, "The place even smells like dragon wind."

"It was cheap," I said.

"So's pneumonia."

Without stopping anywhere for chop, we headed straight to

the police station. This time the commander was in, a man who introduced himself as Captain Peik Du-han. We shook hands and he spoke in English.

"I understand you were in last night requesting an arrest."

Briefly, I explained the situation to him. He nodded, his expression calm, but I noticed that his fists were beginning to knot.

"*Kei-sikki*," he said finally. Born of a dog.

Ernie came alert at that. His Korean vocabulary is limited mostly to cuss words. Captain Peik caught our alarmed expressions and said, "Not you. My duty officer last night. He should've listened to you. Or at least called me at home."

"Why?"

Captain Peik sighed heavily. Then he stood up and grabbed his cap off the top of his coat rack. "Come on," he said. "I'll show you."

General of the Army Douglas MacArthur, floppy hat atop his head, corncob pipe gripped in his teeth, hands on his hips, stared out across an expanse of lawn and over a cliff that fell off into the misty expanse of the churning Yellow Sea.

"Doug, baby." Ernie slapped the back of MacArthur's shin.

South Korea is one of the few countries in the world, outside of the United States, to have landscapes studded with statues of famous Americans. Up north at Freedom Bridge just south of the DMZ stands a statue of White Horse Harry Truman. In June of 1950, if he hadn't made the decision to fight to save South Korea, this country wouldn't exist today. MacArthur's contribution was the invasion of Inchon: cutting North Korean supply lines so US forces could manage to break out of the Pusan Perimeter, retake Seoul, and push the North Korean Communists all the way north to the Yalu River, their border with China.

But Captain Peik hadn't brought us here to this place known as *Jayu Gongyuan*, Freedom Park, for a history lesson. While MacArthur stared thoughtfully at the Yellow Sea, Peik led us into the heavy brush beneath a line of elm trees.

"*Chosim,*" he said.

I understood and managed to avoid the two mud-covered stone steps that led downward into the brush. Ernie stumbled over the hidden masonry. I caught him before he fell.

"*Chosim* means 'be careful,'" I told him. "When are you going to start taking those Korean language classes on post?"

"When you stop bugging me about it." Ernie pushed away my hand and straightened his jacket.

Some of the bushes in front of us had already been cleared and strips of white linen surrounded the area, the Korean indication of a place of death.

The body of Clerk Lee Ok-pyong lay in a muddy ditch.

"Shit," Ernie said.

Lee had changed out of his T-shirt and pajama bottoms. Now he wore slacks and an open collared white shirt that had been spattered with dirt. His head had been bashed in with something long and heavy. All I could think of was an MP's night stick.

Blue-smocked technicians milled around the body. Ernie and I tried to think of something to say, but there was nothing to be said. We'd screwed up royally this time. If only we'd collared Dubrovnik last night when we'd had our chance.

A KNP sedan pulled up to the edge of the park. Two officers climbed out and one of them held the back door open. A woman dressed in black emerged. Holding both her elbows, the two officers escorted the woman across the damp lawn. She kept her head bowed and a veil of black lace covered her face.

As they approached, she glanced up at me and even through the flimsy shroud I recognized the beautiful face of the wife of Clerk Lee. The look she gave me would've cooled Hell by about twenty degrees.

Keeping her eyes on me, she navigated the stone steps with ease and then paused in front of the body and turned her attention to what lay before her. The escorting officers backed up and Captain Peik approached. He stood silently next to her for a few moments and then began to whisper soft words. When he finished, she nodded slowly. Captain Peik thanked her and the two officers escorted her back to the waiting sedan.

When she was gone, Captain Peik turned to us. "That's her husband all right. She says he left the house shortly after midnight. Had to meet someone, she doesn't know who. Now, you fellows want to tell me what you know about this?"

We nodded and walked back to General MacArthur. As Ernie explained about Sergeant Dubrovnik and our screw-up last night, I studied the granite statue and noticed that it even had shoelaces. Doug seemed to be listening to Ernie and Captain Peik. I strode across the expanse of lawn to the cliff and gazed down at foamy breakers crashing against rocks a hundred feet below. From here, I guessed I could throw something about a quarter mile out into the Yellow Sea.

When I turned around, General MacArthur was staring at me, reading my thoughts.

Ernie and I caught hell back at 8th Army.

The Foreign Organization Employees' Union had lodged a formal protest about our conduct. Harassing one of their employees at his home and later not protecting him when he went to his rendezvous with death. Of course, everyone assumed that Sergeant Dubrovnik was the man who had summoned Clerk Lee to the park overlooking the Yellow Sea and there proceeded to bludgeon him to death. Why had he done it? Maybe because Sergeant Two wanted to keep Clerk Lee quiet about the nefarious activities they had engaged in together. Maybe. More likely they had an argument. Maybe Clerk Lee threatened to rat Dubrovnik out. Right now we could only speculate. What we needed to do was catch Sergeant Dubrovnik. Ernie and I checked with his MP company. Of course, the man hadn't shown up for morning formation and, according to the Commanding Officer, no one in the unit knew where he had disappeared to.

Ernie and I were about to start searching for Dubrovnik when the CID First Sergeant pulled us aside.

"You're off the case," he told us. When Ernie started to protest the First Sergeant held up his palm. "Your first suspect escapes, right from under your noses. And then your second suspect, a Korean National who you shouldn't even have been messing with, turns up dead."

Ernie's face flushed red and he started to sputter.

"Keep your trap shut, Bascom," the First Sergeant barked. "The Provost Marshall is still deciding whether or not to bring you two up on charges. A Status of Forces violation. Harassing a Korean civilian and misuse of your military police powers. Not to mention gross incompetence."

With that, we were assigned to the black market detail.

Two weeks passed by. Two weeks of watching Korean dependent housewives to make sure they didn't sell duty-free liquor or cigarettes down in the ville. Clerk Lee was buried, Sergeant Dubrovnik was still at large, and the Provost Marshall was still holding the threat of charges over our heads. Then we got the call.

Stiff found in the village of Songtan-up.

The corpse belonged to Sergeant Ivan Dubrovnik. He'd been shot once through the heart at close range, apparently with his own Military Police issued .45, which was found beside him. He lay in a cobbled alleyway lined with nightclubs and beer halls and cheap room-rent-by-the-hour *yoguan*s. Songtan-up served the 5,000 or so US airmen stationed at Osan Air Force Base. The sun was just rising above the rooftops of the two- and three-story buildings that surrounded us. The Korean cop who'd found the corpse at two in the morning told us that no one in the neighborhood had heard or seen anything. Five hours more of canvassing the neighborhood didn't change that story.

The Security Police at Osan classified Dubrovnik's death as a suicide. The only other person who'd been involved in the plot was the driver, who'd been long since locked up. He couldn't have been the killer.

And that also closed the case neatly. Now that justice had been done, the Foreign Organization Employee's Union dropped their formal protest against Ernie and me. Everyone had suffered enough, they figured. The Provost Marshall put us back on regular duty status and signed off on the finding that no charges would be brought against us. Still, he kept us on the black market detail.

Dubrovnik's body was shipped back to the States. It was over. All killings had been accounted for. Nothing left but to burn incense at their graves.

The blue silk of her dress hugged the curves of her body like wet paper clinging to a baby's cheek. Her face was a smooth oval with shining black eyes and full lips. I recognized her immediately. The wife of the late clerk, Lee Ok-pyong.

We stood at Gate 4 on the edge of 8th Army's Yongsan Compound near the district of Seoul known as Samgak-ji. She had asked the security guards at the gate to phone me at the CID headquarters and when I received the mysterious call I hurried out.

Holding a black patent leather handbag in front of her waist, she nodded to me, sort of a half bow. Then she spoke in Korean, telling me that she wanted to talk. Signing her on compound would be a hassle; she'd have to give up her Korean National Identification Card, and it would be a long walk back to the CID office. Instead, I gestured toward Samgak-ji. She nodded again and we strode about a half block down the road until we found a tea shop that was open. Once we were seated, she ordered *boli cha*, tea made from barley, and I ordered the more expensive ginseng version. The pig-tailed teenage waitress brought us our drinks. When she left, I sipped on mine and waited for Mrs. Lee to begin.

She kept her head bowed for what seemed a long time. I spent the time admiring her. She was a good looking woman, a widow now, no children. Her perfume smelled of orchids. Probably she'd be remarried in no time. But why had she come to visit me? Finally she spoke, using measured and simple Korean that I could follow.

"I am sorry for having been angry with you. At the time, I blamed you and your friend for my husband's death. For having destroyed our tranquility. Now I realize that the fault was with this man Sergeant Two."

"Sergeant Dubrovnik," I said.

She nodded. "Yes. And also my husband was much to blame. He hoped to make enough money so we could go into business for ourselves. Maybe buy a little teashop like this one." She looked around at the sturdy wooden furnishings and then turned her moist eyes back to mine. "But he wasn't a criminal. This was the first time he'd ever done anything like that."

I nodded, waiting for her to tell me why she had come. Was it just to apologize for being rude to a cop? If I wasn't used to that, I'd have to get out of the business.

She lowered her head once again, thinking over what she would say next. "I have a job, on the American compound where my husband used to work. In the same office."

The Port of Inchon Transportation Office. That wasn't unusual. The Foreign Organization Employees' Union is the most powerful union in the country. When one of their members dies an untimely death, they take steps to provide as best they can for the surviving family members. There's no welfare in Korea. No food stamps or social security. The only thing the union can do is use its influence to land a job for an able bodied member of the surviving family. In this case, Mrs. Lee herself.

A handkerchief emerged from her handbag and Mrs. Lee dabbed her eyes.

I knew it was coming now, the reason she'd gone to all the trouble to find me. I was prepared for a surprise but this one took me completely off guard.

"I want you to meet with me," she said. "I want you to tell me everything about the case, about what happened to my husband."

"We can talk about that right here," I said.

"No. You have to get back to work and there are too many people around."

I studied the layout of the teahouse again, to make sure I hadn't missed something. There were about a half-dozen customers, two waitresses, and one young man behind the serving counter, none of them within earshot of our conversation.

She looked boldly into my eyes. "I want to meet you," she said. "So you and I can be alone."

I'm dumb but not that dumb. As coolly as I could, I agreed.

For the next two weeks, all my off-duty time was spent with the Widow Lee. She had to work in Inchon and I had to work about thirty miles away in Seoul. Some nights we met in between, at a Korean-style inn with a warm *ondol* floor in the city of Kimpo right near the big airport that services the capital city. We'd lie together and hear the big jets fly over us and listen to Korean music and, when we found time, eat Korean food. It was a lovely time for me and she seemed so desperately in need of someone to be near her.

She told me about her job. She filled out the bills of lading for the imported American goods that were transported from the Port of Inchon to the Main PX in Seoul. The same thing her husband had done. Gradually, she started to tell me of the mistakes her husband had made. Before she could go on, I changed the subject. The next time we met, she brought it up again.

Ernie clicked his fingernail against my coffee cup.

"Wake up," he told me. "We have to go to work here in a minute and you're still sleeping."

We sat in the 8th Army snack bar on Yongsan Compound, wearing clean white shirts and ties and jackets, having one last cup of java before heading up the hill to the CID office to begin our regular workday.

"And you're developing bags under your eyes," Ernie

continued. "The Widow Lee is putting you through one serious workout."

"Can it, Ernie."

"Oh. That much in love, are we?"

I pushed my coffee aside, placed both my hands on the small formica-covered table, and stared him straight in the eye. "So what if I am?"

Ernie's eyes widened and he leaned back. "Easy, pal. I didn't know you were taking this so seriously."

"Yeah. I've been taking it seriously. I've been taking her seriously. The last couple of weeks have been about the best couple of weeks of my life."

"Okay. Fine. So what's bothering you?"

"What's bothering me is that I don't know what to do."

"Hey, relax and enjoy it. Just don't get married."

"That's not what I'm talking about."

Ernie's eyes crinkled in puzzlement, something that doesn't happen to him much. He has the world figured out. Or at least he thinks he does.

"Then what *are* you talking about?" he asked.

"I'm meeting her tonight at the same *yoguan* in Kimpo. Drive me out there in the jeep. Hang around. You'll see what I'm talking about."

Before he could ask more questions, I rose from the table, strode out of the big fogged-glass double doors of the snack bar, and marched up the hill to the CID office.

That night the Widow Lee and I went to the best restaurant in Kimpo. I ordered *kalbi*, marinated short ribs braised over an open charcoal fire. When we were finished, we walked arm in arm back to the *yoguan*. After we hung up our coats and relaxed, she pulled a wad of paperwork out of her purse. She sat next to me on the warm floor and held my hand and spoke earnestly to me for what must've been almost an hour. Most of what she said, I didn't listen to. The bills of lading she handed to me, those I did pay attention to. Duplicates. With differing amounts of product listed on each.

I guess I knew from the day out at Freedom Park overlooking the Yellow Sea. Maybe General MacArthur had made me aware of it. Or maybe it had been the hidden stone steps that Ernie and I had stumbled on, and almost every Korean cop who approached the scene; she had breezed past as if they were an item of furniture in her front room.

She'd been there before, and recently, to the murder site of her husband.

Sergeant Dubrovnik, an experienced MP and a man on the run for his life, had either shot himself in the ribs with his own .45 or he'd allowed someone he trusted to stand very close to him. Who else but a woman? And a woman he knew well?

And the job she'd received on compound. Sure, the union would work very hard to make sure that, as a widow of one of their deceased members, she found employment, but starting as a billing clerk? That was a relatively high paying job that required extensive experience. The union gets people jobs but usually the job is at the lowest entry level and the person who lands it is happy to get it. The work is steady, the benefits better than most jobs in Korea, and advancement will depend on how hard they work.

The Widow Lee had started near the top. Somebody, probably a man, had cleared the way for her.

And now me. I was next on her list. She'd learned from her husband's mistakes; Sergeant Dubrovnik, an MP, was no longer in the picture. A CID agent was her next step up.

And now I held the duplicated bills of lading in my hand. The proof I needed. Ernie was waiting in a nearby teahouse, the jeep outside.

But could I do it?

▪ ▪ ▪

Her eyes widened when I told her.

"A drive? Why should we go for a drive?"

"Because I say so." I ripped her coat off the peg in the wall and tossed it to her. "*Kapshida*," I said. Let's go.

She refused so I slapped her once—something I never do to a woman. But she was no longer a woman to me. She was a criminal.

At the police station in Inchon, Captain Rhee studied the bills of lading and listened patiently to my explanation. She wanted me to go into the scam with her. She had taken her husband's job and now I would take Sergeant Dubrovnik's place. And working in the CID headquarters, I'd be in even a better position to cover things up. Captain Rhee nodded, understanding what I said.

He held the Widow Lee overnight for questioning.

In a way I was proud of her. Captain Rhee told me later that she denied everything.

The Korean National Police re-covered the ground they'd covered before but this time they were asking different questions. Between the home of Lee Ok-pyong and the park overlooking the Yellow Sea, they canvassed local residents who'd been out on the night he was murdered. Previously, no one had seen two men walking together, one of them a Korean, the other an American. This time the police asked them if they'd seen a Korean man walking with a woman. A few of them had. One of them, a sweet potato vendor, even mentioned that she'd seen the couple, deep in conversation, pass the statue of General MacArthur and disappear into the brush. Later, the woman had come out alone, stood by the sea for a moment and had then thrown something over the cliff. A stick maybe. Maybe a *mongdungi*, a heavy club that women in Korea use to beat dirt out of wet clothing. Then the woman had hurried out of the park.

In Songtan-up, bar girls and local shop owners remembered a robust American GI walking arm in arm with a beautiful Korean woman. Both of them were strangers in these parts. They'd entered a narrow back alley and one of the bar girls assumed it was for a late night tryst. After only a minutes or two, the woman had left alone, in a hurry, and the bar girl assumed that she'd changed her mind about her affection for the big GI.

Had the bar girl heard a gunshot? No. The rock music blaring from the outside speakers that lined the narrow lane was much too loud.

Captain Rhee personally interviewed the local union leader. As an experienced cop, he knew enough to be circumspect in his questioning and didn't press the union overly hard. There was too much power involved. Too much chance for the union and therefore all Korean employees to lose face. And, after all, how could you prove such an allegation? That a union leader had allowed a beautiful young widow to influence him and land her a better-than-average job? The union leader, however, was smart enough not to stonewall the Korean National Police completely. He confirmed to Captain Rhee that what he suspected, that the Widow Lee had received extraordinary assistance, was within the realm of possibility.

"You knew it was coming, didn't you?" Ernie asked me.

Once again we were sitting in the 8th Army snack bar on the morning after the Widow Lee was convicted of the murder of her husband and Sergeant Dubrovnik.

"I guess I knew. Somewhere. But I didn't want to know."

"I don't blame you." Ernie nibbled on his bacon, lettuce, and tomato sandwich. "She was a good looking woman."

I sighed.

"Unlucky in love," Ernie said.

"You got that right."

"You could've gone along with the plan," Ernie told me. "Made some money for yourself. And you'd still have her."

I set my coffee down and looked into his green eyes. "I never thought of that."

"Sure you didn't," he said.

THE OPPOSITE OF O

"**N**ever the twain shall meet," a wise man once said.

He was referring to the Occident and the Orient but as a criminal investigator for the 8th United States Army in Seoul, Republic of Korea, I can assure you that the two worlds often meet. And in the case of Private First Class Everett P. Rothenberg and Miss O Sung-hee, the two worlds collided at the intersection of warm flesh and the cold, sharpened tip of an Army-issue bayonet.

Ernie and I were dispatched from 8th Army Headquarters as soon as we received word about a stabbing near Camp Colbern, a communications compound located in the countryside some eighteen miles east of the teeming metropolis of Seoul.

Paldang-ni was the name of the village. It clings to the side of the gently-sloping foothills of the Kumdang Mountains just below the brick and barbed wire enclosure that surrounds Camp Colbern. The roads were narrow and farmers pushed wooden carts piled high with winter turnips and old women in short blouses and long skirts balanced huge bundles of laundry atop their heads. Ernie drove slowly through the busy lanes, avoiding splashing mud on the industrious pedestrians. Not because Ernie Bascom was a polite kind of guy but because he wasn't quite sure where, in this convoluted maze of alleys, we would find the road that led to the Paldang Station of the Korean National Police.

Above a whitewashed building, the flag of *Daehan Minguk*, the Republic of Korea, fluttered in the cold morning breeze. The yin and the yang symbols clung to one another, red and blue teardrops embracing on a field of pure white. Ernie parked the jeep out front and together we strode into the station. Five minutes later we were interrogating a prisoner: a thin and very nervous young man by the name of Private First Class Everett P. Rothenberg.

"They were sisters," Private Rothenberg told us.

"Who?" Ernie asked.

"Miss O. And the woman she shared a hooch with, Miss Kang."

"Sisters?"

"Yeah."

Ernie crossed his arms and stared skeptically at Rothenberg. Rothenberg, for his part, allowed long forearms to hang listlessly over bony legs. The three-legged stool he sat upon was too low for him and his spine curved forward and his head bobbed. He looked like a man who'd abandoned any hope of receiving a fair shake.

"Didn't it ever trouble you," Ernie asked, "that the two women had different last names?"

Rothenberg shrugged bony shoulders. "I figured they had different fathers or something."

I asked the main question. "Why'd you kill her, Rothenberg?"

He tilted his head toward me and his moist blue eyes became larger and rounder. "You don't believe me, do you?"

"What's to believe? You haven't told us anything one way or the other."

"I told *them*." He pointed to the three khaki-clad Korean National Policemen standing outside the cement-walled interrogation room. Their arms were crossed, fists clenched, narrow eyes lit with malice. Rays from a single electric bulb illuminated the interrogation room, revealing cobwebs and dried rat feces in unswept corners.

"What'd you tell the KNPs?" I asked.

"I told them I couldn't have killed Miss O."

"Why not?"

Rothenberg, once again, allowed his head to hang loosely on his long neck. "Because I love her," he said.

Ernie smirked. Virtually every young GI who arrives in Korea and finds his first *yobo* down in the ville falls in love. The US Army is so used to this phenomenon that they require eight months' worth of paperwork for an American GI to marry a Korean woman. What with a twelve-month tour of duty, a GI has to fall in love early and hard to be allowed permission to marry. Why all the hassles? Simple. To protect innocent young American GIs from the sinister wiles of Asian dragon ladies. At least, that's the official rationale. The real reason is flat-out racism.

"Where were you last night, Rothenberg?"

"You mean after curfew?"

"Yes. But let's start from the beginning. What time did you leave work?"

I dragged another wooden stool from against the wall of the interrogation room and sat down opposite Private First Class Everett P. Rothenberg. I pulled out my pocket notebook and my ballpoint pen and prepared to write. Rothenberg started talking.

Ernie leaned against the cement wall, arms crossed, and continued to smirk. The KNPs continued to glare. A spider found its web and slowly crawled toward a quivering moth.

Our first stop was the Full Moon Teahouse.

Miss O had worked here. And, according to Rothenberg, she was the toast of the town, the tallest, most shapely, and best looking business girl in the village of Paldang-ni. The front door was covered with a brightly painted façade; a replica of a gateway to an ancient imperial palace. The heavy wooden door was locked. Ernie and I strolled around back. Here the setting was more real. Piled cases of empty *soju* bottles, plastic-wrapped garbage rotting in rusty metal cans, a long-tailed rat scurrying down a vented drainage ditch.

The back door was open. Ernie and I walked in. The odor of ammonia and soapy water assaulted our nostrils. After a short hallway, light from a red bulb guided us into the main serving room. Wooden tables with straight-backed chairs covered most of the floor. Cushioned booths lined the walls and behind a serving counter a youngish-looking Korean woman sat beneath a green-shaded lamp, laboring over heavy accounting ledgers. When she saw us, she pulled off her horn-rimmed glasses and stared, mouth agape.

I flashed my ID. Ernie found a switch and overhead fluorescent bulbs buzzed to life. The woman stared at my Criminal Investigation badge and finally said, "*Weikurei nonun?*" No bow. No polite verb endings. Just asking me what I wanted. A Korean cop would've popped her in the jaw. Being a tolerant Westerner, I shrugged off the insult.

"What we're doing here," I said, "is we want to talk to Miss Kang Mi-ryul."

She touched the tip of her forefinger to her nose. A hand gesture not used in the West. She was saying, that's me. I started to explain why we were there but she'd already guessed. She said, "Miss O," and pulled out a handkerchief. After a few tears, she calmed down and started to talk. In Korean. Telling me all about her glorious and gorgeous friend, the late O Sung-hee. About Miss O's amorous conquests, about the job offers from other teahouse and bar owners in town, about the men—both Korean and American—who constantly pursued her.

Miss Kang closed the accounting books and after shrugging on a thick cotton coat, walked with us a few blocks through the village. It was almost noon now and a few chop houses were open. The aroma of fermented cabbage and garlic drifted through the air. Miss Kang led us to her hooch, the same hooch she and Miss O had shared. She allowed us to peruse Miss O's meager personal effects. Cosmetics, hair products, a short row of dresses in a plastic armoire, tattered magazines with the faces of international film stars grinning out at us. Kang told us that Miss O's hometown was Kwangju, far to the south, and she'd come north to escape the poverty and straight-laced traditionalism of the family she'd been born into. When I asked her who had killed Miss O, she blanched and pretended to faint. It was a pretty good act because she plopped loudly to the ground and a neighbor called the Korean National Police, a contingent of which had been following us anyway.

In less than a minute they arrived and glared at us as if Miss Kang's passing out had been our fault. One of the younger cops stood a little too close to Ernie and Ernie shoved him. That caused a wrestling match and a lot of cursing until the senior KNP and I broke it up.

So much for good relationships between international law enforcement agencies.

As we left, Miss Kang was still crying and two of the KNPs, God bless them, were still following us.

Camp Colbern wasn't much better.

Rothenberg worked in the 304th Signal Battalion Communications Center. Electronic messages came in over secure lines, then were printed, copied, and distributed to the appropriate bureaucratic cubby holes. Apparently, Camp Colbern had two functions. First, as a base camp for an army aviation unit, boasting a landing pad with a dozen helicopters and associated support personnel and second, as a relay station for the grid of US Army signal sites that runs up and down the spine of South Korea. When I asked the signal officers a few technical questions, they clammed up. I didn't have a "need to know," they told me.

"How do they know what we 'need to know'?" Ernie asked me. "This is a criminal investigation. We don't know what we need to know until after we already know it."

I shrugged.

Private Rothenberg had been a steady and reliable worker, I

was told. A good soldier. He had no close buddies because his off duty time was spent out in the village of Paldang-ni, apparently mooning over Miss O Sung-hee.

Ernie pulled a photograph from his pocket, one he'd palmed while we rummaged through O's personal effects at Miss Kang's hooch. It was of Miss O and Miss Kang standing arm in arm, smiling at the camera, in front of a boat rental quay on the bank of a river. The sign in Korean said Namhan-kang, the Namhan River, not far from here. Miss O was a knockout, with a big beautiful smile and even white teeth and a figure that would make any sailor—or any GI—jump ship. Miss Kang, by comparison, was a plain-looking slip of a girl. Shorter, thinner, less attractive. Her smile didn't dazzle as Miss O's did, Rather it looked unsure of itself, slightly afraid, wary of the world.

Atop her head, at a rakish angle, Miss O wore a black baseball cap. Using a magnifying glass, I examined the embroidery on the front. It was a unit designation: 545th Army Aviation Battalion, Company C. In smaller print on the side was a shorter row of letters. It took stronger light for me to make them out. Finally, I did: Boson. I handed the photograph back to Ernie.

Ernie took another long look at the gorgeous Miss O and then slipped the photo back into his pocket. Something told me he had no intention of letting it go.

The air traffic controllers at the Camp Colbern aviation tower told us that Chief Warrant Officer Mike Boson was due in at sixteen thirty—four thirty P.M. civilian time. Ernie and I were standing on the edge of the Camp Colbern helipad when the Huey UH-1N helicopter landed. As the blades gradually slowed their rotation, a crewman hopped out and then the engine whined and the blades slowed further and finally the co-pilot and then the pilot jumped out of the chopper. Chief Warrant Officer Mike Boson slipped off his helmet as he walked toward us and tucked it beneath his arm.

"The tower told me you wanted to talk to me," he said.

Ernie and I flashed our identification. I asked if there was a more comfortable place to talk.

"No," Boson said. "We talk here. What do you want?"

The chopper's engine still buzzed. The crewman and the co-pilot hustled about on various errands, all the while listening to what we were saying. Boson, apparently, wanted it that way. We asked Boson where he had been last night, the night of the murder.

"In the O Club." The Officers' Club here on Camp Colbern. "For dinner, a couple of beers, and then to the BOQ for a good night's rest." The Bachelor Officer's Quarters.

"You didn't visit Miss O Sung-hee?" Ernie asked.

"No."

"Why not?"

Boson shrugged. "I don't run the ville when I have duty the next morning."

"You were scheduled to fly?"

"Yes. To Taegu to pick up the Nineteenth Support Group commander. And then south from there."

"When did you hear Miss O was dead?"

"Just before I left out this morning. Everyone was talking about it."

"Did you realize you'd be questioned?"

"No."

"Why not?"

"Because I knew her but a lot of other guys knew her too."

"Like who?"

He shrugged again. "I don't know their names."

We continued to question Warrant Officer Boson and he finally admitted that he'd spent more than just a few nights with Miss O Sung-hee and that he'd also escorted her and Miss Kang to the Namkang River the day the photograph Ernie showed him had been taken. They'd rented a boat and rowed to a resort island in the middle of the river and a few hours later returned to Paldang-ni where Boson spent the night with Miss O.

"In her hooch?" I asked.

Warily, Boson nodded.

"It's tiny," Ernie said. "So where did Miss Kang sleep?"

For the third time, Boson shrugged. "I don't know."

"But she lived there too, didn't she?"

"Yes. But every time I stayed with Miss O, she'd disappear. I figured she bunked with the landlady who owns the hooch."

"But you weren't sure?"

"Why would I care?"

We asked if he knew Rothenberg. He didn't.

"You didn't know a lot of things," Ernie said.

Boson bristled. "I'm here to fly helicopters. Not to write a history of business girls in the ville."

"And not to murder anyone?"

Boson dropped his helmet and leapt for Ernie's throat. I thrust my forearms forward, blocked him and managed to hold Boson back, although it was a struggle. The chopper crewman and the co-pilot ran over. I shoved Chief Warrant Officer Boson backward, they held him, and I dragged Ernie off of the helipad.

Night fell purple and gloomy over the village of Paldang-ni. But then a small miracle happened. Neon blinked to life: red, yellow, purple, and gold. Some of it pulsating, some of it rotating, all of it beckoning to any young GI with a few dollars in his pocket to enter the Jade Lady Nightclub or the Frozen Chosun Bar or the Full Moon Teahouse. Tailor shops and brassware emporiums and drug stores and sporting goods outlets lined the narrow lanes. Rock music pulsated out of beaded curtains. A late autumn Manchurian wind blew cold and moist through the alleyways but scantily clad Korean business girls stood in mini-skirts and hot pants and low-cut cotton blouses, their creamy bronze flesh pimpled like plucked geese.

The women cooed as we passed but Ernie and I ignored them and entered the first bar on the right: The Frozen Chosun. They served draft OB, Oriental Brewery beer, on tap. We jolted back a short mug and a shot of black market brandy, ignored the entreaties of the listless hostesses scattered around the dark enclosure, and continued on to the next dive. At each stop, I inquired about Miss O Sung-hee. Everyone knew her. They all knew that she'd been murdered brutally and they all assumed that the killer had been her jealous erstwhile boyfriend, an American GI by the name of Everett P. Rothenberg. But a few of the waitresses and bartenders and business girls I talked to speculated further. Miss O had Korean boyfriends—a few of them. Mostly men of power. Business owners in the bar district. But one of the men stood out. It was only after I'd laid out cash on an overpriced sweetheart drink that one under-weight bar hostess breathed his name. Shin, she said. Or that's what everyone called him: Mr. Shin. He was a dresser and a player and had no visible means of support other than, she'd heard, playing a mean game of pool and beating up the occasional business girl that fell under his spell.

"A *kampei*," I said to her. A gangster.

She shook her head vehemently. "No. Not that big. He small. How you say?" The overly made up young woman thought for a moment and then came up with the appropriate phrase. "He small potatoes."

In addition to buying her a drink, I slipped her a thousand *won* note—about two bucks. The tattered bill disappeared into the frayed waistband of her skirt.

When Ernie and I entered the King's Pavilion Pool Hall, all eyes gazed at us.

There was no way for two *Miguk*s to enter the second-story establishment surreptitiously. It was a large open room filled with cigarette smoke and stuffed with green felt pool tables from one end to the other. Narrow-waisted Korean men held pool cues and leaned over tables and lounged against walls, all of them puffing away furiously on cheap Korean cigarettes and all of them glaring at us, eyes narrow, lips curled into snarls, hatred filling the air even more thickly than the cloud of pungent tobacco smoke. This pool hall wasn't for GIs. It was for Koreans. The GIs had their bars, plenty of them, about two blocks away from here in the foreigner's bar district. Nobody, even the man who collected money at the entranceway, wanted us here.

Ernie snarled back. "Screw you too," he whispered.

"Steady," I replied.

In Korean, I spoke to the bald-headed man collecting the fees. "Mr. Shin?" I asked. "*Odiso*?" Where is he?

The man looked blankly at me. Then he turned to the men in the pool hall. From somewhere toward the back, a radio hissed and a Korean female singer warbled a rueful note. I said it again, louder this time, "Mr. Shin."

The snarls turned to grimaces of disdain. Korean cuss words floated our way. A few men laughed. More of them turned away from us, lifting their cues, returning their attention to eight balls and rebound angles and pockets. Nobody came forward. Nobody would tell us who Mr. Shin was or, more importantly, where to find him.

Ernie and I turned and walked back down the stairway. At the next pool hall, we repeated the same procedure. With the same result.

Later that night, we stood at the spot where Miss O had been murdered.

The site was located atop a hill overlooking both Paldang-ni and Camp Colbern. On the opposite side of the hill, to the north, moonlight shone down on the sinuous flow of the Namhan River. One or two boats drifted in the distance, fishermen on their way home to straw-thatched huts. On the peak of the hill stood a tile-roofed shrine with a stone foundation and an enormous brass bell hanging from sturdy rafters. No one was there now but I imagined that periodically Buddhist monks walked up the well-worn path to sound the ancient-looking bell.

"When did they find her?" Ernie asked.

I pulled out a penlight to read my tattered notebook.

"Zero five hundred this morning," I said. "Just before dawn. Two Buddhist monks who came up here to say their morning prayers. She was laying right here."

I pointed at the far edge of the stone foundation, nearest the river.

"Stabbed in the back once," I continued. "And then four or five times in the chest. She bled to death."

"And the murder weapon?"

"Never found. The KNPs assume it was a bayonet for two reasons, the size and depth of the entry wounds and the fact that Rothenberg, being a GI, would've had access to one."

"His bayonet was found in his field gear."

"He could've stolen another one. Happens all the time."

"Or," Ernie replied, "the killer could've bought one on the black market."

I nodded. Ernie was right. The KNPs were taking a big leap in locking up Rothenberg. So far, they had no hard evidence linking him to the murder. Still, public opinion had to be mollified. When a young Korean woman is murdered, someone has to be locked up, and fast. Otherwise, the public will wonder why they're spending their hard-earned tax dollars on police salaries. Someone has to pay for the crime. Like the yin and the yang symbols on the national flag, harmony in the universe must be restored. Someone is murdered, someone must pay for that murder. Everett P. Rothenberg wouldn't be the first American GI convicted in Korea of something that there was no definitive proof he'd actually done. But if that was the case, harmony would come to his defense. If there was little or no evidence proving that he did it, Rothenberg would receive a light sentence, maybe four years in a Korean jail and then deportation back to the States. So far, no one—including me and Ernie—had any real idea who'd murdered Miss O Sung-hee.

Rothenberg's alibi was sketchy. After finishing the day shift at the 304th Signal Battalion Comm Center, he'd eaten chow, showered, changed clothes and headed to the ville. At about eighteen hundred hours, he'd arrived at the Full Moon Teahouse. There, he'd sat in a corner sipping on ginseng tea while Miss Kang and Miss O Sung-hee worked. Miss Kang did most of the actual serving and preparation. Miss O sat with customers—Korean businessmen, small groups of American officers—adding beauty and charm to their evening. Before the midnight curfew, according to Rothenberg, Miss O convinced him that she was too tired to see him that evening and he should return to Camp Colbern. He did. Since he returned to his base camp before the midnight-to-four curfew, the MPs at the main gate didn't bother to log in his name. Lights were already out in the barracks. In the dark, he'd undressed, stuffed his clothes and wallet in his wall locker, and hopped into his bunk. None of the other GIs in the barracks had any recollection of his arrival.

Ernie walked over to the bell and rapped it with his knuckles. A low moan reverberated from the sculpted bronze, like the whispered sigh of a giant. We started back down the trail. It was steep. Boulders and thick brambles of bushes blocked our way on either side. We stepped carefully, inching forward, watching our step in the bright moonlight.

"Why'd we bother coming up here?" Ernie asked.

As he spoke, the earth shook—just slightly, as if something heavy had thudded to the ground. I looked back. I could see nothing except Ernie staring at me quizzically, wondering why I had stopped. Then two more thuds, one after the other, shallower this time, as if something were skipping forward, becoming louder, rolling toward us.

It emerged from the darkness above Ernie's head, looking for all the world like a steam roller from hell.

"Watch out!" I shouted.

I leapt to the side of the trail and Ernie, not yet fully understanding, followed suit. He dove into a thicket of branches and I landed atop a small boulder and scrambled over it to the opposite side away from the trail.

The noise grew deafening, one crash after another, and then an enormous metal cylinder flew out of the night, rolling down the trail, careening to the right and then left; barreling down the trail and smashing everything in its path. It clipped the edge of the thicket and missed Ernie by a couple of feet. I crouched. The huge metal rolling pin crashed against the boulder and the cylinder flew over, only inches above my head. After it passed, Ernie and I sat up, staring at moonlight glistening off the cylinder. The careening monolith continued its pell-mell rush down the side of the hill, smashing an old wooden fence outside a small animal shelter and then hitting the shelter itself. Lumber flew everywhere. The cylinder kept rolling until it slowed and finally landed in a muddy rice paddy with a huge, sloppy splat.

"What the hell was that?" Ernie asked.

I rose slowly to my feet, checking uphill to make sure nothing more was coming at us. "The bell," I said.

"The what?"

"The bronze bell. Come on."

We ran back up the pathway. At the top of the hill, the shrine stood empty. Using my penlight I examined the weathered ropes hanging beneath splintered rafters.

"Sliced," I said.

"With what?" Ernie asked.

"Can't be sure but with something sharp. Maybe a bayonet."

Mr. Shin found us.

So did about five of his pals. Light from a yellow streetlamp shone on angry faces, all of then belonging to young punks with grease-backed hair and sneers on their lips.

"Why are you looking for me?" Shin asked in Korean.

We stood in an alley not far from the King's Pavilion Pool Hall Ernie and I had stopped in earlier today.

"Your girlfriend," I told him, "Miss O Sung-hee, was murdered last night. Where were you while she was being killed?"

Shin puffed one time on his cigarette—overly dramatically—and then flicked the flaming butt to the ground. Ernie braced himself, about one long stride away from me, his side to the Korean man nearest him. He was ready to fight. Five to two were the odds, but we'd faced worse.

"Not my girlfriend," Shin said at last, switching to English. "No more. Break up long time ago."

"How long?"

"Maybe one month."

A long time all right. "Miss Kang didn't mention your name to the Korean police. Why not?"

"She no can do."

"'No can do?' Why not?"

"She my . . . how you say? . . . sister."

"She's your sister?"

"Yes. Kang not her real name. Real name same mine. Shin."

"So you met Miss O through your sister?"

"Yes."

"Why'd you break up with Miss O?"

Shin shrugged. "I tired of her."

I didn't believe that for a minute. Shin was a tough guy all right and like tough punks all over the world there would be a certain type of woman available to him. Women who thought little of themselves. Women who, in order to build up their self-esteem, flocked toward men who were on the outs with the law. Men who they considered to be exciting. Korea, like everywhere else, had its share of this type of woman. But from everything I'd heard about Miss O Sung-hee, I didn't believe she was that type. She went for cops and attorneys and helicopter pilots. Men of power. Men of real accomplishment. Not men who were broke and hung around pool halls.

"She dumped you," I said.

"Huh?"

"Miss O. She think, 'I no like Shin anymore.' She tell you *karra chogi.*" Go away.

Shin's sneer twisted in anger. "No woman tell Shin go away."

Ernie guffawed and said to me, "Is this guy dumb or what?" He stepped past me and glared at Shin. "So you took Miss O to the top of the hill and you used a knife and you killed her."

Shin realized that he was digging a hole for himself. "No. No way. I no take. That night, I in pool hall. All night. Owner tell you. He see me there."

Shin mentioned the pool hall owner because even he knew that nobody would believe the testimony of him and his buddies. I crossed my arms and kept my gaze steady on Shin's eyes. He was a frightened young man. And when he'd heard that Ernie and I were looking for him, he'd voluntarily presented himself. Both these points were in his favor. Could he have murdered Miss O Sung-hee? Sure he could have. But something told me that his alibi would hold up. Otherwise, he wouldn't be standing here anxious to clear his name. If he'd murdered her, he'd be long gone. Still, I'd check with the pool hall owner as soon as I could.

Ernie had his own way of testing Shin's sincerity. He stepped forward until his chest was pushed up almost against Shin's. Ernie glared at Shin for a while and then snarled. "Out of my way."

Shin seemed about to do something, to punch Ernie, but indecision danced in his glistening black eyes. Finally, he sighed and stepped back, making way for Ernie and me. Grumbling, his pals made way too.

We ran the ville.

Shots, beers, business girls on our laps. Ernie was enjoying the rock music and the girls and the frenzied crowds and gave himself over to a night of mindless pleasure. Me, I sipped on my drink, barely heard the music, and ignored the caresses of the gorgeous young women who surrounded me.

"What the hell's the matter with you?" Ernie asked.

I shook my head.

"Come on," he coaxed. "What could possibly be wrong? We're

away from the headshed, on temporary duty, we have a pocket full of travel pay, and we're surrounded by booze and bands and business girls. What more could you possibly want?"

"A clue," I answered.

"A clue?"

"A clue as to who murdered Miss O Sung-hee."

Ernie shrugged. "Maybe the KNPs were right all along. Maybe it was Rothenberg."

And maybe not.

When the midnight curfew came along, GIs either scurried back to Camp Colbern or paired up with a Korean business girl. Ernie found one for me and the four of us went to their rooms upstairs in some dive. In the dark, I lay next to the girl, ignoring her. Finally, I slept.

Just before dawn, a cock crowed. I sat up. The business girl was still asleep, snoring softly. I rose from the low bed, slipped on my clothes and, without bothering to wake Ernie, walked over to the Korean National Police station.

The sun was higher when I returned. After gathering the information I needed at the police station, I'd walked over to Camp Colbern. There, in the billeting room assigned to me and Ernie, I'd showered, shaved, and then gone to the Camp Colbern Snack Bar. Breakfast was ham, eggs, and an English muffin. Now, back in Paldang-ni, I pounded on the door to Ernie's room. The business girl opened it and let me in. Ernie was still asleep.

"Reveille," I said.

He opened his eyes and sat up. "What?"

"Time to make morning formation, Sleeping Beauty."

"Why? We don't know who killed Miss O so what difference does it make?"

"We know now."

"We do?"

I filled him in on the testimony I'd received this morning from Private First Class Everett P. Rothenberg. When I finished,

Ernie thought about it. "You and your Korean customs. Why would that mean anything to anybody?"

"Get up," I told him. "We have someone to talk to."

Ernie grumbled but dressed quickly.

We wound our way through the narrow alleys of Paldang-ni. Instead of American GIs and Korean business girls, the streets were now filled with children wearing black uniforms toting heavy backpacks on their way to school and farmers shoving carts piled high with garlic or cabbage or mounds of round Korean pears. We passed the Dragon Lady Teahouse and just to be sure, I checked the doors, both front and back. Locked tight. Then we continued through the winding maze, heading toward the hooch of Miss Kang.

What I'd questioned Rothenberg about this morning concerned his friendship with Miss Kang. How they'd both sat up nights in the hooch waiting for Miss O. But Miss O would stay out after curfew and then not come home at four in the morning and often Rothenberg had to go to work before he knew what had happened to her. But sometimes she'd be back early with some story about how she stayed at a friend's house and how they were having so much fun talking and playing flower cards that the time had slipped by and she hadn't realized that midnight had come and gone and she'd been trapped at her friend's house until after curfew lifted at four in the morning.

"You knew it was all lies, didn't you?" I asked.

Rothenberg allowed his head to sag. "I guess I did."

"But Miss Kang knew for sure."

"Yeah," Rothenberg said. "Miss O had a lot of boyfriends. I realize that now."

Private Everett P. Rothenberg went on to tell me that sometimes Miss O made both him and Miss Kang leave the hooch completely.

"She'd tell us that family was coming over for the weekend.

And she didn't want them to know that a GI like me was staying in her hooch. So Miss Kang helped out, she took me to her father's home near Yoju. It was about a thirty-minute bus ride. When we arrived at her father's home they were real friendly to me. I'd take off my shoes and enter the house and bow three times to her father like Miss Kang taught me. You know, on your knees and everything."

"You took gifts?"

"Right. Miss Kang made me buy fruit. She said it's against Korean custom to go 'empty hands.'"

"And you prayed to her ancestors?"

"Some old photographs of a man and a woman."

"And you went to their graves?"

"How'd you know? To the grave mounds on the side of the hill. We took rice cakes out there and offered them to the spirits. When the spirits didn't eat them, me and Miss Kang did." He laughed. "She always told me that food offered to the spirits has no taste. Why? Because the spirits take the flavor out of it and all you're left with is the dough."

"Is that true?"

"It was for me. But I never liked rice cakes to begin with."

I stared at Rothenberg a long time. Finally, he fidgeted.

"Hey, wait a minute," he said. "If you think there was something between me and Miss Kang, you're wrong. Sung-hee is my girl. Miss O. I was faithful to her."

"You were," I said softly.

His head drooped. "Right," he said. "I was."

Miss Kang wasn't in her hooch.

"She go pray," the landlady told us.

"At the shrine at the top of the hill," I said, pointing toward the Namhan River.

Her eyes widened. "How you know?"

I shrugged. Ernie and I thanked her, walked back through the village and started up the narrow trail that led out of Paldang-ni, over the hills, and eventually to the banks of the Namhan River. On the way, we passed the bronze bell. It still hadn't been moved and sat amongst a pile of rotted lumber.

At the top of the hill, we found her. She squatted on the stone platform of the shrine, just below where the bell would've been. Ernie walked up to her quickly, shoved her upright, pressed her against one of the wooden support beams, and frisked her. He tossed out a wallet, keys, some loose change and, finally, an Army-issue bayonet.

Miss Kang squatted back down, covering her face with her hands. Narrow shoulders heaved. She was crying.

Ernie backed away, rolling his eyes, exasperated.

After she shed a few more tears, maybe she'd open up to us. I was about to whisper to Ernie to be patient when, behind me, a pebble clattered against stone. Ernie was too busy staring at the quivering form of Miss Kang to notice. As I turned, something dark exploded out of the night.

Ernie shouted.

For a moment, I was gone. Darkness, bright lights, and then more bright lights. I felt myself reeling backward and then I hit something hard and I willed my mind to clear. The darkness gave way to blurred vision. Ernie slapped me on the cheek.

"Sueño, can you stand?"

I stood up.

"Come on. He hit you with some sort of club and when I lunged at him I tripped on this stupid stone platform. He and Kang took off."

"Who?"

"Mr. Shin."

I followed Ernie's pointing finger. Fuzzy vision slowly focused. The early morning haze had lifted and more sunlight filtered through bushes and low trees. In the distance, two figures sprinted down the pathway, heading back toward Paldang-ni.

"Come on!" I shouted.

"My sentiments exactly," Ernie said. "But watch out. She took the bayonet."

And then we were after them.

A crowd had gathered in the central square of Paldang-ni. It was like a small park, surrounded on either side by produce vendors, fishmongers, and butcher shops. No lawn but a few carefully tended rose bushes were ringed by small rocks. Under the shade of an ancient oak tree, old men—wearing traditional white pantaloons and blue silk vests and knitted horsehair hats—squatted on their heels, smoking tobacco from long-stemmed pipes. Groups of them gathered around wooden boards playing *changki*, Korean chess.

*Halaboji*s, they were called. Grandfathers.

One of the *halaboji*'s horsehair hat had fallen into the dust. So had his long-stemmed pipe. Shin held him, his back pressed firmly against the trunk of the old oak. Miss Kang stood next to him, the sharp tip of her bayonet pressed against the loose flesh of the grandfather's neck.

"Get back!" she screamed at me in English. "We'll kill him."

I stood with my arms to my side. Ernie paced a few cautious steps away to my left. I knew what he was thinking. Could he pull his .45 and take a clear shot at Kang's head before she could slice the old man's throat? But at that distance, over ten yards, it would be risky.

"Put the knife down," I told Miss Kang.

"Go away!" she shouted. "My brother and I will leave Paldang-ni. We'll never come back."

A crowd of local citizens had started to gather. Their mouths were open, shocked at what they were seeing. Elders were revered in Korea, never abused like this. Mumbled curses erupted from the crowd.

"The KNPs are on the way," I said. "Put the knife down."

Of course I had no idea if the KNPs had been alerted but they would be soon. Ernie was inching farther to the left, attempting to evade Kang's direct line of sight. I had to stall for time, before Ernie chanced a shot or Miss Kang decided that one less grandfather wouldn't be missed one way or the other.

"You had good reason for what you did," I told Miss Kang.

Her eyes widened. Perspiration flowed down her wrinkled forehead, forming a puddle beneath her eyes. "Yes," she said, surprised. "That's what I told my brother. I had good reason. Miss O made me do it."

People were shutting down produce stands now, running to the back of the crowd to stand on tiptoes to see what was going on.

Miss Kang kept talking. "She was using him."

"Who?" I asked.

"Miss O. She was using Everett."

She meant Private Rothenberg. "How so?" I asked.

"She tricked him. Took his money. Never slept with him. Only had fun, changing from one boyfriend to another. Making me leave my own room. Never paying her share of the rent. So I took Everett. I was nice to him. He met my family. He prayed at our grave mounds. He liked me."

Using her free hand, the one without the bayonet, Miss Kang wiped flowing perspiration from her eyes and stared directly at me. "He liked me. I know he did."

"But you talked to Miss O one night. Atop the hill at the shrine with the bronze bell. You argued."

"No!" Miss Kang shook her head vehemently. "We didn't argue. I told Miss O about everything she did wrong. She didn't argue. She agreed. She *knew* she was doing wrong. But after I told her everything and told her she should leave Everett alone, she laughed at me."

Miss Kang stood incredulous, lost in her own story. Lost in the memory of the unbridled temerity of the arrogant Miss O Sung-hee. "She said that she would take Everett's money and use him for as long as she wanted to and there was nothing I could do about it."

388 ■ MARTIN LIMÓN

Shin looked about frantically, knowing that as the crowd grew his chance of escape grew less. He shouted at his sister to shut up. Her head snapped back toward him.

Ernie by now had the position he wanted, on the extreme left of Shin's peripheral vision. He reached inside his jacket and unhooked the leather shoulder holster of his .45. Miss Kang's head was bobbing around while the old man leaned his skull backward, trying to avoid the sharp tip of the bayonet that pointed into his neck. Tears rolled down the *halaboji*'s face.

Maybe it was the sight of these tears that enraged the crowd most. Whatever it was, suddenly a barrage of garlic cloves was heaved out of the crowd. They smacked the trunk of the oak tree, barely missing Shin and the old man. Enraged, Miss Kang shouted back at them to stop. The crowd roared. This time it was a head of Napa cabbage that exploded at Kang's feet. She hopped. Ernie pulled his .45, held it with both hands in front of him. Still no shot. I took a couple of steps forward. Miss Kang swung the tip of the bayonet my way.

That was the signal for the crowd to unleash their rage. Amidst shouts of anger, more produce flew at Shin and the grandfather and Miss Kang. Garlic, persimmons, fat pears, even a few dead mackerel.

Then the enraged citizens of Paldang-ni surged forward. Ernie raised the barrel of his .45 toward the sky, holding his fire. I tried to run at Miss Kang but a woman bumped me and, to avoid falling on her, I slowed. The entire mob pushed forward, some of them brandishing sticks, some hoes, some with nothing more than their bare fists.

For a second, Miss Kang held her ground; eyes wide with fright, bayonet pointed forward. But then, like a swimmer being drowned by a tidal wave, the crowd enveloped her. Shin screamed and let go of the old man and tried to run. He didn't get far.

Fifty people surrounded the old oak tree. Kicking, screeching, pummeling.

Ernie fired a shot into the air. No one seemed to notice. Rounding a corner at the edge of the square, a phalanx of KNPs ran across pounded earth. Wielding riot batons, swinging freely, they forced the crowd to disperse.

Only Miss Kang and Mr. Shin lay in the dust. Shin was hurt. Leg broken, compound fracture, maybe an arm. I knelt next to Miss Kang Mi-ryul. Her nose was bashed in, the one she'd pointed to only yesterday. Also bashed in was her forehead and the side of her skull. Using my forefinger and thumb, I pinched the flesh above her carotid artery. The skin was still warm but the flow of blood, the force of life-giving fluid, had stopped.

Back at 8th Army I typed up my report. Private First Class Everett P. Rothenberg had already been released by the Korean National Police. Mr. Shin, the pool player, had been taken to a hospital and was recovering nicely, although he was facing hard time for the Korean legal equivalents of aggravated assault and aiding and abetting a murderess.

Miss O Sung-hee was scheduled to be buried by her family in a grave mound back in Kwangju. Miss Kang Mi-ryul, on the other hand, would be cremated. That's all her family could afford.

What they did with her ashes, I never knew.